SIX TO ONE AGAINST

Lyndon Stacey

HUTCHINSON
LONDON

First published by Hutchinson in 2006

3 5 7 9 10 8 6 4

Copyright © Lyndon Stacey 2006

Hutchinson
The Random House Group Limited
20 Vauxhall Bridge Road, London SW1V 2SA

Random House Australia (Pty) Limited
20 Alfred Street, Milsons Point, Sydney,
New South Wales 2061, Australia

Random House New Zealand Limited
18 Poland Road, Glenfield,
Auckland 10, New Zealand

Random House (Pty) Limited
Isle of Houghton, Corner of Boundary Road & Carse O'Gowrie,
Houghton 2198, South Africa

Random House Publishers India Private Limited
301 World Trade Tower, Hotel Intercontinental Grand Complex,
Barakhamba Lane, New Delhi 110 001, India

The Random House Group Limited Reg. No. 954009
www.randomhouse.co.uk

A CIP catalogue record for this book is available from the British Library
Papers used by Random House are natural,
recyclable products made from wood grown in sustainable forests.
The manufacturing processes conform to the environmental
regulations of the country of origin

Typeset by Palimpsest Book Production Limited, Polmont, Stirlingshire
Printed and bound in Great Britain by Mackays of Chatham plc

ISBN 9780091796655 (hardback – from Jan 2007)
ISBN 0 09 179665 2 (hardback)
ISBN 9780091796754 (trade paperback – from Jan 2007)
ISBN 0 09 179675 X (trade paperback)

SIX TO ONE AGAINST

By the same author

Cut Throat
Blindfold
Deadfall
Outside Chance

To Patsy, Ray and Howard, for friendship, good food and
long evenings of enjoyable discussion.

ACKNOWLEDGEMENTS

With thanks to the usual suspects. Also Tina Parham at Wiltshire Ambulance Service Emergency Operations Centre, and to Dave Baker of Hotline Electric Fences for answering some very unusual questions without demur.

PROLOGUE

THE NIGHT BREEZE WHISPERED through the trees and around the weathered stone of the tower, sending a handful of dead leaves skittering playfully along the base of the wall. It rippled through the white cotton shirt of the young man high on the ledge, evaporating the perspiration on his skin, and ruffling his fine blond hair.

The youth stood like a statue, his jaw set and eyes fixed in mesmeric fascination on the jumble of stones below. It was quiet now, almost peaceful; the voices that had driven him here – mercilessly tormenting him – had died away, but there was no going back.

He stepped forward, the grit under his shoe sounding loud in the silence. The wind had dropped. It was as though the night was waiting.

A shadow raced across the parkland as the moon slid behind a streamer of cloud. When it emerged again the ledge was empty and the fickle wind rose once more, carrying with it the memory of a thin, high scream.

ONE

GIDEON DIDN'T HEAR THE shot that killed Damien Daniels. In fact, despite the sporadic gunfire from the clay-pigeon shooters in the field beyond the wood, it didn't immediately occur to him that Damien *had* been shot.

They had been discussing Damien's horse; Gideon being, among other things, an animal behaviourist and Nero being a horse as troubled as he was talented.

One moment they were riding down the grassy woodland track congratulating themselves on the encouraging progress the horse had made over the past few weeks; the next, both animals had jumped forward, accelerating like a pair of drag racers. Gideon grabbed at his reins, rapidly shortening them to bring his horse under control, and was surprised to see Damien's riderless horse shoot past him.

Instinctively soothing his own mount, he twisted in the saddle and looked back.

Damien was lying unmoving, tumbled on the soft, hoof-pitted turf of the track.

This in itself wouldn't have been remarkable, if the man hadn't, until just a few years before, been one of the leading jump-jockeys in the UK. Now, at thirty-eight, he had given up his competitive career and was busy building a considerable reputation as a National Hunt trainer, but he was still, without a doubt, one of the best horsemen that Gideon had ever worked with. The horse's startled leap might have been expected to cause problems for a novice, but it seemed inconceivable that it should have unseated someone as experienced as Damien.

After his initial rush forward, Nero only moved half a dozen steps further before turning to look back at his rider, eyes and nostrils wide, his face reflecting the bewilderment that Gideon was feeling.

'Damien? You all right, mate?' he called, though as soon as the words had left his mouth he could see that he wasn't. He appeared to have fallen awkwardly, landing on his head and one shoulder, and now lay more or less face down with his neck twisted at an unnatural angle.

Gideon went cold with shock.

'Oh, shit!'

He swung his leg over his horse's neck and slid off, leading the animal to the side of the track where, with shaking hands, he looped the reins over a sapling before hurrying to Damien's side.

What could be seen of his face, between the crash cap and the ground, was smudged with dirt; the one visible eye half open but its gaze fixed.

'Oh, God!' Gideon breathed. 'Damien! Can you hear me?'

He didn't really expect an answer and he didn't get one. Kneeling down, he placed two trembling fingers against the man's neck, feeling for a pulse. He tried several positions without success, watching the back of Damien's navy bomber jacket for any perceptible rise and fall, as he did so.

There was none.

'Come on, Damien. This is stupid.' Gideon couldn't get his head round what had happened.

4

In any other circumstances the obvious course of action would be to begin resuscitation, but first-aid training had drummed into him the cardinal rule that you must never move anyone with a suspected neck injury. Here, it was a case of damned if you do – damned if you don't, Gideon thought desperately.

Fighting against panic and the growing conviction that it was too late to help, he took his mobile phone from its pouch on his belt and keyed in three nines.

'Emergency services,' a female voice said, after a blessedly short space of time. 'Which service do you require?'

'Ambulance. Quickly! It's a riding accident and I think he's got a broken neck. I can't find a pulse.'

'Right; I'm transferring you through to someone who'll take your details. Please hold the line . . .'

There was a faint click and another woman said in a broad Scottish accent, 'Ambulance Emergency. What is the address of your emergency?'

When she'd pinpointed Gideon's location, the operator asked for a brief description of what had happened, and Damien's condition.

'You must hurry, please!' Gideon said, as he finished.

'OK, Gideon, try and keep calm. The ambulance is already on its way. Stay on the line. I'm going to hand you over to a paramedic who'll talk you through what you should do for the casualty.'

Before Gideon could thank her, she'd gone and a masculine voice said, 'Hello Gideon, I'm Rick. Now, what's the condition of the patient?'

Gideon was still kneeling beside Damien. He described the way he looked, and felt for a pulse again with the same negative result as before.

'And he's not breathing?' the paramedic asked, when Gideon told him. 'Right; well, we need to get him breathing again. Don't worry, I'll talk you through it.'

'I know how, but he's face down and I can't move him if his neck's broken . . .'

'I'm sorry, but I'm afraid we don't have any option. It's crucial that we restore heart and lung function and we can't afford to wait for the ambulance to reach you. Exactly how is he lying?'

Following the step-by-step instructions of the calm voice on the phone, Gideon began to turn the injured man with gentle hands, breaking into a sweat as he strove to do so without causing further damage. As he carefully lowered Damien's body onto its back, the blue jacket fell open, revealing a small red-rimmed hole in the centre of his white tee shirt. Gideon recoiled in shock.

'Oh, Christ!' he said faintly, staring in horrified fascination; struggling to take it in. *He'd fallen off his horse for God's sake!* He felt bile rising and swallowed hard.

On the ground by his knee, his mobile phone emitted a short burst of tinny vocals and he reached for it, noticing, with a fresh surge of distaste, that he had blood on his hand. Where had that come from? Wiping his fingers in the grass, he picked the handset up.

'Yes, I'm here.'

'How are we doing?' the voice enquired, calmly.

'I think he's been shot,' Gideon heard himself say, quite composedly, the words stating what his mind refused to admit. He *couldn't* have been shot – ordinary people don't just get shot for no reason. It was a Sunday morning in Somerset, not a war zone.

'Where?' The paramedic asked.

In the woods. The inappropriate humour caught Gideon unawares, and he was glad he hadn't spoken aloud. With an effort, he dragged his eyes away from the obscenity of that neat, round hole. He knew the trainer had been wearing a back protector; presumably that had prevented the wound being visible from behind. A cautious investigation revealed that blood had soaked his shirt. Under the Kevlar shield, Damien's back was a mass of torn flesh.

'Gideon?'

'Yes?' He swallowed hard.

'Did you say he's been shot?'

'Yes. In the chest. He's dead.' Gideon's whole body had started to shake, and he clenched his jaw, trying to stay in control. How could he be dead? They'd been talking. Even now, his face looked peaceful, bronzed, healthy; as if he was just sleeping.

'Are you sure?'

'Yes.' Gideon checked the sarcastic retort that rose to his lips. After all, the man was just doing his job. He couldn't see the awful finality of the hole in Damien's chest and the irreparable chaos of his back.

'Right. I'll inform the police. Don't touch anything else. I suggest you vacate the area, as a precaution. You have to consider the possibility of danger to yourself.' There was a pause, during which a fresh burst of gunfire broke out in the adjacent field, then the voice came again, full of urgency. 'Gideon, are you all right?'

'Yes. They're shooting clays. I'm not in any danger.'

'But your friend has been shot,' the paramedic reminded him.

Incredibly, Gideon, still grappling with the enormity of the first discovery, hadn't even considered the possibility that he might also be a target. This had been no accidental shooting. Shot from the clay shooters' guns would have dispersed harmlessly long before it reached the track through the woods and Damien's wound clearly hadn't been made by lead shot, but a bullet. Someone must have lain in wait. Was Gideon even now being watched? Were the gun's sights now lined up on *his* chest? He looked swiftly round.

Nothing.

The broad grassy ride stretched away for perhaps a hundred yards in either direction, edged in places by sprawling brambles and flanked by conifers in dense, regimented rows. Above the branches of dark green needles the sky was blue and, a few feet away, roused by the April sunshine, an early bumblebee buzzed around a clump of pale yellow primroses.

Was that movement in the trees?

He stared, his heart thudding heavily, but could see nothing more than branches stirring in the breeze.

7

How far away had the gunman been?

He had no idea.

It was an intensely unnerving sensation. He wondered if there would be any brief realisation before all form of awareness was snatched away, or would everything just cease. The concept was beyond his imagining.

'Gideon? Are you still there?'

'Yeah. I'm OK.' He pulled himself together. 'I think if he was going to take a shot at me, he'd have done it by now.'

He wished he felt as confident as he sounded, but the fact remained that Damien had been shot by what the evidence suggested was an extremely competent marksman. As Gideon had no clear idea where he might be hiding, there appeared to be little he could do to avoid the same fate, if it was, indeed, on the cards.

'Listen, I've got to catch his horse,' he told the paramedic. The situation was bad enough without the added worry of having tens of thousands of pounds' worth of racehorse going AWOL when the emergency services arrived. At the moment Nero was calmly grazing on the soft grass at the edge of the track but he was an unpredictable beast at the best of times, and Gideon placed no dependence upon the mood lasting.

Pocketing the phone, he stood up, feeling intensely vulnerable. He wasn't even wearing a back protector; but then, Damien's hadn't done a lot for *him*.

Nero saw him coming and lifted his head, jaws champing. He'd stepped through the circle of his reins as they trailed, and feeling the pull on his neck he threw up his head and stepped back in alarm.

'Steady, lad.' With an effort, Gideon tried to calm the turmoil in his own head and concentrate on the matter in hand.

Another burst of gunfire made him jump, but it was only the clay shooters again. He noticed, with a kind of detached satisfaction, that Nero had hardly reacted to the sudden noise. It was one of the problems they had been treating him for, and the reason they'd been riding in the wood on a shooting day.

After a couple more steps backward, Nero allowed Gideon to take hold of his rein, but then he was left with another problem: the horse wasn't good about being tied up. Gideon suspected that somewhere in his past, something had frightened him in that situation, and left him with an unreasoning fear of restraint. It was something else they'd been working on together, and Nero was improving, but this certainly wasn't the time to put him to the test. He was quite capable of breaking his reins and galloping off into the sunset.

It wasn't going to be easy to deal with police and ambulance men while hanging onto a borderline-neurotic horse, but the only alternative wasn't really an alternative at all. A call to the stables would doubtless bring help running – but there was no way he would willingly expose any of Damien's family or staff to the horror of the scene before him.

He looked across to where his own, more placid, mount had stripped the new foliage off the sapling he was tied to and was now making a start on the bark. He, at least, seemed content.

Gideon's thoughts returned to Damien's family. The trainer had shared Puddlestone Farmhouse and the adjacent cottage with his parents, his younger sister – who was also his assistant trainer – and his wife and three-year-old son. They were a close family unit and he dreaded to think of the effect this was going to have on them.

Unbuckling Nero's reins to free them, he ran the stirrups up and slackened the girth. Guessing that the police, when they arrived, wouldn't want any more hoof and boot prints than strictly necessary in the vicinity of the crime scene, he unhitched his own horse and led them both twenty yards back down the track.

The sun shone on, determinedly cheerful, and a fly alighted on Gideon's hand. He shook it off, imagining the flies that were almost certainly collecting on Damien's ravaged body. The thought was disgusting, but it was a fairly warm day and Gideon was only wearing a rugby shirt, and no jacket that could be taken off and used to cover the dead man.

He glanced at his watch. Ten to twelve.

How long had he been waiting? It seemed like for ever.

How soon could he expect help to arrive?

Gideon longed for the weight of responsibility to be lifted from his shoulders. He was way out of his depth.

It was quiet in the woods. The clay shoot had stopped, he realised, and in the distance he could hear the faint swish of traffic on the road. Seconds later he heard the first far-off sounds of a siren, growing steadily louder. From past study of the map, Gideon knew that the ambulance couldn't be more than four hundred yards away when it eventually wailed to a halt, but the trees were too thick for him to see its flashing lights.

For several minutes he waited, straining his eyes and ears for any sign of the crew, and then his phone trilled, making him jump. He hoped to God it wasn't any of Damien's family ringing to find out where they'd got to. What the hell could he say?

'Gideon? Do you have a blue and white shirt and two horses?' The male voice was accompanied by a certain amount of heavy breathing and background noise. 'OK; we've got a visual and we'll be with you very shortly.'

Gideon assumed it was the ambulance crew, on foot and hurrying, and sure enough, within moments he could see two figures in Day-Glo jackets approaching through the undergloom of the conifers from the direction of the clay shooters' field. The horses lifted their heads, still munching, and watched them come.

They emerged onto the track, one – young and almost bald – carrying a folded-up stretcher and heading straight across to where Damien lay; the other middle-aged and rather portly, pausing beside Gideon, ostensibly to check on him but, in reality, breathing hard and needing a moment to recover.

'All right, mate?' he asked between breaths.

'Yeah. What about you?'

The ambulance man bent double and shook his head.

'Stitch,' he said succinctly. 'Not as fit as I used to be.'

It took only a matter of moments for the younger man to confirm death, which verdict he relayed to his colleague by straightening up, pursing his lips and shaking his head. He made his way back to them, and Gideon didn't miss the wary glances he cast at the surrounding trees as he did so.

A crashing sound startled the horses and presaged the arrival of two uniformed police officers, one swearing as he attempted to disentangle himself from the vicious grasp of a blackberry runner and the other evidently finding it highly amusing.

Seeing Gideon and the paramedics close by, the second man swiftly sobered up, and after receiving the news that Damien Daniels was, in fact, dead, produced a notebook and took down not only Gideon's name but also those of the two ambulance men, while his colleague stood by, gingerly removing bramble prickles from his trouser leg.

Shortly after, the paramedics – made redundant by the absence of life to preserve – took their leave and trudged off through the trees, down what seemed set to become a well-worn track. Hardly had their fluorescent jackets disappeared into the murky depths of the wood when two more men came into view, this time in plain clothes but somehow, Gideon thought, still just as obviously policemen. The foremost of these fell prey to the same arching bramble stem that had snared the first man, and swore, if anything, even more vehemently. It would have been funny if the circumstances had been different.

Gideon watched as the newcomers exchanged a few low-voiced words with the two uniformed officers, who were quite clearly relaying the information they had gleaned from him. The elder of the plain-clothes men was fiftyish, with thinning grey hair, a grey suit and an almost avuncular look about him. The other was perhaps twenty years his junior, a dark-haired, unsmiling man in jeans, a tee shirt and a black leather jacket.

It was this younger man who presently introduced himself to

Gideon as Detective Sergeant Coogan and began by asking if he couldn't tie the horses up somewhere.

'Well, actually – no.' Gideon explained his dilemma.

'But presumably someone else could hold them,' Coogan said. 'I'm allergic to the bloody things.' He called the uniform back. 'You – Fletcher – come and look after these horses, would you?'

Judging by his expression, Fletcher wasn't too keen on the idea but Coogan wasn't big on sympathy.

'Oh, come on! How difficult can it be? They won't eat you.'

Fletcher took the horses' reins from Gideon, regarding the two animals much as one might a couple of hungry lions, and trying to keep at arm's length from them both.

'Good. Now take them away, down the path, they've done enough damage as it is – trampling all over the crime scene!' Coogan turned to Gideon. 'Right, suppose you tell me what happened here.'

Gideon sat staring into the plastic cup standing cradled between his hands on the tabletop before him. The liquid it contained was scalding hot, but that was all that could honestly be claimed for it. He had asked for coffee but the muddy-brown, machine-generated brew had little smell and even less taste.

He was sitting, as he had been for the past three and a half hours, in an interview room at Chilminster police station. Fluorescent strip lights lit the small, windowless room, which had black vinyl on the floor, shiny cream paint on the walls, and one massive Victorian radiator that either didn't work or hadn't been turned on. The surface of the heavy wooden table at which he sat was defaced with inkstains, scratches and cigarette burns, and his chair was of red moulded plastic and was to comfort what Punch and Judy was to political correctness. High above the door, an extractor fan whirred constantly, producing a rattling vibration every six seconds.

Apart from the visit from the cheerful young PC who had brought him the coffee, Gideon had been alone for the last three-quarters of an hour, and felt cold, depressed and utterly drained.

In spite of the passage of time, a feeling of unreality dogged him. It was still difficult to accept that the cheerful, energetic man he'd ridden out with that morning had anything to do with the lifeless body he'd left behind him in the woods.

His mind went back to the scene as it had been when he was led away: the area cordoned off by quantities of red and white striped tape, half a dozen men and women in stark white coveralls busily searching the track and surrounding forest with meticulous care, and a uniformed photographer documenting the tragedy from every angle. A helicopter scanned the neighbouring countryside for any sign of the gunman, backed up on the ground, Gideon knew, by four pairs of armed-response officers, and two dog handlers.

All the while, Damien, lying face up as Gideon had left him, stared sightlessly into the cloudless blue sky.

The door of the interview room opened and Gideon glanced up just in time to see a head withdraw as it closed once more.

'Hey!' he called, getting to his feet. 'Hey. When can I go?'

There was no response, and he banged his fist on the table in frustration. He was beginning to feel more like a suspect than the innocent witness to a crime; a feeling reinforced by the fact that on arrival at the station he had had his hands swabbed and his clothes taken away.

'Sorry, sir, it's routine,' he was told, and was left to change into a white all-in-one garment fashioned from some sort of papery fibre. It looked like the sort the CSI team had worn.

He could call someone to get some clothes brought in if he wanted, he was told, so he'd called Graylings Priory where Giles Barrington-Carr, his friend and landlord, lived with his sister Pippa. Gideon knew Pippa was out drag hunting, but left a message with Giles' answering service.

He'd been taken to the interview room where, before long, Coogan and another plain-clothed officer joined him, and the questions began.

Did Gideon often ride with Mr Daniels?

This was the fifth time.

Did they often take this particular route?

Yes, they had the last three times, to accustom the horse to the sound of the guns. It was part of the therapy.

Had Gideon noticed anyone in the wood that morning?

Only a dog walker . . .

Could Gideon describe the dog walker?

To be honest, he'd been more interested in the dog – a rather handsome Rottweiler. As far as he could remember, the owner was female, middle-aged, plump and dark-haired; not your average sniper material.

'And how many snipers do you know, Mr Blake?' Without a flicker of humour.

'OK, point taken,' Gideon said wearily.

Had Mr Daniels seemed his normal self that morning?

Yes.

Not worried about anything, or distracted?

No. Full of plans for the future.

Was Gideon aware of any trouble within Mr Daniels' family – had he said anything about relationship problems?

'Look,' Gideon said with a touch of irritation. 'I'm an animal psychologist, not a marriage-guidance counsellor! As far as I know, he was happy with his home life, but I couldn't say for sure. I don't – didn't – know him that well. We mostly talked about the horse.'

'Would you say Damien Daniels was hot-tempered? Confrontational?'

'No. He's – he was – very easy-going. He got on with most people.'

'You say most people – who didn't he get on with?'

'Well, *I* don't know,' Gideon said, exasperated. 'I didn't mean anyone in particular, but I expect there were people – nobody hits it off with absolutely everyone, do they?'

'And what about you? Have you ever quarrelled with him?'

'No. And before you ask – I didn't quarrel with him this morning, and I didn't shoot him.'

He was the recipient of a long, calculating look, then Coogan changed tack.

'When did you first realise that Mr Daniels had been shot?'

Gideon had already related the events of the morning twice, but previous experience of police procedure had taught him that it did no good to kick against it, so he swallowed his impatience.

'Not until the paramedic on the phone told me to turn him over. I hadn't moved him before because I thought his neck was broken.'

'And you say you didn't hear the shot because of the noise from the guns next door.'

'That's right.'

'Did you think perhaps he'd been hit by a stray shot from there?'

'No. Not when I saw the wound.'

'You're familiar with firearms, then, Mr Blake. Do you own one?'

Gideon's eyes narrowed.

'No, I don't. But you don't have to be an expert to know that wound wasn't made by a shotgun. I should imagine most country people would know the difference between a shotgun and a rifle, and we were way out of range for a shotgun.'

Another long look, a scribbled note, and the questions went on.

How well did Gideon know the Daniels family?

Not well. Only since he'd been working with the horse.

How did he come to be doing that?

He'd started working on Nero with his previous owners and Damien had wanted him to continue.

Was he having a relationship with Damien's sister?

No, he was not.

What about Damien's wife, Beth, wasn't it?

No. Not with Beth, either.

Was Gideon gay, perhaps?

Gideon looked heavenwards. No, he had a girlfriend, but she wasn't related, in any way, shape or form, to Damien Daniels.

'Mr Blake, we have a job to do,' Coogan said then. 'I appreciate that you've had an upsetting morning, and I'm sure you'd rather be anywhere but here, but if we can just keep this civilised, it'll be easier all round.'

The other officer cleared his throat.

'I'm sorry if some of our questions seem intrusive, but it's important that we have a clear picture of the situation. Now, can I ask what your girlfriend's name is and where she lives?'

Gideon hesitated, unwilling to draw Eve into it, but he really didn't see that he had any choice.

'Eve Kirkpatrick. She owns an art gallery in Wareham – the Arne Gallery,' he added, anticipating the next question. 'She lives in a big Georgian house, I could take you there but I don't know the address.'

'Not with you, then?'

'No. I live near Blandford,' he pointed out, with tenuous patience. They already knew that. He'd given his details at least six times that afternoon. He was getting tired of the double questioning. It was as if they were trying to catch him out.

Coogan favoured him with another of his long looks and Gideon gave in.

'She likes to be near the sea, and she *has* to be near the gallery. We have a casual relationship.'

There was a knock at the door and a head peered round.

'Have you got a minute?' it asked, and Coogan nodded.

'Please wait here, Mr Blake. We'll be back shortly.'

They weren't.

Half an hour passed before Gideon saw Coogan again, and then he brought with him a different sidekick.

This time it was clear that someone had dug out his file, for the questioning took on a new slant. Gideon had been involved in bringing a noted criminal to book, two years before, and although he couldn't really see what bearing those events could have on Damien's shooting, he went along with it, fervently hoping that he didn't contradict anything he'd told the police at that time. For his part, what he'd told them then had been on a need-to-know basis, and there'd been a fair amount he hadn't felt they needed to know.

After another twenty minutes' grilling, Coogan had got suddenly to his feet and gone out, taking his almost silent colleague with him.

So Gideon was left alone once more, and after three-quarters of an hour he was beginning to think that even Coogan's company would be preferable to the empty room and the constant muted, echoey voices he could hear through the door.

The door wasn't locked but his one foray into the world beyond it had resulted in a pleasant but firm request that he wait inside, and the cup of grim coffee. He'd been told that his presence was not compulsory, but supposed they could be fairly certain he wouldn't try to leave the building dressed – as he was – in what was basically a paper romper suit.

The door opened once more and he glanced up.

'Gideon Blake, isn't it?'

Not Coogan, this time, but his grey-suited senior colleague from earlier, and carrying what looked like a bundle of clothes.

'That's right.'

'DI Rockley. I'm sorry you've been stuck in this dismal place all afternoon, but we didn't have another room free. I expect you'll be glad to have these,' the man said, coming forward and placing them on the tabletop next to the coffee cup.

He wrinkled his nose. 'Tell you what. Why don't I go and see if I can find something that's at least drinkable, while you change? Won't be a tick.'

By the time he returned, some five minutes later, Gideon had stripped off the paper suit and replaced it with the corduroys, cotton shirt and leather jacket that Giles had supplied from Gideon's own wardrobe. The difference, both physical and psychological, was immense.

Rockley placed two white china cups of coffee on the table and next to them an unopened packet of milk chocolate digestives, which he'd carried wedged under his arm.

'I expect you'd rather have a Big Mac or something, but I'm afraid this is all I've got. Came from my private stash,' he admitted, with just a trace of undisguised regret. He had a been-there-and-seen-it-all kind of face, but without the overt cynicism this often engendered.

For the first time, Gideon realised how hungry he was, and it seemed Rockley was too, for he wasted no time in opening the packet, following the *Tear Here* instruction on the wrapper.

The inspector helped himself to two and pushed the packet towards Gideon.

'They always put the pull strip about a third of the way down, so you have to eat at least four to stop them falling out, and seven or eight if you want to seal it again,' he complained, his eyes twinkling under a pair of impressively bushy brows. 'At least, that's my excuse.'

Gideon took two, and thanked him, grateful to be talking to someone human. Coogan had all the warmth and character of the speaking clock.

'Now, I realise you've had a pig of a day and you've probably been through all this at least half a dozen times already, but could you bear with me and go through it just once more?'

Sighing, Gideon nodded. He felt deeply, unutterably weary but one more time wasn't going to make a lot of difference, and the coffee and biscuits had bought Rockley quite a chunk of credit.

'Thank you.' Rockley looked genuinely grateful. 'And then we'll see about getting you home – or to wherever you want to go.'

TWO

T HE POLICE RANGE ROVER dropped Gideon at the
 end of the driveway to Puddlestone Farm Stables. It had
given him a lift on its way to follow up a report of stolen farm
machinery some miles further on. The young PC at the wheel
had been quite prepared to take him right up to the front door.
He wasn't in any hurry, he said, but Gideon had preferred to
walk, needing the time to organise his thoughts.

After the long hours of inactivity it felt good to be on the
move again, stretching the kinks out of his legs and getting some
fresh air into his lungs, and yet, given the choice, he would rather
be going almost anywhere than to the farm, to face the unimag-
inable grief of Damien's family.

What on earth was he going to say to them if they wanted
him to describe exactly what had happened? How do you tell a
family that their loved one has been shot by a trained marksman;
that when he'd fallen from his horse he'd broken his neck, and
that the last time you saw him, he'd been lying in the mud with
a hole over his heart and a gory mess where his back should have
been?

It had in all likelihood been a soft-nosed bullet, Rockley had told him when he'd asked. Specially modified to disintegrate upon entering the body, thus leaving the trademark small entry wound and large exit. Only the back protector had prevented the carnage being immediately obvious.

Gideon shook his head, pushing the memory away. For Damien's family, shooting probably conjured up the kind of sanitised image it had for him – until that morning. At least they would be spared the appalling reality.

At the end of the drive he hesitated and then turned into the stableyard, telling himself he was checking that the two horses had got back safely, but knowing he was only delaying the moment. The horses would have been back and settled long ago; he'd been assured of that.

It was half past five – nearly feeding time – but the usually busy yard was quiet. The door to the tack room was closed, as was the door to the cottage adjoining the yard, which the four Puddlestone stable lads shared. Heads appeared over many of the stable doors as Gideon walked through, and the tabby cat that lived in the hay store strolled out to greet him, but there didn't seem to be anyone about until a slim girl, with dyed-blonde hair scraped back in a ponytail, came out of one of the boxes carrying an empty haynet and a muck sack. She half-stopped when she saw him, and Gideon recognised her as one of the 'lads', the mainstay of any racing yard.

'Hi,' Gideon said, because he patently had to say something. 'Anything I can do to help?'

The girl shook her head in silence and walked by, casting him a reproachful look from swollen eyes, as if he was somehow to blame for not having been shot instead. He knew from his previous visits that the staff were fiercely loyal to the yard and Gideon suspected that, even though he'd been married, at least two of the three female 'lads' had fancied themselves in love with their dashingly handsome boss.

The girl disappeared into the hay store, pulling the door shut behind her with a gesture of finality and, after visiting the two horses, Gideon turned his steps reluctantly towards the grey stone farmhouse. This stood out of sight across the lane from the yard, with Damien's tiny cottage tucked against its flank, like a duckling against the mother duck.

Gideon's old dark green Land Rover stood where he'd left it that morning, next to the Daniels' more modern vehicles in front of the pretty walled garden, and he'd have given a lot to be able simply to get in it and drive away. He was little more than a stranger to most of the family, but having been with Damien when he died, he couldn't just leave without seeing them.

He knocked on the door and stood looking down at the worn stone of the step. The old house had doubtless weathered the tragedies of many families, but it was hard to imagine one as cruel and senseless as this.

After a few moments, the door opened to reveal Damien's sister, for which Gideon was grateful. As Damien's assistant trainer, Matilda − or Tilly − Daniels was the family member he knew best. There was a strong family resemblance, Tilly having her brother's height, fair good looks and ready smile, though at the moment the smile was understandably absent and her grey-blue eyes were reddened with weeping.

'Hi,' she said, miserably, then stepped back into the hallway. 'Come in.'

'Look, I don't want to intrude . . .'

'No, please. It must have been awful for you, too. Are you all right?'

She sounded genuinely concerned and Gideon was touched.

'I'm all right − apart from the shock. I'm sorry I couldn't come before, I've been at the police station all afternoon.'

'I know. They said. I opened the door and there were two policemen standing there. When they told me, I couldn't take it in at first; it didn't seem real, you know? They were very kind, but then they started asking questions. It was as if they thought we knew something about it − about why it happened . . .'

Gideon looked at her with compassion, remembering some of the things Coogan had asked him.

'I suppose they have to,' he said. Rockley had told him that around ninety per cent of murders were committed by the victim's family or close friends. However unsympathetic it might appear, it obviously made sense for the police to start their enquiries there. 'Oh God, Tilly, I'm just so sorry . . .'

Tilly shook her head. 'No, there was nothing you could have done — they told us that. I just don't understand—' Her voice broke.

Gideon stepped towards her instinctively and suddenly she was in his arms, sobbing hard into his shirtfront. He rubbed her back, helplessly trying to give comfort. At thirty-five, she was, surprisingly, still single and it was probably at times like this that it mattered the most.

'I don't understand, either. It all seems crazy,' he said.

'But how can this have happened?' she asked between sobs. 'I just can't believe it.'

'I know,' he agreed. 'I know.'

Over her shoulder, he saw his reflection in a mirror on the wall. Thick, weather-bleached, dark blond hair, grey-green eyes and fairly symmetrical features; it seemed somehow strange that the shocking events of the morning had left no visible sign on the face that looked back at him.

Tilly pulled back, wiping her nose on a handkerchief she was clutching, and then looked searchingly into his eyes. 'Did he . . . I mean — was it quick? He didn't suffer, did he?'

Under that intense gaze, Gideon was glad to be able to answer with complete honesty. 'No. It was instantaneous. He couldn't have felt a thing.'

Her eyes scanned his face for a moment longer, then she put her hand on his arm and said, 'Thank you. We'd better go in; they'll wonder where I've got to. Oh, and Gideon . . . Mum's not coping too well. She's . . . well, you'll see; I just wanted to warn you. There's a policewoman here, too. She's a liaison officer or something. Anyway, she's just here to help, apparently – if we need anything. She's very nice.'

The room they entered was the only room of the house that Gideon had been in before. It was the kitchen, and was, like many farmhouse kitchens, the hub of day-to-day life, a function reflected by its comfortably chaotic, lived-in look. A hotch-potch of units, old and new, a Rayburn and a huge Belfast sink; it was the kind of shabby-aged look that the editors of glossy magazines loved. Here he'd sat, just that morning, discussing Nero's progress and drinking Damien's overstrong tea from one of the stoneware mugs that were stored on hooks under the shelves of the big, cream-painted dresser.

Now all the family were present, with the exception of Damien's father, Hamish, who Gideon knew was away for the day at a farm sale. Damien's wife Beth was there, petite and dark, with Freddy, the couple's three-year-old son, sitting on her knee. She looked up briefly as Gideon came in, but then her gaze dropped to the coffee cup she held, her large brown eyes swimming with tears and her hands visibly shaking. Freddy, fair like the rest of the family, snuggled close, burying his face in the soft wool of his mother's jumper, aware of the atmosphere but nowhere near to comprehending the scale of the tragedy.

A uniformed Asian WPC sat next to Damien's mother. Barbara Daniels was a trim sixty-something with mid-length, greying blonde hair and skin that bore the evidence of a lifetime spent outdoors. Always fiercely proud of her children, Gideon had expected her to be the worst affected, but in spite of Tilly's warning, she seemed surprisingly calm and composed. The reason for this soon became clear.

As Tilly offered their visitor a seat and a cup of coffee, her mother looked up with a smile and said brightly, 'Ah, Gideon, isn't it? I'm afraid Damien's still at school, but he won't be long. In fact, I ought to see about getting his tea . . .'

There was a moment's awkward silence, during which her daughter and daughter-in-law exchanged anxious glances, and then she continued, waving a hand at the policewoman, 'Oh, this is Yvonne something-or-other – she's been very kind, haven't you dear?' She paused, looking uncertainly at the other woman, as if wondering to herself just why she was there.

The young WPC smiled, then looked at Gideon and shrugged slightly, clearly at a loss.

She wasn't the only one. Gideon didn't know how to respond so he greeted Barbara with a smile, said 'Hi,' and was thankful when Tilly, coming across with his coffee, said quietly to him, 'The doctor's on his way. She's been like this ever since she heard.'

'Oh, God!' Beth said, suddenly bursting into tears. 'I can't believe this is happening – it's a nightmare! I just can't believe it. He only went for a ride, for God's sake! How can he be dead?'

Within the curl of her arm, Freddy's tears flowed in sympathy. Beth hugged him tighter and kissed the top of his head. 'If he'd had a riding accident, it would've been one thing – but this . . . It just doesn't make sense. How could anyone be *that* careless?'

Gideon had been wondering how much the family had been told, but Beth's words clearly indicated that, as yet, they knew comparatively little.

'Don't cry dear,' Barbara said, stretching a hand across the table towards her daughter-in-law. 'Damien and Marcus will be back soon; they'll sort it out.'

'Oh, Mum!' Tilly pleaded. 'Please don't do this – I can't bear it!'

'Who's Marcus?' the WPC asked Tilly, quietly.

But it was Barbara who answered, her face shining with pride. 'He's my youngest. He's going to the Olympics.'

The policewoman raised her eyebrows at Tilly, who shook her head slightly and mouthed 'No,' a look of desperation in her eyes.

Beth began to sob even harder and Freddy, frightened by what he didn't understand, wriggled out of her grasp and ran to Tilly.

Through the kitchen window, Gideon saw a newish saloon car pull up, followed immediately by Hamish Daniels' four-wheel drive.

Putting his coffee mug down, he turned to Tilly. 'I think the doctor's here. Tell you what, Freddy – would you like to come and ride Laddie? He could do with some exercise, he's getting big and fat like you!'

Freddy's face brightened. 'I not big and fat!' he responded indignantly, but nevertheless let go of Tilly's hand and toddled across to offer his small fist to Gideon.

Damien's sister mouthed 'Thank you,' over his head.

More than three-quarters of an hour passed before the doctor emerged from the farmhouse and went on his way. While he was waiting, Gideon had – with the doubtful benefit of Freddy's help – caught, brushed and saddled Laddie, the Daniels' elderly Welsh pony, and then led him several times round the paddock behind the stableyard, with the youngster perched on his back.

Never nursery-nurse material, by the time Hamish appeared to relieve him of his charge, Gideon was heartily glad to hand the boy over and, judging by the cry of glee with which Freddy greeted his grandfather, the feeling was reciprocated.

Hamish was a big, heavily built man, only an inch or two short of Gideon's six foot four, and had blue eyes and a mop of curly greying-blond hair that, according to Damien, were a legacy from a Scandinavian mother. He swung his grandson off the back of the pony and round onto his own back, where the child clung happily.

'Gideon, thank you,' he said in his soft, deep voice. 'The doctor's given Barbara a sedative and she's asleep now, thank goodness. He says she'll probably sleep through till tomorrow morning. I just hope she's better when she wakes up. He says it's a reaction to the shock, but he can't – or won't – say how soon she's likely to get over it.'

Gideon ran the stirrups up on the pony's saddle and they started to walk back to the stables, Freddy still riding piggyback on his grandfather.

Hamish himself was an indifferent rider, and devoted his time to running the eight hundred acres or so of Puddlestone Farm. Gideon knew it was farmed organically and produced – amongst other arable crops – all the hay for the horses, besides supporting a large and much acclaimed herd of Aberdeen Angus cattle.

In the yard, the boy wriggled to get down and then sat playing contentedly with a handful of pebbles and a water bucket, while Gideon took care of the pony.

Hamish turned to Gideon, and the strain of remaining in control was obvious.

'The girls don't seem very clear about what's happened,' he said quietly. 'And the WPC isn't saying much, even if she knows. I gather you were with Damien . . .'

Gideon sighed. 'Yes, I was. It was all over in the blink of an eye. One moment we were riding through the wood – the next, Nero jumped forward and Damien fell backwards over his rump. I had no idea he'd been shot, at that point. I mean it's the last thing you'd think of, isn't it?'

'Tilly and Beth seem to think it was someone out rabbiting – an accidental shot, or something. It seems the police were a bit vague about it.' Hamish was watching him closely, and Gideon could see his scepticism.

He hesitated, unsure as to how much he should say, but then, he hadn't specifically been told not to talk to the family, and surely they had a right to know.

'It wasn't a shotgun,' he said. 'And it wasn't an accident. I'm afraid whoever it was knew exactly what they were doing. It can't have been an easy shot.'

Hamish frowned and shook his head. 'But – I don't under-stand. Why would anyone want Damien dead? He's so popular. Everybody likes him.' He paused, putting a hand to his eyes as he lost the battle with his emotions. 'I'm sorry . . . It's just – I don't think I can cope with all this again. After Marcus . . . it's too much . . .' His shoulders began to shake.

'It's all right . . .' Gideon tailed off, feeling painfully inadequate. He'd never done much more than pass the time of day with the man before now, and was at a loss to know how to comfort him. After all, what can you say to a father who's just lost his son? Surely, nothing would ever again be completely all right for Hamish or any of the family.

Because of the manner of his death, Damien Daniels' body would not be released for burial until the investigation was over, which only added to the trauma for his family. The jockey turned trainer had been a well-known and popular figure, and for a few days the media coverage was intense. When Gideon phoned Puddlestone Farmhouse the next day, Tilly told him despairingly that they had been besieged by reporters and photographers to the point where the police had had to be called to move them on, and one officer had remained to stand guard at the end of the drive for a few hours.

As a result of the publicity, the family was soon flooded with letters and cards of condolence from Damien's many friends and fans. In response to repeated enquiries as to the date of the funeral, they decided to hold, in the meantime, a service of commemoration. Instead of flowers, it was requested that donations should be sent to the Radcliffe Trust, a charity that reschooled ex-racehorses for a life away from the track. As a trainer, it was a cause that Damien had enthusiastically supported.

In the ten days between his murder and the memorial service, the police appeared to make little progress towards finding Damien's killer. Their enquiries had been thorough; Gideon had himself been questioned twice more and he knew, from contact with Damien's family, that they too had had several sessions with Rockley and his men. The inspector had appeared on the television news, two nights running, appealing for information, and from media reports Gideon knew that roadside checks and house-to-house enquiries had been carried out in the vicinity of the crime. If these had thrown up any useful information, the police were keeping it strictly to themselves.

Gideon's friends, Giles and Pippa, had known the Daniels family since childhood, and Pippa had even dated Damien a time or two, so Gideon hadn't enjoyed the task of breaking the news to them on his return from Puddlestone Farm at the end of that first dreadful day. Pippa had just returned from a long day's drag hunting, tired but still buoyed up with the exhilaration of the chase. When Gideon arrived with his tale of tragedy, she and her boyfriend, Lloyd, had been drinking soup in the Priory kitchen, bootless but still wearing their mud-spattered clothes. He'd spared them the gritty details, but even so they had reacted with deep shock.

'Oh, God!' Lloyd had exclaimed. 'That's why there were so many police cars about on the road. The meet was only about ten miles away,' he added, for Gideon's benefit. 'My mare pulled up stiff at the end of the first line, and I walked her back along the road to get my second horse. There was a chopper going round and round, too.'

'Yes, *I* noticed that,' Pippa remembered. 'Oh, God! Poor Damien! And poor Tilly! I can't believe it. It just doesn't make sense.'

Gideon had a question.

'Who's Marcus? Both Barbara and Hamish spoke of Marcus, but Tilly obviously didn't want to talk about him.'

'Marcus! Oh, my God, I'd forgotten Marcus,' Pippa said instantly. 'He was Damien's younger brother. He committed suicide about ten or twelve years ago. It was awful! He was on a training course, trying out for the Olympic Pentathlon team, and threw himself off the top of a building. He was only seventeen and everyone thought he was happy. The family were absolutely devastated. And now this has happened. Oh God, it's so unfair! Poor Barbara, poor Tilly.'

This conversation was running through Gideon's mind as he waited for Giles to pick him up on the morning of the commemoration service.

Pippa and her older brother lived in the rambling stone priory that Giles had inherited after the untimely death of their parents some years before, and Gideon had been living in the gatehouse, largely rent-free, for the past couple of years. He shared the sixteenth-century lodge with an Abyssinian cat called Elsa and a two-year-old brindle mongrel that answered – when it suited him – to the name of Zebedee.

Gideon stared out of the stone-mullioned, diamond-paned window at the strip of garden in front, his unfocused gaze fixed on the sprinkling of daffodils that nodded under the brown-leaved beech hedge. After several dull, wet days, the sun was shining again and the grass was sorely in need of cutting, but, at that moment, nothing was further from his mind.

Why Damien? If there was one thing this tragedy had shown above everything, it was just how universally liked the trainer had been. Tributes had been made, both publicly and privately, on TV, in the newspapers and by letter, and the recurring theme was of his generosity, helpfulness and good humour. Nobody seemed to have a bad word to say about him.

Nevertheless, somebody somewhere had had a falling-out with him: one that had resulted in that person hiding in the woods and shooting Damien as he rode by. That was some quarrel.

The roof of Giles' Mercedes four-by-four slid into view along the top of the hedge and Gideon shook off the unprofitable thoughts and reached for his navy wool jacket.

Inside the vehicle, he found not only Giles but also Pippa.

'Hi. No Lloyd today, then?' he asked, surprised. Pippa had been seeing boyfriend and would-be Member of Parliament, Henry Lloyd-Ellis, for the last two months, and he seemed to be forever at the Priory. Gideon had assumed they would go to the service together.

Pippa shook her head, looking neat and unusually elegant in a black trouser suit, with a velvet-trimmed hat on her short, light brown curls.

'He's hoping to catch us up later. He's got some last-minute campaign business to take care of before this countryside march on Saturday. He'll be gutted if he misses the service – he and Damien go way back.'

Gideon settled himself in the front seat, feeling that there was very little that couldn't be postponed for an hour or so to attend the commemoration of a friend, even urgent political business, but he held his tongue.

He'd known Pippa for almost as long as he'd known her brother, having spent a number of holidays at Graylings Priory when he and Giles were at school together. After leaving university he'd lost touch with Pippa until a chance meeting had thrown them together again, and they picked up their brother-and-sister relationship as if the intervening ten years had never been. It was only lately that things had become a little strained – since around the time Pippa had started dating Lloyd, in fact. Normally very even-tempered, she had begun to be moody and unpredictable, until even Giles – who wasn't known for his intuition – had noticed the change in her.

'You look very nice, Pips,' Gideon said, turning to survey her through the gap in the front seats. Not conventionally pretty, she had the kind of classic bone structure that would stand her in good stead in years to come, when her more sweet-faced contemporaries had gone to seed.

'She still scrubs up quite nicely, doesn't she?' Giles observed as they set off.

'Yes – considering my age,' she agreed acidly. At thirty-three she was three years younger than the other two, and eight years younger than the absent Lloyd.

Gideon wondered if this was an oblique reference to his own current relationship with an older woman, but dismissed the thought; Pippa had never made any comment about Eve's age before – at least not in his hearing.

'Are the police any nearer to catching the bastard who did this?' Giles enquired, recalling the business of the day. 'Have you heard anything?'

Gideon shook his head. 'I had another session with Coogan yesterday, but if they've made any breakthroughs he wasn't about to tell me. I rather think they're stumped. There's a lay-by on the side of the road beyond that wood, and it's very popular with dog walkers, so there are often one or two cars parked there. Tilly says the police were back there this Sunday, stopping cars and questioning people, but she doesn't know if they came up with anything. I suppose it would be easy enough for someone to walk off into the trees with a gun held under their coat – especially if it was one of the sort that comes apart.'

'Somebody must have known you would ride that way, though,' Giles pointed out, frowning as he accelerated smoothly onto the Blandford road.

'Well, we'd ridden that way the last three times. We were trying to get Nero used to the noise of the guns, but I think it was a regular route of Damien's, anyway.'

'So why did the police want to see you again?' Pippa asked.

'I should imagine it's routine. I expect they're just hoping I'll remember some vital fact that I've hitherto forgotten, although Coogan always gives me the impression that he thinks I'm hiding something.'

'Oh, for heavensakes! Surely he doesn't think *you* had anything to do with shooting Damien . . .'

'No, I don't think I'm a suspect exactly, but . . .'

'But what?'

Gideon shrugged. 'I don't know. It's probably just his manner, and anyway, I guess they have to cover all possibilities.'

There were, Gideon estimated, upward of two hundred mourners at Damien Daniels' memorial service, and it became clear that the choice of the minster instead of the parish church had nothing to do with any perceived idea of status and everything to do with practicality. As it was, extra chairs had to be found, and there were still an unlucky few standing along the side aisles.

As well as Damien's friends and family, Pippa pointed out several of his fellow trainers with their families, and a number of jockeys he had either ridden against, or who had, more recently, ridden for him. There were even – she told him in lowered tones – a couple of minor royals attending; the result, no doubt, of his having worn the Queen's colours a time or two.

The press, predictably, were out in force, and a news team from both the BBC and a local TV station had been outside the lychgate to film the arrival of the mourners. Gideon saw one or two of the celebrities being asked to say a word or two, and hoped nobody would point him out as the man who'd been with Damien when he'd been shot. Somehow, his name and address had became known and, after being caught unawares once, he'd spent the last week checking his front garden before venturing out.

Thankfully, on this occasion, nobody came his way.

In due course, the family processed through the nave, all the ladies hatted and veiled, with Freddy, smart in grey and navy, stumping solemnly at Beth's side.

Gideon noticed that in contrast to the bowed heads of the other family members, Barbara Daniels, arm in arm with her husband, was looking about her at the massed ranks of mourners and, even through the gauze, she looked plainly bemused. His heart sank. It seemed that even this formal acknowledgement of her son's passing had failed to pierce the self-protective bubble she had formed around herself. He wondered what would happen when reality finally filtered through, and feared for her. In the meantime, he knew it was making a difficult time much worse for her family.

Due to the number of people who wished to say their piece, the service was fairly long and, by the time the congregation filed out into the spring sunshine, many of the younger members had become fidgety and complaining, and a baby at the back of the building had started to cry fitfully.

As Gideon's party left the cool of the minster, a tallish man in grey corduroys and a tailored leather jacket appeared beside them and tucked his hand proprietorially through Pippa's arm.

'Lloyd!' she exclaimed, looking pleased. 'How long have you been here?'

'Oh, quite a while – I don't know, twenty minutes? Half an hour? I managed to get away earlier than I'd expected. I think it was about half past eleven. I arrived in the middle of "Abide With Me", but I had to stand at the back. What a turnout! Old Damien would have been flabbergasted! Hi, Giles; Gideon.'

Recently separated, with two young children, Henry Lloyd-Ellis had grey-flecked wavy brown hair that was beginning to show signs of receding and an athletic figure that was showing signs of doing the opposite. In his youth and early twenties he had been a competitive, all-round sportsman who, Gideon knew, had represented England in the triathlon. Generally popular, it was often said that he was impossible to dislike, but somehow, Gideon managed.

'Henry,' he nodded briefly, enjoying the flicker of annoyance his use of Lloyd's given name invariably produced.

Born into a wealthy family, and heavily involved with the local foxhounds ever since leaving full-time education, Lloyd had switched successfully from fox hunting to drag hunting following the countrywide ban, and was now Master of the Tarrant and Stour Drag Hounds. He had, at the same time, ridden the tide of ill feeling the ban caused and put himself forward to stand on countryside matters in the upcoming parliamentary elections. His was very much a rural constituency and the general consensus was that he had a very good chance of success.

Joining the flow of people, the four of them moved on to the car park and in due course headed for the hotel and the reception, Pippa abandoning Gideon and Giles in favour of Lloyd's Range Rover.

Looking at the busily chattering throng from his position near one of the tall Edwardian sash windows, Gideon supposed that the reception would be accounted a success but, for his part, he hoped that Giles wouldn't want to stay too long. This was, he knew, a rather forlorn hope, because Giles was one of life's born socialisers and never happier than when in a room full of people.

He sighed. If he'd thought of it, he would have made some excuse of having to get away early, declined the lift and made his own way to the service. He found his eyes straying, not for the first time, to where Pippa and Lloyd sat sharing a window seat and, shaking off the mild irritation that this provoked, wondered if Eve would be waiting for him when he got home. He glanced at his watch, supposing – when a decent amount of time had passed – that he could feign a headache, say his farewells and call a taxi.

Somewhere between the minster and the hotel, Barbara had disappeared, presumably taken home by a relative. A sensible decision, Gideon thought; she could only be further confused by the occasion, and it saved both family and guests from possible embarrassment. Much easier and kinder to say that she didn't feel able to face everyone.

After half an hour or so of small talk, canapés, and waiters who tried to top up his glass every time he took a sip, the room was becoming stuffy and Gideon's claim to a headache could be made in all sincerity. Disengaging the grasp of a portly individual with a red-veined nose and watery eyes, who insisted on clutching Gideon's sleeve while he regaled him with doubtful tales of his part in Damien's success, he went in search of Giles to inform him of his change of plan.

Pippa's brother, true to form, was surrounded by a group of rather more females than males, and appeared to be having a fine time, entirely forgetting, Gideon suspected, the reason they were all there.

Gideon approached from behind, laid a hand on his shoulder, and spoke close to his ear.

'Going to make my own way home, Giles. Say goodbye to Pippa for me.'

Giles swung round, an elegant brunette on his arm. 'Gideon! Say hello to Leila, she's an air hostess.'

'*Flight attendant*,' the girl corrected, transferring her blue gaze to the newcomer with every appearance of appreciation. 'Hi, Gideon.' She made the two words a full-on flirtation.

'Hi,' he said with a brief smile.

'Look, if you're really going now, why don't you take the Merc?' Giles suggested. 'I probably shouldn't be driving anyway – I think I've probably had rather too much to drink. These waiters fill up when you're not looking!'

'Yeah, well I changed onto orange juice for the same reason. OK. I'll do that. I'll just say my goodbyes to the family.'

Giles held out his car keys and the ticket for the car park and, with another smile for the others, Gideon collected his jacket from the chair-back he'd draped it over, and began to thread his way through to where he could see Hamish's curly blond mop showing over the heads of the other guests.

He found Damien's father in a small group that included his daughter-in-law, a big fair-haired man who might have been a brother, and two younger Japanese men, who quite obviously weren't.

'Thank you for coming, Gideon,' Hamish said, after he'd said his piece. 'It's wonderful that so many people wanted to pay their respects.'

Before he could say anything else, a look of distraction came over him and he put a hand into the inner pocket of his jacket, withdrawing a mobile phone.

'It's on silent,' he said, by way of an explanation. 'Excuse me.'

Hamish turned away to speak and, as Gideon took his leave of Beth, he could sense from the low, urgent tones that the phone call was important.

Then Hamish was back. 'Has anyone seen Tilly, lately?'

'I think she went to the loo,' Beth told him. 'Is there a problem?'

'Just got to nip home for something,' Hamish said, avoiding the issue.

Beth's look sharpened. 'It's not Barbara?'

'No. Nothing like that.'

Hamish gave his daughter-in-law a significant look and Gideon sensed that he didn't want to share his news with all and sundry.

'Well, you guys obviously have family business to discuss, so

I'll be on my way,' he said, hoping the other men would follow his lead.

Thankfully, they did, and Hamish shot Gideon a grateful look as the three of them turned away.

As a result of the quantities of orange juice Gideon had consumed, and with the prospect of a longish drive home in mind, he paid a visit to the men's room on his way out, and when he emerged from the rear entrance of the hotel into the crowded car park, the first person he saw was Hamish. The farmer was standing staring in frustration at a Volvo and a sports saloon that were blocking his own vehicle in.

'Hell and damnation!' he exclaimed as Gideon approached. 'This is all I bloody need!'

'Anything I can do?'

'I wanted to slip out quietly but these morons have double-parked! It's going to take for ever to sort out, and by the time we've finished, everybody'll be wanting to know where I'm going and why.'

'Well, I could give you a lift,' Gideon offered. 'I'm taking Giles' car and he's getting a taxi later. We parked in the multi-storey round the corner because we thought this might get a bit chocker.'

For a moment, Hamish hesitated.

'You don't have to tell me anything,' Gideon said.

'But it's way out of your way . . .'

'No problem.'

'OK, thanks.' Suddenly Hamish was striding towards the car park exit and Gideon had to hurry to catch up.

'That was Barbara's sister on the phone. She took Barbara home after the service; we thought it was best.'

'I meant it,' Gideon assured him. 'You really don't have to explain.'

'Well, you'll hear soon enough, anyway. I just didn't want a fuss in there – you know. It's bad enough already with the way Damien died, and the press and everything. I kept hearing people talking about it, and then they'd go quiet when they realised I was near.' He broke off as they turned towards the town centre. 'Oh, I suppose you can't blame them, but now, on top of everything else, we've been broken into. The farmhouse, I mean. When Lucy and Barbara got home they found the glass in the French windows broken. Some bastard's taken advantage of us all being out, and helped themselves!'

'Oh, God!' Gideon was appalled, immediately thinking of the effect this further calamity would have on Damien's mother.

'I managed to persuade Beth and Tilly to stay and keep up appearances, but I don't envy them. God knows what they'll say if anyone asks where I am. They'll have to make up some excuse.'

In the multi-storey, Gideon paid for the time the Mercedes had been parked and they hurried up the steps to the next level.

'I'm sorry,' Hamish said presently, as he settled himself into the passenger seat. 'You said you had to get home – this is going to delay you . . .'

Gideon shook his head. 'That's all right. To be honest, I'd just had enough. I'm not one for crowds.'

'That's good. That's good. Neither am I,' he replied, distractedly. 'Oh, God, we could have done without this!'

Gideon stopped the Merc at the barrier, fed his ticket into the machine and waited while the bar was raised. Easing out into the town-centre traffic he asked, 'Was there no-one at the farm?'

'Well, most of the girls wanted to come to the service, but Megan was there – she's our house-help and extra groom. The house was locked but not alarmed, because she needed to get herself some lunch. Normally she'd be in or around the yard, within sight of the house . . .'

'But today . . . ?' Gideon prompted.

'Well, apparently two of the horses got out, so she had to go and round up a couple of the farm workers to help find them.'

'Got out, or were let out?'

'That's what I was thinking,' Hamish agreed. 'We didn't advertise the service but, as you saw from the numbers, it wasn't exactly a secret. Oh, God! You hear about this happening but you never really think it will happen to you, do you? Lucy says Barbara's in a bit of a state.'

Gideon drove as fast as he dared but nevertheless, when they reached the farm some fifteen minutes later, there were already two police cars and a van parked by the low garden wall. The front door stood open, and Hamish leapt out of the vehicle almost before it had stopped moving and headed up the garden path.

Gideon parked the Mercedes and then followed more slowly, passing a uniformed policeman in the doorway. The officer, perhaps assuming he was one of the family, didn't question his right to be there, so Gideon went on in, lured partly by a desire to help and partly by good old-fashioned curiosity.

Out of habit, he made for the kitchen, glancing through the open lounge door as he passed. Two men in white coveralls were at work in there, bent over the huge oak sideboard on the far side of the room. Their starkly clinical figures looked incongruous standing on the deep-pile carpet, amidst the cosy luxury of the sitting room, like white paper cut-outs on a velvet-draped stage. Thankfully the room didn't appear to have been too badly desecrated.

In the kitchen he caught up with Hamish, and found also Barbara, an older woman who was presumably her sister Lucy, and Detective Inspector Rockley. Gideon paused in the doorway just in time to hear Barbara say, in a voice that shook piteously, 'But why did they have to mess up the cottage? I was trying to keep it nice for when Damien comes back. They've spoiled it. Damien will hate finding it like that; he's so tidy.' Tears shining in her eyes, she looked up at her husband who stood with his hand on her shoulder. The black of mourning accentuated the lacklustre quality of her skin, and she looked desperately frail.

'We'll put it right again,' Hamish promised, as one might to a child, but this time it seemed she was not to be comforted.

'You can't,' she said brokenly and, with aching sympathy, Gideon witnessed the dawning of the full, devastating truth. 'He isn't coming back. He's gone; my baby's gone. Why did he have to leave me? Why? Why Damien? Why?'

She cried out the last words with a sudden rush of grief and then began weeping with terrible keening sobs, rocking to and fro as if the pain was physical.

'No, Babs, please . . .' Hamish pulled her towards him and held her tight but the wailing continued unabated. He looked helplessly round at the others, and it was Rockley who said decisively, 'She needs a doctor. Do you have a number?'

By the time the doctor arrived, just over fifteen minutes later, Barbara Daniels' heart-rending sobs had quietened but she still rocked constantly in her husband's arms, eyes wide open and tears streaming down her cheeks.

Rockley beckoned to Gideon and led the way outside, wandering down the path with every appearance of enjoying the sunshine, and stopping to rest the seat of his grey trousers against the garden wall.

Gideon did the same. The rough stone was warm, and aubretia sprouted from the cracks to tumble down the sides in purple and white cascades. A fly buzzed and settled on his hand. He shook it off.

'Hamish a particular friend of yours?' Rockley asked after a moment.

Gideon shook his head. 'No. Actually, I hardly know him. I drove him back from the reception because his car was blocked in in the hotel car park, that's all.'

'What was Damien's relationship with his father like, do you know?'

'OK, I think. I'm not really sure. Surely you're asking the wrong person . . . One of his family – Tilly or someone – would know much more.'

'No. I'm asking the right person. You strike me as more than averagely perceptive, and I'm interested to know what *you* think.'

Gideon was surprised. 'All right,' he said slowly. 'For what it's worth, I think the whole family are very close. I also got the impression, from a couple of things he said, that a certain amount of pressure was brought to bear by Hamish to get Damien to give up his racing career, but I don't think that came between them at all. After all, it was understandable, don't you think? Jump racing is a dangerous game, and having already lost one son . . .'

'Some families don't seem to have much luck, do they?' Rockley pushed a pebble round with the toe of his shoe, watching it with apparent concentration. Suddenly he kicked it away. 'And what about you? Have you remembered anything else about the morning Damien was shot?'

Gideon shook his head. 'Nothing. I've told you everything.'

'Perhaps you'd go through it again for me . . .'

'I went over it again with Coogan, just two days ago.'

'Nevertheless, if you don't mind,' Rockley said placidly.

Gideon swallowed his frustration and complied. After all, the police had a job to do, and he wanted Damien's killer found, as much as anyone. The constant repetition, though, was keeping the horror fresh in his mind.

'And other than the dog walker, you didn't see a soul?' Rockley asked when he'd finished.

'No.'

'And on your previous rides, can you remember whether you saw anyone then? Maybe more than once?'

'No, sorry. If we did, then I don't remember. Do you have any ideas about the motive yet?'

'We always have ideas — it's finding the right one that's the problem.'

'In other words — mind your own business,' Gideon observed. 'I suppose it's no good asking if you're making any progress?'

'The release of information has to be very carefully thought out,' Rockley told him. 'A careless word could warn our murderer that we were onto him. He might destroy evidence or even flee the country. It's safer to say nothing.'

'On the TV they said you were looking for the drivers of a white van and a red hatchback . . .'

'Only to eliminate them from the investigation. We made a list of vehicles that people remembered seeing in the lay-by on the main road, and so far those are the only two we haven't traced, but to be honest, if the owners don't choose to come forward, there's not much we can do. It won't necessarily be important.'

'So, do you think this is related?' Gideon waved a hand towards the house.

Rockley pursed his lips. 'Can't say for sure, at this point, but the possibility can't be ignored. Unfortunately this kind of burglary is all too common, as you probably know, targeting a house when the family are at a funeral. The Danielses did the right thing in leaving someone to keep an eye on the house but it seems, in this case, that the thieves were prepared for that.'

'So, does that make a connection more likely?'

Rockley shrugged. 'Perhaps. Perhaps not. We'll know more in a day or two.'

THREE

GIDEON LEFT PUDDLESTONE FARM as the rest of the family and staff began to return from the reception. It was late afternoon, and he called Giles on his mobile to reassure him that he hadn't driven the Merc into a ditch — or anything else, for that matter.

'If you're not doing anything, why don't you come for supper?' Giles was apparently none the worse for wear, which didn't surprise Gideon. He seemed to have been born with an astoundingly hard head where alcohol was concerned, and had been notorious at university for being able to drink anyone under the table.

'I'd say yes but I'm not sure whether Eve's coming over.'

'If she is, bring her along. I was going to show you the plans for the launch, and with her background she might have some useful suggestions.'

Eve was very much her own woman, and Gideon hesitated to make plans on her behalf. He'd have liked to ask whether Lloyd would be there, but good manners forbade it.

'I'll see, but I'll get the Merc back to you, whatever.'

'OK, well let me know.'

When Gideon finally turned between the stone gateposts at the end of the drive to Graylings Priory, the first thing he saw, parked outside the Gatehouse, was Eve Kirkpatrick's cream-coloured Aston Martin. He stopped the Mercedes behind it, shaking his head in mild exasperation at the haphazard way she had parked. Never one to slot into one space if there were two available, she had left the rear end of her expensive sports car jutting some eighteen inches out into the lane, just asking to be hit by a careless driver. Admittedly, it was a private drive, but Gideon knew she'd have parked the same way anywhere. His own Land Rover was parked on the short drive in front of the shed-cum-garage.

The lights were on in the Gatehouse, one burning in almost every room, as far as Gideon could see, and smoke curled from the central chimney pot.

'Hi,' he called, opening the heavy oak front door.

'Hiyah.' The response came from the kitchen, at the back of the house, and Eve came through to the hall, tall and stately, with a glass of red wine in her hand. Born of an English father and Jamaican mother, she was six feet tall and had olive skin and wavy black hair that, worn loose, reached the small of her back. More striking than beautiful, she was forty-two, the widow of a property developer, and had been left, by her own admission, quite disgustingly well off. She worked from choice rather than need, and the small art gallery she ran had become one of the most prestigious on the south coast.

'This isn't half bad,' she said, holding the glass up. 'Where did you get it?'

'Giles,' Gideon said, putting a hand down to greet Zebedee who came, wagging delightedly, to meet him.

'You've been a long time. How did it go?' Eve asked, leaning forward to kiss Gideon on the cheek. 'Sorry I couldn't make it.'

'The service went OK, but there was a bit of a drama afterwards,' he said, going on to tell her about the break-in at the farm. 'Actually, I've just been talking to Giles. I've got to take the Merc back, and he wondered if we'd like to come to supper – both of us.'

'That's kind of him,' she said in her rich, musical voice. 'What time?'

The evening was as pleasant as it could be, following, as it did, on the heels of such a day. They dined 'in state' as Giles dubbed it, in the wood-panelled dining room, with candles for light and a CD of Gregorian chants playing softly in the background.

Eve, a child of the Sixties, was dressed, as often, in long flowing garments of Indian cottons and silks, this evening in gold and amber, which lent her whole being a kind of ethereal glow in the soft light. Around her neck hung a huge red and gold pendant, and countless bangles and bracelets jangled on her wrists. Gideon thought she looked like a dancer from some Eastern land, and felt a warm contentment that it was *his* bed she was sharing, that night.

Lloyd *was* there but, for once, his presence didn't grate on Gideon. He seemed a little preoccupied, and Gideon wondered if it was reaction to the service, overindulgence at the wake, or a combination of the two. Pippa sat next to him, her jeans and lambswool jumper a sharp contrast to Eve's ethnic finery. Gideon caught her eyes on the older woman a couple of times, and wondered what she was thinking. Being based primarily on a mutual sexual attraction, his four-month-old relationship with Eve was mostly a thing of the night, and it was pretty much the first time Giles and his sister had had a chance to get to know her properly.

The conversation during the first course was inclined to dwell on the events of the day, but as the lamb pasties were polished off and fruit salad passed round, Giles changed the subject to that of his latest business venture.

After years of flirting with first one outrageous idea, then another, he had finally come up with a possible winner. The Graylings estate had, amongst many other resources, several acres of extremely productive orchards, said to have been planted by the Franciscan brothers who'd inhabited the original priory, long since gone. A certain amount of scrumpy cider had always been made, but a foray into the world of winemaking had led to Giles blending apple juice with the grapes from the age-old vines in the greenhouses, and developing a light, sparkling apple wine that he was now preparing to launch onto the market under the name Graylings Sparkler.

They had, in fact, been drinking Sparkler with their meal, and to Giles' delight, Eve, who had a far more discerning palate than the rest of them, had pronounced herself agreeably surprised.

'To be honest, I expected it to be nothing more than a glorified cider,' she admitted. 'But it's really rather good. There's grape in there too, isn't there?'

'Just a little.'

'It works,' she said, and Gideon knew that she wouldn't have said it unless she meant it.

'I'll buy a case,' Lloyd agreed, nodding.

Pippa gave him a dig in the ribs. 'You'd buy anything remotely alcoholic,' she said, laughing.

'You make me sound like some old soak,' he protested. 'I only buy what I like – it's just that I tend to like most things.'

'So how are you planning to promote this?' Eve enquired of Giles, ignoring the other two.

Given this invitation, Giles immediately started to run through his plans for the launch and marketing of the wine, which kicked off with a grand reception at the Priory in just over a week's time.

'You've invited the press and local hoteliers, I presume?' Eve broke in, arching black brows drawn down over equally black eyes.

'Yes, and the local TV and radio stations.'

'Good. What are you feeding them?'

'Just canapés and stuff. Pippa's taking care of that,' Giles told her, and they became immersed in the details.

Eve was clearly in her element. Her deceptively languorous air hid a razor-sharp mind, and Gideon guessed there was nothing she would like better than to be planning a marketing coup.

Be careful, Giles, he thought, as he watched the pair. You'll find you've got yourself a business partner before the night's out.

When the supper party broke up, just before one o'clock, the sky was clear and moonlit, and Gideon and Eve turned down the offer of a lift back to the Gatehouse in favour of walking the quarter-mile or so.

As the door shut behind them, Eve wrapped her long, woolly coat around her and, tucking her arm through Gideon's, said, 'I like Giles and Pippa.'

'Good,' he responded, trying not to dwell on the way Lloyd's arm had wrapped possessively around Pippa as they'd turned back into the house.

'Have you ever dated her?' Eve asked after a moment.

'Who, Pippa? No. We're just friends. I've known them for ever.'

'You don't like her being with Lloyd.'

'I don't think he's good enough for her.'

'Is that all?'

'Yes . . . Why?'

Eve didn't answer. For a moment there was only the sound of their footsteps crunching on the gravel, then she said, 'I don't think they're in love.'

'Lloyd and Pippa?' Gideon was surprised. 'But he's obviously staying the night.'

'So am I,' she pointed out.

The following morning brought a telephone call from Tilly Daniels.

It was past nine and Gideon had been lying in bed listening to the birdsong outside his window and enjoying the play of the sunshine on his closed eyelids.

He opened his eyes. Beside him, Eve lay sprawled on her back, apparently asleep, her dark hair tousled on the pillow and her long lashes touching the smooth caramel skin of her cheeks. She had only the faintest of laughter lines and no hint of silver in her black mane; Gideon imagined she'd probably look the same for another fifteen or twenty years.

The phone trilled on the bedside cabinet on Eve's side of the bed, and without opening her eyes she reached out a slim brown arm and located it, handing it across to Gideon.

'Hello?'

'Gideon? It's Tilly here – Tilly Daniels. It's not too early, is it?'

'No – not at all,' Gideon said. 'How can I help?'

'Well, it's about Nero. I was lying awake last night, worrying about him. The thing is, you and Damien were getting on so well with him, but since . . . well, you know . . .'

'Yeah, sure.'

'Well, since then he's been a real pig, and I'm not sure I can cope with him. It's partly the lack of time. One of my lads didn't turn up for work yesterday and I've still got a yardful of horses to deal with – except for a couple whose owners whisked them away as soon as they heard about Damien. Nero needs more attention than I can give him, and the lads that I've got left aren't too happy about managing him . . .' Her voice tailed off.

'And you'd like me to have him for a while, and continue his training,' Gideon said.

'I hate to ask, but would you, Gideon? It'd be a weight off my mind. I don't really want to sell him – even if I could in his present state – because Damien thought such a lot of him, but just at the moment . . .'

'Well, I'll have to check with Pippa, but I'm pretty sure she's got room.'

'Oh.' Uncertainly. 'I didn't realise – I mean, I just assumed you had stables yourself.'

'I'm sure there won't be a problem. Listen, I'll get back to you as soon as I can.'

Eve was already out of bed as Gideon leaned over to put the handset back. Yawning, she wrapped a black satin housecoat around her and padded across to the door, winding her hair into a knot in preparation for her shower.

'You don't have to get up, if you don't want to,' he told her.

'Oh, but I do,' she said with a smile. 'I've got a gallery to open and I'm late as it is. I'll only be five.'

As predicted, Pippa raised no objections and the Daniels' cream and brown horsebox delivered the problem horse just after three that same afternoon. Tilly backed the vehicle right up to the stone arched entrance to the Priory stableyard, so that Nero, should he somehow get free, would only have the run of the yard.

'Thanks guys, this is brilliant – such a help,' she called, jumping down from the cab as Pippa and Gideon went to meet her.

'That's all right,' Pippa said. 'How are you? Gideon told us about the break-in; how awful!'

'Yeah, it's been pretty bloody, but at least they didn't take too much.'

'How's your mum?' Gideon asked.

'Much quieter, thanks. She's still sedated but at least she's finally facing up to everything. We were beginning to wonder if she ever would. It's been awful, and what makes it worse is not being able to have Damien's body for a proper funeral. It makes it hard to move on, you know?'

From within the lorry came a heavy banging as Nero began to complain at being kept waiting, and Tilly made a face.

'Oh, he's done that all the way over. Every time we stopped at a junction he'd start up: bang, bang, bang. It was almost driving me mad!'

'Well, let's get him in. Have you got time for a cuppa before you start back?' Pippa enquired.

'Oh, I'd love one,' Tilly said, going round to the back of the lorry. 'Where do you want him?'

'In the end box,' Gideon said. 'Shall I bring him down?'

'Be my guest.'

Nero had worked up a sweat and came out of the lorry with a rush, pulling right to the end of the extra-long lead rope Gideon had fastened to his headcollar. Once in the yard he went into rapid reverse, his head held high and shod hooves drumming a frantic tattoo on the cobbles. Gideon went with him for a few strides, offering no resistance and avoiding eye contact until the brown horse backed himself into a corner and stopped. Then, still not looking directly at Nero, he moved slowly up the rope, soothing him with a steady stream of nonsense. Gradually the animal's head came down and when Gideon was finally close enough to reach out a hand and rub him between the eyes, Nero sighed and relaxed.

'All right now? Come on, you daft bugger,' Gideon said. 'Let's go and see your new home.'

With the horse safely installed, Tilly fetched his saddle and bridle from the lorry, and Pippa followed with a big canvas bag containing a number of rugs and blankets.

'He has to have his own saddle because he's got such a high wither,' Tilly said, meaning the bony part of a horse's anatomy, at the base of its neck. 'And we always keep separate rugs for each horse, so I've brought those, too.'

Ten minutes later, happy that Nero was settling, the three of them made their way across the yard, through the boot room and into the huge kitchen, where heat from the old-fashioned range banished the chill of the cold wind outside.

The Priory kitchen was one of Gideon's favourite places on earth. Cavernous and cosy at one and the same time, it had dark beams, warm ochre-painted walls and a wide, diamond-paned window over the biggest earthenware sink he'd ever seen. The uneven stone floor was scattered with rugs and supported, among other things, a range of cupboards and shelves, an oak table, three armchairs that had seen better days, and two dog beds.

Giles was already in the kitchen and, anticipating their need, had the kettle boiling. His greeting woke the dogs, who'd been occupying both beds *and* armchairs, and for a moment all was chaos as five assorted canines pressed forward to welcome them.

'Oh, my goodness! What a crowd!' Tilly exclaimed. 'Are they all yours, Pippa?'

'No, one of them's mine,' Gideon admitted, adding, 'the well-behaved one,' whereupon he was immediately shouted down by Pippa and Giles.

'Hallo, sweetie, what's your name?' Tilly said, leaning down to fondle the ears of Pippa's black Labrador.

'That's Fanny,' Giles told her. 'The two handsome Jack Russells are Yip and Yap – they're mine. The other two are Fanny's pups; the black one is Bella, and the brindle monster is Zebedee – he belongs to Gideon.'

'They're gorgeous. I love dogs but Damien's allergic – *was* allergic – so we've never had one. We could have done with a couple in the house yesterday . . . But Zebedee? Why on earth Zebedee?'

'Because he bounces,' Gideon explained. 'You remember *The Magic Roundabout*?'

They talked dogs while Giles made and served the coffee, but after a while they drifted inexorably back to the subject of the break-in.

'Honestly, it's just the lowest of the low,' Pippa said. 'And Gideon said they let the horses out. Did you get them back OK?'

Tilly nodded. 'It was only two of them. Megan – she's our Girl Friday – found one of them straight away – he'd only wandered a little way down the lane and started eating grass – but she couldn't find the other one anywhere. She was distraught, poor girl! I mean, what a nightmare – left in charge and twenty minutes later two of the horses go missing!'

'So where was the second one?' Giles asked.

'Well, actually, he'd never been out at all. Whoever did it was a clever sod. I suppose he guessed that we'd find them pretty quickly in the lane, so he shut one of them in the haybarn in the corner of the field. He was tucking in happily when we eventually found him, but of course, Megan never thought to look there. You wouldn't, would you? She'd got the Land Rover out and been all round the nearest villages – told the police and everything. All kinds of people got involved in the search.'

'But you didn't lose too much in the house?' Giles said.

'No, thankfully. Mostly small stuff, although that's bad enough. Mobile phones, the two laptops and some disks and stuff. They didn't take the PCs but the police said they often don't – they're so heavy, and unless they're state of the art, they're not worth the trouble. Damien's digital camera had gone and they'd made pretty much of a mess of his and Dad's offices. They turned the cottage upside down, too, and I think that's what finally got to Mum. She kept saying she wanted to keep it nice for when . . .' Tilly's eyes swam with tears and she fished a handkerchief out of her pocket to mop them. 'It was really hard on Beth. And the worst thing is that the house doesn't feel safe any more. It's like it's been defiled. I keep thinking about these people wandering round the house, touching things – our things – and I feel like I want to have it fumigated from top to bottom! I threw away everything in the fridge and larder, and put every single piece of crockery and cutlery, and all the pots and pans and casserole dishes through the dishwasher last night, after the police had gone. Absolutely everything; but still it doesn't feel clean.'

'Oh, God! You poor thing! That must be terrible.' Pippa put her hand over Tilly's and she responded with an apologetic smile.

'I'm sorry. It sounds horribly melodramatic, but it's just how I feel. I suppose it's partly because it's come at such an awful time . . .'

'And the police don't have any clues?'

'No, except they know the thieves were still in the house at quarter to twelve because they broke a carriage clock that was one of Mum and Dad's wedding presents, and it stopped at quarter to twelve.'

'More coffee, anyone?' Giles asked, getting to his feet. 'Tilly?'

'I should really be going,' she said. 'There's so much to do.'

'Oh, go on. Ten minutes either way won't make a lot of difference,' Pippa said.

Tilly pulled a face, weakening. 'OK, thanks. Actually, it's nice to get away for a while. I know that probably sounds awful, but it's just so *intense*, at the moment. Sometimes I just feel like I want to scream!'

'What's happening with the horses?' Gideon enquired. 'Will you be able to carry on training them?'

'Well – yes, for the moment, but I can't, long-term, because I haven't got a licence. I mean, I can still train the point-to-pointers, but most of our horses are running under rules now. That's where the money is – obviously. I shall have to apply to the Jockey Club to see if I can take over Damien's licence. I've already made enquiries and there shouldn't be a problem, but God knows how long it'll take. Most of the owners have said they'll hang on for a bit, but they won't wait for ever. And then there's the sponsors – we're not sure whether Skyglaze will continue to support us without Damien. It was his name that carried the deal, you see.'

'But surely they can't pull out now?' Pippa put in. 'You've got a contract, haven't you?'

Tilly shook her head, sadly.

'It was a two-year contract and unfortunately it's due for renewal in a couple of months. Damien was just starting negotiations, but of course everything's up in the air now.'

'Oh, that's really bad luck!' Pippa said.

Tilly shrugged. 'Yes, well, I suppose you can't blame them, really. It's business, after all, and Damien was the high-profile one.'

'So what about Nero?' Gideon asked. 'Will you keep him?'

'Well, I'd like to, if we can get him straightened out. As you know, he actually belongs – belonged – to Damien, and he was convinced he'd be brilliant one day, if we could just get to the bottom of his problems.'

'Gideon says he came from the Radcliffe Trust,' Pippa said. 'I thought that was where racehorses went to when they'd *finished* racing, or weren't good enough. I didn't realise you could actually get them from there.'

'No, well normally you wouldn't, but Nero was different. He's very well bred and should have had a decent career on the flat, but there's just no way he was ever going to go in the starting stalls. Until Gideon started working with him, it was a major operation just to get him into a horsebox, but he's improving all the time. Damien had an incredible eye for a horse and he had this grand scheme to buy difficult horses for a song, train them on until they started to win, then sell shares to a syndicate. That way he'd still get to train them but someone else would pay the bills. Nero was the first one. Damien was very keen to help the Radcliffe Trust – in fact he'd promised them a percentage of anything Nero won. They do a wonderful job, as Gideon knows. Do you still help out there, Gideon?'

'Yeah. Actually, I'm due there again tomorrow. Thanks, Giles,' he added as a coffee appeared at his elbow. 'But Damien was right about Nero. He might have been bred for the flat but he jumps like a stag. I've never seen anything like it. I know Damien hoped he might be a Grand National horse.'

'Yes, he did, and it's probably silly, but I feel if I could make something of him, I'd be doing it for Damien. Does that sound daft?'

They assured her that it didn't, and Gideon wondered who she'd get to jockey him. Brilliant or not, Nero was never going to be everybody's horse.

By the time Tilly got up to leave, the best part of another half-hour had passed and Gideon thought she looked a lot more relaxed than she had when she'd arrived. In the main, he felt this was probably due to having shared some of her worries with someone outside her immediate family, but also, he sometimes wondered, fancifully, if the old house didn't have some kind of healing quality about it. It was as though, within its walls, one was enveloped in a warm, comforting cocoon; as if the outside world could somehow be kept at bay for a few precious moments.

Pippa had been called away to the phone, so Gideon walked Tilly out to the horsebox, accompanied by four of the five dogs. Nero was looking over his half door, shifting restlessly and tossing his head.

'Goodbye, lad. Be good,' Tilly called. Then to Gideon, 'You'll find a folder in the bottom of the bag with the rugs and stuff in. Damien keeps – kept – notes on all the horses. You know the sort of thing. What they're eating, what work they're doing, which items of tack we've tried, which fitness regime, veterinary notes – the lot. A complete history. I thought it might be useful, though I expect you know most of it.'

Gideon *had* been through most of it with Damien, but he thanked her, nevertheless.

They stopped by the lorry, and Tilly turned, running her fingers through her long blonde hair and looking up at him with a measure of desperation.

'Oh, Gideon, I keep thinking when this is over we'll get back to normal. And I find I'm including Damien in that; as if this is just a temporary thing and he'll somehow be back. But then I remember it's never going to be over, and I get such a sudden rush of panic and fear that I don't feel I can cope. I just don't know how I can bear it . . .' Her blue eyes scanned his face, as if hoping to find the answer there. 'I mean, it's bad enough losing your brother, but when he's your business partner, too . . . There seems to be no part of the day when I'm not reminded of him. Whenever I have to make a decision about anything in the yard, I find myself thinking I must check that with Damien. The lads are depressed – though they've been very supportive – and even some of the horses seem a bit below par; I think they pick up on the general atmosphere. And of course, Damien had a way with them.'

'Yes, he did,' Gideon agreed. 'Look, Tilly – I don't know what I can say that you haven't heard before, but the reason you'll have heard it before is because it's true. It'll take time, but you *will* get through it, you know. I'm fairly sure that the panic is normal.

Just take one day at a time and – whatever happens – don't forget you've got friends here who really want to help. We're not just saying that; we mean it, OK?'

'Thanks.' Tilly managed a smile as she swung herself up into the cab. 'And thanks for taking Nero off my hands. I'll be in touch, but if you want to know anything, just give me a ring.'

'Will do. And Tilly . . . Damien would have wanted you to carry on with the horses. He was very proud of his little sister, you know.'

Tilly looked up and away, out of the windscreen.

'Did he say that?'

'Oh, yes,' Gideon stated, and, if it wasn't the literal truth, he didn't intend to let his conscience trouble him.

Gideon's visit to the Radcliffe Trust, near Bath, was part of an ongoing programme of rehabilitation for some of the centre's most difficult horses. It was never any hardship, as he enjoyed both the challenge and the company of the Trust's excellent staff. He was a great believer in the work the centre was doing, as he knew Damien had been. If it had been necessary, he would happily have given his services for free, but Angie Bowen, the centre's energetic manager, wouldn't hear of it. She insisted that the Trust could afford to pay him, so Gideon submitted an invoice each month for a token amount that covered his travelling expenses, and duty was felt to have been done on all sides.

The centre did indeed appear to be thriving. A new block of ten stables had been built in the eight months since Gideon had first visited and, even now, work was under way on a covered school to enable work with the horses to continue uninterrupted during the winter months.

Gideon was looking at the detailed plans of the new development in the staffroom when Angie came to find him that morning.

''Sgoing to be quite something!' he commented, after they'd exchanged greetings. 'Your mysterious benefactor's still coming up with the goods, then?'

'Yes, thank goodness. Regular as prunes.' Angie was fortyish, with uncompromisingly straight, collar-length, hennaed hair, a plain – if pleasant – face, and a figure that remained stubbornly plump in spite of a punishing workload. She lived and breathed horses, and had reportedly given up a well-paid position in a bloodstock agency to run the centre and take care of just a few of the countless racehorses that she had previously seen falling by the wayside due to age, injury or just plain lack of talent. 'It must be nearly ten months now, though whether there'll be any more now, after – well, you know . . .'

'I'm sorry?' Gideon *didn't* know.

Angie looked a little awkward.

'Well, I did wonder – I mean, he was always so interested in everything we were doing here – but it's probably a stupid idea. He was a smashin' fella but just because he had a couple of horses off us, doesn't mean he'd do something like that . . .'

The penny dropped. 'You mean Damien? Surely you didn't think *he* was your fairy godfather?'

'Well, he was the only person I could think of . . .'

'But where on earth would he get that kind of money? I mean, I obviously don't know exactly how much we're talking about here, but it must surely have been thousands – if not tens of thousands – by now; I can see that by the work you're having done. I'm not saying his family's poor, because they're not, but even though Puddlestone has been incredibly successful, it is only a small yard, as yet. It wouldn't make sense for him to be shelling out huge amounts like that on a regular basis.'

Angie raised her eyebrows, pursed her lips and shook her head.

'I admit it doesn't seem likely, but who else? People are wonderfully generous, but most of our supporters are in the ten or twenty pounds league, with just the odd hundred or two, here or there. All gratefully received, but nothing like this. We'd been through a really rough patch just before this started, and I mean really rough. We were struggling to keep going, and the directors were within a whisker of throwing in the towel. That first envelope was a complete bolt from the blue – a godsend. When I finally managed to convince myself that it wasn't a mistake – that someone wasn't going to turn up and ask for it back – I just sat down and howled with sheer relief!'

'What about one of the big trainers, or somebody that used to own one of your horses?'

'Well, I suppose it could be. Actually, I did wonder whether it could be a syndicate, because the cash always comes in five separate envelopes inside the one big one; varying amounts in each but always the same combination and the same total.'

Gideon frowned. 'That doesn't sound like one person then, does it?'

'Well, no. I suppose not. But at the end of the day, money is money, however it comes, and even if it does stop now, I shall be eternally grateful to whoever it was.' She turned and led the way out into the yard.

'I think you probably have to accept that you may never know,' Gideon said, following. 'Now, who're we going to do first? Pumpkin or Boomer?'

'Well, I've told Katy to get Boomer ready. Did I tell you, I've got someone coming to see him on Wednesday? Quite experienced, from what I can gather. They want him for riding-club stuff. Anyway, I thought we'd best do him while it's cloudy; you know what he's like with the flies – can't keep his mind on anything.'

'Good thinking,' Gideon approved. 'Let's see what kind of mood he's in today . . .'

'I wish you and Lloyd got on better, he's a really nice guy.'

Pippa and Gideon were hosing Nero down after a fairly successful session in the schooling arena. The horse had been with them a week now, and was improving daily.

'I've never said I didn't like him,' Gideon hedged.

'You don't *have* to say it. It's obvious. And Lloyd's noticed, too. He asked me if I knew what he'd done to upset you.'

Blast Lloyd! Gideon thought, turning the hose off and slapping Nero on his wet rump.

'That'll do you,' he said, thinking that he wouldn't have got away with it when the horse had first arrived.

'So what did you tell him?' he enquired.

'What *could* I tell him? I said I didn't know.' She busied herself with tidying up the hose. 'Did you know he went over to the Daniels' place the other day to see if he could help out at all?'

'No, I didn't. What brought that on?'

Pippa rounded on him. 'See, there you go again! He just wanted to help, of course. He's a friend. Why do you always look for something else?'

And why are you so touchy about him? Gideon could have replied, but he held his tongue for the sake of peace. His impression of the man was that he rarely did anything that didn't have some positive benefit for number one, but he wasn't about to say that to Pippa.

'I was just surprised because I know how busy he is with the election coming up.' He untied Nero, preparatory to taking him back to his box. 'Look, it's not that I don't like him, but we don't have to be best buddies, Pips. He's *your* friend. As long as *you're* happy, that's what matters. Come on, Nero, old boy. Let's get you in and fed.'

When he'd settled the horse, he found Pippa in the tack room.

'Everything sorted for tomorrow night, then?' he asked, determined to steer the conversation into safer channels. Both Pippa and Giles had been working hard all week, preparing for the Sparkler launch.

'I think so,' she murmured, her attention apparently focused on a piece of paper she was holding. 'This is odd.'

'What is?' Gideon went closer to look.

'This. I found it tucked in one of the plastic pockets of Nero's case file, between two sheets of paper. It just appears to be a series of letters and numbers.'

Gideon tilted his head sideways to look.

It was a piece of lined paper with a ragged top, such as might have been torn out of a spiral-bound notepad, and bore three columns, written in blue ballpoint. In the first column were six pairs of letters, and next to each of these were a six-digit number in the second column and then a three-digit one in the third. The top row of letters and numbers had been crossed through, and at the end of each of the others was a tick, as if someone had been checking them off, one by one.

Underneath these columns had been written, heavily under-scored several times, 6–1 Against, and around the margins were a number of elaborate doodles.

'Something to do with betting, perhaps,' Pippa said, shrugging. 'I've never really understood the mechanics of it.' She turned the paper over but the other side was blank.

'Maybe. I can't think it's got anything to do with Nero. Which reminds me, I've been meaning to take his file home and have a good look through it again. I'll put it in the Land Rover, so I don't forget.'

'Better put this back where I found it, I guess. Are you going to stop for lunch?'

'Thanks. Don't mind if I do,' Gideon said, glad the quarrel seemed to have blown over.

The following day was sunny and surprisingly warm for April, and as evening fell, the setting sun bathed the golden stone of the Priory in a warm glow and glinted on the tiny, uneven windowpanes.

The effect that greeted the guests to the Graylings Sparkler launch was magical, and exactly what Giles had hoped for.

When Gideon and Eve joined the steady stream of elegantly dressed people making their way through the arched front doorway and into the cavernous entrance hall, they heard count-less exclamations of delight and Gideon basked in vicarious pride.

The guests were guided into the main hall, where ladies dressed in Elizabethan costume moved among them bearing pewter trays with glasses of ice-cold water and intriguing canapés. Soft, lilting music filled the hall, and as Gideon glanced appreciatively around, he spotted a group of three musicians at the far end. High above the growing throng, torches burned in wall sconces, throwing dancing shadows way up into the vaulted ceiling and, around the lower walls, rich tapestries hung, interspersed with an impressive array of swords, pikes and shields. The setting was perfect; even Gideon, who was comfortably familiar with the hall, was wowed by the atmosphere.

'If this doesn't sell a few dozen cases, then nothing will,' Eve murmured in his ear. 'By the way, have I told you how devastatingly handsome you look in that dinner jacket?'

'Actually, I think you have, but I'm quite happy to hear it again. Come to that, you look quite passable yourself. I like that dress, it suits you.'

She smiled and inclined her head graciously, looking tall and willowy in a sheath dress of copper-coloured silk, with a fringed and beaded pale gold shawl draped over her arms. She was certainly a head-turner, her colouring still fairly unusual in rural Dorset, and Gideon had seen several people of both sexes watching her admiringly.

'These canapés are to die for,' she said then. 'Pippa's a genius. Why on earth would she want to mess around with horses when she can cook like this?'

Gideon shrugged. 'It's a calling, I guess. Horses sort of get under your skin.'

'My skin's obviously a closer fit,' Eve commented. 'Giles is looking rather dashing tonight, don't you think?'

Gideon pursed his lips. 'OK, I guess. But he's not really my sort.'

Eve put her head on one side, watching Giles as he moved among his guests, smiling and chatting easily.

'Ah, and there's Pippa. Doesn't she look nice?'

Gideon followed her gaze to the top end of the hall, where Pippa had come in and was having a word with the musicians.

She was wearing a dark red dress and had done something different with her hair; he couldn't quite decide what, but he liked it.

'I wonder where Lloyd is?' Eve said, echoing his own thoughts, but even as she said it, Lloyd appeared, sauntering across to slip an arm round Pippa's waist and whisper something in her ear.

She turned, laughing, then shot him a glance of mock severity.

'Speak of the devil,' Gideon observed.

Judging from the animated faces and many overheard comments, the evening was a great success. The actual moment of the Sparkler launch was stage-managed to perfection, complete with a drum roll, and with a profusion of fizzing sparklers positioned round the ceremonial bottle. When all the guests had been given glasses of wine and speeches made, the first of what Gideon knew was to be a spectacular display of fireworks started to go off at the back of the house. With exclamations of surprise, many of the visitors started to move out of the hall, through what was known as the garden room, then through the open French windows to the patio beyond. The reporter and his team from the local TV station hurried on their heels, just as if fireworks were something new.

'I'm just going to nip out and check on Nero,' Gideon said, speaking close to Eve's ear. 'He can get a bit upset by loud noises. Won't be a minute.'

As he made his way across the hall, Gideon caught sight of Pippa and pointed in the general direction of the stableyard. She nodded and gave him the thumbs up, showing that she understood, and he made his way through the kitchen, where the chaos of preparation covered every available work surface, and out through the boot room into the yard beyond.

Here he found the security light already on, activated – probably – by one of the semi-feral cats that made the outbuildings their home.

Gideon made his way along the nearest range of stables to Nero's box, speaking reassuringly to the horses who were gazing nervously at the colourful explosions just visible over the roof of the house.

Nero had his head over his half door.

'All right, lad? You're a brave fella,' Gideon said soothingly. Earlier in the day he'd fitted Nero with earplugs, and a fringed ear guard of the sort that had originally been designed as fly protection. Damien had told him that riders often used this combination to deaden the noise when showjumping on highly strung animals, and it certainly seemed to be doing the trick. Nero was restless and a little wide-eyed, but his neck felt dry and cool.

'You're fine, aren't you, old chap?' Gideon patted him and walked on round the yard.

Under the overhang, his presence didn't affect the light sensor, and consequently, after a moment, it went out, leaving only the light from the waxing moon.

Passing the tack room, Gideon glanced at the door and stopped short. The padlock on the bolt was hanging, unfastened.

'Tut, tut, Miss Barrington-Carr,' Gideon muttered, deciding that it would be as well to check that everything was in order before he locked it.

Opening the door, he stepped inside and reached for the light switch, thinking that Pippa must have had her mind on the evening ahead; she was normally meticulously careful.

In that instant, something hit him a cracking blow across his head and left shoulder, sending him spinning down into darkness.

FOUR

THE FLOOR WAS EXCEEDINGLY cold and hard and, for a moment, Gideon couldn't think why he should be lying on it. He was face down, with his cheekbone pressed to the concrete and his left arm twisted awkwardly underneath him, but, in spite of his discomfort, it took a considerable effort of will to move. His first attempt was rewarded by the onset of a heavy, throbbing pain in his head and neck, and a wash of dizziness.

'Oh, shit!' he said aloud, closing his eyes.

Fighting the vertigo, he sat up with his back to the wall and ran his fingers gingerly through his hair, wincing as they located a sizeable lump, above and behind his left ear. It was oozing, and Gideon had to stop himself wiping his hand on his trousers, remembering in the nick of time that he was wearing his best pair.

Damn.

The launch party. Eve would be wondering where he was.

With a groan, he pushed himself to his feet with the aid of the wall and, for the second time, reached for the light switch.

Blinking in the sudden brightness, he found the door had been pulled to, but not shut – which was encouraging; at least he hadn't been locked in. Glancing around, he did a swift mental inventory and decided there was little, if anything, missing, although one or two things had been moved and a couple of drawers were open, their contents pulled out.

It seemed Gideon had arrived on the scene just in time and, having hit him, the would-be thief had presumably lost his nerve and run off.

Gideon wiped his hands on an old tea towel that was used for tack cleaning and then, switching the light off again, went out into the yard, shutting and locking the door. He had no idea how long he'd been unconscious but, over the roof of the house, the night sky was dark and silent, and Gideon imagined that the guests were back in the warmth of the hall, enjoying the wine, and the cheese and biscuit supper that Pippa had prepared. Feeling decidedly muzzy, he made his way back to the house and into the kitchen, where he cast a look of longing at the old armchairs before going across to the sink and dampening his handkerchief under the cold tap.

The door at the far end opened, letting in a wash of sound from the hall beyond.

'Gideon?' Eve was standing there. 'I wondered where you'd got to . . .'

'Sorry. Won't be a moment.'

The door shut, and Eve came towards him.

'Was there a problem with the horse? Hey – are you all right?'

'Not really,' he admitted.

'Oh, good God!' she exclaimed, seeing him properly for the first time. 'Here, give me that. You're getting blood all over your collar. Did the horse do this?'

Gideon surrendered the damp handkerchief gratefully.

'No, it wasn't Nero. I – er . . . surprised someone in the tack room, helping himself to the gear.'

'It looks more like *he* surprised *you*,' Eve observed, pressing the folded cloth gently but firmly to his head. 'You mean they'd broken in?'

'Well, actually, no. It rather looks as though someone forgot to lock up.'

'So what happened? Did he get away?'

'Yeah, 'fraid so. I never even saw him. I don't think he took much but I can't tell for sure. Pippa'll have to look. I suppose he'd only just got in, but he'll be well away by now, that's for sure. What *is* the time, anyway? I've no idea how long I was out for.'

'Ten to ten. You were gone about fifteen minutes, in all,' she told him. 'I suppose it should be reported but it's a bit difficult, isn't it? Giles won't want the police turning up with all this going on. It'd be disastrous, especially when it's going so well. There, I think it's stopped bleeding. If I comb your hair down, it won't show at all. It just looks a bit wet.'

'Good. No, I think you're right about the police. I should tell Pippa, though. I'd better see if I can find her.'

'Tell you what, you wait here and I'll find her. It'll do you good to sit down for a minute.'

'I won't argue with that – but play it down, can you. It'd be better if Giles didn't know for now.'

'I shall be the soul of discretion,' Eve promised, washing her hands and drying them on a convenient dishcloth. 'Are you sure you're OK?'

'I'll survive. And Eve . . .'

'Yes?' She stopped on her way to the door.

'Thanks.'

'Well, I could have just turned round and gone back to the party, I suppose,' she said thoughtfully. Then, with a smile, she was gone.

Gideon eyed the armchairs once more, but settled for a seat at the table. For one reason, he felt that if he sank into cushioned comfort, it might take more will power than he had at present to dig himself out of it; and for another, if Pippa found him resting there after what Eve was about to tell her, he was almost certain she would take it as evidence of his imminent demise, and call a doctor without delay.

It seemed only moments later when the door reopened and Pippa came in with Lloyd on her heels.

'Hi. Eve told me what happened – are you OK?'

'Yeah, just a sore head. Look, I didn't think you'd want a fuss but you might want to check if anything's missing.'

'In a minute. First things first; let's have a look at that head.' She started towards him.

'No need,' he said. 'Eve's done a brilliant job.'

'Oh.' She hesitated, as if this possibility hadn't occurred to her.

'Go and check the tack,' he urged. 'But – take Lloyd with you, just in case.'

Pippa and Lloyd were gone only a matter of minutes before reporting back that all was quiet and nothing appeared to be missing.

'I've been trying to remember if I definitely locked it,' Pippa said as she took off the coat she'd wrapped around her semi-bare shoulders. 'But the thing is, I can't. It becomes automatic. You come out at the end of the day, turn round and lock the door. If you asked me five minutes later, I'd probably have to go and check.'

'You've had so much on your mind, these last few days, it wouldn't be surprising if you'd forgotten it, love,' Lloyd said.

'Yeah, I know, but it's not like me,' she protested. 'I've never ever found it unlocked in the morning. And if I did forget it, isn't it just Sod's Law it has to be the one night someone comes prowling?'

'Yeah, but you don't know how many times he might have come and found it locked,' Lloyd pointed out, and Pippa frowned.

'Oh, thanks! That's made me feel much better! The thought that someone was hanging around, watching and waiting.'

'Oh, I'm sure it wasn't like that,' Gideon reassured her. 'Just an unhappy coincidence or, at the most, someone taking advantage of the comings and goings. But it wouldn't hurt to be careful for a day or two, all the same, now he's seen what's in there.'

'It's a horrible feeling, though, isn't it?' she said. 'Kind of creepy! I know exactly what Tilly meant now, and it must be ten times worse if someone's actually been in your *house*.' She shuddered. 'Well, I don't think there's any point in calling the police tonight, but what about you? You really ought to see a doctor, if you were actually knocked out. You're probably concussed.'

He groaned. 'I'd really rather not. I've just got a bit of a headache. I'm sure it's nothing a couple of aspirins and a good night's sleep won't fix.'

'But it can be dangerous,' she persisted.

'Hey, what about Monty Sinclair?' Lloyd suggested suddenly. 'He said he couldn't stay late, but I'm sure he was still there when Eve came to find you. Shall I go and see if he'll come? He'd be completely discreet.'

'Brilliant! Yes, I'd forgotten him. Go and see if he's still there. If not, I'll run Gideon to casualty as soon as this thing's over. It can't go on much longer, surely?' Pippa looked at her watch.

'Who's Monty Sinclair?' Gideon asked as the door closed behind Lloyd.

'Oh, he's an old friend of ours – a doctor. I'm sure he'll come, if he's still here. He's ever so nice. He's patched Lloyd up on the hunting field more than once.'

Monty Sinclair was, as Pippa had promised, very nice. Slim and fairly tall, he had greying hair and wire-rimmed glasses, and Gideon estimated that he was probably around fifty. He knocked on the kitchen door a couple of minutes later and came in, saying Lloyd had sent him. After introductions had been performed, he examined his patient with brisk efficiency and strongly recommended a trip to A & E, which provoked a protest from Gideon.

'All right. Look, I'll write you a note,' the doctor said. 'If you won't go tonight, you should definitely run along tomorrow and get it checked out, OK?'

Gideon thanked him, and with a cheery wave, he was gone.

It was fairly late the next morning when Gideon drove in through the stone arch of the Priory stableyard. He'd bowed to pressure from Eve and allowed her to drive him to the A & E department of the local hospital, where he'd been examined and given the all clear.

On their return to the Gatehouse, she'd made him a cup of coffee, advised him to take it easy, and departed to Wareham to open the gallery for the Saturday tourists. Ten minutes after she'd left, he'd collected his coat, Zebedee, and the keys to the Land Rover, and was on his way out of the front door.

'Shouldn't you be resting?' Pippa came out of the tack room as he stepped out of the vehicle.

'No, I'm fine. Officially.'

'You went to the hospital?' She sounded surprised. 'That must have been Eve's doing. So how is it? Still aching?'

'Very little,' he said truthfully.

'But you drove here . . .'

He normally walked or pedalled.

'It's raining, and I didn't particularly want to squeeze my hat on over the bruise, all right? Inquisition over?'

Just at that moment, Lloyd came to stand in the doorway behind Pippa.

Gideon nodded. 'Henry. Quiet day on the hustings?'

'Just giving Pippa a hand clearing up,' Lloyd replied, evenly. 'How are you, this morning?'

'OK, thanks. My neck's a bit stiff but otherwise I'm not too bad, considering.'

'Make you think twice before you go tackling burglars again,' Lloyd observed.

'Actually, if I'd had any idea there was anyone in there, I'd have shut the door and locked it, then called the police.'

'Oh, and I had you down as a have-a-go hero. From what Pippa's been telling me, you're a regular Indiana Jones.'

Gideon smiled thinly. 'It's not like Pippa to exaggerate,' he said. 'But anyway, that's all in the past and much best left there.'

The mild snub seemed to affect Pippa more than it did Lloyd.

'I didn't tell him anything,' she said defensively. 'Nothing that mattered, I mean.'

This time it was Lloyd's turn to look less than pleased and, if Gideon had been in a better mood, he would have found it funny but, as it was, he effectively dismissed the subject by asking if Giles was around.

'He's in the snug, I think,' Pippa told him. 'At least, he was when I last saw him. Bella's in the doghouse, this morning. Somehow she found her way in there and knocked his antique paperweight off the desk. God knows what she thought she was doing! Sod's Law, it had to hit the edge of the hearth and break.'

Adjoining the library, the snug was a small room that Giles used as an office, and Gideon did indeed find him there, shuffling through files and papers with an expression of intense frustration.

'Argh!' he muttered, without looking up, and as Gideon tapped on the open door, 'Millie, have you been tidying my desk again?'

'How many times have I asked you to stop calling me that?' Gideon demanded, going in. 'It ruins my street cred!'

Giles glanced up with a grin. 'Idiot! Mrs Morecambe looked in a moment ago and offered me a cup of tea. I thought you were her.'

Mrs Morecambe had been employed by the Barrington-Carrs since Giles and Pippa were in the nursery, first as a nanny and then as a housekeeper, and she plainly regarded her duties as being somewhere between the two.

'I saw her in the kitchen and asked her to put another cup on the tray. I gather Bella's in disgrace.' Gideon strolled forward and picked up two chunky pieces of coloured glass. 'Whoops . . .'

'Yes. I don't know what she thought she was going to find. I don't keep any food in here — at least not since a packet of boiled sweets got shoved to the back of the drawer and forgotten. When I found them, God knows how long after, they'd turned to liquid and run all over the year's bank statements. My accountant wasn't amused!' Giles chuckled at the memory. 'Anyway, I've kept it a food-free zone since then. Even biscuit crumbs leave fatty stains.'

'Perhaps Bella was chasing a fly,' Gideon suggested. 'You know how crazy she goes then.'

'Yeah, could be. So what did you think of last night, eh? The feedback was absolutely brilliant and I've had three calls already . . .' He faltered. 'Oh, Christ, I'd forgotten – Pips said you had a bust-up with a tack thief in the middle of it all! Are you OK?'

'I think a "bust up" is putting it a bit strongly. I walked in – he clobbered me; end of story,' Gideon said ruefully. 'But – no, I'm fine. Just a bump on the head and a stiff neck. I've had worse. Are you going to notify the police, or not?'

Giles shrugged. 'Oh, I don't know. Pippa doesn't think anything's missing. It hardly seems worth all the hassle. Unless you feel strongly about it . . . ?'

'Good Lord, no! I've spent more than enough time with the cops lately. If you're happy, I am. After all, it must be a million-to-one chance they'll ever catch the bastard. So . . .' he went on in a lighter tone, 'Graylings Sparkler is officially launched and has the wind in her sails.'

'Yes, it's amazing! If I'd known starting my own business would give me such a rush, I'd have done it ages ago!'

After a lazy morning, Gideon stayed to lunch at the Priory, where the talk alternated between the attempted theft and the ballooning success of Giles' apple wine. Three more calls had come in: two from customers wanting to place orders and the third from a regional paper, keen to do an interview with Dorset's newest entrepreneur.

'Eve's ideas were brilliant – just added the final touches,' Giles told Gideon. 'Especially those perfume burners, or whatever you call them. It was very subtle, but it made all the difference.'

'Yeah, she's done a fair bit of research into that sort of thing.'

'Feng shui,' Lloyd put in, knowledgeably.

'No, not feng shui. The whole business of marketing. Apparently it's a proven fact that adding just a trace of the right scent into the retail area – not even enough for people to be aware of it – can improve sales dramatically. Eve uses something in the gallery, and it seems to work. She's been very successful. She sold two of mine last week.'

'Wow! It must be good!' Giles joked.

Gideon laughed.

'OK, I asked for that, didn't I? Actually it's a mixed blessing, because if she sells too many, I'll have to get on and do some more. But anyway, I'll pass on your gratitude.'

'Yes, please do. And why don't you bring her over one evening for a celebratory meal? How about tonight?'

Gideon shook his head. 'Can't do tonight. I know that right away. She's got a "do" on at the gallery. She wants me there, too. She says she's got someone coming who may be interested in commissioning me for a portrait. But I'm sure she'd love to come, another time. She said how much she enjoyed it last week.'

'I'm probably going to be out tonight, anyway,' Lloyd announced.

'Oh? And what made you think *you* were invited?' Pippa enquired, echoing Gideon's thoughts.

Lloyd pulled a face at her.

'So, where are you going tonight, then? You didn't say anything earlier,' she queried.

'No, I've only just remembered – Gideon saying about the "do" at the gallery reminded me. Amber's school are putting on a fashion show, and I promised to be there. Amber's my daughter,' he added for Gideon's benefit. 'Not exactly my idea of a fun evening – a bunch of flat-chested ten-year-olds modelling home-made clothes – but it means a lot to her.'

'Well, of course she'd want her daddy there!' Pippa exclaimed. 'And you'll be clapping just as hard as everyone else, when it comes to it.'

'OK, so I'm really a big softy,' Lloyd admitted, smiling at her. 'But you didn't have to tell everyone!'

Gideon felt he'd had enough.

'Well, if I'm going to do anything with my troubled friend out there, I'd better get moving,' he said, pushing his chair back and getting to his feet. 'Eve's expecting me at six, and I've got to brush my hair and clean my nails before then!'

★

Gideon supposed the evening exhibition could be counted a success – inasmuch as he apparently said the right things and was given the commission to paint three golden retrievers belonging to a retired colonel and his wife – but he couldn't truthfully have said he enjoyed it.

Eve was in her element, looking stunning in a flowing silk garment the colour of pewter, and wearing the biggest and most elaborate mother-of-pearl necklace Gideon had ever seen.

'It *is* a bit OTT, isn't it?' she agreed, when he commented on it. 'But you see, it's kind of expected of me. It gives people something to talk about, and it's no bad thing to have a trademark. I think some of the ladies only really come to see what I'm wearing; I'd hate to disappoint them!'

By day, the gallery – a barn conversion full of glass and oak beams – seemed to catch and reflect the light, giving it a kind of luminescence, and the effect after dark was equally impressive, the windows turning into black mirrors and the pictures glowing under the clever spotlighting. Gideon spent the evening mingling with Eve's guests, sipping drinks he didn't really want, and wishing he could take his throbbing head home and lay it on a pillow.

It was gone eleven when the last lingering visitor had been waved off the premises and Eve was able to switch off the lights and lock up.

'Thanks for coming, and staying,' she said, putting her arms round Gideon as they stood on the gravel outside. 'I know it's not really your thing.'

'No, it was OK; I enjoyed it.' She smelled faintly of some musky, exotic spice and, despite his headache, he pulled her against him, imagining the pewter silk sliding off over her smooth golden curves.

'Liar. You hated it.'

'OK, I did, but I got a commission out of it, so I can't complain.'

Eve pulled back a little.

'I meant to ask you about that. That price you quoted – did I hear right?'

'Did you see the car they came in?' Gideon countered.

'You know, you're wicked!' Eve told him, leaning against him once more and laying her cheek against his. 'It's a good job I like bad boys . . . Come home with me?'

'I can't,' he said. 'I'm sorry, but I have to let Zebedee out. He'll be sitting cross-legged as it is.'

Eve sighed. 'Much as I love animals, that's the one reason I wouldn't have one; they tie you down so, and I love to be free. Oh well, I suppose I'll just have to come home with you.'

'You're welcome to, of course, but I must warn you, I have the mother and father of all headaches.'

'That's not very original,' she murmured, then more sharply, 'Oh, your head! I'd forgotten. Why the hell didn't you say something?'

'It's been coming on gradually.'

She scanned his face with a certain amount of concern.

'Do you think you should see a doctor?'

'No,' Gideon said firmly, 'I don't. It's just the natural result of being clobbered and then spending an evening making small talk and smiling a lot. It'll probably be better by tomorrow.'

'Will you promise to see a doctor if it isn't? Oh, God, listen to me, I sound like your mother!'

'Actually,' he said, amused, 'you sound more like my mother than my mother does – if you see what I mean. She's an artist, too, and she gets completely immersed in her work. It was nothing unusual for her to forget meals when my sister and I were growing up. We learned, very early, to be self-sufficient. But anyway, thank you – you're very sweet.'

She gave him another searching look.

'Are you sure you'll be all right?'

'Positive.'

'Well, in that case, I think I'll love you and leave you. I've got to open up tomorrow, and I'm pretty well dead on my feet. But – ring me in the morning, OK?'

'So you know I've made it through the night?' he quizzed. 'Be a bit late if I haven't.'

'Oh, don't say that!'

Laughing, he drew her closer and kissed her soundly before seeing her to her car.

The roads were fairly clear on the way home, and Gideon drove with the window open to keep him awake. The night air was refreshing, and he found himself wishing – not for the first time of late – that he were on a motorbike. It had been a couple of years since he'd wrapped his treasured Norton around a tree, through no fault of his own, and Giles and Pippa had given him the Land Rover. At first, comfort and convenience had kept him content, but the call of two wheels had never entirely gone away and had, over time, grown steadily stronger.

With the promise of a financial boost from the portrait commission, he found the idea of getting another motorcycle very quickly put down roots and flourished, and by the time he reached the Gatehouse he was only left with the pleasurable task of deciding what sort of bike to buy.

Zebedee greeted him with his usual wild exultation, exhibiting the bouncing technique that had earned him his name. Gideon had tried, unsuccessfully, to train him out of it, but as he didn't actually jump *at* people any more, but only up and down on the spot, he now let him get on with it. It was a harmless expression of his excitement, and Gideon championed individuality.

Closing the front door, he looked round for Elsa, who sometimes got 'bounced', but she was nowhere to be seen, which was unusual. She spent a lot of her time on the Aga, and almost always appeared to welcome him when he'd been out. Shrugging, he quieted Zebedee and went through to the kitchen to make himself a cup of coffee before he went to bed. The cool air had soothed his head and he no longer felt the need for painkillers so, after calling for the cat a time or two with no success, he let the dog out into the garden for five minutes, then switched the light off and made his way upstairs, half-expecting to find Elsa curled up on his duvet.

She wasn't.

Frowning, Gideon stood his mug on the bedside cabinet and began a search of the upstairs rooms. There was only another bedroom and a bathroom, and both doors had been shut, but he looked anyway, on the off chance that she'd got shut in before he left. She was nowhere to be seen.

Really puzzled now, Gideon went back downstairs, turning the lights on again and stepping over Zebedee, who was lying in his customary place against the bottom step. The dog looked up and wagged his tail sleepily as Gideon stepped over him and went on into the sitting room.

'Elsa?'

He glanced round hopefully but there was no sign of her.

'Now where the hell have you got to?' he muttered, going back into the hall and opening the door of his studio. Another blank.

Where had he last seen her?

In the hall, when he left at half past five. He was almost sure she'd been sitting in the kitchen doorway looking reproachful, as was her custom when he went out several times in one day. The doors and windows had all been shut, so she had to be in the house.

Deep in thought, he heard a whine, and became aware that Zebedee wasn't with him. Normally the dog shadowed him, wherever he was in the house. Another whine, and Gideon went through to the sitting room once more. Zebedee was standing on the rug in front of the wood-burning stove, ears cocked and head on one side, gazing intently at the chimney breast.

'What're you up to, Zeb?' Gideon asked, suddenly interested. 'What've you found?'

He went over to the fireplace and, putting one hand on the huge oak bressummer beam above it, he bent down and peered up into the gloom.

There, on a dusty, cobwebby shelf, crouched Elsa.

'Hello, little one,' he said softly, and was rewarded with a pathetic, long-drawn-out meow.

When he reached up to lift her out of her refuge, she drew

back, but the ledge was too small for her to hide, and within moments, after a brief frightened struggle, he had her in his arms.

Murmuring comfortingly, Gideon carried the cat into the kitchen and put her in her favourite place on top of the Aga. Brushing the dust and cobwebs from her sleek, tawny-flecked coat, he opened a small tin of sardines and poured her a saucer of milk, wondering, all the while, what could possibly have sent her scurrying for such a hiding place. Surely Zebedee hadn't been chasing her? He'd never shown any inclination to do so, and Gideon suspected that if that had been the case, the dog's guilty conscience would have given the game away as soon as he got home. He often confessed to his misdemeanours before Gideon was even aware they'd been committed.

After eating two mashed-up fishes, and drinking most of the milk, Elsa settled down on the folded blanket where she normally slept, and began to wash, purring with apparent contentment. Gideon switched off the light and took himself back to his bedroom and a cooling cup of coffee.

Gideon rose late the next morning, and had a leisurely breakfast before turning his attention reluctantly to the mounting pile of correspondence in his studio. He'd got as far as sorting it, several days previously, into order of urgency, with the items nearest the top those that should have been answered over a month ago, and those at the bottom, less than a week. The whole added up to a stack that teetered precariously on the brink of sliding onto the floor from its position on the corner of his desk.

With a sigh, Gideon sat down with what remained of his second cup of coffee, picked up the top envelope and removed the contents. For a moment, he stared at the papers in his hand. It was a telephone bill. Nothing strange in that, except that he could have sworn he'd sorted it to more than halfway down the pile. Surprised, he looked for the date and found that he still had three days before it became overdue – nowhere near urgent, then.

Frowning slightly, Gideon reached for the next item and found another more recent invoice, but then a much older one that he'd actually written 'Urgent' on. Beneath this there were two or three envelopes, address-side down. That certainly wasn't right. He knew damn well he hadn't left them like that.

He sat back and took a sip of his coffee, then looked around thoughtfully. Everything appeared much as he'd left it, except . . . Across the room, on an easel, was a portrait of Pippa's horse, Skylark, that he was painting for her birthday and, seen in the light of day, he noticed a faint smudge mark across the nose, as if someone had walked carelessly close and brushed it with their sleeve. It was too high to have been one of the animals, even had they been in there, which, as far as he knew, they hadn't.

Eve perhaps, although she wasn't in the habit of coming into the studio on her own.

His frown deepening, Gideon opened each of the drawers in his desk.

If he hadn't specifically been looking for signs of disturbance, he probably wouldn't have noticed any because, on the face of it, there didn't appear to be anything missing. His desk was, essentially, his office, but he had no PC or laptop, and his mobile phone lived in his jacket pocket, for the most part. The desk drawers contained such unfashionable things as writing paper, pencils and pens, bulldog clips, an account book with carbon paper, and Sellotape. Never particularly tidy, Gideon couldn't have sworn to it that anything had been moved; but the muddle just didn't look quite the same muddle he was accustomed to seeing.

The telephone rang, making him jump, and he reached out a hand for the receiver.

'Is that Gideon Blake or a paramedic?' Eve's voice enquired dryly.

Too late, Gideon remembered his promise to call her.

'I'm sorry. But I did survive,' he said, injecting a note of self-congratulation.

'So I gather.'

'Actually, I've not long been up, and the reason I forgot to call is because my headache has completely gone.'

'And here I was, making myself ill with worry, and wondering whether I should ring there or the hospital . . .'

'Yeah, yeah,' he said. 'Make the most of it . . . Listen, Eve . . . did you by any chance go into my studio when you were here last?'

'Er . . . no, I don't think so, but I might have done. Why?'

'Well, remember that huge pile of mail I was sorting through when you arrived the other day?'

'The one you kept swearing at?'

'That's the one. Well, now it's unsorted.'

'What do you mean?'

'Well, it's all higgledy-piggledy again. I left it ready to deal with, in order of importance, and now it looks as though someone's knocked the whole lot onto the floor and picked it up again in a hurry.'

'Well, it wasn't me,' Eve said positively. 'I'd have remembered that. One of the animals?'

'And picked it up?' Gideon queried, sceptically.

'Ah, yes. See what you mean.'

'And there's another thing.' He told her about finding Elsa hidden in the inglenook. 'Something frightened her,' he finished.

'You think someone broke in?'

'Well, got in somehow. There's no obvious sign, but I might go and check again.'

'But have they taken anything? What do you think they were looking for?'

'I've absolutely no idea,' he admitted. 'I've only just discovered this, so I haven't really looked to see if anything is missing. They didn't take my electricity bill, more's the pity!'

After he rang off, he sat staring into space for a few moments. He couldn't really imagine what might be missing. He had a fairly good music system but no TV, video or DVD player.

His camera!

In a flash, he was on his feet and heading for the sitting room, where his state-of-the-art digital camera was kept out of sight in a cupboard, along with several hundred pounds' worth of lenses.

It was still there, and so were the lenses, nestling in their case.

What then?

Why break in, if not to steal?

He recalled his conversation with Eve, and set off, with Zebedee at his heels, to recheck all the windows and doors for signs of entry.

There were none.

The only possibility he could see was the bathroom window, which didn't fit as closely as it should and could conceivably be opened from the outside by someone with a ladder and the appropriate tool. But that would presuppose that the person in question knew about it, and it certainly wasn't obvious from the ground.

Shaking his head in bewilderment, Gideon made a mental note to remind Giles about the window, and went back downstairs.

'Will you call the police?' Eve had asked before he rang off. But what was he supposed to tell them? Somehow he didn't think they'd get overexcited about an untidy pile of correspondence and a frightened cat. He was a fair way to thinking it was a product of his blow to the head, himself.

Glancing unenthusiastically at the paperwork, he consulted his watch and decided it was probably time he thought about going up to the Priory. Tilly Daniels was due to come and see how Nero was progressing, and he wanted to be there.

The horse did them proud. His general demeanour was much calmer now, and although he was by no means problem-free, his progress over the nine days he'd been in the Priory yard augured well for the future.

With Pippa and Tilly following on foot, Gideon rode Nero out of the yard and round the back of the stables to the conifer-screened outdoor school behind. One of Nero's foibles was a tendency to nap, or baulk, at leaving the yard, but today, although Gideon felt his slight hesitation as he passed under the stone arch, he doubted whether either of the girls would have noticed it. Once in the railed-off area, the horse didn't put a foot wrong. Gideon put him through his paces, doing a warm-up, a little elementary dressage, and finishing over two low jumps that Pippa had erected across the diagonal of the rectangle.

It was only the second time he'd jumped the horse, but Nero gave him a wonderful feeling and it occurred to him that if he didn't ever make good on the track, he might prove to be a terrific showjumper or eventer, given time. As he began to slow the horse up, Pippa called out, 'Keep him going, Gideon. I'll pop it up a peg or two.'

Obediently Gideon sent Nero on round the outside of the school, concentrating on keeping him calm and collected, and it wasn't until she called for him to come again, and he swung into the turn, that he saw just how high she'd raised the poles.

Gideon had never been more than a hobby rider. Although his behavioural work sometimes called for him to climb aboard, this only normally involved ensuring that the horse would perform the basics, such as hacking across country, behaving in traffic, and any other everyday situation it might be having difficulties with. He'd never, in his life, faced a jump the size of these two, and wondered why Pippa had put them so high.

He was given little time to consider it, for, whatever other problems Nero might have, jumping wasn't one of them. He saw the first obstacle and was away, finding his own stride, bunching his quarters and sailing over. In the nick of time, Gideon shifted his weight forward, sliding his hands up the brown neck to give the horse the freedom to stretch, and they touched down on the other side in perfect harmony. Two strides later, the performance was repeated, and Gideon turned the horse in a circle before riding it back to the gate, where he saw that Giles had now joined the two girls. They were all smiling.

'Wow!' Gideon exclaimed, as he drew to a halt. 'Suddenly the

Grand National doesn't seem such a wild ambition! That was all down to him, that last time; he's a natural.'

'He's not the only one,' Tilly observed. 'You didn't look too shabby yourself!'

'Just what I keep telling him!' Pippa put in. 'But he doesn't believe me. He's never had a lesson in his life.'

'Do you want to ride him?' Gideon asked Tilly, feeling it was high time to change the subject. Every now and then, Pippa tried to persuade him that he was good enough to compete, and he had no interest in the concept whatsoever.

'I'd love to, if you don't think it'll upset him.'

'No, I don't think so. Just keep your hands as light as you can; too much contact panics him at the moment. I rode him in a headcollar when he first came in to the Trust.'

'That would cause a stir at Aintree!' Tilly laughed, pulling her crash hat on.

With his new rider on board and the stirrup length adjusted, Nero moved off willingly enough and, on the whole, behaved well, but after a few minutes it became clear that some of his self-doubt was creeping back in.

Even Giles noticed it.

'He looks kind of worried,' he said, watching their progress.

'He is,' Gideon agreed. 'He's a very insecure person.'

Tilly and Nero approached, trotting down the side of the school, the horse's ears flicking back and forth nervously and his stride noticeably shortening.

'He feels a little bit tense,' she called as they passed. 'Do you want me to stop now?'

'Just pop him over the jumps, he'll enjoy that,' Gideon suggested.

She nodded and sent Nero on into a canter, her long blonde hair flopping up and down on her back with the rhythm of his stride. Gideon hadn't seen her ride before – other than in and out of the yard at Puddlestone – and was impressed by her. If anything, he thought her a better rider than her brother had been; she had more sympathetic hands.

As Nero approached the fences again, his uncertainty left him. His ears pricked forward, his eyes became eager and his whole attention was focused on the job in hand. Tilly sat quietly, leaning forward as the horse took off, her legs close and still, and her hands giving as he stretched.

'That was amazing!' she said, pulling up beside them. 'He's a different horse when he sees a jump. What a talent! I can see why Damien was so excited about him but, having said that, he didn't go as well for me as he did for Gideon, did he?'

'I call him the witchdoctor,' Pippa said. 'All my horses go better for him than they do me; it's infuriating!'

'He's basically insecure,' Gideon told Tilly. 'We just have to get him to see you as his herd leader. Perhaps, when you've got time, we could try join-up. It's the basis of all animal psychology, really.'

To his relief, Tilly showed no cynicism. 'Oh, right. I saw a demonstration, once. It was fascinating. How long will we need?'

'Not long for the actual join-up session,' Gideon said as she dismounted, ran the stirrups up and loosened the girth. 'But you'll need to follow it up; build on it, and really give him a chance to bond with you.'

'Well, I'm up for it,' she said, as they began to walk back to the yard with Nero. 'I'm over the moon about what you've done so far. He was being such a pig, I was beginning to despair. He's so much more relaxed now.'

In Gideon's pocket his mobile began to vibrate, silently, the ringtone having been turned off in deference to Nero's nerves. He fished it out and glanced at the display.

Angie Bowen.

'Just going to answer this,' he told the others, indicating the phone and dropping back. With the Trust, there was always the possibility of an emergency.

'Hi, Angie.'

'Gideon? Not interrupting anything, am I?'

'No, not at all. What's up?'

'Well, it's two things. One is to ask if it would be at all possible to change the day of your next visit?'

'I'm sure that won't be a problem but I haven't got my diary handy, at the moment. I'll have to ring you back on that one.'

'OK, that's fine. It's just that we've got the trustees visiting, and I'd rather like them to meet you and see you work.'

'OK.' Gideon could think of things he'd like better, but he supposed they needed to see where the money was going. 'And . . . ?'

'Oh, and just to tell you that Boomer's gone to his new home. They came to try him on Wednesday, then brought their vet out, Friday, and picked him up this morning.'

'That's brilliant! So he behaved himself, presumably?'

'He did. He was the perfect gentleman. I explained about the flies, but they didn't think it would be a problem. It's a lovely home.'

'Wonderful. I'm really pleased. A few more pennies for the coffers, then.'

'Yes. Oh, that reminds me. You know when we were talking about our mystery benefactor the other day, I said that the money always came in five separate envelopes? Well, this time there were only four. What do you make of that?'

'You're still convinced this has to do with Damien?' Gideon lowered his voice instinctively, even though the others were, by this time, some way ahead.

'No – not convinced, but it does seem a bit of a coincidence, doesn't it?'

'Well – yes, I suppose it does . . . But to be honest it could well be just that – a coincidence. And short of asking Tilly outright – which I'm not about to do at the moment – we'll probably never know.'

FIVE

WHEN GIDEON CAUGHT UP with the others he found that Tilly had already received, and accepted, an invitation to stay to lunch.

'I'm under orders from my staff to take the day off,' she said. 'They're a bossy lot, and they said they didn't want to see me around the yard until teatime.'

'Right, then after lunch I'll take you down to see the honkers,' Giles told her. 'If you'd like to?'

Tilly looked puzzled. '*Honkers?*'

'Donkeys,' Pippa explained. 'You've heard about our sanctuary, I expect. Giles calls them honkers because of the noise they make.'

'I'm thinking of renaming the sanctuary "Honkers' Hollow",' he said. 'You can come and help me sign in two new arrivals.'

'She's supposed to be taking the day off,' Pippa protested. 'That's a bit of a busman's holiday.'

Tilly laughed. 'Actually, I'd love to come and see them. I love donkeys, and I'd much rather be busy.'

'Great.'

Gideon thought Giles looked particularly pleased, and felt a little uneasy. It was nothing unusual for Pippa's brother to show interest in an attractive female, in fact he'd have been more surprised if he hadn't, but his relationships weren't known for their longevity, and Tilly could do without any more heartache at the moment.

Just as Mrs Morecambe was putting a ploughman's-style lunch on the table, Lloyd turned up, wearing mud-spattered breeches, a white shirt and a Puffa jacket, having spent the morning drag hunting.

He greeted both Tilly and Pippa with a kiss, and collapsed onto one of the armchairs with a theatrical groan.

'I'm knackered! We had a bloody brilliant morning, though. Huge turnout and hounds went like the wind. We lost half the field in the first ten minutes and they didn't catch up until the start of the third line!'

'I wouldn't have thought *they* had a brilliant morning, then,' Gideon observed.

'Well, we can't hang about for the stragglers,' Lloyd declared. 'If they're not up to it, they shouldn't come.'

'You can hardly call half the field stragglers,' Tilly put in, voicing Gideon's own thought, and he was reminded that Lloyd was an old friend of the Daniels family.

'Yeah, well maybe it wasn't quite half,' he amended with a grin. 'But still, I think we might have to organise special days for the unfit and the novices. Lay a trail with smaller jumps and put more breaks in it, to slow things up.'

'You want to be careful – if it gets too popular, nobody'll want to chase foxes any more and you'll lose your political platform!' Gideon warned.

'Rubbish! Drag hunting's OK, but it's not a patch on the real thing. Besides, there's still fishing and shooting; with hunting banned, everyone's scared shitless the bastards will start on those next.'

'*Lloyd*,' Pippa warned, with a nod towards Mrs Morecambe, who had stopped on her way out of the kitchen and was looking back with an expression of strong disapproval.

He put up his hands. 'Sorry – sorry! Language – I know. It's what comes of spending the morning with the lads from the kennels. I apologise. But, getting back to the hunting, the trouble is, if we organise extra days, I shall have to get a couple more horses. Prince is OK but Badger's getting a bit past it, and Lady hasn't been right since that day I had to walk her back to the box.'

'I don't know why you took her,' Pippa commented. 'You said you thought her back wasn't quite right.'

'Well, I wouldn't have done if Prince hadn't bashed his leg on the gatepost and given himself a big knee. They always do it the day before hunting – that's why you need a spare. Course – I could hire one of yours . . .' he said, with a sideways look at her.

'Oh, no, buster! Think again. I know how you ride, and I'm not having any of *my* horses brought back on their knees!'

'Hey, I'm not *that* bad!' Lloyd protested, assuming a deeply wounded expression, but Gideon got the impression that he was rather proud of his hard-riding reputation. His opinion of the man slipped another notch.

'So, how come you're back early today?' he asked. 'I thought these things went on all day.'

'Yeah, they do, normally, but one of the whips has got flu and Pete – our huntsman – had a big family do to go to, so we just laid three short but very fast trails.'

Over lunch, the conversation was light-hearted and touched on many things, including the ongoing triumph of Giles' business venture.

'The launch went brilliantly. We were even on the local TV news – did you see us?' Giles asked Tilly, but she shook her head.

'Sorry, I don't have time to watch much TV, but I'm glad it all went well.'

'Don't worry, he'll probably show you the video,' Pippa said. 'We've all seen it at least a dozen times. But actually, there was one blot on the evening; someone tried to help themselves to our tack.'

'What – one of the guests?' Tilly asked incredulously.

'No, I didn't mean that, but I reckon someone took advantage of us being busy with the launch. After all, it was well advertised. It nearly worked, too. If Gideon hadn't gone out to check on Nero when the fireworks started, they'd have got away with it.'

'Gosh!' Tilly looked at Gideon. 'Did you catch them in the act?'

He shook his head ruefully. 'I'd like to be able to say I was the hero of the hour, but the truth is—'

'He blundered in and got clobbered over the head,' Lloyd cut in. 'That is, if there ever was a burglar. My theory is that he tripped up and knocked himself out, then invented the story of a break-in to cover up his embarrassment!'

'Damn! You've sussed me,' Gideon said, with a smile that didn't reach his eyes. 'Could you pass the pickle, Giles? Thanks.'

'Did they do much damage?' Tilly asked. 'Breaking in, I mean.'

'No. They didn't really have to break in, as such,' Pippa said. 'It seems I must have left the door unlocked, though I can't imagine how – I'm usually so careful.'

'Haven't you got an alarm?' Tilly looked surprised.

'No. We should have, really,' Giles said. 'Who do you use for security?'

'Actually, we had ours updated last year, when there were a lot of tack thefts locally. An old friend of Damien's did it – or at least, his company did. Julian Norris. Norris Security Systems. Did a good job, too. It's a doddle to use.'

'Old Nervous Norris,' Lloyd said, nodding. 'Perfect line of work for him. Isn't he dead now?'

'Yes. Actually, it was rather sad because it was the day his company finished the work for us that he was killed in the car crash,' Tilly said. 'It was a hell of a shock. He came to see us that evening – to check we were happy with the work, I suppose, Damien spoke to him – and then, on the way home, his car went off the road and hit a wall. We didn't find out about it until a couple of days after.'

'So what happened – did he fall asleep?' Gideon queried.

'Possibly. Nobody really knows.'

'I heard it was suicide,' Pippa said.

'Yes, I heard that rumour, but there wasn't any proof,' Tilly said. 'They held an inquest and the verdict was accidental death. Damien and I had to give evidence because we were the last people to see Julian alive. They wanted to know what his state of mind was – you know, did he seem worried about anything, that sort of thing.'

'Ha! That's a laugh!' Lloyd exclaimed derisively.

'Why?' Gideon didn't understand.

'Because you're talking about the most miserable bugger I've ever met! He was always worrying about something or other, and if he couldn't find anything to worry about, he'd invent something. That's why we called him Nervous Norris.'

'He *was* a bit of a worrier,' Tilly agreed. 'I think he suffered from depression, but he was a really nice chap. Actually, on that night, he seemed quite cheerful, which made it all the more tragic when we heard what had happened. Damien was quite cut up about it.'

'Yeah, I'll admit, he *was* a nice chap,' Lloyd conceded. 'Just a bit of an old woman, at times. God – it's hard to believe they're both gone! What a waste!'

There didn't seem to be much to say following this observation, and there was an uncomfortable silence for a few moments, then Pippa said brightly, 'Well, I can't sit around here all day – I've got horses to ride. Are you coming, Gideon? Blackbird could do with the exercise, he's getting fat!'

'He's not fat!' Gideon retorted. Pippa's horses were never fat, unless they were out at grass, and even though Blackbird was nominally *his* horse – because he flatly refused to behave for anyone else – Gideon knew she kept him well exercised when he couldn't find the time to do so himself. 'But I'll come, anyway.'

'Lloyd?' Pippa enquired.

'No, not me. I'm for home and a hot bath; get out of these

sweaty clothes. That faint hum you can hear is my socks!'

'I wondered what it was,' Giles commented.

'Does that still hurt?' Pippa asked sympathetically, watching Gideon ease his crash cap off and rub his head.

'It is a bit tender,' he admitted. 'But the swelling's gone right down. I wouldn't like to have tried putting my hat on yesterday.'

'Well, I'm really sorry it happened but at least it wasn't in vain. I've been through everything and it doesn't look as though they got away with anything at all. They must have panicked after hitting you, and run off empty-handed.'

Gideon made an ironic bow. 'Glad to be of service, but I think maybe an alarm might be a good idea. I don't think my head can stand many more clobberings.'

'Well, Giles is going to ring the security people tomorrow. He was talking about getting the house updated, while they're at it, and maybe even your place.'

'Actually, that's not such a bad idea,' Gideon said, and told her about Elsa and the papers, and his conclusion.

She was shocked.

'Are you sure?'

'Well, ninety-nine point nine per cent, yes. It's either that or I'm going completely off my trolley!'

'And they didn't take anything?'

'Not a sausage. I didn't say anything earlier because I didn't think it was worth worrying Tilly with, just as she's looking a bit brighter.'

'She is, isn't she? I was thinking that,' Pippa agreed. She bent to look at the inside of her horse's fetlock. 'Oh, Sky! You've kicked yourself, you clumsy great oaf. I'll have to wash that off; it's got dirt in it.'

'I'll get you some water,' Gideon offered, having already put Blackbird back in his stable. In due course he delivered to her half a bucket of warm water from the kitchen, and a handful of cotton wool.

'Thanks,' she said. 'Oh damn! That's my phone. You couldn't just answer it for me, could you? It's in my coat. It might be Giles . . .'

Gideon obediently located the phone and flipped the lid.

'Hello?'

'Oh. That's not Pippa Barrington.' A woman's voice.

'Well spotted,' Gideon said, amused. 'But I can pass you over.'

'Well, actually, it was Lloyd I wanted. He's not answering his phone. Can you tell him the kids were ready half an hour ago? He was supposed to be taking them to the pictures. It's bloody unfair – poor little loves! I'm his wife – ex-wife, Harriet,' she added somewhat unnecessarily.

'Well, he left here,' Gideon consulted his watch, 'about an hour and a half ago. But he did need a pretty major clean-up.'

'Thinks more about his bloody hunting than he does his own kids!' Harriet Lloyd-Ellis complained. 'Well, I suppose he'll turn up here eventually – when he's good and ready – but it'll be too late for the cinema. It's such a shame when Archie was so excited. How do you tell an eight-year-old that his daddy can't be bothered to take him out?'

The phone clicked off before Gideon had time to answer, which was just as well, really, as he hadn't a clue what to say.

'I wouldn't want to be in Lloyd's shoes when he finally shows up,' Gideon said, reporting the conversation to Pippa.

'He's probably fallen asleep in the bath,' she laughed. 'But I should imagine Amber and Archie have a pretty good idea what their dad's like by now.'

'Where does Harriet live?' Gideon asked. 'The code looked familiar. I thought for a minute it was somebody at Tilly's place.'

'Yeah, same area. A couple of miles up the road from the farm,' Pippa said, coming out from under Skylark's belly. 'There, that should do you, old boy. It's not very deep. I'll put a bit of purple spray on and it should be fine. Oh, and by the way, talking of Lloyd – have you still got that bit of paper we found in Nero's things? Lloyd knows a fair bit about betting and bookies, and I wondered if he might be able to make sense of it.'

'It's still in the folder – in the Land Rover,' Gideon said, surprised. 'I'd forgotten about it. Why the sudden interest?'

'Just curious, you know me,' Pippa said, but she avoided his eyes and he wondered, with insight, whether the request had actually originated with Lloyd. It would be just like him to want to show off his superior knowledge.

'All right, I'll do you a copy. But I think we ought to leave the original where it is, as it's really none of our business.'

'Oh well, if you don't think we should . . . I didn't mean to be nosy. Perhaps we should show it to Tilly first.'

But Tilly, when she was shown the paper, later that afternoon, exhibited little interest in it.

'Oh, that was typical of Damien. He always used to scribble memos to himself in some kind of personal shorthand that no-one else could understand. Sometimes even *he* forgot what he'd meant by it, so I shouldn't think there's much chance of us being able to decipher it. I should bin it, if I were you.'

'It looks as though it's something to do with betting. *Did* Damien bet on his horses?' Pippa wanted to know. 'I'm surprised it's allowed.'

'Yes, it's quite legal. Jockeys can't, of course, but trainers can. Not that Damien did very often. He always said it was a mug's game.'

In spite of Tilly's obvious indifference, Gideon didn't feel it was his place to destroy or bin the paper, so he decided to make a copy for Pippa that evening and leave the original where they'd found it.

He was sitting in his study at the Gatehouse, looking at the columns of letters and figures written in Damien's bold, rounded script, when a hand bearing a glass of red wine came over his shoulder.

'You're not going to do that lot tonight, are you?' Eve asked, looking at the pile of correspondence. 'Why don't you leave it till tomorrow and come in by the fire. It's bloody cold in here!'

'That's exactly what I was going to do.'

'So what's that all about?' She nodded at the paper he held. 'Are you thinking of risking your worldly wealth on a horse?'

'No, actually, this isn't mine. Pippa found it in Nero's file, but it doesn't make a lot of sense. At least, it didn't . . . We thought it had something to do with betting, but now I'm wondering if these aren't phone numbers.'

'They don't look much like phone numbers,' Eve said doubtfully.

'Ah, but that's because of the way they're written down. If you rearrange the numbers so the first column has three and the second six, then put oh-one in front of them, they suddenly look exactly like phone numbers, and the letters in front could be initials.'

'Well, I see what you mean, but it's a bit of a stab in the dark, isn't it? I mean – any set of nine numbers would look like a phone number if you put oh-one in front of them, and why write them down like that, anyway?'

'I agree, it does sound a bit far-fetched, but look . . .' Taking another sheet of paper, Gideon copied the numbers out as he had suggested. Tapping the result with his finger, he looked up at Eve. 'Tell me what you see?'

She frowned slightly. 'Three of them are local codes. OK – you might actually have something. Not just a pretty face, are you? I'm impressed.'

Gideon shook his head.

'Much as I hate to disillusion you, I have to come clean. The truth is I recognised one of the numbers – or at least, I think I did. I'll have to check, but I think this bottom one is Lloyd's ex-wife's. Harriet rang Pippa's mobile this afternoon, and I answered it. I probably wouldn't have recognised the number if it hadn't ended in four fives, and I couldn't swear to it even now.'

'Why don't you look in the directory?'

'I did. She's not listed, and neither is he.'

'So what are the letters?'

'Initials. H.L. Harriet Lloyd-Ellis. Or Henry, for that matter.'

'Oh, I didn't realise he was a Henry. But you said it was his ex-wife's number . . .'

'Well, it depends when the list was made. He only moved out about four months ago. Strictly speaking, she's still his wife; they're only separated.'

'And the other numbers?'

'I've no idea,' he admitted.

'Six to one against . . .' she read. 'So, what do you think it is? Some kind of betting syndicate?'

'I don't know. I suppose that's possible,' Gideon mused.

Eve straightened up, trailing her fingers across his shoulders and up into his hair.

'Well, Sherlock, when you've finished your investigation, I'll be waiting for you in the other room. It's too bloody cold in here; I'm getting goosebumps.'

'I'll come right now. There's no great mystery about a list of phone numbers, even if they were disguised. Tilly said that was nothing unusual.'

'Well, if you wanted to be really nosy, you could always ring them,' Eve suggested.

Gideon laughed and got to his feet. 'I can think of more enter-taining ways to spend the evening,' he said, slipping his arm round her waist.

The following morning, after Eve had departed, Gideon drove to Bournemouth and spent the best part of two hours trying to explain to the doting middle-aged owner of a shih-tzu that the only way to stop her little darling growling at her husband was to make sure that the dog knew its proper place within the family pack. Feeding it at the table, letting it sleep on the bed and barge through doorways ahead of them, and sitting somewhere else rather than move it from the sofa, were all adding to the precocious creature's sense of its own worth, he told the woman, as tactfully as he could.

'You have to make sure Chi-Chi knows that your husband comes above him in the pecking order,' he said for the umpteenth time, and the doubtful look on his client's face spoke volumes.

He gave her a printed copy of the guidelines he had laid down for such cases, promised to send his account, and left, completely confident that Chi-Chi would continue to reign supreme. There was little point and no satisfaction at all in trying to help those who refused to acknowledge the truth. He just wished they wouldn't call him in the first place; they sent his blood pressure rocketing.

In the afternoon he travelled to Lymington to photograph the retired colonel's retrievers, took a twenty per cent deposit payment and somehow, on the way back, found himself detouring to take in a couple of motorcycle dealerships.

'You look pleased with yourself,' Pippa observed, when he turned up to exercise Nero.

'Just got a deposit for a portrait,' he said, omitting to add that he'd also already spent it. He was almost certain that she wouldn't approve, and he had no wish to engage in a lengthy argument on the perils of motorcycle riding.

'Oh, good. Maybe you'd like to contribute a little something towards the upkeep of your horse,' she suggested, with a sweet smile. 'By the way, if you haven't got anything specific planned for today, how about coming down to Home Farm with me? I thought of taking Toddy round part of the cross-country course, and I'd like to see how he handles jumping in company before I go hunting on him next week.'

'Lloyd's really got you hooked on that, hasn't he?'

'Well, it's good training for eventers, besides being great fun. You ought to try it one day. Blackbird would love it.'

'Mm, I'm sure he would.'

'Well, don't sound so enthusiastic. You never know, you might enjoy it yourself.'

'Mm,' he said again.

They hacked the horses down the lane and through the ford to Home Farm, where their plans almost came to nothing when Nero caught sight of what was obviously his first donkey.

For several long moments he took root in the gravel of the track, whilst the donkey began the bellows action of working itself up for a call. Then, when the trumpeting finally started, Nero panicked, turned on his haunches and attempted to retrace his steps to the yard at top speed.

With an effort, Gideon managed to halt his charge and turn him back to face the object of his fear, which had now come forward to put its head over the fence and had, moreover, been joined by several others.

Pippa stifled her mirth and rode Toddy closer to the long-eared onlookers to demonstrate that they were harmless and, after much coaxing, Nero was persuaded to go past.

The cross-country jumping course at Home Farm had been Pippa's thirty-first birthday present from Giles, and had more than paid for itself in the last two years, through hiring out for the use of riding clubs and private schooling. Putting the episode with the donkey behind him, Nero threw himself into the session with great enthusiasm, jumping fast and clean and giving Gideon a super ride.

'Damien was right, he's going to make a terrific steeplechaser,' Gideon told Pippa as they pulled up with some difficulty at the end. 'It almost makes me wish I was eight inches shorter and ten years younger.'

'To say nothing of four stone lighter,' she remarked.

'Thank you for that.'

'Actually, I'm glad you enjoyed it so much because I wanted to ask a little favour . . .'

'Why do I get the feeling I'm not going to like this,' Gideon pondered aloud.

'You know Lloyd and I are doing this team chase thing later this month . . .'

'Yeah,' he said slowly.

'Well, we've got a bit of a problem – you see, William Hadley's had to drop out, so we've only got three riders . . .'

'O-oh, no! No you don't. You know I don't do competitions.'

'It's for charity. The Turkish earthquake appeal.'

'I'll make a donation.'

'But if we don't find a fourth rider, none of us will be able to take part.'

'That's blackmail,' Gideon pointed out.

'I know. But it's true.'

'Surely there are other people you could ask. What about all Lloyd's hunting friends?'

'The entries had to be in weeks ago. Anyone who wanted to take part is already in a team.'

'Well, it's no good anyway. Even if I wanted to – which I don't – there's no way I'm going to risk someone else's horse doing something like that.'

'Oh, I know that. I didn't mean on Nero, I meant Blackbird.'

'Oh, that's even better! Two complete novices, together.'

'It's for charity,' Pippa repeated. 'No-one takes it seriously.'

'Maybe, but I doubt if it's meant to be a comedy.'

'You're quite capable of doing it – you should have more self-belief.'

Gideon had a brainwave. 'Tell you what. Why don't I lend Blackbird to this William person, then everybody's happy.'

Pippa shook her head.

'William's got a broken arm.'

'Don't tell me – he did it on one of these team chase things.'

'No. Out hunting, actually. Oh, come on, Gideon. Be a sport. It'd be fun.'

'Remind me to look up the definition of fun again. My dictionary's obviously got it wrong.'

The horses had stopped for a drink in the ford, and Toddy began to paw at the water with his forefoot. Pippa pulled his head up and they moved on.

'Lloyd said you wouldn't do it,' she said, after a moment or two. 'I said you would.'

'Then he was right and you were wrong,' Gideon observed. 'And that was well below the belt, Miss Barrington-Carr.'

'Well, you're so infuriating!' she declared.

When they got back to the yard, Lloyd was sitting on the mounting block waiting for them, talking animatedly on his mobile phone. His two liver and white springers were quartering the cobbles with heads down and stubby tails no more than a blur.

'How'd they go?' He snapped the phone shut and got to his feet, reaching for Toddy's rein as Pippa dismounted. 'Missed you,' he added, putting his arm round her shoulders and kissing her.

The two dogs came wagging across to greet them, milling around the horses' feet fearlessly.

'They were good,' Gideon answered, jumping down. 'It was fun.'

Lloyd looked questioningly at Pippa.

'Well, did you ask him?'

'Yes, I did, but—'

'I said I'd have to check my diary, but it shouldn't be a problem,' Gideon put in, the words as much a surprise to him as they no doubt were to Pippa. It had just been something in the way Lloyd had looked when he asked her. Moments later, Gideon could have kicked himself. What did it matter what Pippa's boyfriend thought of him? He didn't even like the man. He didn't normally let pride get in the way of his decision-making.

Pippa turned to him, out of Lloyd's line of sight, her eyes wide and incredulous.

'Well, it's time Blackbird did something for his keep,' he added without a flicker, and had the satisfaction of seeing Lloyd momentarily nonplussed.

'She did tell you that you have to do at least one day's hunting with the Tarrant and Stour, to qualify?'

Ducking under Nero's neck to run his offside stirrup up, Gideon gave Pippa a look that promised payback, and said casually, 'Is that a problem?'

'No. No, of course not,' he answered, perhaps a touch too heartily, and Gideon wondered, with amusement, if Lloyd actually *wanted* him on the team, or whether he'd just seen the opportunity to make him appear in a bad light to Pippa. If that was the case, it showed how little Lloyd understood her. And, if it *was* the case, then the prospect of being a thorn in the man's side provided the whole affair with at least one redeeming factor.

When he'd returned Nero to his box, Gideon found Lloyd in the tack room with Pippa.

'Oh, I did you a copy of that paper of Damien's,' Gideon said, taking it from the pocket of his jeans and giving it to him. 'Pippa said you wanted to see it, though I'm not sure why . . .'

'Oh, no real reason. Just thought I might be able to help you out with it,' Lloyd said, glancing at the paper.

'Well, to be honest, I don't think it's any of our business,' Gideon remarked, watching him. He'd decided to keep his discovery to himself, interested to see if Lloyd recognised the last number for what it was. He showed no sign of having done so, however, merely folding the sheet and slipping it into his pocket. Gideon had been hoping for some reaction, however slight, and wasn't sure whether the lack of it betokened incomprehension, or prior knowledge. If, as Eve had suggested, the paper was a list of members of a betting syndicate, then maybe Lloyd had already known what to expect when he asked for it.

'I don't want to feed until Toddy and Nero have rested for a bit, so I vote we have a cup of coffee first,' Pippa said. 'Anyone interested?'

'You go on, I'll be with you in a minute,' Gideon said, pretending to rub at a stubborn mark on Nero's snaffle.

He'd just spotted Pippa's mobile on the window sill and, as soon as she and Lloyd disappeared in the direction of the house, he left the bridle and picked up the phone.

Feeling faintly guilty, he scrolled through the menu, found

Records, and Calls Received, and there it was: just a number –
no name, because it presumably wasn't among Pippa's stored
contacts – but it was, without doubt, the same as the number on
the bottom of Damien's list.

Gideon exited the menu, thoughtfully, and put the phone back
where he'd found it. So it *was* Harriet's number; where did that
get him?

Exactly nowhere. However, the mystery continued to nag at
him and that evening, having gone into the study for a session
on the Skylark portrait, Gideon found himself picking up the list
of numbers once more. In his mind, he heard Eve's voice from
the night before.

' . . . *if you wanted to be really nosy, you could always ring them.*'

Well, why not?

With sudden decision, he carried the piece of paper out to
the telephone in the hall and dialled the first of the numbers.

It rang no more than four times before a voice said, peremp-
torily, 'Sam Bentley.'

Gideon's mind went blank.

'Sorry. Wrong number,' he said, and the voice at the other end
made a noise of exasperation and put the phone down.

Sam Bentley. S.B. The initials beside the number.

Damn! Gideon was annoyed with himself for not having
thought out his approach. It was as if, in spite of having verified
Lloyd's number, he hadn't really believed his theory until Sam
Bentley answered his phone.

He needed a plan.

Leaving the list where it was, he went through to the sitting
room, put another log on the fire and poured himself a glass of
wine. Eve was getting him into bad habits, he thought, as he sat
back on the sofa, to the delight of Zebedee, who immediately
came and sat with his chin on Gideon's thigh. Fondling the dog's
silky ears, he put his mind to the problem.

It was difficult to see what he *could* say, when he had absolutely
no idea what the connection was between Damien and the six

people on the list. Or five – if you discounted the one that had been crossed off. Were the five known to one another, or only to Damien? How old was the list? He'd been assuming it was recent, because of where they'd found it, but that wasn't necessarily so.

Nero's case file.

Gideon remembered Tilly saying that Damien had been intending to sell shares in the horse to help finance his keep and the expansion of the Puddlestone Farm yard. Well then – could it have been a list of prospective owners? Perhaps Damien had already rung them, which would explain why one was crossed out and the others ticked.

'I bet that's it!' He spoke out loud, and Zebedee raised his head to look at him. 'I think I've got it, Zeb,' he said. 'And you were no help at all.'

Zebedee wagged his tail happily.

Back in the hall, Gideon looked at the list. With the five ticked numbers and Damien himself, that would have been six; could the other have been the one against? It made as much sense as any previous theory.

With this in mind, he dialled the second number.

It rang, maybe seven or eight times, and then there was a click as an answerphone cut in, and through a certain amount of static a voice said, 'You have reached the home of Robin and Vanessa Tate. I'm afraid neither of us are available to take your call at this time, but please don't hang up. Leave a message after the tone and we promise to get back to you.'

Gideon put the receiver down and wrote Robin Tate on the pad, underneath Sam Bentley.

After this promising beginning, the third call was a bit of an anticlimax. In the first place, an automated voice informed him that the number had not been recognised and that he should check it and try again. He did so, with the same result, before it occurred to him that the number might just be a mobile one. Substituting oh-seven for the oh-one, he tried again, and this time was rewarded with a ringtone. Unfortunately that was as far as he got. The phone rang on for a short time and then the Orange answering service suggested he leave a message. Gideon declined.

The fourth number was answered by a woman's voice simply saying, 'Yes? Hello?'

Thinking fast, Gideon said, 'Is that Lynette Turnbull?'

'No. I'm afraid you've got the wrong number.' The voice was middle class, with a hint of Essex.

'Oh, sorry.' Before she could hang up Gideon read out the number he'd just dialled. 'Isn't that you?'

'Yes. That's the number.' The woman sounded puzzled. 'But my name's Tetley, not Turnbull.'

'Oh. Is your husband there, by any chance?'

'I'm divorced. He doesn't live here any more. But my boyfriend's here. Look, who *are* you and what do you want? Where did you get this number?' She began to sound a little edgy.

'It was given to me, in connection with a racehorse syndicate.'

'Oh, and I suppose you think that's funny, do you? Look, I don't know what your game is, but if you don't leave me alone I'll—'

'It's all right,' Gideon interposed soothingly. 'I'm a old friend of Damien Daniels.'

'Oh, is that right? Well, you're no bloody friend of Adam's then! Do you know what he said when he heard what'd happened to him? I'll tell you: he said it couldn't have happened to a nicer guy! Now get off the fucking line before I report you for harassment!'

She hung up and Gideon replaced his receiver, glad that he'd had the foresight to withhold his number.

Unwittingly, in spite of her antagonism, she'd given him the name he'd been after, but her reaction to his mentioning Damien's name had been interesting, to say the least. Not the attitude he'd have expected from someone whose husband had been contemplating a mutually beneficial business partnership, even if they *were* now divorced. Had something gone badly wrong?

This put a new complexion on Lloyd's interest in the note.

Gideon rubbed his chin meditatively.

Everyone had said Damien had no enemies. He'd heard it time and time again at the reception, but it seemed this wasn't strictly true. As fantastic as it might seem, this scrap of paper with its list of initials and telephone numbers could turn out to be important, after all. Was it even possible that it could have some bearing on the trainer's murder?

Gideon had a strong suspicion that he should turn the list over to DI Rockley with no further ado, but there was Lloyd to consider. Personally, he owed the man nothing at all, but he was Pippa's boyfriend, and Gideon owed her a hell of a lot.

It was a tricky situation.

Gideon found he was still staring at the list and, almost as a way of postponing a decision, he decided to ring the only number he hadn't yet tried – the one that had been crossed through.

The phone rang twice, then there was a click and a taped voice said, 'This is Norris Security Systems. The office is now closed. Please ring back during business hours: eight-thirty to five, weekdays, and Saturdays from nine till one. Alternatively, leave your name and number after the tone and we'll get back to you at the earliest opportunity. Thank you.'

Gideon put the phone down, thoughtfully.

Julian Norris.

Crossed off the list, not because he didn't want to buy shares in a racehorse, but because he was dead.

SIX

B Y THE TIME GIDEON got up the next morning, he'd
decided on a plan of action. The first thing he did when
he went downstairs was ring Puddlestone Farm, and ten o'clock
found him parking the Land Rover in the stableyard.

There were three horses in the small holding paddock that
flanked the lane to the gallops, mounted and circling calmly at
the walk while their riders chatted. In the yard, three more horses
stood waiting, tacked up and with blankets thrown over their
saddles. Tilly was there, fitting protective boots on the legs of a
rangy dark brown gelding, aided by a short wiry grey-haired man
whom Gideon didn't know.

Tilly straightened up as Gideon drove in.

'Hi. Comet's ready for you,' she called, as he stepped out of
the Land Rover, carrying his crash cap. She indicated a big, well-
made chestnut, on the far side of the yard. 'He should be well
up to your weight.'

'I'll pretend not to take offence at that remark,' Gideon said.

Tilly laughed.

'You know what I mean. By the way, this is Ivan, an old friend of Damien's, who's very kindly helping out while we're short-handed.'

The wiry man glanced up at Gideon, pursed his lips and nodded.

'Hi. Ivan . . . ?'

'Mundy,' he supplied.

'The jockey. I thought I recognised you! Pleased to meet you.' Gideon held out his hand.

'Ex-jockey,' Ivan said, but he looked gratified.

'Well, I think we're about ready,' Tilly said, pulling her helmet on. 'It worked out just right, you calling like that,' she added to Gideon. 'Beth rode out with the second lot but then she had to go to the dentist, so we'd still have been one short if you hadn't been coming over.'

Under his blanket, the chestnut gelding wore a general-purpose saddle that looked as though it had seen better days, but was, nonetheless, more inviting to Gideon than the postage-stamp-sized racing saddles the others wore.

He led Comet across to the stone mounting block and swung aboard, lengthening the stirrups to suit his long legs as the horse moved forward.

'I'd put them a hole or two shorter than your normal,' Tilly advised. 'It'll make it easier for you to get the weight off his back on the gallops.'

They clattered out of the yard and joined the three from the holding paddock in the lane, with Tilly and one of the lads taking the lead, and Gideon and Ivan bringing up the rear.

After displaying an initial tendency to jog, the chestnut settled into a long-striding walk; one ear forward and one to the side, where Ivan's mount jigged and sidled with suppressed energy.

The ex-jockey seemed disinclined to talk, but Gideon was quite happy immersed in the atmosphere of the morning. The temperature had dropped overnight and Dorset lay cocooned in a low-lying mist, which lent the rolling hills and valleys a mystical quality, bushes and small trees appearing adrift in a milky sea.

'Worse than this earlier,' Ivan said suddenly, as they approached the gateway that led onto the gallops. 'Couldn't see a bloody thing. Good job there's no rabbit burrers in this field.'

'There *are* rabbits about, though,' Gideon said. The evidence had been plain to see ever since they left the yard; scattered piles of round pellet-like droppings abounded on the grassy verges and banks.

'Gotta a man takes care of the gallops, haven't they? Lives up in the cottage in the woods. Gotta couple of ferrets to keep the rabbits down; looks after the sheep, fills in any holes that appear and picks up flints and such that the horses might tread on.'

'Does he live on his own?'

'Bit of a hermit, by all accounts,' Ivan said, nodding.

They filed through the gate onto the sheep-cropped turf, and at once all the horses' heads came up, ears sharply pricked in anticipation, plumes of steam hanging in brief clouds around their muzzles. As if it were contagious, Gideon felt an answering thrill of excitement fizz through his own veins.

At the front, a tall grey started to plunge its head towards the ground, trying to weaken its rider's grip, and Tilly called out, 'Circle him, Gavin. Keep in behind the others until you're ready to go. I don't want you getting carted! Girths, please, everyone.'

She swung round to come alongside Gideon, who was pulling the chestnut's girth one hole tighter.

'We'll go first, Gideon, then I can watch the others work. Keep Comet's nose level with Mojo's flank, if you can. We'll go steady along the bottom of the valley until we get just past that clump of bushes, then swing uphill and let them stretch out a little. Three-quarter speed will be quite fast enough, but don't worry if you can't hold him; he'll be blowing pretty much by the time he reaches the top. OK?'

'Fine,' Gideon confirmed.

'Right, you lot,' she called to the others. 'Come on my whistle. Ivan's in charge, OK?'

She clicked her tongue at her mount and they were off,

trotting at first, then easing into a canter. Keeping Comet's bobbing head roughly in line with Mojo's powerful quarters, Gideon leant forward over the chestnut's withers and revelled in the sensation of latent power.

As they approached the bushes, Tilly glanced back.

'OK?'

'Fine.'

'Right, sit tight!'

Gideon had the fleeting impression of a figure standing in the lee of the bushes, but a split second later his concentration was fully on his riding as the two horses rounded the corner and surged forward up the hill, their heads lowering as they met the rising ground.

The misty valley fell away behind them as they powered diagonally across the slope of the twenty-acre field towards its boundary and then followed the post and rails to the summit, the speed of their passage snapping the fabric of Gideon's jacket and whipping tears to his eyes. For the time being, reality was the rhythm of thudding hooves, short snorting breaths, and the blur of the rails racing past.

At the top of the hill, the two horses swung away from the fence in perfect accord to run along the crest, both slowing appreciably now, and Tilly threw Gideon a look over her shoulder.

'OK? Keep him going until we get to the clump of trees up ahead.'

When they eventually slowed to a trot and circled to a walk, she glanced at him again.

'How was that?'

'Incredible!' Gideon shook his head. 'Absolutely amazing! Wow!'

Tilly laughed.

'You did really well. I wish some of my lot followed instructions like that.'

'Well, actually I think most of that was down to this fella,' Gideon admitted. 'He was a perfect gentleman.'

'Ah, "the Gideon factor",' Tilly said.

'Sorry?'

'It's what Pippa calls it. Didn't you know? "The Gideon factor". Comet's not always that well behaved.'

'It's probably my great weight,' Gideon joked. 'By the way, when we passed those bushes down in the valley, I thought I saw someone standing watching, did you?'

'Oh, that was probably Reuben; he nearly always watches the horses being exercised.'

'Reuben?'

'Yes. He lives in an old charcoal burner's hut on the edge of the copse, and looks after the gallops for us. I don't know how old he is – could be anything from fifty to seventy – but he's been there since before I was born. Just turned up one day, apparently.'

'Oh, yes, Ivan mentioned him. Lives on his own, he said.'

'Yes. Well, he's got an old collie dog but he's a bit of a recluse, really. Dad takes him a box of groceries once a week and picks up a list for the next week. That's his wage. We don't pay him, as such. Nobody can remember his other name – if we ever knew it, which I doubt. I shouldn't imagine he exists on any electoral roll, because that old hut only appears on the map as a ruin, and I don't suppose he's been off the farm for the last twenty years or more. We don't often see him, he kind of blends into nature, but I think he watches the horses, most days. Melanie and Sue say he gives them the creeps but he doesn't bother me, and Damien used to visit him regularly when he was growing up.'

'It's kind of comforting to think that you can still slip through the net in this day and age,' Gideon said.

'Absolutely. I agree.'

They drew up, facing down into the valley, and Gideon could see they'd travelled through a rough U-shape, ending up almost level with the horses that still circled below. Tilly took a teacher's whistle from her jacket pocket and blew strongly, and after a few moments two of the riders detached from the others and started along the valley bottom.

Well before they reached the bushes, the horses were travelling at a fierce pace, first one then the other getting its nose in front.

Tilly groaned out loud.

'No, no, no, Gavin!' she said, even though they were too far away to hear. 'Keep hold of him. Hands down, you idiot! Oh, for Pete's sake!'

This last cry of despair came as the rider on the grey finally lost his struggle for control, just before the bushes, and his horse shot past his training partner and away up the hill, gaining lengths in no time at all. Left behind, the other horse fought unsuccessfully for its head then suddenly jinked right, tipping its rider over its shoulder, and galloped in pursuit of its stable companion, leaving the girl sitting on the turf.

'Oh bugger!' Tilly said. 'Poor old Melanie. She's brilliant in the yard, but she needs bloody superglue on her saddle. And that bloody Gavin . . . !'

'That bloody Gavin' came thundering towards them along the brow of the hill, still travelling strongly and looking as though he might well go straight past without stopping. The loose horse followed in his wake.

'Hands down; sit down; turn him in a circle!' Tilly shouted, and eventually the grey slowed to a shambling trot.

'Shall I try and catch the other one?' Gideon offered, his eyes on the approaching animal.

'You can try, but she can be a bit of a devil. It wouldn't be the first time we've had to ride home and let her follow on behind.'

She sounded stressed and Gideon felt sorry for her.

The bay mare cantered towards them, eyes and nostrils wide with excitement. One stirrup lay across her saddle and she'd trodden on her reins, leaving the broken ends to trail in the grass. Fifteen or twenty yards away she came uncertainly to a halt, anxiously eyeing the waiting group and, without a word, Gideon slipped off Comet and handed his reins to Tilly.

Keeping his head and body inclined at forty-five degrees from the loose horse he walked quietly to within ten feet or so, and slightly out to one side.

She was tense; watching him. Head high and eyes wary.

Sensing she was on the point of whirling round and away, he stopped, crouched down, and gazed into the distance. Out of the corner of his eye he watched her and, after perhaps half a minute, she lowered her head and regarded him curiously, her nostrils flaring to the rhythm of her heaving flanks.

With his mind, he invited her; blanking everything else out; picturing her stepping closer; trying to radiate security and calm.

For a moment, he thought it wasn't going to work. He hadn't taken the time he normally would, knowing he couldn't expect Tilly to keep the other horses waiting in the chill air. But then he heard the mare's hooves swishing in the grass, and something bumped gently against his shoulder. Warm breath huffed in his ear and her whiskers tickled the side of his face.

'Hello, sweetheart,' he murmured, and with a slow hand took hold of the rein that trailed from her bit. 'There's a good girl.'

Rubbing her soft muzzle, he rose smoothly to his feet and patted her steaming neck, before leading her across to join the others.

'I'd give you ten thousand pounds if you could teach me how to do that,' Tilly said frankly. 'But I know you couldn't. That was way beyond technique.'

Gavin had dismounted from the grey and now stood sulkily beside it, viewing Gideon with disfavour.

'Shall I take the mare down to Melanie?' Gideon asked.

'No, that's all right. We'll be going round again, so she'll make her way back to the bottom. I'll just bring the last two up.'

The whistle was blown again, and Ivan's two set off, making the run in an orderly manner, much to Tilly's relief and Gavin's added humiliation.

With Ivan switched onto the grey, the whole process was repeated with no further drama, and the cavalcade set off back down the lane to the yard, much to Gideon's relief. By the end of the second gallop, his calf and thigh muscles had been on fire with the strain of the unaccustomed position. The horses were quiet now, and Tilly dropped back to ride with him.

'You said you wanted to ask me something? Is it about Nero?'

'Well, not exactly. At least, I don't think so. Not directly. I had another look at that list . . .'

Tilly looked puzzled.

'You know, the one we showed you, the other day. It's actually a list of names and phone numbers.'

'Really? Whose?'

Gideon slowed the chestnut a little so that they dropped back from the pair in front.

'Julian Norris; Sam Bentley; Robin Tate . . .'

Tilly was shaking her head slightly, lips pursed. 'I know Julian, of course – I told you about that.'

'Adam Tetley . . .'

'Tetley. *Adam Tetley.*' Tilly turned sharply to look at Gideon, causing her mount to throw its head up and fidget sideways. 'My God! I'd forgotten about him.'

'Who is he?'

'He was a friend of Damien's from way back; I think from his pony-club days. We didn't hear anything of him for ages, and then, soon after Damien started training, Adam called and asked if we'd train a couple of horses for him. He was one of our first owners. Actually, strangely enough, Comet was one of his.'

'Was . . .'

'Yes. It was all rather messy, really. He bought the horses in his company's name, and when they ran it was good advertising – you know the kind of thing. Only, after a while, he became very unreliable. The training fees began to come through weeks late and then stopped altogether. Adam always had an excuse – you know – cash-flow problems; just waiting to finalise such-and-such a deal and then he'd be fine. I think Damien gave him more leeway than normal because of old times, but eventually he had to put his foot down. He told Adam that if he didn't pay, we'd have to sell one of the horses to cover the debt.'

'So is that what happened?'

'More or less. But, when the chips were down, it turned out that Adam didn't actually own the company, after all. He was only the financial director, and the first his boss knew about the horses was when our solicitors contacted him direct, with our ultimatum.'

'Ah . . .'

'Yes. As you can imagine, he was given his marching orders like a shot, and the horses came to us in settlement.'

'But you didn't sell them.'

'We sold one, but we'd just got this sponsorship deal from Skyglaze, so Damien decided to keep Comet. This all happened five or six years ago. He was a good horse in his day, but he's getting a little long in the tooth now.'

'Well, that explains the ex-wife's attitude, anyway.'

'Did you ring him, then?'

'Yeah, I did. You see, I only had initials until then. When I mentioned Damien, the former Mrs Adam Tetley was hostile, to say the least.'

'I'm not surprised. Adam must have been creaming the company profits for some time, because the two of them were living the life of Riley. The horses were just part of it. When it all came apart – it came apart big-time! He lost his job, his five-bedroomed house, and three cars. And then his wife walked out on him. He was lucky the company didn't take him to court, but it was all a fearful mess and I suppose they didn't want that kind of publicity.'

'It's hard to believe Tetley thought he'd get away with it,' Gideon said. 'Surely he must have known he'd be found out eventually.'

'Damien reckoned he had a gambling habit. You know, convinced the big win was just around the corner and he'd be able to pay the money back, with no-one any the wiser.'

'So, does Rockley know all this?'

'I don't know. *I* didn't tell him. I'd forgotten all about it,' Tilly said. 'Oh, my God! You don't mean . . . ? No – Adam would never have done something like that.'

'Someone did,' he reminded her. 'And it sounds as though this guy had ample motive.'

'Oh, my God!' she said again.

'You ought to tell Rockley.'

'Yes, I will. But I still can't believe he did it. Adam hit rock bottom, that's for sure, but I never heard that he blamed Damien – even if his wife did.'

'If he's in the clear, he's got nothing to worry about,' Gideon pointed out.

They'd dropped well behind the others by now, and the front pair had reached the gate and gone through into the yard. As they covered the last hundred yards or so Tilly seemed lost in her thoughts, and Gideon reflected that this new twist had blown his racing-syndicate theory right out of the water. There was no way that Damien would have wanted to do business with Tetley again after what had happened, old friend or not. In fact, it made it very unlikely that he'd have wanted to contact the man at all.

Did that mean the list was an old one? Compiled before he'd known Tetley for what he was? But that didn't really fit because Julian Norris' name had been crossed out and – according to Tilly – he'd only died the previous year.

Back to square one. The difference now was that in place of mild interest, Gideon had a burning curiosity.

'Er – Tilly. Could I ask a favour?'

'Yes – sure.' She raised her eyebrows, questioningly.

'When you talk to Rockley, could you not mention the list just yet?'

'Well, OK. I suppose I could say I just remembered about Adam. I could say you asked about Comet and that reminded me. But why?'

Gideon hesitated, realising he had no choice but to confide in

Tilly. It wasn't fair to expect her to withhold information from the police without offering an explanation.

'I just want a little bit more time to try and work out what the list is all about. I mean, it's not as if it can have anything to do with what happened to Damien anyway, because Julian Norris' name is on there.' He paused, seeing that she still didn't look convinced. 'The thing is, Lloyd's name is on there, too. Or his wife's, I'm not sure which – their initials are the same.'

'Lloyd is? But that's weird.'

'Yeah. I know. But that's why I didn't want to show it to Rockley just yet.'

'OK. Have you asked Lloyd about it?' Tilly said, as they turned into the yard.

'No, I haven't, yet, but he's got a copy of the paper – I hope you don't mind.'

She shook her head. 'No, not at all.'

'But I haven't said anything about the phone numbers. I wanted to see what he came up with himself. Pippa doesn't know either – can we leave it that way for now?'

Tilly slid her feet out of the stirrups and dismounted. 'Gavin, get that horse away from the others before he kicks somebody! Honestly! You haven't got the sense you were born with! And that wasn't much,' she added, under her breath.

She turned back to Gideon. 'Don't you think you might be playing this list thing up too much? I told you, Damien was always writing stuff down in a kind of shorthand. It doesn't neces-sarily mean anything sinister.'

Gideon dismounted and looked at her across Comet's back.

'Humour me. Please?'

She shrugged. 'OK.'

'And you won't mention it to Lloyd or Pippa?'

'Not if you don't want me to. But let me know if you find anything, won't you?'

★

Spurred on by the sudden realisation that Pippa's birthday was only a couple of weeks away, and aided in his resolve by what the weatherman had called 'prolonged showers', Gideon spent most of Tuesday working on the portrait of Skylark. With classical music on the radio, a slice of cold quiche for lunch, and no interruptions, he worked through until late afternoon, at which time he pushed aside his tray of pastels, stretched, and informed an eager Zebedee that it was time to go for a walk.

It was still raining and, after trudging round the Graylings woods for an hour or so, Gideon returned to the Gatehouse, firmly shut the front door, pulled the curtains on a darkening world and lit the fire.

In due course he fed Elsa and Zebedee, and was standing with the fridge door open, wondering what he could concoct that might be even remotely appetising from half a tin of salmon, a cold baked potato, and a pot of strawberry yoghurt, when the telephone rang.

'Hi, handsome. Want some company?' a husky voice enquired.

'Now, which one are you?' Gideon wondered aloud.

'I'm the rich bitch that's going to give you a clip round the ear if you don't behave!' Eve warned him. 'I was going to say I'd come over, but now I'm not sure I will . . .'

Gideon laughed. 'Oh, please! Please come and see me.'

'That's better. And again . . .'

'Please come – I haven't seen you for three days and I've missed you . . .'

'OK, OK – you can stop now. I'll be there in about three-quarters.'

'I've missed you dreadfully,' Gideon continued as if she hadn't spoken. 'And if you happened to pass a fish and chip shop, mine's a large cod and chips with salt but no vinegar.'

'You cheeky bastard!'

'Well, I've got nothing in the fridge.'

'You don't deserve me!' she told him, and put the phone down.

Left to kick his heels for the best part of an hour, Gideon

switched on the light in the porch, put a bottle of wine to chill and went back into his studio to take a critical look at the portrait. After a period away from the easel he could often see better where – if anywhere – he was going wrong.

This time, he was pleased with his work. Skylark's handsome head looked out of the paper at him, eyes shining and coat looking soft to the touch. All it needed was tidying up, adding the whiskers and other delicate finishing touches, and it would be ready for the framer.

Whistling softly with satisfaction, Gideon turned out the light and went back into the hall.

There, on the table beside the telephone, lay the list and, on a whim, he picked up the receiver and dialled the one number that had remained unanswered the night before.

For several seconds it looked as though he was going to be out of luck again but then, just as Gideon was on the point of giving up, there was a click and a male voice said, in the tone of one whose patience had been stretched to the limit, 'If that's you, Hodgkins, I'll string you up by your balls from the flagpole!'

'Well, that's one way to get rid of nuisance callers,' Gideon said with amusement.

'Oh, that's not Hodgkins, is it? I do apologise. Who is it?'

'I was about to ask the same.'

'Sorry. Garth; Garth Stephenson. Somehow the boys have got hold of my mobile number and they've been plaguing me with calls and text messages, night and day, since the day before yesterday. I'm going to have to ask Orange to give me a new number.'

'You're a schoolteacher?'

'Yes. PE. Sorry, who did you say you are?'

'I didn't, actually.' Gideon decided to opt for the partial truth. 'I'm a friend of Tilly Daniels. She found your number amongst her brother's things, but no name. I offered to check it out for her.'

'Tilly . . . ? Oh, good Lord! Damien Daniels' sister. I heard about that. What a terrible thing to happen. They don't have much luck, do they?' Stephenson didn't appear to find anything strange in Gideon's rather weak excuse for ringing.

'Why do you say that?'

'Well, I mean, with Marcus' suicide and everything.'

'Oh, I see. No, they don't. Would you have any idea why Damien would have your number written down? Were you in touch with him recently?'

'No. As far as I can remember, I've never spoken to him personally in my life. I knew Marcus – but not well . . .' The voice on the end of the phone tailed off then came back strongly. 'No, I'm sorry, I can't help you.'

'Well, do you by any chance know Sam Bentley?'

'Listen, I'm sorry – Mr er . . . ?'

'Gideon.'

'Yes, well, I'm sorry, Gideon – I really have to go. I'm supposed to be on duty in the prep room in five minutes. Give my condolences to Damien's sister. Goodbye.'

Gideon put the phone down and stood looking at it, wondering what, if anything, could be gleaned from the conversation, apart from the fact that an evening prep class presumably denoted a boarding school.

Considering Gideon's flimsy pretext, Stephenson's reaction to his call had been remarkably patient, and Gideon couldn't really blame him for his eagerness to terminate it. What he couldn't decide was whether the man would have rung off just as quickly if Gideon hadn't mentioned Sam Bentley. Unfortunately, there was no way of knowing.

It was three o'clock in the morning when Gideon awoke.

For a moment he lay still, heavy with sleep, wondering what had woken him. Eve lay close, her cheek and one arm on his chest, and he could hear her breathing, quiet and steady. It hadn't been her, then.

A short burst of barking sounded from downstairs, and Gideon sat up, carefully displacing Eve, who turned over, sighed deeply and snuggled down again.

Zebedee very rarely barked at night and, even muffled as it was by thick stone walls and heavy oak doors and floorboards, Gideon could sense the dog's urgency. Something was bothering him.

Quickly and quietly, Gideon got out of bed and crossed to the window. It was almost pitch black outside, and although he could just make out the cream-coloured roof of the Land Rover beyond the front hedge, he could see little else. Feeling for his clothes, he pulled on jeans and a jumper, and pushed his feet into moccasins before leaning across to give Eve's shoulder a gentle shake.

'Wha . . . ? What's the matter?'

'Shh! Zebedee's barking, and after the other night, I think I'd better just check it out.' Anticipating her next move, he said quickly, 'No, don't put the light on.'

The bedclothes rustled as she sat up.

'I'll come too,' she whispered.

'No, you stay there. It's probably just a badger or something.'

'I'd like to see a badger.' She slid across and got out of bed.

'Honestly, Eve. It's probably nothing.'

'Last time you just went to check on something you got clobbered,' she reminded him. 'You need someone to look after you.' Her body showed as a faint silhouette as she hopped, stepping into her trousers.

'OK, but be quick and quiet. No lights; if there is someone there, we don't want to scare him off.'

'Speak for yourself. Personally, that sounds like a great idea.'

Gideon ignored her, easing the door open and pausing to listen.

From the foot of the stairs came a low, rumbling growl.

'All right, lad. I'm coming,' he said softly.

By the time Gideon reached the bottom of the stairs, with Eve close behind him, he could see that Zebedee was standing staring at the front door, ears and hackles up.

Gideon picked up a torch from the hall table, and Eve touched his arm.

'Wouldn't it be better to call the police, Gideon? Please.'

'For a badger?'

'You don't know it's a badger.'

'Well, unless they've got a car in the area, who or whatever it is'll be long gone by the time the police get here. I'll just take a look, but I'll be careful.'

'Take Zeb, then.'

'No, I'd rather he was here with you,' Gideon told her.

'Now you're sounding really scary.'

His hand on the front-door bolt, Gideon dropped a kiss on her brow.

'I just don't want him chasing badgers,' he said, slid the bolts back and turned the key. 'Have you got him? He'll try and make a run for it.'

Moments later he was out in the cold night air and closing the door quietly behind him. After the unlit house, the darkness in the garden was less intense, and he was easily able to make out the path leading to the front gate, the roof of the Land Rover parked in the lane, and the dark swell of trees beyond. Cloud masked the moon, and all but a scattering of stars, and a chill wind rustled the dry brown leaves of the hedge.

Gideon stood still, all his senses straining to catch whatever it was that had upset the dog.

Nothing.

No sight or sound of anything unusual.

Gideon relaxed a fraction, but supposed he'd better check the Land Rover and the shed before he went back inside.

Stepping over the low shrubs that bordered the path, he trod silently across the grass to the wicket gate, feeling the dew begin to soak the thin leather of his moccasins almost straight away. With his hand on the gate latch he became aware of a dim glow inside the Land Rover.

Hefting the rubber-covered torch in his hand, Gideon carefully operated the latch and started to open the gate. As he did so, the door on the far side of the vehicle shut with a muffled thunk, and a male voice muttered, 'Fucking hell!' in tones of extreme frustration.

In the Gatehouse, Zebedee began to bark once more and, beside Gideon, the gate hinge emitted a dry squeal as he eased it open.

Instantly, the prowler took to his heels and sped away down the lane towards the road. Abandoning caution, Gideon tore after him.

It was a hopeless effort. For one thing, the man in front had a five-or-six yard head start, and for another, he presumably wasn't wearing moccasins.

After only two or three strides, Gideon lost both of his, and from then on the outcome of the chase was never in doubt. He pulled up, hopping and swearing, just a few paces later, and switched the torch on. The feeble beam of light completely failed to reach the fugitive's fast-retreating form, and Gideon glanced at the fading bulb with irritation.

'Hell and bloody damnation!' he said out loud, and making a mental note to renew the torch batteries, he began to retrace his steps, using the dim circle of light to locate his fallen shoes.

Reshod, he gave the Land Rover and the shed a cursory examination and then headed for the house, where he found Eve waiting for him on the step, her hand still in Zebedee's collar.

'Badgers?' she enquired wryly.

'Well, maybe not.'

'What happened? Are you OK?'

'Yeah, I'm fine – except for a bruised foot. My moccasins came off when I tried to run after him. But the bastard's slashed the canvas on the Land Rover.'

'Oh, no, you're kidding! Was he trying to steal it, d'you think?'

'I don't know. I rather got the impression he was looking inside it, but I can't imagine what he hoped to find.'

Eve shivered. 'Well, if you've finished chasing burglars, shall we go inside? I'm freezing to death here.'

'Why on earth didn't you wait inside?'

'Because I couldn't see what was happening, and I thought you might need some help. D'you think it was the same person who broke in before?'

Gideon followed her into the relative warmth of the hall and shut the door.

'I don't know. They had all evening to look around last time. Why would they come back?'

'Well, to search the Land Rover, I suppose. It wasn't here that night, was it? Because you'd driven over to the gallery.'

'But what the hell did he think he was looking for? I don't have much in the house, but I've got even less in the car.'

He sat down and kicked the moccasins off, stretching his damp feet towards the Aga.

'Doesn't all this bother you?' she asked. 'You know, I wasn't just shivering with the cold out there, I was really frightened!'

'Oh, I'm sorry,' Gideon said, reaching out to rub her arm. 'Well, obviously I'm not exactly overjoyed about it, but until I know who he is and what he's looking for, there's not a lot I can do. But at least he doesn't seem too eager for a confrontation, that's one thing.'

'You're a strange one, you know, mister? When I first met you I thought you were pretty much of a big softy, but now I'm not so sure. You're so laid-back it's untrue, but you're soft like a polar bear is soft, and I wouldn't want to get on the wrong side of one of those.'

Gideon shrugged, embarrassed. 'I'll fight if I'm cornered, but basically, you got it right the first time.'

The truth was that behind his habitually relaxed exterior, he was beginning to feel a faint stirring of unease. Damien's death, and the manner of it, had shaken everyone up, and it was natural that it should take some time for things to settle down, especially while his murder remained unresolved. But now, it seemed, someone was taking an unhealthy interest in Gideon, and the feeling was not a pleasant one. What if, for some reason, the murderer was having second thoughts about letting him live?

Admittedly, the intruder hadn't been eager for a confrontation, but maybe that wasn't his style. What possible defence was there against a long-range sniper's bullet?

The answer was as clear as it was chilling.

None at all.

SEVEN

T HE NEXT MORNING GIDEON paid his rescheduled
visit to the Radcliffe Trust stables.

It was the day Angie Bowen was to play host to the Trust's directors, and she came hurrying out of the office as Gideon parked
the Land Rover and got stiffly out. He thought she looked tense.

'Hello, Gideon. Are you all right?'

'Yeah. I went and rode work with Tilly Daniels yesterday, and
I'm not as fit as I thought I was,' he said ruefully. 'But don't
worry, I'm fully functional – just a little creaky!'

'Oh, good. But they're not here yet. I'm sorry. They told me
half past ten. I think everything's ready . . .'

'Hey, it'll be fine,' Gideon said. 'They can't fail to be pleased
with what you're doing here.'

She gave him a brief, nervous smile. 'I thought we'd start with
Ping Pong, the new lad who arrived on Monday. He came from
a jumping yard up north. I don't know much about his history
but he's very nervous and I wondered whether you could do a
join-up session with him? Would you mind? I know you don't
really like an audience.'

'But I'll do it for you, my dear,' he said, assuming an expression of martyrdom.

'You're daft, you know that? Oh 'eck! Here they come.'

Gideon turned to see a gleaming dark blue Daimler nose into the yard. It pulled up next to his own dusty vehicle, with its taped-up slashed canvas, and two men got out: one tall and lean with wire-rimmed spectacles, and the other a good eight inches shorter and rather overweight. They were both attired in cavalry twills and tweed jackets; immaculate to the toes of their polished brown shoes. The effect was rather as though they had visited a Bond Street tailor and asked to be kitted out for a visit to the country.

Angie stepped forward to perform the introductions.

'Colonel Havering, Dr Camberwell; Gideon Blake. Gideon's our behaviourist.'

Handshakes were exchanged and comments made about the lovely spring weather, and then their tour of the facilities got under way. The new stable block was inspected and the benefits of the proposed covered school discussed, and then they met the horses currently in residence.

The two men took an intelligent interest in everything they were told, and Gideon rapidly revised his first impression of them. When they had seen everything else, he slipped a headcollar onto the new grey gelding and led it into the boarded round pen.

Unclipping the rope, Gideon let the horse loose and it immediately shied away from him and went to stand on the other side of the circle, eyeing him warily. Stepping towards its hindquarters and flicking the loose end of the lead rope, Gideon clicked his tongue and sent the animal plunging into a canter round the outside of the pen. Out of the corner of his eye, Gideon saw Angie and the two men settling themselves into the seats on the viewing platform and, trusting her to explain the procedure to them, turned his full attention onto the horse.

Ping Pong was an exemplary pupil, displaying all the behavioural patterns that illustrated the join-up technique perfectly.

After an initial period of sending the horse away from him, Gideon took the pressure off and let him slow a little. Instantly Ping Pong lowered his head and started to make chewing and licking actions, plainly indicating his willingness to submit. At this cue Gideon turned away, dropping a shoulder and bowing his head: an invitation to the horse to come into the centre, to follow him and accept his leadership. Within moments, the grey was standing next to him and, after rubbing its forehead reassuringly, Gideon moved away, confident that Ping Pong would be right behind.

He was.

Gideon wandered this way and that in the round pen, with the grey horse following like a devoted puppy, and then stopped and clipped the rope on once more. The whole episode had taken less than ten minutes.

The directors, it seemed, were impressed.

'I have to say, I've never seen anything like that in my life!' Colonel Havering exclaimed, as Gideon emerged from the pen with Ping Pong in tow.

'I'm afraid I can't claim it's anything new. There are dozens of people using this method now.'

'But Angela would have us believe you're somewhat exceptional,' the colonel said. 'She says you have a real gift.'

Gideon wasn't sure how to reply to this.

'That's kind of her. I suppose I've always had an instinct for it,' he said. 'But she's the one who puts in all the hard work to back it up.'

Excusing himself on the pretext of needing to return the horse to its box, Gideon made his getaway and, by the time he'd settled Ping Pong, the two men had taken their leave and swished quietly away in the Daimler.

'I think that went well. You were brilliant, and this fellow was an absolute star,' Angie declared, coming into the grey's stable as Gideon rubbed him down with a cactus cloth. 'Have you got time for a celebratory coffee?'

'Just try and get rid of me without! So you think Laurel and Hardy went away happy?'

Angie laughed. 'They only needed the bowler hats, didn't they? Yes, they seemed very upbeat. It's the Trust's tenth anniversary later in the year, and they're talking about trying to get some TV coverage, which would be good.'

They left Ping Pong munching on a net of hay, and headed for the staffroom and the promised cup of coffee, but halfway there they were interrupted as another vehicle entered the yard.

'No, no. Go away. I want my coffee,' Angie muttered as they turned to meet the newcomer.

A monstrous four-by-four pulled up, and a slim woman with short dark hair and a Mediterranean tan jumped down from the driver's seat.

'Hello, Vanessa,' Angie said, with what Gideon judged to be a genuine smile of welcome. 'Did you have a nice holiday?'

'Yes, too short, though. Morocco was divine.' Her dark brown eyes flickered over Gideon with interest.

'Oh, this is Gideon Blake,' Angie told her. 'Gideon; Vanessa Tate. Vanessa's had two horses off us.'

'Hi,' he said, stepping forward to shake her hand briefly.

'Hi. And now I'd like a third, if you've got anything suitable,' Vanessa announced, turning to Angie once more.

'We might have,' Angie said. 'But do you think you could possibly wait five minutes while we grab a cup of coffee? Gideon and I have been entertaining the charity's top brass. In fact, if you've got time, why don't you come and have a cuppa with us?'

Vanessa looked at her watch. 'Well, OK. I've got an appointment at two o'clock, but that still gives me a couple of hours. Thanks.'

In the staffroom they surprised a young lad and a girl who were sitting close together on one of the orange-covered, boxy sofas. They moved apart instantly, as if an electric charge had passed between them, and the boy, who had lank dark hair and teenage skin, pushed a hand through his fringe in a gesture of self-consciousness.

'Ah, Warren. Conniston's tack needs cleaning,' Angie said briskly. 'And make sure you oil that new noseband, it's horribly stiff. Julie, could you go and catch Pinto and Twiggy?'

'Yeah, um . . . where shall I put them?' Julie was blonde with dark roots, a sulky pout and a nose stud.

'Any of the spare boxes. They won't be in for long.'

The two youngsters left the room together, and broke into audible giggles as the door swung to behind them.

'I don't know what she sees in him,' Angie remarked as they disappeared. 'Must be pheromones, I suppose. Coffee or tea?'

Vanessa Tate, it transpired, had a daughter of fifteen, and the two women disappeared into the tiny kitchen area to discuss the vagaries of the lovelorn teenager while Angie prepared the drinks.

Gideon was glad to be temporarily excluded from the conversation; it gave him a chance to decide how best to take advantage of this completely unheralded good fortune. There was no real doubt in his mind that this was the Vanessa Tate whose telephone-answering machine he'd listened to, three days before. And if there had been any doubt, it would have been stilled moments later, when Vanessa carried her coffee over to the sofa and sat down, saying, 'Robin's determined that Poppy should go to boarding school in September, but any mention of it brings on a strop of gigantic proportions!'

She gave Gideon a friendly smile.

'Do you have any children, Gideon?'

'No, just a dog and a cat,' he responded. 'So, what sort of horse are you looking for?'

'An eventer – or at least, a potential one. The two I had from here last year are coming on terrifically well.'

'Three's a lot to cope with, or does your husband ride, too?'

'I've actually got five,' she said. 'All at different stages of their careers. No, Robin doesn't often ride any more, but I have a girl to help me.'

'How sad, to give up like that,' Angie put in. 'When he used to ride such a lot.'

'Yes, but to be honest, I think he only really rode because it was necessary for the pentathlon. He always preferred the shooting and the fencing. And now he's got his motorbikes. Fifteen of them, at the last count!'

'Ah, I can identify with that,' Gideon said warmly. 'I've just put down a deposit on a new bike myself.'

'Really? I never saw you as a biker,' Angie commented.

'Dyed in the wool,' he assured her. 'Only been without for a couple of years since I was eighteen.'

'Like Robin,' Vanessa agreed. 'You should meet up.'

'You know, I can't help thinking I've heard the name Robin Tate somewhere recently,' Gideon said, injecting a note of thoughtfulness into his voice. 'He wasn't a friend of Damien Daniels, was he?'

Vanessa shook her head. 'Not unless it was before I knew him. Wasn't that a dreadful thing? Have they caught anyone yet?'

'Not that I know of. Robin Tate – would it have been something about a racing syndicate?'

'No, I think it must definitely have been another Robin Tate. My Robin's got no interest in racing whatsoever.'

'What about Sam Bentley? Do you know him?' That was the name he fancied had struck a chord with the PE teacher.

Vanessa shook her head again, but with no apparent disquiet. 'No. Sorry. We know a Sam Potter, but not Bentley.'

'Sam Potter? Is that Ian and Sarah's boy?' Angie enquired. 'How is Sarah these days? I heard she was rather ill. Breast cancer, wasn't it? How's she getting on?'

The conversation moved on and, in due course, Angie took her visitor out to look at the two horses Julie had brought in, and Gideon went thoughtfully on his way, to spend the afternoon clearing a space in his shed-cum-garage for the new motorbike.

★

'What on earth's that?' Pippa asked.

Arriving for Giles' dinner party, Gideon and Eve had ridden the bike up the drive right behind Pippa in her brother's four-wheel-drive Mercedes, and had now stopped beside it in the yard.

'It's a motorcycle,' Gideon said, helpfully.

'I can see that, but whose?'

'Mine. Picked it up this afternoon and we've just been out for a ride round.'

Eve took her helmet off and shook out her long hair. At the dealer's she'd calmly kitted herself out in almost a thousand pounds' worth of clothing and boots, and now looked like one of the more decent adverts in the bike magazines.

'It's brilliant! I'm tempted to get one myself,' she said, balancing her helmet on the seat and unzipping her fringed leather jacket.

'D'you like it?' Gideon asked Pippa, looking proudly at the black and chrome cruiser.

'Lovely,' Pippa said tightly. 'I thought you'd got over that stage when you crashed the last one.'

'One doesn't just *get over* motorbikes,' he told her. 'It would be like telling you to *get over* horses. Can't be done. And anyway, I didn't just crash it, if you remember. I had a little help!'

'Wow! I thought I heard a bike.' Giles had emerged from the back door. 'Don't tell me – a Harley?'

'No, actually it's a Triumph,' Gideon said. 'I couldn't afford a Harley, and besides, I'd rather buy British.'

'It's beautiful. You kept quiet about that, didn't you?'

'I've only just got it. It was a spur of the moment thing that's been coming on for the last eighteen months. I sold a couple of paintings at the gallery and decided to go for it.'

'Well, if you'll excuse me, I'll leave you lot to admire Gideon's new toy while it's still in one piece, and go check on supper,' Pippa said. 'It should be ready in about half an hour.'

'Oh, dear. Someone's not happy,' Eve observed as the door closed behind Pippa.

'We had a cousin who was killed in a bike accident when she

was about sixteen. She idolised him,' Giles explained. 'But she'll get used to the idea again, don't worry. I think she just thought that when Gideon had the Land Rover, he'd forget about bikes. I didn't.'

Apart from Lloyd unwarily mentioning it and earning himself a frosty look from Pippa, the subject of the motorcycle was left severely alone over supper, the conversation dwelling for some time on Gideon's projected initiation into drag hunting, the coming Saturday.

This topic was as unwelcome to Gideon as the other had been to Pippa. Barely a day had gone by when he hadn't regretted having risen to Lloyd's challenge. It wasn't that he was anxious about the riding side of it – although he was by no means sure how Blackbird would behave in such an inflammatory atmos-phere – more that he was aware that he'd be venturing onto Lloyd's territory, where Lloyd, as Master of the Tarrant and Stour Drag Hounds, would be in charge. The thought rankled.

'So have you dusted off your bowler hat and boots?' Giles teased.

'Bowler hat? Where have you been for the last century?' his sister demanded. 'Gideon's got a black jacket though, haven't you?'

'Have you?' Eve asked, intrigued.

'I have, actually. I bought a second-hand one last year when I had to take a horse to the New Forest Show, for a client. It was a heavyweight hunter that used to get ring fright and go into high-speed reverse in the middle of the arena.'

'And did you sort it out?'

'Yeah, I think it was more a rider problem.'

'And the rest!' Pippa exclaimed. 'He only went and won reserve champion hunter!'

'Well, I can't claim any credit for that. It was a good-looking horse.'

'And it went like a dream.'

'So you've got the gear,' Lloyd said, bringing the subject back to hunting. 'If you're riding Blackbird, you ought to put a green ribbon in his tail.'

'Very pretty,' Eve murmured.

'It's to warn the other riders that he's untried and might be unpredictable,' Pippa explained. 'If you know you've got an excitable animal that's likely to kick, you use a red ribbon instead.'

'So what exactly does a drag hunt consist of? What's actually dragged, for instance?'

'Right,' Lloyd was now in his element. 'Basically the hounds follow a scent laid down twenty minutes or half an hour before the start . . .'

'I think this is where I go and sort the dessert out,' Pippa cut in, rising to her feet.

Lloyd didn't seem to notice. 'They used to use aniseed mixed with animal droppings, or even human urine, but nowadays we use a special chemical crystal, mixed with water and oil. The runner dips a cloth in it and then runs along dragging it behind. If we want a fast run they keep it pretty continuous, but to make it more realistic and challenging for the hounds, they can double back or leave breaks in the trail, or splash through water, you know the sort of thing.'

'So do you know where the runner is going to go, or is it a surprise to you?'

'No, we have to plan it in advance. Because we're on private land, we have to keep to the areas that the farmer or landowner specifies, to avoid damaging crops or disturbing livestock. Also, there are jumps along the way; sections of clipped hedge or fences and walls that are safe to jump, so they have to be included. Each trail, or line – as we call them – is usually around two to three miles long, and there are maybe three or four of them in a day's hunting, sometimes more, with breaks in between.'

'It sounds exciting,' Eve said. 'Are spectators allowed?'

'Oh, no,' Gideon groaned.

'Yes. We get quite a few on a fine day,' Lloyd told her.

'So do you use foxhounds?'

'We do, but you can use any type of hound, really; beagles, otterhounds, bloodhounds. Although bloodhounds just follow a human scent, of course. They call it hunting the clean boot.'

'OK, so what happens if the foxhounds come across a fox while they are following a trail? Would they chase that instead?'

'Almost certainly.'

'So what happens then? Can you stop them?'

'Well, it's not easy, but it can be done,' Lloyd said, adding with a twinkle, 'but usually we all have to ride after them to try to get them back. It can take absolutely ages . . .'

Eve wasn't stupid.

'I imagine it might,' she said. 'So all this stuff about hunting people being out of work was rubbish, was it? They're still busy hunting.'

Gideon's breath hissed between his teeth as he cringed in anticipation.

'Absolutely not!' Lloyd said forcefully. 'Drag hunting's all very well, but it can never completely take over from the real thing. For one thing, a drag hunt covers a much bigger area, so where there might have been two or three foxhound packs, there's now only one drag hunt. That's a sixty per cent cut in employment before you start . . .'

By the time Pippa returned with a large tiramisu and a jug of cream, Gideon and Giles, who had heard Lloyd's political pitch before, were bordering on comatose, and even Eve, to whom it was apparently new, was beginning to look as though she wished she'd not asked. She had played devil's advocate to start with, but it soon became obvious that she was sparring with an obsessive.

'Time up!' Pippa said, placing her burden on the table. 'Put the soap box away, Lloyd.'

'I surrendered five minutes ago, but I don't think he noticed,' Eve said laughing. 'He's a natural for politics, I'll give him that.'

'Oh, sorry! You should have stopped me.'

'A chance would have been a fine thing,' Giles remarked, good-humouredly. 'Once you get going you don't stop for breath!'

Lloyd put his hands up. 'OK. I won't say another word. But you really should come and watch a drag hunt, anyway. And if you do, come and find me before the off, and I'll tell you where the best vantage point is likely to be.'

'OK, I'll do that,' Eve said, and Gideon was surprised and a little dismayed to see that she seemed to be seriously considering it.

The morning of Gideon's drag-hunting debut dawned with watery sunshine and a low-lying mist, but by eleven thirty when the Tarrant and Stour Drag Hounds met at Catsfinger Farm near Sherborne, it was shaping up to be a beautiful day.

Gideon and Pippa had boxed the horses to the meet, with Eve following on behind in her car, and now joined the fifty or so other members of the field on the half-moon of pea-shingle in front of the farmhouse. Most of the horses were plaited and all the riders wore breeches, boots and jackets; some black, and some hacking jackets in shades of olive and fawn. The huntsman, his two whippers-in and Lloyd himself, as Field Master, all wore the traditional scarlet coats.

'It's called "hunting pink",' Pippa told Eve. 'Don't ask me why, it's just one of those things.'

'Perhaps, in years gone by, the coats faded,' she suggested practically. Then waving a hand in the direction of a corpulent middle-aged man with a florid complexion, she said to Gideon, 'Look, I'm going to hitch a lift in that kind man's Range Rover. Lloyd introduced us – he says he knows the best vantage points – so I'll be off in a minute. By the way, did I tell you, you look extraordinarily dashing in that get-up?'

'That's what I said,' Pippa agreed.

'Well, I should hope I do, after the hours of blood, sweat and tears I spent tying this stock,' Gideon put in, fingering the neat white neckcloth.

'*You* did?' Pippa exclaimed. 'I like that! You'd still be standing in front of the mirror now, if I hadn't taken over!'

'I bring out her maternal instincts,' he said in an aside to Eve, and then swayed sideways to dodge a slap.

Eve laughed and moved away to find her cross-country taxi service, looking, in corduroy trousers, Aran jumper and a waxed jacket, as though this was the way she spent every weekend.

Their hosts, the owners of the oddly named Catsfinger Farm, moved among the mounted throng with trays bearing mulled wine and nibbles, and the hounds, with their wide-smiling faces, milled around getting under everyone's feet.

Blackbird was undeniably excited, but being extraordinarily good. He stood beside Skylark, looking alert and handsome, with his black mane plaited and his feet oiled, and fairly quivering with nervous anticipation. So far it had been Pippa's horse, Skylark, who was the more fidgety, every so often diving his head downwards to try and loosen her grip on the reins, and once suddenly swinging his quarters towards Gideon's mount, causing him to shy violently sideways in his turn.

'Get that bloody animal under control!' someone exclaimed furiously from behind Gideon, and after steadying Blackbird, he turned to see a good-looking young man scowling blackly at him from the back of a tall bay horse.

'Sorry.'

'Bloody first-timers!' the man muttered. 'It's you should be wearing the ribbon, not the bloody horse!'

'It was my fault,' Pippa called across. 'I'm sorry. My horse barged into him. He didn't kick out, did he?'

'No thanks to matey here.'

'Look, it was nobody's fault,' Gideon said. 'And no-one got hurt, so shall we drop it? I did apologise, after all.'

But the rider on the bay obviously didn't want to be mollified. He kicked his horse forward, leaning towards Gideon as he passed.

'You just make sure you keep out of my way,' he muttered.

Gideon raised an eyebrow at his departing back.

'*Charming!*'

'But it wasn't even your fault,' Pippa protested, bringing Skylark round and alongside Blackbird, who glanced crossly at the other horse. 'Or mine, come to that. Some idiot backed into Sky – that's what started it. I can't believe that guy was so rude to you . . .'

Gideon shrugged. 'Forget it. He's not worth it.'

'Who isn't?' Lloyd rode his brown horse up on the other side of Pippa, leaned across and kissed her.

'Some moron who threw a wobbly because Blackbird nearly bumped his horse.' She explained what had happened, for Lloyd's benefit. 'He was way out of line!' she finished, hotly.

'I'm sorry. D'you want me to have a word with him?' Lloyd offered. 'Which one was it?'

'It was . . .' Pippa twisted in her saddle to scan the other riders. 'It was a man on a big bay horse. Damn! I can't see him now.'

'It really doesn't matter,' Gideon said.

Lloyd looked at his watch. 'Well, I'd better go and get this thing under way,' he said. 'You ready?'

This last was directed at Gideon, who nodded. 'As I'll ever be.'

Lloyd rode to the edge of the gravel and stood in his stirrups, raising his voice to call, 'Can I have your attention please?'

Gradually the chattering died away and everyone turned expectantly towards him.

'Thank you,' he said, settling back into the saddle. 'We'll be moving off in approximately five minutes, so please drink up and don't forget to tighten those girths. For those of you who are riding with us for the first time, I'll just run through the rules of the chase . . .'

Watching Lloyd, as he addressed the field, Gideon was reluctantly impressed. From the occasional comments, it was clear that he was regarded with both liking and respect by the regulars amongst them.

Most of what he had to say, Pippa had already explained to Gideon, though Lloyd added a few pointers about etiquette and went on to say that those on less fit horses could, by dint of a short hack, miss out the third line of the day and meet up with the rest of the field at the break, ready to start the final one.

'Just follow Penny, with the white armband. She'll take you through,' he advised, waving at a trim, grey-haired lady on a grey horse, who waved back. 'The first line isn't particularly taxing. There are two biggish gates — fences five and eight — but there are alternatives. Again, look for Penny. Well, that's it for the first line. We're hunting twelve couple of hounds, and your dragsman for the day, back by popular demand, is Steve Pettet. Have a great day, and our hosts have promised us a slap-up tea at the end of it.'

A concerted cheer greeted this last piece of information, and almost immediately the huntsman, who'd been waiting a little way off, blew a series of short notes on his horn, riding his horse down the gravel drive towards the road. At once the hounds began to percolate through the forest of equine legs, as if they were all attached by some invisible thread to the man in the red coat.

The note of the horn had a similar effect on both horses and humans. All talking stopped. The riders sat up straight and shortened their reins, and the horses pricked their ears, tossed their heads and began to sidle impatiently. Even Gideon, who had hitherto had no close association with hunting, felt a thrill buzz through him, and Blackbird was almost transfixed with excitement, head high and nostrils flaring. Gideon ran his gloved hand down the damp black neck, and spoke quietly to him.

When the last hound had joined its fellows in the dash after the huntsman, the two whips fell in behind to chivvy the stragglers, and Lloyd swung his horse round to follow. Within moments, the whole field was on the move.

Gideon held back, intending to tuck in at the rear of the field, and, for a moment, he thought Blackbird was going to explode. He began to move rapidly up and down on the spot like a footballer warming up, his hooves churning the shingle, but when Gideon gave him the office to move he settled into a bouncy jog next to Skylark.

Gideon and Pippa followed the other riders through a gateway and into a field, and from there they watched while the huntsman led the hounds to the start of the trail. Almost immediately a lemon and white dog gave tongue, its tail — or stern, as it was known in the hunting world — waving high. Two more hounds went to join it, adding their voices, and suddenly the whole pack was in full cry, heading across the grass to a low rail in the corner. The huntsman blew the 'Gone Away' and put his horse at the rail, and after a suitable interval Lloyd led the field in pursuit.

That first line of the day passed in something of a blur for Gideon. The unseen dragsman had laid a short and clear opening trail, and the hounds hunted it briskly. As the field set off, Blackbird's excitement finally bubbled over, and not all Gideon's soothing powers could stop him giving a series of quite sizeable bucks going towards the first fence. Gideon wrapped his long legs round the horse and hung on grimly. Luckily the rail was no more than three feet high, with only the shallowest of ditches on the far side, and seeing it at the last moment, the black horse had no problem negotiating it. This done, he settled into a ground-covering stride and applied himself enthusiastically to working his way to the front of the field.

Five hedges, two post and rail fences, and both the gates later, Gideon brought the horse to a halt at the end of the line, in time to see the huntsman showering the pack with some kind of biscuit or dried meat from his saddlebags.

The hounds scrabbled eagerly for their reward, a seething mass of hard-muscled brown, yellow and white bodies and waving sterns, until every last morsel was gone and their heads came up, grinning broadly, tongues lolling.

Gideon patted Blackbird's hot neck and looked down at his heaving flank. The horse was breathing deeply, but not excessively so. The fifteen-minute break should easily see him ready to tackle the second run.

'I'm looking for the guy on the black horse who said he was

going to ride quietly at the back of the field,' a voice said, and he turned to find Pippa steering Skylark towards him through the other horses.

Gideon grinned.

'The black horse had other ideas.'

'So I noticed. Did he cart you?'

'Actually, no. But he was going so well, it seemed a shame to stop him. I didn't want to risk him starting bucking again. He jumped like a stag!'

'He looked smashing,' Pippa agreed. 'I've already had an offer for him. Someone who saw us together at the meet and asked about him.'

'Did you accept?'

'Of course not,' she said with a quick frown. 'He's yours. And, even if he wasn't, you know what a pig he is normally. He's a real one-person horse. Oh, here's Lloyd . . .'

'How did you enjoy that?' Lloyd asked, coming up to Gideon.

'It was brilliant – once this fella settled down.'

'Good.' Lloyd looked genuinely pleased, and Gideon wondered if he'd misjudged the man. 'There's a couple of biggish fences in this next line, but nothing you can't handle. Just watch for the ditch on the other side of the long hedge, it gets wider the further right you go. But it's flagged, so just keep between them and you'll be fine. Oh, well, I'd better go and do my little speech. I hope Dan's got my second horse waiting at the next stop; Badger will have had it by then, won't you, old boy?' He tugged on one of the horse's plaits, causing him to shake his head in irritation.

Five minutes later, after Lloyd had repeated the information about the ditch to the assembled riders, the huntsman marshalled the hounds and they all hacked the hundred yards or so to the start of the next line.

This time, when the field set off, Gideon was ready for Blackbird, and foiled a half-hearted attempt to buck by hauling his head up and driving him forward. As the first fence flashed a good foot below the black's belly, Gideon really began to enjoy himself. Pippa ranged up alongside at one point, and they flew a substantial hedge side by side.

'He's going beautifully,' she called across, and Gideon smiled and nodded.

Moments later they were separated, and Gideon took the next bank and ditch in the company of a woman on a breedy chestnut and a man on a tall, heavily built bay. As they crossed the next field, the bay horse accelerated and Blackbird instinctively length-ened his stride to keep up. The chestnut fell behind, and a grey took its place.

As they thundered along, three abreast, Gideon could see Lloyd up in front, taking the next fence, a solid-looking post and rail with a ditch on take-off.

The horses either side of him were very close now – unnec-essarily so, Gideon thought, as they approached the rails – their stirrups clashing with his. Three strides out, they suddenly surged forward, catching him unawares and gaining almost a length on Blackbird. With a shout of 'Hup!' the bay and the grey rose smoothly into the air and, way too early, Gideon's horse rose with them.

They were in flight for an eternity. It didn't seem to Gideon that Blackbird had a hope of clearing the rails from where he'd taken off, but somehow he did it. He pecked heavily on landing, his muzzle somewhere down by his front hooves, and Gideon fell forward onto his neck, but the next moment they were up and away again.

Gideon regained his seat, gathered up his reins and took a pull.

The man on the grey looked back and called airily, 'Sorry, mate.'

Gideon didn't trust himself to answer.

Across another field, down a muddy lane through a copse, and through a remote yard between two barns and a tractor shed, Blackbird powered on. Steadying to take the turn through a narrow gateway into a field, Gideon found that there were only three or four horses between himself and Lloyd, in front.

The pace picked up once more and the next jump loomed: a long, clipped hedge with a flag at either end. Outside the flags the brush was a good eighteen inches higher, and to the right the ground dropped away, looking damp and reedy. This, then, was the hedge Lloyd had warned him about. Gideon started to ease Blackbird towards the left, with the intention of taking the centre line, as the horses in front were doing, but suddenly the big bay was there again, blocking his intended move and bearing him steadily to the right.

Gideon looked ahead. The fence was no more than sixty yards away and he was being pushed inexorably towards the right-hand flag. At this rate, it wasn't so much a case of having to jump it at the widest end – he seemed more likely to miss the flagged area altogether.

'Hey, move over, mate,' he shouted, wondering if the bay was losing its nerve and trying to run out.

Its rider totally ignored him. The distance to the hedge was halved now and rapidly closing.

'Oi! Move over, damn you!' Gideon yelled furiously, glancing across.

This time he recognised the bay's rider as the one who'd bawled him out at the meet, and he was grinning.

EIGHT

A T THE SPEED THEY were travelling, and with the right-hand boundary of the field now only a few yards away, Gideon had no hope of turning or stopping in the available space, even if he could have prevailed upon Blackbird to do so. The horse, however, was galloping full pelt, clearly a little annoyed at the encroaching behaviour of the bay, and completely unaware of the potential hazard ahead.

Three strides . . . two . . . one . . . They were outside the flag, where the tops of the untrimmed blackthorn shoots reached six or seven feet high and the ground was poached and boggy. Undeterred, Blackbird lowered his head, bunched his quarters and launched skyward. Gideon, throwing his weight forward to give the horse all the help he could, felt the whippy stems rattle against his boots as they brushed harmlessly through the top foot or so and, from this elevated position, the full extent of the danger became all too apparent.

The ditch that ran along the far side of the hedge was more in the nature of a small stream and, at the point that Blackbird had been forced to jump it, widened considerably, with a hoof-pitted muddy slope forming the far bank. The black horse reached forward with outstretched hooves, but gravity won out, and his forefeet landed on the treacherous incline and slid backward into the stream. His head ducked sideways, he hit the bank with his shoulder and the momentum carried his hindquarters over, propelling Gideon onward to land clear, several feet away, with a thud that rattled his teeth and expelled every last ounce of breath from his body.

He rolled twice and sat up, his chest a mass of pain as he fought to get air back into his deflated lungs. Through watering eyes he could see the black horse, half in the muddy stream, struggling unsuccessfully to regain his feet, and a split second later four or five more horses came flying over the clipped hedge, to land with varying degrees of finesse and gallop on. Another group followed and suddenly it seemed that Gideon's plight had been noticed, as two or three riders peeled off and came cantering back.

Pulling up on a snorting, foam-spewing chestnut, just yards from Gideon, one woman called, 'Are you OK?'

Gideon nodded. Breathing was now a distinct possibility in the not too distant future, but speech was still some way off. He waved an arm towards the stream and the stricken Blackbird.

'It's all right. They're looking after your horse,' she said, speaking over her shoulder as the chestnut strove to follow the latest wave of horses that passed. 'Do you need a doctor?'

Gideon shook his head, inhaled a painful quarter-lungful and wheezed, 'Just winded.'

'Well, if you're sure . . . ?' The woman was quite obviously losing her battle with the chestnut and, when Gideon nodded again, the pair of them took off, thoughtfully showering him with mud and turf.

His first attempt to climb to his feet led to him sitting back down with a bump, and the realisation that one side of his body was completely soaked in mud and water. On his second attempt he made it to a crouch, where he paused, trying for more breath, frustrated at not being able to go to his horse.

From that position he could see that three riders had stopped to help Blackbird, one holding the horses, while the other two were endeavouring to push and pull the black horse to a position where he could get his legs under him, and stand.

'Gideon! Are you OK? I saw what happened.'

Pippa, this time. She jumped off Skylark and squelched towards him.

'Will be,' he said. 'What about Blackbird? Can you see?'

'I think they're trying to get him down into the bottom of the stream where it's more gravelly. Here, do you want some help?' she offered, holding out a gloved hand.

'Thanks.'

As Gideon made it to his feet with Pippa's aid, he saw Blackbird give a huge lurch and scramble up the slippery bank to safety. Once there he shook himself vigorously, showering his rescuers with dirty water, and then gave vent to a shrill neigh, his body shaking with the effort.

Slipping and sliding on the uneven ground, Gideon went over to the horse. One man was holding him while the other tried to look him over, but Blackbird, typically robust and headstrong, had other ideas, and began to fidget and circle, eager to rejoin the chase.

'As far as I can see, he's OK,' the man said. 'He certainly doesn't seem any the worse for wear.'

'Thanks. You did a brilliant job,' Gideon said. 'I'd never have managed on my own.'

'No problem,' the man replied. 'But – next time – I should stick to the course, if I were you. The flags are there for a reason, you know.'

'Yeah. Tell the other guy! He swerved into me.'

'Oh, bad luck! These things happen.'

'Yeah, well, thanks again. I'll be fine now, if you want to catch up with the others.'

They quite patently did, and after enquiring once more if he was quite sure it was OK, they mounted and rode off in the direction the rest of the field had taken.

Quieting Blackbird, who had responded to the disappearance of the other horses by whirling round him in tight circles, Gideon tried to wipe his saddle clean with the sleeve of his jacket. Miraculously, both stirrups were still intact, and even more miraculously, so were his reins. Blackbird himself seemed remarkably untroubled, both physically and mentally, by his crashing fall. Gideon didn't see why he shouldn't remount, and said so.

'Are you sure?' Pippa looked doubtful. 'I don't mind walking back with you, if you'd rather.'

'No, I'll be fine, and I expect it'd be better for Blackbird to keep moving, too. If he's as wet as I am, he'll be getting cold.'

In spite of his reassuring words, getting back into the saddle wasn't the most comfortable experience, but once there, things began to settle down. The saddle was wet and slippery, but felt unbroken, and the laced leather reins provided good grip for his fingers. Blackbird's sodden ears looked unusually long and narrow, and there was a tuft of muddy grass caught in the headpiece of his bridle, but he felt strong and sound beneath Gideon, and strode out eagerly beside Skylark.

'Some guy swerved into you . . . ?'

'Yeah, in a manner of speaking,' Gideon said sourly, leaning forward to remove the grass.

'And he didn't stop?'

'No, and if he's got any sense, he won't stop until he's in the next county. You remember the rude man at the meet?'

'It wasn't him?' Pippa swivelled in her saddle to look at Gideon. 'Are you saying he rode you off course intentionally?'

'I'm damn sure of it!'

'Oh, for heavensakes! I mean it's one thing to be arsey about a bit of jostling but this was downright dangerous! Are you really sure? Couldn't he have just lost control?'

'Well, if he had, he was looking pretty happy about it!' Gideon told Pippa exactly what had happened.

When he'd finished she said decisively, 'You must tell Lloyd.'

'Later, maybe. But to be honest, what can he do? It's only my word against the other guy's.'

It was the best part of another mile to the end of the second line, and when Gideon and Pippa arrived huntsman, hounds and field had already moved on. Three riders remained, one of whom was Penny, the lady with the white armband, whose job it was to show the less fit participants the short cut to the start of the last line.

She waved a hand as the two of them rode up.

'Hello Pippa. Everything OK? I heard there was a nasty fall. Oh . . .' Her eyes twinkled as she took in Gideon's muddied state. 'Looks like you found a soft place to land, anyway!'

'Could have been worse,' he agreed. 'Thanks for waiting.'

'No problem. Right, if you'd like to follow me, I'll take you on to the next halt. And then I can head you in the right direction to get back to the farmhouse, unless of course you want to hunt on.'

'I might do,' Gideon said. 'He seems OK.'

'And it would be good to finish on a high note, wouldn't it? See how you go then.'

After hacking quietly along the edge of some plough and down a muddy lane, they emerged into a high, open field with views over the surrounding countryside. Here they sat and waited until the pricking of the horses' ears alerted them to the approach of the hunt.

'Look. There's one of the hounds,' Pippa said, pointing, and within moments the whole pack were streaming under and over the stile in the far corner of the field. Giving tongue sporadically they headed towards a pile of half a dozen plastic-wrapped hay bales, where they gathered round, pushing and shoving one another for best position.

'Is there something there for them to find?' Gideon asked Penny.

'Just a few bits of meat,' she said. 'Gives them extra incentive. Ray – the huntsman – will give them all something when he gets here.'

As if on cue, the huntsman and one of his whips jumped into the field over the stile, followed closely by the second whip, and galloped to where the hounds were. Moments later Lloyd appeared, riding his second horse, and on his heels, the rest of the field.

If there was any doubt about Blackbird's eagerness to rejoin the action, it was swiftly banished now. As the other horses came into sight, he suddenly plunged his head between his knees in an attempt to loosen Gideon's grip, and, when that didn't work, began to paw the ground with an impatient foreleg.

When the field had come to a halt, many of them dismounting to rest their tiring horses, the waiting group rode over to join them. Gideon's eyes searched in vain for the man on the bay. With so many horses and riders, some now on foot or facing the other way, it was impossible to get a good look at all of them without riding round and among them.

Lloyd spotted Pippa and led his horse across.

'Everything all right? Oh, dear! What happened to you?'

'Blackbird put his foot in the ditch,' Gideon said.

'And the rest!' Pippa said explosively.

Lloyd looked questioningly at each of them in turn, but Gideon merely shook his head slightly.

'Not now.'

'Something I should know?'

'Later maybe,' Gideon said. 'How long will this line be? Do you think it'll be all right for this fella after his fall?'

'Oh, yes, I should think so. It's about three miles but Steve usually lays a trickier line for the last one – more breaks and less jumps, because the horses are tiring. Makes the hounds work. It's more like the real thing.'

Within ten minutes they were under way, and to Gideon's relief Blackbird seemed unaffected by his experiences at the hedge and ditch, and continued to jump eagerly and apparently without fear. Gideon couldn't decide whether this was due to bravery or stupidity, and said as much to Pippa during a pause in the run.

'Actually, I think it's because he trusts you,' she said, as they watched hounds quartering the headland in search of scent. 'His ears are constantly flicking back and forth. For some reason the old bugger listens to everything you say. Never mind that I'm the one who feeds him and sees to his every need!'

'I've heard it said that horses are incredibly good judges of character,' Gideon said, straight-faced.

'But then, everyone makes a mistake, once in a while,' she replied sweetly, as first one hound and then another picked up the trail and began to give tongue excitedly.

Seconds later the whole pack was streaming across the field in full cry, robbing Gideon of the opportunity of comeback.

At the end of the day, with horses installed in their trailers and boxes, rugged up and pulling at haynets, the members of the field and foot-followers were treated to hot soup and garlic bread in the barn at Catsfinger Farm.

'Is he here?' Pippa asked, coming across to where Gideon and Eve sat on hay bales against the wall. She was wearing a polo-necked jumper over her white shirt and a Puffa jacket in place of her black one, but her cream breeches were saddle-stained and splashed with mud. 'Oh, hi, Eve. I was just telling Lloyd what that idiot did but I couldn't see him anywhere.'

'I think he must have gone on home. I couldn't see him either,' Gideon said. He'd changed into a spare pair of jeans and a jumper that he'd had the foresight to bring with him.

'Well, Lloyd was furious. He asked a couple of people if they knew who the guy was and they seemed to think he wasn't from round here. Not a regular, anyway. So I don't think there's a lot we can do . . .'

'Gideon was just telling me what happened,' Eve said. 'What a bastard! Just because you accidentally bumped his horse. It's not as if you meant to do it. What about the other one, is he still here?'

'What other one?' Pippa said sharply, looking at Gideon.

'I'd forgotten after the fall, but earlier on there was another bloke on a grey horse, and the two of them came up either side

and tried to put Blackbird off his stride. I wasn't sure it was delib-
erate, at the time, but in light of the other . . . But I'm afraid I
didn't get a good look at the one on the grey.'

'It was a grey horse that started it all by backing into Sky at
the meet,' Pippa said, frowning.

'Yes, but there had to be at least half a dozen greys in the field,
if not more,' Gideon reminded her. 'I guess we just have to accept
the guy was a complete moron and forget it. It's not likely I'll
ever see either of them again, anyway.'

'It's a shame, though,' Pippa said. 'I so wanted you to enjoy
today . . .'

'Well, I did enjoy it,' he told her. 'I admit I didn't think I would,
but Blackbird was brilliant, and I had great fun – in between
times.'

'You know you're all completely mad, don't you?' Eve remarked,
turning to meet Lloyd as he came over.

Lloyd quite patently had news. 'Have you heard the latest about
Damien's murder?' he asked, ignoring Eve's last comment. 'They've
just said, on the news, they've arrested someone – well, taken
him in for questioning, but it's all the same thing. What's more,
it's someone I know! You would, too,' he said to Pippa.

'Well, who is it?' she said impatiently.

'Adam Tetley.'

'What, Adam Tetley from our pony-club days?' Pippa said,
astounded. 'Little Adam Tetley who used to keep falling off and
getting nosebleeds?'

'Well, I imagine he's grown up a bit since then,' Lloyd said
with amusement. 'They said on the report that he's thirty-eight
and a security guard.'

'But why would he want to kill Damien?'

'They're not saying, but the police must have had some reason
for taking him in. He's a crack shot, I can tell you that. He used
to do pentathlon when I was doing it.'

'What *is* pentathlon?' Eve asked. 'Excuse my ignorance, but
sport isn't really my thing.'

'Riding, shooting, running, swimming and fencing,' Pippa told her.

'It was the fencing I always liked the best,' Lloyd put in. 'Matching your skill against another human being, just like the duellists of old . . . Well, except for being wired to a buzzer, of course.'

'I 'ave buzzed you, M'sieur, and I declare that honour 'as been satisfied,' Eve said, putting on a haughty French accent.

'It loses something, doesn't it?' Lloyd agreed, laughing.

'But why would he want to kill him?' Pippa repeated, not diverted by Eve's play-acting. 'I mean you'd have to have had a pretty big falling-out to want to kill somebody. You'd think Tilly would have heard about it.'

Gideon could have enlightened her but to do so would, no doubt, bring a barrage of questions down on him, to say nothing of betraying his success in deciphering the coded list. He kept silent, and it was left to Lloyd to answer.

'Well, if he did do it, I expect we'll find out why, in the end, love. But for the time being, let's just be glad they've caught him.'

'It's hard enough to come to terms with the fact that someone you know has been murdered – but to find that the murderer might also be someone you know, or knew . . . It makes you wonder how well you really know anyone,' Pippa said. 'It's a horrible feeling.'

'Talking of knowing people,' Gideon said, 'do you know a lady called Vanessa Tate? I met her at Angie's the other day. She's got eventers, and *her* husband used to do pentathlon.'

'I know *of* her,' Pippa said. 'I've often seen her name down in the entries for competitions, and I think I may have met her at Wilton, last year, but I don't exactly know her.'

'I know Vanessa,' Lloyd put in. 'She comes hunting occasionally. Nice lady. Never really knew Robin, but then, I did more *triathlon* than *pentathlon*.'

'I gather he isn't particularly horsy, these days.' Gideon let the remark hang in the air.

'He's something in the City,' Lloyd supplied. 'They've got stacks of money. Live in a massive house out at Wimborne St Giles with acres of land.'

'Is there anyone you *don't* know?' Pippa enquired.

'A politician has to know his constituents,' he declared grandly.

'All right, then. How about Sam Bentley?' Gideon asked, seizing the opportunity. He watched Lloyd closely.

'Bentley? Mm . . . don't think so,' he said, appearing to consider the matter then shaking his head. 'Why? Who is he?'

'Just a name that came up in conversation with Tilly the other day. I think it was someone Damien knew but she didn't.'

'Oh, I see. Well – no, me neither, sorry. Does he live round here?'

'I'm not sure. That's why I asked.'

It wasn't until the gathering began to break up, and Gideon and Pippa headed back to the lorry to take their weary horses home, that Gideon had the chance to ask her whether Lloyd had ever mentioned the list again.

'No. I did ask him about it some time ago, but he said he couldn't make head nor tail of it. I think he threw it away.'

'It wasn't anything to do with betting, after all, then?'

'No, I don't think so. Actually, thinking about Nero's file, I was going to ask you if it says anything about feedstuffs in there. I've had him on the coarse mix I give my lot, but he seems to be getting very itchy and I wondered if he had a problem with one of the ingredients.'

'OK, I'll have a look,' Gideon promised.

It was past seven o'clock by the time Gideon had helped Pippa settle and feed the horses, and, just as they were finishing, Giles came out to the tack room with a tray of hot toddies.

'I knew there was a reason I picked you for a friend, all those years ago,' Gideon said, taking a glass and inhaling the boozy vapours appreciatively.

'*You* picked *me*?' Giles queried. 'I was under the impression that

I took pity on you and played the good Samaritan. If I'd had any idea that I'd still be saddled with you nearly twenty years down the line . . .'

'If you ask me, you're a couple of misfits who deserve one another,' Pippa put in. 'But what I can't work out is what I've done to deserve being lumbered with the two of you!'

'Well, if you become the second Mrs Lloyd-Ellis, you won't have to worry about us misfits any more,' Giles suggested lightly.

Pippa's face flushed red.

'Don't be ridiculous!'

'Why's it so ridiculous?' her brother enquired.

'Because we haven't even discussed it and anyway, he's not divorced yet.'

'Whoops! Have I touched a nerve? I'm sorry, Pip.'

'No, you didn't. It's not an issue – I mean, it's between me and Lloyd.'

Planting her glass back firmly on the tray, she brushed past Giles on her way to the door, saying over her shoulder, 'I'm going in to soak in a long, hot bath.'

A hot bath was exactly what Gideon had in mind when he finally got back to the Gatehouse, tired and somewhat achy. However, his wasn't destined to be a long soak because, uncharacteristically, Eve had been busy in the kitchen.

'I was beginning to think you'd decided to eat at the Priory and all my efforts would have been for nothing,' she called out, as he closed the front door behind him and responded to Zebedee's exuberant greeting.

'I wouldn't do that to you,' Gideon protested. Cooking aromas wafted out of the kitchen and he recognised onion and lamb. 'That smells wonderful, but I absolutely must have a bath first.'

'You've got half a hour, and not a minute more!' Eve warned.

'Join me?' Standing in the kitchen doorway, he took in a scene of chaotic domestic industry. The sink was piled high with bowls and utensils, the fridge door was half open, a bag of flour lay

on its side and a bottle of milk stood, uncapped, on the Aga.
'Or . . . maybe not.'

She turned round incredulously, a smudge of grease on her
chin. 'What, with all that mud? Anyway, I can't leave this, it's at
a crucial stage.'

Closing the fridge door on the way, Gideon crossed to the
range, moving the milk bottle from its warm surface to the table
and recapping it.

Eve was leafing through the pages of a recipe book with an
air of distraction. Her hair lay down her back in a long black
plait from which several strands had escaped, and she wore an
apron over her ankle-length red dress.

Regarding her affectionately, Gideon completed his circuit of
the kitchen, leaning to kiss her cheek as he passed.

The combination of a hot bath, excellent meal, and a crack-
ling log fire was sufficient to reduce Gideon to a state of drowsy
torpor, and his eyelids were drooping as he sat on the comfortably scruffy leather sofa with Eve's head resting in his lap. He'd
undone her inefficient plait and now her hair lay in a silky riot
around her face and over his knee.

Eve's day, however, had been less demanding than Gideon's,
and her mind was still active.

'Those names you were trying out on Lloyd – were they from
that list you've been puzzling over?' she asked suddenly, dragging
him back from the brink of sleep.

'Mm.'

'So I take it he doesn't know you've deciphered it.'

'No, not yet.'

'Why haven't you told him?'

'Because I wanted to find out what it was all about first. And
because I wanted to see whether he worked it out, himself.'

'And do you think he has?'

'I'm not sure. He told Pippa he hadn't.'

'But you don't believe him?'

'I'm not sure,' Gideon said again.

There was a long pause while he stroked her hair, listening to the gentle hiss and spit of the cedar log on the fire and watching the flickering glow play on her olive skin.

'Have you tried putting the names into an Internet search engine?' Eve asked suddenly.

'No. It may have escaped your notice, but I don't have a computer.'

'Oh, no, I forgot. You're still in the Middle Ages, aren't you? Well, I've got my laptop in the car, we could use that.'

'In the car? That's a bit chancy, isn't it?'

'Well, it's locked in the boot, of course.' She sat up. 'I'll go and get it.'

Gideon groaned. 'Must you? Surely it won't work, anyway – without an Internet connection?'

Eve stood up, laughing down at him. 'I was wrong. You're not medieval; you're prehistoric. It's a wireless connection. Or I can use my mobile phone. Won't be a minute . . .'

By the time she returned, Gideon had resigned himself to the fact that he wasn't going to be allowed to doze comfortably on the sofa for the rest of the evening, and had put the kettle on for a restorative cup of coffee.

'Where's this list, then?' Eve called from the sitting room.

'In the ring binder on the bookshelf. You'll find it tucked in the last pocket.'

Gideon finished making the drinks and took them through to where Eve sat, intent on the small screen in front of her. He sat down beside her and picked up the discarded binder, remembering his promise to look up Nero's feeding history.

He found the information printed on a sheet of A4 and, tucked behind it in the same plastic sleeve, another torn sheet, on which a feed order had been scribbled in Damien's slightly disjointed handwriting. One corner of this sheet was turned back, as if it had been hastily pushed into the pocket, revealing what looked like the very dark photocopy on the reverse.

With mild curiosity, Gideon drew the sheet out and looked

more closely. It was indeed a photocopy, but very underexposed and indistinct, so that much of it was illegible. It appeared to be an image of a page from a book, showing the splayed edges of the other pages at one side and the central fold at the other. What little could be read was handwritten, but the script, a beautiful copperplate, was clearly not Damien's.

Gideon lifted it and leaned nearer to the light, concentrating hard. From the partial phrases he could make out, he quickly recognised it as a page from someone's diary or journal but much of it was illegible.

'. . . *that Major Clemence is a bastard. I was running as fast as I could . . .*' he read, and then, further down, '. . . *I'd leave, but I promised Damien and I don't want to let . . .*' Another obscure section. '. . . *tonight, the others were teasing me but I need . . .*'

Feeling almost guilty, Gideon read on, peering closer as the words became even less distinct. There was a gap in the script, a short line that might have been a date, and then the writing continued, but this time more slanted and far less clear, as if the writer was working fast and under some emotion.

'. . . *Oh God, this is a nightmare! I still can't believe . . .*'

'. . . *keep thinking I'll wake up – God, I wish I could! What the hell am I . . .*'

'. . . *didn't have a chance to speak to them. I don't think I could have faced . . .*'

'. . . *every time I close my eyes I hear that terrible . . .*'

'. . . *again today and I was terrified they would want . . .*'

'. . . *can they be? I'm so scared. I still want to tell the truth. Gary wants . . .*'

At this point the script disappeared completely, infuriatingly, into the encroaching photographic gloom, with only the odd word surfacing. Gideon was forced to abandon his attempts to decipher it. He read it through again with mounting frustration. It was like a half-heard conversation, or someone mumbling and refusing to repeat themselves.

'Found Robin Tate,' Eve said suddenly, breaking in on his

thoughts. 'Member of the Modern Pentathlon team at the Dubai Olympics. We were just talking about that this afternoon, weren't we? Pentathlon, I mean. Strange, isn't it? This morning I hadn't a clue what it was and now here it is again.'

Gideon frowned, trying to remember where else the subject had cropped up recently, but the answer eluded him.

'Ah,' Eve went on. 'Adam Tetley – that was the guy's name, wasn't it? The one they're questioning. He's here, too.'

'Who else? Any of the others?'

'No . . . Adam Tetley, Robin Tate, Timothy Landless, and Philip Proctor. The reserve was Ian Duncan, and Stuart Wells competed as an individual. The team coach was Harry Saddler. That's all the names mentioned.'

'Oh, just for a moment, I thought we might be onto something, but I suppose that would have been too easy. Not that it would have explained why Damien should have their names written in code. Talk about a riddle! You know, I don't think I'm cut out to be a detective. Maybe I should just give the paper to Rockley, after all, and have done with it.'

'And what about Lloyd and Pippa?'

Gideon sighed. 'Yeah, I know . . .'

There was silence for a moment, and a log spat and whined on the fire as a pocket of sap heated up and exploded. Eve's fingers tapped the keyboard and Gideon's gaze fell on the photocopy once more. He held it out to her.

'What d'you make of this? It was in the folder.'

Her brows drew down in concentration as she scanned the sheet in her hand before exclaiming, 'Oh, isn't that annoying! If there was only just a little bit more. It's like finding a treasure map with the X missing! It looks like someone's diary, don't you think?'

'Yeah, that's what I thought. Whoever it is sounds pretty desperate, don't they?'

'Didn't you say Damien's brother committed suicide? Perhaps it was his.'

Gideon took the paper back and looked at it again.

'You know, you might just have something there. But why would Damien photocopy it if he had the original? It doesn't make sense.'

'No idea.' Eve shrugged, her attention back on the screen.

'I've got Sam Bentley here,' she announced presently.

'Pentathlon again?'

'Nope. Owner-manager of an extremely prestigious health club, by the look of it. Bentleys of Bath. Spas, mud baths, saunas, every kind of massage known to man, and then some, spray-on tanning, toning tables, seaweed therapy, whatever that is, body-wraps, reiki healing, aromatherapy, acupuncture, shiatsu – good God, the list is endless! We've got pictures, too. Shiny tiles, mosaics, gold-plated taps, fluffy gold-coloured towels by the dozen and carpet pile so deep you could get lost in it. This is seriously opulent. The website's huge, too. It even gives sample itineraries and menus, and you wouldn't want to go there to lose weight, I can tell you, although it says you can . . . About the only thing it doesn't tell you is the price.'

'*If you have to ask, you can't afford it.*' Gideon leaned over her shoulder to take a look. 'What makes you so sure it's the right Sam Bentley?'

'Well, it's the same contact number,' she said on a note of triumph.

'Well, well. Maybe I should go and pay Mr Bentley a visit,' Gideon mused.

'I think I should come too.'

'I wasn't thinking of booking in,' he said, with amusement. 'It's a bit beyond my touch, to say nothing of it not being exactly my scene. I was thinking more of laying siege to the reception area until he agrees to see me. Maybe a message containing the words Damien Daniels might do the trick. Any luck with the other names?'

'Well, Lloyd turns up all over the place, of course. He has his own political website; he's on the Countryside Alliance one, and the drag hounds one. I can't find anything on Garth Stephenson – at least not one that was likely to be ours – but Julian Norris is there under Norris Security, and I've also found an account of his death in the archives of a regional paper.'

'Oh? What does it say?'

'It's only short. Here, it's easier if you look.' She pushed the laptop towards him.

'*Local Businessman Killed in Car Crash*' was the unimaginative headline, and it continued, '*Respected local businessman Julian Norris, founder of Norris Security Systems based in Sturminster Newton, died on Friday night when his Vauxhall estate car left the road and hit a wall in Winterbourne Whitechurch. It is believed that Mr Norris, who was thirty-nine and married with two young children, died at the scene when the stone wall collapsed, crushing the vehicle. The reason for the crash is not yet clear, but no other vehicle was involved and police would like to hear from anyone who witnessed the accident. The family request that donations be sent to . . .'*

Gideon read it through again, then looked up.

'That's odd.'

'What is?'

'Well, Tilly said Julian crashed on his way home from their place – Puddlestone Farm – and it says here that Julian Norris lived at Stur. So what was he doing in Winterbourne Whitechurch? It's not exactly en route.'

'It says his *business* was based at Sturminster Newton; it doesn't say he actually *lived* there,' Eve pointed out.

'That's true. I'll have to ask Tilly. Anything else?'

'Not on Robin Tate, but Vanessa Tate's mentioned a couple of times in three-day-eventing news and results. Adam Tetley's mentioned again, too. Did you know he used to have horses in training with Damien?'

'Well, yes, actually I did,' Gideon confessed apologetically. 'Tilly told me the other day. They had some trouble. He didn't pay his training fees and eventually it turned out he'd bought the horses with company money and couldn't pay it back. Needless to say, he lost his job, and I gather his wife sent him packing, too.'

'Why does that make him a suspect? Surely he couldn't blame Damien for that. It was patently his own fault.'

'Well, apparently it was Damien that dropped him in it, in the end, by contacting his boss, but I agree, it seems a bit hard. Unless there's more to it than meets the eye. It all happened five or six years ago.'

'You didn't say anything about that, this afternoon.'

'No. I don't want Lloyd to know I've figured out the list.'

'But you mentioned Sam Bentley,' she reminded him.

'I know. I took a chance, and I wanted to see his reaction, but there wasn't one, really, was there?'

'You know, if you told Lloyd about the names, he might be able to clear up the whole mystery, had you thought of that?'

'Well, yes, obviously. But . . .'

'But you're not going to.'

'Maybe. But not just yet.'

Eve tipped her head on one side and looked at him.

'Are you sure this is about protecting Pippa?'

'Yes,' Gideon said, surprised. 'What else?'

Eve watched him for a few more lingering moments, then pursed her lips and shook her head.

'I don't know. Ignore me. Well, we're finished here. Let's get to bed, huh?'

NINE

BENTLEYS OF BATH WAS, in fact, on the outskirts of Bath, rather than in the city centre. The business was housed in a huge, purpose-built complex, which was a clever mix of old and modern styling, and stood, the website had stated, in sixteen acres of its own landscaped grounds. The name was inscribed on a large polished bronze plaque, to the right of the smoked-glass double front doors.

Gideon had taken advantage of a bright, cloudless morning to give his new motorcycle an outing and, as the deep, burbling note of the powerful engine died away and he took his helmet off, he caught sight of a couple of curious faces at one of the downstairs windows. Even as he glanced at them, they were hastily withdrawn, and he unzipped his leather jacket with a private smile. Visitors to Bentleys were probably not in the habit of turning up on two wheels.

Through the front doors, which opened silently at his approach, he found himself in a sumptuous reception area, carpeted in gold and furnished in bronzed metal and golden-veined marble. Two tall, well-built men stood, one on either side of the doors, but the smart brown and gold uniform did nothing to disguise their function. Something about the look in the eye and the set of the jaw proclaimed them as security; probably ex-army, Gideon decided, and as he advanced across the acres of carpet, he fancied he could feel their eyes boring suspiciously into his back.

'Good morning, sir. Welcome to Bentleys of Bath.' The twenty-something girl on the other side of the marble-topped reception desk had perfect teeth and nails, and just-out-of–the-salon burnished copper hair. Her smile faltered almost imperceptibly as she took in the appearance of the visitor, but training took over and she recovered immediately. 'Can I help you?'

Gideon could have left his helmet and gloves outside with the bike but it was no part of his plan to conform, so he dumped both on the polished marble in front of him and smiled at the girl.

'I'd like to speak to Mr Bentley, please,' he said pleasantly.

'I'm sorry, sir. Mr Bentley is in a meeting.'

'Ah, yes, I thought he might be. And, no doubt, this meeting is expected to last most of the morning.'

She relaxed a little.

'Yes, sir. I'm afraid so.'

'And this afternoon?'

The wary look was back.

'I'm sorry?'

'I'm in no hurry. Is the meeting expected to last all day?'

'Um . . . I'd have to speak to his secretary, sir. I couldn't say.'

'All right.' Gideon took up the attitude of someone who was prepared to wait as long as it took, and saw the girl's eyes flicker nervously towards the two bouncers by the door.

'Er . . . if you'd like to take a seat, sir – I'll see if I can find out for you,' she said then.

'I'm fine standing,' Gideon said helpfully. 'I've been sitting all the way here. You carry on.'

Robbed of the chance to speak privately with her colleague, the receptionist reached for the phone, a tinge of pink creeping into her cheeks.

'Janet? I've got a gentleman here who wants to speak to Mr Bentley . . .'

Gideon was close enough to hear the secretary ask if he had an appointment, and before the girl could relay the query, answered, 'No, he hasn't.'

The receptionist's face flushed darker and the voice on the other end of the line said, 'What is it in connection with?'

The girl looked at Gideon helplessly, and he raised his eyebrows and held out his hand for the receiver. 'Wouldn't it be easier if I talked to her?'

'He wants to talk to you,' she told the secretary.

'All right, put him on,' came the reply.

Gideon took the bronze-coloured, cordless handset.

'My business with Sam is private, but it won't take long,' he informed her.

'I'm sorry. Your name is . . . ?'

'Gideon Blake, but he may not remember me. Tell him it's to do with Damien Daniels.'

'I'm sorry, Mr Blake. I'm afraid Mr Bentley is an extremely busy man, and doesn't see anyone without an appointment. If you'd like to leave your name with our receptionist, with a short note explaining the nature of your business, we'll do our best to get back to you at the earliest opportunity to arrange a mutually acceptable date.'

'I'm afraid that won't do. You see my business is rather time-sensitive,' Gideon declared grandly, dredging the phrase up from his subconscious and feeling rather pleased with it.

'Mr Blake – Mr Bentley can't be expected to drop everything without warning. His diary is completely full for the next—'

'I'll wait,' Gideon cut in, and handed the receiver back to the startled receptionist while Sam Bentley's secretary was still blustering. Picking up his helmet and gloves, he retired ten or twelve feet to where two dark leather sofas flanked a smoked-glass coffee table, laden with upmarket magazines.

The foyer was warm, and Gideon removed his jacket before

sinking into the squidgy-soft upholstery. The leather smelt new and squeaked as he eased himself into a comfortable position and prepared to wait, crossing his booted feet.

The receptionist cast him a look of palpable dismay, then spoke into the phone.

'No, he's sitting down . . . OK.'

Replacing the receiver she began to busy herself, rather unconvincingly, with moving things around in her work area and straightening the piles of leaflets and brochures that sat on the counter.

Minutes passed and, just as it seemed as though it was going to be a waiting game, the telephone trilled and the girl picked it up.

'Yes, he is,' she said after a moment. 'OK . . . OK.'

Putting her hand over the mouthpiece of the phone she said to Gideon, 'You can go up now; Mr Bentley will see you. Take the lift in the corner – second floor.'

'Oh, meeting over already?' Gideon feigned surprise, and was rewarded with a sour look as he gathered his gear and stood up.

When the lift doors hissed softly open on the second floor, a slim blonde female in a short-skirted suit stood waiting for him on the gold carpet outside. Her eyes flickered over Gideon's sizeable person and the motorcycle gear, but if he was not the usual sort of person to grace the polished interior of Bentleys, she was too well trained to give any sign of it.

'If you'd like to follow me, Mr Blake,' she said coolly, and led the way at a brisk pace down a corridor between rows of cream, brass-furnished doors, her neat behind twitching from side to side provocatively.

Gideon found himself wondering if Sam Bentley was married and, if so, whether his wife had ever met his secretary.

At the end of the passage there was a door marked Private which opened onto a large, well-lit room with a desk, several filing cabinets, an L-shaped cream leather sofa, and a kitchen area in one corner. Gideon dumped his jacket, helmet and gloves on the sofa.

The secretary crossed to her desk, pressed a button and spoke into an intercom.

'Mr Bentley will see you now,' she said, and moments later a door slid open soundlessly just feet from where Gideon was standing.

Inclining his head calmly, as if such surroundings were his natural habitat, Gideon passed through the open doorway, hearing the faint click as it closed behind him, seconds later.

The room he'd entered was vast – more like an open-plan living space than an office – with floor-to-ceiling windows in one wall, steps up to a desk complex and a luxurious seating area built around a raised circular fireplace. Cream, gold and bronze still predominated, as did leather, marble and velvet. The whole effect was very, very expensive.

Bentley turned from looking out of the window and Gideon went forward, seeing a slightly overweight, medium-height man of about his own age, or slightly older.

'Ah, Mr Blake – *Gideon* Blake, I believe.'

'That's right.'

'I'm almost certain we have never met before – I feel sure I would have remembered that name – so tell me why on earth I should want to see you now?' he enquired, in a voice that proclaimed a privileged upbringing and a public school education.

'Suppose *you* tell *me* why I'm standing here. You agreed to see me,' Gideon countered. 'I'd say my mentioning Damien Daniels had something to do with it, wouldn't you?'

'Well, what about him?' Bentley said with a touch of impatience.

'How well did you know him?'

'I didn't, but I knew his brother. Not that it's any business of yours.'

'You didn't know Damien at all?' Gideon was puzzled.

'I just said so, didn't I? Look, what's this all about?'

'If you didn't know him, how come you agreed to meet me

on the strength of my mentioning his name? And how come he'd made a special note of your name and phone number?'

'He had?'

'Amongst others,' Gideon nodded.

Bentley regarded him closely.

'What are you, some kind of private investigator?'

'Just a friend of the family.'

'Did they send you here?'

'I'm helping Damien's sister sort a few things out.'

'She your girlfriend?'

'With respect, I don't think that's any of your business,' Gideon told him.

Bentley shrugged.

'Well, I've absolutely no idea why he should have my details,' he said, sauntering across to his desk and picking up a beautiful marquetry cigar box. Opening the box, he offered it briefly in Gideon's direction before selecting a cigar for himself and lighting it with a match from a gold case. 'So, what *were* the other names?' he added, casually.

'Henry Lloyd-Ellis; Garth Stephenson; Robin Tate . . .'

'Was that all?'

'No. Julian Norris and Adam Tetley . . .'

'Julian's dead,' Bentley stated flatly, drawing on his cigar.

'I know he is. Did you know him?'

Again the shrug.

'A long time ago. We lost touch – you know how it is.'

'How long ago?'

'I don't know . . . Ten years, maybe twelve – what does it matter? Look, I don't really see where you're going with this, anyway. Damien's dead now, and whatever reason he had for writing the names down presumably died with him. I can't help you.'

Bentley leaned over his desk and pressed a button on the intercom, but before he could speak Gideon said, 'Yeah, you're right. I should probably just hand the list over to the police and let them deal with it.'

Bentley paused. A thin wisp of smoke curled from the end of the cigar.

'Now why would you want to do that? What possible interest could it be to them? I mean, it's obviously out of date, for a start. It must have been a year ago, or more, that Julian Norris died.'

'Somebody shot Damien Daniels,' Gideon reminded him. 'And the police have taken Adam Tetley in for questioning. I think they might be very interested that his name appeared on a list that Damien made, don't you?'

That had unsettled him. A distant voice emitted from the intercom and he bent his head to say, 'Sorry, Janet. Give me five, will you?'

He transferred his attention to Gideon and said harshly, 'All right. What do you really want? Is it money? Is that it? How much?'

Gideon hesitated, out of his depth now.

'How much is it worth to you?'

Bentley drew in and expelled a lungful of aromatic smoke, eyeing Gideon thoughtfully. Then he relaxed and smiled.

'You don't know, do you? You know nothing about this at all. You're bluffing. Tell me – if you're just a friend of the family – why haven't you turned this over to the police already?'

Having lost the edge he'd held for a few short moments, Gideon saw no reason not to tell him.

'One of the other people on the list is a friend; I wanted to find out what it was all about before I did anything.'

'Well, tell me this, Mr Blake. If he's a friend, why don't you ask him, huh?' He pressed the button on his intercom again. 'Janet. Mr Blake is just leaving.'

Riding home, Gideon went over the conversation in his mind. On the face of it, he'd not learned an awful lot, but Bentley's reactions had been telling. He'd said he hadn't known the trainer, yet what other reason could he have had for agreeing to speak with Gideon if it wasn't because of the mention of Damien's name? And for someone who professed no interest in the whole affair, his response to Gideon's suggestion of letting the police have the list was surely hugely significant. He'd dismissed it as of no account but suddenly he was offering to buy Gideon off, which must mean that he had a very good idea what it was all about, but he wasn't going to admit it.

If Gideon had learned anything at all from the encounter, it was only that there was something of importance *to* learn. Not a lot for a round trip of more than a hundred miles, but even so, it left him feeling rather unsettled. Why should Sam Bentley have been so quick to offer him money? And what, precisely, had he been offering money for? For a list of names and phone numbers? For information? With a sense of growing unease, Gideon acknowledged the most likely reason.

To buy his silence.

The offer had been an impulsive one on Bentley's part, just as quickly rescinded as he realised that Gideon had been bluffing about telling the police. But the mere fact that the businessman was so ready to pay out was worrying. Just what had Damien been up to? And Lloyd? What was his part in all this? It was true that Gideon didn't like him, but that was only on a superficial level. He was honest enough to admit that he'd have been quite prepared to tolerate Lloyd's overconfidence and occasional insensitivity if he hadn't been Pippa's boyfriend.

What was it all about?

Why should Damien Daniels, a racehorse trainer, have a list comprising a budding politician; the owner of a health spa; a teacher at a boarding school; a wealthy man who was 'something in the City' and a security consultant, now deceased? If they knew one another, they weren't keen to reveal the fact, and the only thing they appeared to have in common was that they were successful in their chosen field. The odd man out was Adam Tetley, the security guard, now in police custody, whose life had not gone at all to plan.

The only answer that presented itself was not a comfortable one.

Blackmail.

Somehow, Damien had found something that linked the six names on the list; something they would pay to keep quiet. However out of character it might seem, it was the only explanation that fitted the few facts he had. But what could it possibly be that linked such a disparate group of people?

Gideon began to feel that he had opened the proverbial can of worms. The question was, did he press the lid down firmly and hand it all over to the authorities, whatever the consequences to Lloyd, Pippa and Damien Daniels' family, or did he lift it a little further and see what wriggled out?

Throughout the afternoon and a ride with Pippa, Gideon pondered his next course of action. He didn't entertain the option of inaction for long. It might be that he wouldn't be able to get to the bottom of the mystery but having got this far, he found he couldn't just sit back and not try. He did toy for a while with the idea of handing the paper to Rockley, as he'd threatened to do, but in spite of the inclusion of Tetley's name, there was no reason to suspect that it had anything to do with their case, and the thought of the inevitable upset it would cause made him hesitate. What would it do to Lloyd's political aspirations? If Gideon threw a spanner in those particular works, would Pippa ever forgive him?

So it seemed the decision had almost made itself, and when Eve texted him mid-afternoon to say that an old friend had arrived unexpectedly and was taking her out for dinner, Gideon decided to spend the evening chasing down another of the names on the list.

With Tetley currently out of the picture and Julian Norris out of it for good, that left Lloyd, Robin Tate and the schoolteacher, Garth Stephenson.

Although he realised that sooner or later he would have to face Lloyd with the list, Gideon intended to put it off as long as he could. If Lloyd's reaction was anything like Bentley's, it might make relations with Pippa's boyfriend more uncomfortable than they already were and, in turn, damage his own friendship with Pippa herself.

Gideon had a feeling that 'something in the City' Robin Tate might not be easy to find, for he didn't appear to be listed in the telephone directory. Although Wimborne St Giles wasn't a big place, it had its fair share of large houses, and any attempt to ask around would understandably arouse a certain amount of suspicion in the neighbourhood. Even supposing he did find himself on the Tates' doorstep, he thought it more likely that the door would be firmly closed in his face than that he would be invited in to chat, once he'd announced his reason for calling. He dismissed the idea, with some vague notion of furthering his contact by means of Angie Bowen, at a later date.

That left Garth Stephenson, the teacher; the problem in his case being that Gideon only had a mobile number, and no idea of the location of the boarding school he taught at.

After much deliberation, he picked up the phone and keyed in a number he hadn't used for eighteen months or more.

The phone rang seven or eight times, during which period Gideon became increasingly tempted to replace the receiver and forget the idea, but, just before he did so, the dial tone was interrupted and a weary voice said, 'Yeah. Logan here.'

'Sorry. Did I wake you?' Gideon said, trying to remember what PC Mark Logan had told him in the past about shift patterns.

'A chance'd be a fine thing. I'm on lates, and I've had the builders at home all day, knocking down a wall.' He paused. 'Well, well, Gideon Blake! I wondered if I'd be hearing from you . . .'

'You did?'

'Your name's come up in conversation at the nick a time or two, lately. A little matter of murder, I believe, and you're involved. Now why doesn't that surprise me?'

'It's not by choice, I can assure you,' Gideon told him.

'So what can I do for you now? I presume this isn't a social call?'

'I, er . . . wondered if you could trace a mobile phone number for me, if I asked nicely?'

'That depends on whether it's pay monthly or pay as you go,' Logan said. 'If it's pay as you go, and unregistered, it's virtually impossible.'

'I've no idea.'

'You want to know whose the phone is?'

'No. I know his name, I need an address.'

'Are you going to tell me *why* you want to know?'

'Er . . . Not just yet,' Gideon admitted.

'Then why the hell should I do it, huh?'

'For old times' sake?'

'That's crap! What I remember of *old times* was you giving me the runaround, and me having to dig you out of the mess you got yourself into!'

'Yeah, did I ever thank you for that?'

There was an exasperated noise at the other end of the phone.

'What's the number?'

Gideon gave it.

'He's a schoolteacher – boarding school – but I don't know where.'

'This wouldn't have anything to do with the Damien Daniels investigation, would it?'

'Not as far as I know,' Gideon said, with questionable honesty.

'I don't trust you, mister, but I should warn you. DI Rockley's on this one – you've met him, I expect?'

Gideon agreed that he had.

'Well, you needn't think you can put one past him. If you know anything at all that you're not telling about the Daniels murder, you'd better fess up, cos he'll find out, sooner or later, and he won't be a happy man!'

'I'll consider myself warned,' Gideon said, outwardly placid. 'So, can you get the address for me?'

'Buggered if I know why I should,' Logan muttered. 'It might take a minute. I'll get back to you.' And he rang off before Gideon could thank him.

Half an hour later he was in the Land Rover and heading for a village on the outskirts of Chilminster.

Charlton Montague was tucked away in a tree-lined valley, with only its church spire visible until the road ducked under the tree canopy and revealed a couple of dozen stone-built cottages, three or four larger houses, a timbered and thatched pub, and a post office and general stores.

This much Gideon was able to see in the fading light, and he knew, from studying the map beforehand, that the road led only to the village, the school and a couple of farms beyond.

After driving through the village on one narrow road and back through it on another, he slotted the Land Rover into the one remaining space in the car park of the Goose and Ferret inn, and went inside. He'd seen the sign advertising Montague Park School on the far side of the settlement, the words painted in bold black letters on two glossy white boards which were fixed to the wrought-iron railings either side of an impressive gateway. The gates were closed and lighted windows in the lodge suggested that no-one would be allowed to pass through without authorisation. Gideon had decided his best bet lay in enquiring at the village pub.

Ducking under an almost impossibly low lintel, he opened the squeaky door and found himself in exactly the kind of bar that the outside had suggested it would be: black-beamed, with terracotta walls, horse brasses, inadequate lighting and a log fire. The pub was buzzing with conversation and laughter, and one or two people had to move aside to allow him to reach the bar itself, where he stood with his neck slightly bent to avoid the assortment of copper implements that lined the beam above.

After exchanging a few parting words with some customers at the other end of the bar, the barman, a ruddy-cheeked individual with a fringe of greying hair round a shiny bald pate, made his way along to Gideon, still smiling.

'Gawd, you're a tall one!' he exclaimed. 'Mind your head, won't you? I don't want a lawsuit on me hands!'

A couple of those closest to Gideon turned to look him up and down and he smiled in a friendly fashion.

'So what'll it be?' the barman asked.

'Got any good local ales?'

'Yup. Stinking Ferret,' came the answer, with a twinkle. 'Brewed specially for us, a couple of miles up the road. It's a hell of a lot better than it sounds!'

'Well, I'll try anything once,' Gideon said bravely. 'A pint, please.'

'Not from around here, are you?' the barman observed as he drew the ale, unwittingly giving Gideon just the opening he had hoped for.

'No. Been in Brisbane for a year or two.'

'That's Australia, isn't it? Got a cousin lives in Perth,' the other man announced.

'That's strange, because *I've* got a cousin who lives *here*,' Gideon said in tones of wonder, at the same time sending a prayer of thanks winging upwards that Perth was on the other side of the country from Brisbane.

'Small world. Whereabouts?'

'Right here; Charlton Montague.'

'Oh? Who's that then? That'll be two eighty-five, please.' A tall glass of a slightly cloudy golden liquid was placed on the bar in front of Gideon.

'His name's Garth Stephenson and he teaches at the school,' Gideon said, fishing in his pocket for some change. 'At least, I'm told he does.'

'Yeah, I know Garth; top bloke,' the barman said warmly. 'He might be in later. Does he know you're here?'

'Not yet. Thought I'd surprise him. Does he live in the village?'

'No, up at the school.'

'Thought his brother lived in South Africa.' A man to Gideon's left spoke up. 'He was talking about going out to visit him later this year . . .'

'That's his brother; I'm his cousin,' Gideon said. 'Actually, more of a second cousin. I've been doing the family history and I turned up the connection. Now I'm back in England, I thought I'd come and look him up.'

'Oh, so you've never met before? Ah! He will be surprised.'

Won't he just? Gideon thought.

A cover story that he'd invented merely as a sure way to have Stephenson pointed out to him began to assume a life of its own. Gideon had underestimated the community spirit of this small village. The teacher was evidently a popular chap, and everybody seemed to know him and take a personal interest in this unknown relative who had turned up out of the blue.

By the time Stephenson arrived at the Goose and Ferret, at a little past nine, Gideon had had to endure the best part of an hour of gentle interrogation about his business and what had taken him to Australia, and had waited, in dread, for someone to say that they, too, had spent time in Brisbane, and want to compare experiences. Long before the teacher appeared, he had created for himself a wife, two kids and a white-boarded house on the Pacific coast. He had also imparted a great deal of, quite frankly, dubious information about the Antipodean flora and fauna, and was in a state of trepidation lest the subject turn to politics. With every minute that passed he dug himself in deeper and, with every minute, the idea of him leaving without seeing his 'cousin' became ever less conceivable.

The door squeaked open and the barman looked across, and then at Gideon, saying, with an air of high expectation, 'Here he is . . .'

Gideon turned to see a well-built, blond-haired man of perhaps just under six feet ducking under the door frame.

'Garth, lad! Over here!' the barman called out. 'Someone to see you.'

Stephenson made his way through the throng, which parted before him and then closed round, as a number of people jostled for a view. He glanced at the group by the bar, looking puzzled and slightly embarrassed.

'What's going on, Pete?'

The barman indicated Gideon.

'Betcha don't know who this is . . .'

Stephenson glanced at him again, shaking his head in bewilderment, and Gideon felt sorry for him. Everyone in the vicinity had gone quiet, listening. Heartily wishing he'd thought of a different cover story, he stuck out his hand with a smile.

'Hi. My name's Geoff Blaketon; I'm the second cousin you didn't know you had.'

'He's been in Australia,' the barman put in helpfully.

'My cousin? I don't understand . . .' Stephenson shook his hand, nonetheless.

'Second cousin,' Gideon said. 'On your mother's side. It's a bit complicated. Can I get you a drink? Then I'll try to explain.'

'OK.' Stephenson gave him a long look while they waited for Pete, the barman, to draw the pints, and then said curiously, 'Would that be my Auntie Rita's branch of the family?'

'That's right.' Gideon paid and handed him his drink. 'Look, those people are just leaving; let's grab that table.'

A couple of minutes later, installed at a small table near the door, he took a long draught of his ale and wondered how on earth to broach his real identity and reason for coming. The door opened and two more people came in, accompanied by a hefty whoosh of cold air, but Gideon didn't mind. For his purposes, the location couldn't have been better – well away from the friendly nosiness of the group by the bar.

He was in the process of formulating his opening sentence when Stephenson beat him to it, saying abruptly, 'So what do you *really* want, Mr Blaketon? Or is that even your real name?'

'No, it isn't,' Gideon confessed with relief. 'How did you know?'

'I haven't got an Auntie Rita.'

'Oh. I fell for that one, didn't I? My name's Blake, Gideon Blake.' Stephenson looked a little wary.

'As in the Gideon that rang me, out of the blue, the other night?'

'That's right.'

'So what do you want with me? I told you I didn't know Damien Daniels.'

'But you said you knew his brother . . . How?'

'*Who are you?*' Stephenson asked suspiciously.

'I told you. I'm a friend of the family – just trying to sort something out for Damien's sister. She found this list of names among his things and wanted to know if it was anything important; I said I'd help.'

'And what have you found out?'

'Enough to know that it *is* important. That's why I came back to you.'

'Why haven't you taken it to the police? Why didn't she?'

'Do you think she should?' Gideon queried.

'Oh, God, I don't know! I don't know anything any more – I'm just sick of it! It was all so bloody long ago, I'm not sure it even matters now.'

'If it doesn't matter, tell me about it,' Gideon urged.

Stephenson took a long swallow of his beer and then shook his head.

'It's not just me, is it? It's not my decision to make.'

Gideon could have groaned aloud with frustration.

'You know Adam Tetley's been taken in for questioning over Damien's murder?' he said, instead.

'Yes. I saw it on the news. Do they think he did it?'

'I've no idea – do you?'

'How should I know? I haven't seen him for donkey's years. But I suppose they must have some reason to arrest him.'

'His name is on the list,' Gideon told him.

'What the hell's that got to do with it? So's mine, apparently. What are you implying?'

Gideon leaned forward over the table.

'Look, I'm not implying anything. I'm just trying to find out what in God's name this is all about and it would save a hell of a lot of time if someone would just talk to me! So what about it, huh?'

For a moment he thought Stephenson was going to do just that, but then his gaze dropped.

'I can't,' he said. 'If it was just me . . .'

'Who are you protecting? The other people on the list? Tell me, please.'

'I'm sorry.' Stephenson shook his head. 'I can't.'

Although it didn't exactly keep him awake, the infuriating riddle of the list occupied Gideon's mind throughout the rest of that evening, and he woke up thinking about it in the morning. To try and make some sense of it, he wrote the six names and phone numbers down on a fresh notepad, leaving a gap under each to fill in what he'd found out about them, including their addresses and which of the other names they had admitted to knowing.

He ate his breakfast with this notepad propped against the marmalade jar, but couldn't really have claimed that it helped clear his mind much. The strange thing was that although it was Damien who'd made the list, at least three of the people on it had apparently never met him. So if the names weren't friends, or partners in some business venture . . .

The telephone rang, interrupting his fruitless mental wranglings, and he went out to the hall to answer it.

'Gideon? It's Tilly.' There was an undercurrent of excitement in her voice.

'Hello, Tilly.'

'Have you heard about Adam Tetley?'

'I heard he'd been taken in. Any news on that?'

'Ah, you obviously haven't seen the papers.'

'I don't get a paper, I read Giles'.'

'Well, Rockley phoned yesterday. They let him go but now they've rearrested him and charged him. Gideon, they found the gun!'

'What? Where?'

'In a locker at a sports club. Rockley said they found the key when they were searching Adam's house, and eventually – don't ask me how – traced it to this sports club. The gun was in a kit locker, in a case.'

'Good God! That was careless!'

'Well, the locker wasn't held under his own name, of course. Rockley says he imagines Adam was going to get rid of the gun when the heat died down.'

'Well, that's a result. And a relief for you, I imagine?'

'Yes, I suppose so . . .'

'You don't sound too sure.'

'Oh, I don't know. I'm still finding it hard to believe that he'd actually do such a thing. I mean, *why*, after all this time?'

'Who knows?' Gideon said. 'Perhaps he's been harbouring a grudge ever since it happened, building on it all the time. Maybe it just took some other little thing to spark it off. What does Rockley say?'

'Pretty much what you just said, actually. You're probably right. I suppose it's just difficult to take in when it's someone you know.'

'Well, hopefully it'll all be over soon, and you'll be able to put it behind you and move on.'

There was a pause.

'It sounds silly, but I almost feel guilty about wanting to move on. As if I'm sweeping him under the carpet and pretending all this didn't happen.'

'I know how it feels, but getting on with your life doesn't mean you've put him out of your mind, Tilly. What you need to do now is concentrate on becoming one of the top trainers in the country. That would be the best memorial of all. I'm looking forward to seeing you on TV being interviewed by Clare Balding as the winning trainer of the National or the Cheltenham Gold Cup.'

'Oh, I wish!' Tilly laughed. 'Actually, that reminds me of my other reason for ringing; I wondered how Nero was doing, and whether we could have a go at that join-up thing, sometime soon?'

'Yeah, sure. We could do it today, if you like. I shall be going up there in half an hour or so, if you're free?'

'That'd be great. I'll be about an hour, I expect. Ivan'll take the last lot out for me. I've decided to offer him a permanent job. He's going to be my head lad–cum–assistant trainer. It'll only be part-time, but he seems quite chuffed about it and I think I can learn a lot from him.'

'That's a brilliant idea. There'll be no stopping you now. OK; I'll see you later.'

Gideon put the phone down, thoughtfully.

So it *had* been Tetley. He'd had the motive, the skill, presumably no verifiable alibi, and now the weapon had been found. Gideon tried to imagine the kind of festering resentment that would lead to a man hiding in the undergrowth and shooting another man dead with no warning whatsoever. He found he couldn't. He thought that, even if his *had* been the sort of temperament that could get that bitter and resentful, he would gain more satisfaction from facing the subject of his grievance and making sure he knew what he was dying for. But who was he to try and understand the mindset of a murderer?

The join-up session went really well. Tilly grasped the concept instinctively and Nero was very co-operative, with the result that Gideon suggested that he might soon be able to return to Puddlestone Farm and go back into training.

'You've done a brilliant job with him. He's like a different horse!' Tilly declared as they returned to the yard with Pippa.

'Oh, no! You've discovered my secret!' Gideon joked. 'I'd better go and fetch the real Nero.'

'Don't bother. I'll take this one,' Tilly said, laughing. She loosened Nero's girth, then looked round as a muddy Range Rover swept into the yard. 'Oh, here's Lloyd.'

Pippa's boyfriend had been in the yard when Gideon arrived, but left shortly after, saying he'd leave the 'horse shrink' to his work. The words were said lightly, and Gideon couldn't be sure whether there was any real spite behind them. Now he smiled cheerfully and asked how they'd got on with the horse.

'Fine.' It was Pippa who answered. 'You should have stayed to watch.'

'Well, I'm glad you're here now, anyway,' Tilly told him. 'I've got something to ask you all. One of our horses is running at Towcester in a couple of weeks' time and his owner has hired a box for the day. Anyway, she said would I like to bring some guests along. So what d'you think? It's a really nice course.'

'What? All of us?' Pippa asked, holding Nero as Tilly slid the saddle off.

'Yes, as many as you like. She's a sweet little lady, quite elderly, and she hasn't got very much in the way of family. She said it would be much nicer to have a crowd. Her words, not mine!'

'Well, it depends on the crowd,' Gideon observed. 'I mean, do you think she's ready for Giles?'

Ignoring him, Pippa said she'd love to go but she'd have to check her diary.

'I used to keep a diary when I was a kid,' Gideon said, seizing the opportunity to bring the subject up. 'My sister did, too. My mother encouraged it, she said it would be improving; I never did understand why.'

'I didn't know you had a sister,' Tilly said.

'I don't see a lot of her. She's a dancer, and she's married to a vet who runs a wildlife sanctuary – not far from you, actually. Hermitage Farm.'

'Oh, yes, I've seen the sign.'

'So, did anyone in your family keep a diary?' Gideon asked her, careful to keep his tone casual.

'*I* didn't – it was never my thing – but Marcus used to. He was a solitary child, in some ways, and very sensitive. As far as I know, he stopped when he was about twelve. He had a sleep-over and one of his friends pinched his diary and took it to school. You can imagine the humiliation!'

'Some friend!' Gideon remarked.

'I used to keep a diary, too,' Pippa said. 'I wrote down all my teenage angst in it, as I remember. Horrendous; but I suppose that's what you do when you're that age and you think no-one understands how you're feeling.'

Which was exactly what Marcus had done, Gideon guessed. Away from home and feeling isolated and under stress, would it be so surprising if he had returned to the habit of childhood and kept a journal? He thought not.

Eve was waiting for Gideon when he returned wearily to the Gatehouse after an afternoon spent schooling the horses over the cross-country course at Home Farm with Pippa and Lloyd.

'Had a good day, honey?' Eve asked in a fake American accent, reaching up to kiss Gideon as he met her in the sitting-room doorway. She wrinkled her nose. 'Ooh, you have a distinct aroma of horse about you. Shall I run you a bath?'

'Thank you, and one of those,' he added, indicating the glass of red wine she held.

She tutted and shook her head. 'I'm giving you bad habits. It'll be AA before you know it.'

Their evening together was interrupted by two telephone calls.

The first was Gideon's sister, Naomi.

'Hi, big bruv!'

'Hello. I was just talking about you earlier.'

'How nice.'

'So, how are you?'

'I'm . . . fine. We've been very busy, as usual.'

Something in her voice caught his attention.

'OK. So what's the big news?'

'Oh, you wretch!' she exclaimed. 'I can never surprise you, can I?'

'Well, you might. I don't know what it is yet.'

'Well, how would you feel if I said you were going to be *Uncle* Gideon in seven and a half months' time?'

'Naomi! How wonderful. Congratulations! I'd be *thrilled* to be Uncle Gideon.'

They talked for another ten minutes or so before Naomi rang off, saying she had other people to call.

'I'll ring back in a day or two. I just wanted you to be the first to know,' she said.

'Well, I really think you should tell Tim next,' Gideon joked. 'OK. Speak soon, sis. Bye.'

He sat for a moment with a smile on his face before returning to Eve in the sitting room.

'That was my sister, Naomi,' he said, gesturing over his shoulder, as if she had actually been in the hall.

'Yes, I heard. I gather congratulations are in order, and looking at your face, there's no need to ask if you're pleased.'

'It's great news!' Gideon said. 'You ought to meet Naomi. You'd like her. And Tim.'

'Ah. Meet the family,' Eve said, pursing her lips. 'Must be getting serious. More wine?'

'Think I might have a coffee,' Gideon decided. 'Can I get you one?'

'Nope. I'm feeling all warm and fuzzy, and I have no intention of spoiling it.'

Five minutes later, lying diagonally across the sofa with Eve close beside him and Bruch's Violin Concerto on the CD player, Gideon took a sip of his coffee and sighed contentedly.

'You're really stoked about your sister's baby, aren't you?' Eve said suddenly.

'Mm. It's great news,' Gideon murmured.

After a long pause, she asked, 'Do you want kids, yourself?'

'Yeah, one day.'

Eve lay very still and silent within the circle of his arm and, after a moment, he kissed the back of her head.

'Something wrong?'

'No, just thinking.'

'So how was your dinner date last night?'

'OK,' she replied.

'An old friend, you said . . .'

'Yeah, Trevor. Met him when I was married to Ralph. He's an artist, too.'

'Oh? Competition.'

'Not really. He paints huge canvases with lots of colours and gives them pretentious names like *Solitude* and *Serendipity*.'

Gideon tilted his head to look down at her.

'Don't you like them?'

'They're OK, but they're not genuine.'

'What do you mean? They're copies?'

She waggled her head.

'No. I mean his motives are purely mercenary. He slaps paint on with no real thought. Sometimes he lines up a dozen canvases and does them all at the same time – walking along the row and doing a different splodge on each, then changing the colour and going along again. He can do a dozen in half an hour. But the thing is, he's fashionable. He has maybe two exhibitions a year and always sells out. People pay tens of thousands!'

Gideon was impressed. 'So he only needs to work a few days a year. He's got it made.'

'He's laughing at them,' Eve complained. 'There's no integrity.'

'You can't blame him, though.'

'I suppose not. The shame of it is that he's actually a very talented artist, when he puts his mind to it.'

Gideon had another sip of coffee.

'I wondered if he was an old flame, come to reclaim you . . .'

A sharp elbow in his midriff was his answer, and then the phone rang again.

'Oh, God. It's nearly eleven. Why don't you just leave it?' she suggested.

'For that very reason. It might be trouble; Pippa or Tilly.' He slid her weight off him and went out to the hall.

'Is that Gideon Blake?' A male voice, with a slight West Country burr.

'Yes. Who's this?'

'Arthur Willis. A friend tells me you sort out horses.'

'That's right; sometimes,' Gideon said cautiously.

'Oh, I hope you can help me. It's my daughter's pony, see. My wife says he has to go but Katy, she loves that pony. It'd break her heart if he had to go!'

'What's the problem with the pony?' Gideon asked.

'It's unpredictable, see?' Arthur Willis said. 'Mostly he's as good as can be but sometimes he turns really nasty, and we don't know why. My wife's afraid Katy'll get hurt. Couldn't you just come and have a look? It'd break her heart if we had to get rid of him, poor little mite. My friend says you'll be able to tell what's wrong.'

'Well, I might, but I can't promise,' Gideon said, wondering who the 'friend' was and wishing they had been less fulsome. 'All right, I'll come and take a look. When did you have in mind?'

'Tomorrow? Katy's off school tomorrow.'

'OK.' Gideon took details of the pony's whereabouts, arranged to call the following afternoon at two and put down the receiver with the man's heartfelt thanks ringing in his ear.

'You're a pushover,' Eve murmured sleepily, when he slid back onto the sofa beside her.

'Tell me about it. But when it's some kid's pony . . .'

'You're a pushover,' she reiterated firmly. 'Now how about *I* get some attention for a change?'

TEN

GIDEON DROVE THE LAND Rover down the long bumpy track that led to Arthur Willis' rented field, his mind dwelling on his relationship with Eve.

They had fallen into bed just after midnight and, after a brief spell of passion, had lain languorous and content, watching the stars through the bedroom window and talking in the desultory fashion of lovers everywhere.

This morning she had been up before him, bright and cheerful, showering and getting breakfast for them both, before roaring off in her Aston Martin to open the gallery at ten. Gideon had kissed her goodbye with affection, thinking how simple it would be to drift on in this easy-come, easy-go fashion for another twenty years, but as soon as the thought came, he knew that it wasn't enough. Last night in the passionate darkness it had been enough, and even as they lay basking in the afterglow it was enough, but in the morning, facing the new day, there was something missing.

There always was.

Arthur Willis' daughter's pony lived, with several others, in a large, rough-looking, overgrazed field that appeared to double up as a graveyard for used cars and unwanted farm machinery.

Shaking his head in amazement that any animal could live amongst such an array of twisted metal and trailing barbed wire without mortally injuring itself within the first five minutes, Gideon wandered along the row of adjacent semi-derelict buildings, peering through the grimy windowpanes to try and make out something of their original purpose.

The first had sagging double wooden doors facing back down the track, and held, as far as he could see, an old Land Rover, no doubt quietly rusting into oblivion. The next few had half doors, like stables, and he opened one to find it full of mouldering cardboard boxes and plastic crates. Another contained a few opened sacks of horse feed and several bales of hay, which smelled musty, even from a distance. At the far end of the row was a bigger building with a locked door. He couldn't see a lot through the dirty, cobwebby glass, but he got the impression of a largely empty space with a high ceiling and some form of pulley or winch mechanism by one wall.

He turned away, wiping his dusty hands on his jeans. Looking back at the Land Rover, he could see Zebedee's face watching him soulfully through the passenger window.

The field was pretty isolated, situated as it was well back from the road, and the nearest habitation Gideon could see was the back of what looked like a council estate, a couple of hundred yards away to his left, beyond some water meadows.

He glanced at his watch.

Two fifteen. He'd been a little late himself, but Willis was later. So much for his desperation the evening before.

It was cloudy and a cold wind whistled round the deserted outbuildings. Gideon began to feel a little annoyed.

From the description he'd been given over the phone, Gideon guessed that Katy Willis' pony was the rather poorly put together bay that was grazing in the middle of the field, side by side with an equally weedy-looking grey. Beyond watching him from under its shaggy forelock, it showed little interest in Gideon's presence and, looking at the poached ground and pools of muddy water on the other side of the fence, Gideon had no inclination to venture any closer.

He decided to give Arthur Willis ten more minutes, and contemplated fetching his gloves from the car.

It was Zebedee who alerted him to the fact that company had showed up. All of a sudden he started barking furiously, the whole Land Rover rocking with the energy of his efforts.

Gideon walked back along the row of buildings towards the vehicle, where he would get a view of the track.

'That's enough!' he said sharply to the dog, thumping on the bodywork as he passed. 'Quiet now!'

Zebedee took not a shred of notice.

He had his back to Gideon and his tail was windmilling as his front paws jumped with each bark.

'Zeb, be quiet!' Gideon told him again, looking down the empty track. 'There's no-one there.'

He was wrong.

As he passed the rear of the Land Rover, a figure stepped out from the cover of the end wall to stand in his path. His face nightmarishly distorted by a stocking mask, he was holding what looked like a baseball bat in one gloved hand, and thumping it menacingly into the palm of the other.

He didn't say anything, but then he didn't really have to.

For a moment Gideon froze, immobilised by shock, and in that instant he heard the tiniest sound of a displaced pebble behind him, and two strong arms closed round his torso, trapping his own in a powerful hug that was entirely lacking in affection.

Gathering his wits, Gideon threw his head back forcefully, aiming for his attacker's nose. It was a manoeuvre that had worked well for him once before, but this guy was canny and had his head well out of the way so that he only succeeded in jarring his own neck.

His next effort, that of kicking back sharply at the man's shin, was more successful but rewarded by a fist pummelling into his lower ribs on his right-hand side.

It was like being hit by a battering ram. Gideon was a powerful man himself, and it wasn't the first time he'd been punched, but it was without a doubt the hardest. He grunted as the breath left his lungs and his legs turned instantly to jelly. His attacker grabbed him again, keeping him on his feet.

'Hold him.' The man with the bat stepped forward and Gideon raised his head to look at him, trying to make out his features underneath the dark nylon. He'd plainly been set up, but by whom? Just at the moment, though, he was finding it hard to concentrate on anything other than the almost mesmeric thwacking of the satiny blue bat into the leather-gloved palm.

What was intended?

Not my knees! Gideon thought with a flutter of panic. Almost anything but that . . .

Smack . . . Smack . . . Smack . . .

The man was just a matter of inches away now, and Gideon could smell stale tobacco smoke on his clothes. He stopped and raised the bat until it was rubbing gently against Gideon's face.

Inwardly quaking, Gideon tried to keep his eyes steady on the flattened nose and shadowed eyes of his tormentor's masked face, desperate to maintain his pride, at least.

On the edge of his vision he was very aware of the shiny smooth surface of the bat next to his left eye. Suddenly it lifted a little and then cracked painfully, but not dangerously, against his cheekbone.

Gideon couldn't help flinching, which appeared to amuse the man behind him.

'Go on. 'It him again!'

His mate, though, had more practical issues on his mind.

'No. We should get him inside. I don't like it here; we're too exposed.'

'Awright, well, let's get on with it then. He's a big bloke, I'm not sure how long I can 'old him like this.'

'You'd fuckin' better!' the other man warned.

To Gideon's surprise, the man in front of him discarded his weapon, dropping it behind him, where it rolled a short way and then stopped. From his jacket pocket he then took out a polythene bag from which he drew a pad of white cloth, and Gideon's nostrils were immediately assailed by a pungent chemical aroma. He began to writhe, guessing what was on the cards.

'You might enjoy this – the kids seem to,' the man said and, stepping to one side, clamped the hand with the cloth in it over Gideon's mouth and nose.

Gideon made a Herculean effort to break free of his captor, but with his arms imprisoned at his sides his struggles were ineffective, and his attempt to hold his breath was short-lived.

'Come on, you bastard, breathe!' the man with the cloth muttered, and jabbed his fist into Gideon's stomach. It wasn't a heavy blow but it was enough to make him gasp, and the damage was done.

The first deep inhalation sent his head spinning and brought tears to his eyes. He gagged, coughed, and necessarily inhaled again, feeling the thick spirit-laden air burn down into his lungs, seeming to permeate all his senses and rob him of the power of reasoning.

After several more suffocating lungfuls, the sudden rush of euphoria caught him by surprise, lifting him on a tide of well-being, and his head tipped back, eyes open to the sky. Up there, something was circling: large, dark green – a dragon.

There were two now. Huge, predatory; gliding slowly round and round as they searched for their prey. He needed to make for cover before they saw him, but though he struggled, he couldn't move.

They weren't dragons, they were aeroplanes – bigger than ocean liners, with cartoon propellers. All those people; where were they going? It puzzled him for a while but then he realised he didn't care. Let them go . . . They were no friends of his. He didn't need them because he was floating; he could fly. Soon he'd be

Frowning, Gideon watched as the man then untangled the flex, using a crocodile clip on the end to connect it to a length of silvery wire that hung from above.

It said a lot for his woolly state of mind that Gideon only then recognised the metal box for what it was – an electric fencer unit, such as was used to power stock fencing. He knew from experience that the twelve-volt battery delivered a nasty jolt to any man or beast unwary enough to touch it, and, with a growing foreboding, he followed the silver wire upward with his eyes until he saw where it had been wound round a crossbeam, high in the roof space. His position prevented him from following its course along the beam but it wasn't necessary. Directly above he could see his wrists, bound with orange baling twine and wound about with a coil of the same silver wire. As far as he could see, the baling twine was looped over one of several heavy, S-shaped iron hooks that hung from staples driven into the timber. Gideon thought they looked a little like meat hooks.

At his other extremity he could feel the cold floor with his toes, and it took him a moment or two to comprehend the reason for this. His feet were bare. He had no boots on. His cold-induced shaking grew a stage or two worse.

'Ah. 'E's twigged it,' the talkative one said. 'And 'e don't look too 'appy!'

Gideon *wasn't* ''appy'.

His mind was racing. What did they hope to achieve? Did they intend questioning him? Was that what this was all about?

If it was, he had to wonder just what kind of power pack they'd put in their fencer unit. He had no idea what was legally available, even supposing they stayed within the bounds of legality, which was unlikely, given their record so far. He was heartily glad that beyond an antiquated light fitting or two that might or might not be defunct, the derelict site seemed to have no mains electricity supply; no sockets.

The burning pain in his wrists began to seep through the residual muddle in his head, and he tried to take some of his weight on his feet, without success. Although he could just get the balls of his feet in contact with the floor, he couldn't seem to balance that way and he sagged sideways, the movement putting even more strain on his arms.

He spread his feet to steady himself, with just his toes touching. Marginally better.

'What do you want?' he asked. His throat was sore and his voice emerged as not much more than a cracked whisper.

'We don't want nuffink,' Bad Breath told him, coming round in front and looking up.

It was on the tip of Gideon's tongue to ask who'd sent them, but he checked himself. If he'd been meant to know they would have told him.

The fencer rigged up to his satisfaction, the other man came over.

'We're just delivering a message,' he said, his voice a stage or two more educated than his more loquacious companion's.

'You've been pokin' your nose where it don't belong,' Bad Breath put in. 'And we was asked to 'ave a little word . . .'

By whom? Bentley? Surely this wasn't Stephenson's doing? Much easier to believe it was the health-club owner, who'd been openly antagonistic. But then, Gideon didn't really know either of them, in spite of the instinctive liking he'd felt for the teacher.

'Arncha gonna ask who?'

But the other man shook his head. 'He knows we won't tell him. He's a cool customer, this one. Let's just get this done and get out of here.'

Cool? Ye gods! If they only knew!

Clenching his jaw and just about everything else, Gideon watched the man go over to the fencer and reach for the switch. With a click, it was on, and for one blessed moment, nothing happened, allowing him the fleeting and altogether ridiculous hope that the battery was flat.

In the gloom of the musty room, the little orange bulb on top of the unit flashed brightly, and in the next instant, Gideon convulsed as the shock coursed through his body to the floor.

''E didn't like that,' Bad Breath observed with gratification, and as he finished speaking, the fencer pulsed again.

Bad Breath and his mate disappeared somewhere around the tenth or eleventh pulse of current.

Gideon didn't see them go, he was too caught up in his own personal hell of zinging, fizzing pain. Jolt after jolt. Regular as clockwork, anticipated and yet still unexpected, the current used his body as a bridge to the floor. Squinting through screwed-up eyes between pulses, Gideon found himself alone in the gloom, and the discovery was chilling. With the disappearance of his tormentors went any hope of an early end to his ordeal.

Zap!

It felt as though someone was pushing red-hot wires through his bones. With each shock his muscles contracted violently, beyond his control. And with every shock the initiative he was working so hard to muster in each blessed, two-second respite splintered into a thousand pieces.

'You bastards!' he yelled out, suddenly and without premeditation, then his breath caught in his throat with a sob of hopelessness.

Gradually, the repeated pulses of electricity were breaking down his ability to function on any level. His muscles were in spasm, his brain increasingly unable to do anything but focus with agonising expectation on the next jolt, and his will power leaching away through his feet with the current.

His feet.

Bootless and wet; touching down in a puddle of water; completing the circuit and conducting the electricity to the ground.

Bird on a wire.

Birds sat on the high-voltage cables. They did so in total safety because they had no contact with the earth below; they were not part of the circuit.

Ignoring the burning pain in his wrists, Gideon dropped all his weight onto his bound hands and forced his exhausted muscles to somehow lift his leaden feet clear of the floor.

In the semi-darkness under the dusty window the bulb flashed, announcing its delivery of current with a significant click, and such was Gideon's state that he flinched anyway.

It took two more harmless pulses before he could trust what his body was telling him. The shocks had stopped.

So easy. Why hadn't he thought of it before?

But even as he rejoiced in his delivery from torture he knew it was merely a respite, not a solution. The burning soreness in his wrists and the strain on his stomach muscles were evidence enough that he couldn't hold the position for long. Already his feet were sinking inexorably closer to the floor.

Oh think, you stupid bastard! he told himself. *Think!*

To his left, the orange light flashed on. Patient. Waiting for the moment when his exhausted muscles could no longer hold his feet clear of the floor.

If only he could reach the fencer. How far was it?

Too far. Even the most wishful of thinking couldn't deny that. At least eight feet, and sideways at that. It might just as well have been eight miles. He could quite possibly generate a fair amount of swing, forward and back, but because of the orientation of the hook and staple it would be much more difficult to do so laterally.

A jolt took him by surprise and he snatched his feet up, feeling his stomach muscles burn anew as he did so.

How long would the battery last, earthing like that?

Gideon had no idea. Nor could he guess what kind of voltage the electric fencer was putting out, but he was almost certain that sanity would desert him long before the cell went flat.

There had to be *something* he could do . . .

Think, damn you!

All right – if not the fencer itself, then the wire.

Twisting his head awkwardly, Gideon followed the connecting flex upward with his eyes.

It might be possible. It just might . . .

If they'd taken the wire right the way along the beam to the wall before they'd clipped the flex on, it would have been way beyond his reach, but they hadn't. It began its downward slant less than four feet away from him.

Experimentally, Gideon tried using his legs to initiate some sort of sideways movement but only achieved a kind of undignified wriggling, which would have been funny in any other situation. The twine cut deeper into the skin on his wrists and he was forced to touch down, briefly, once again.

This time he managed to pick up before the current zapped him, and the accomplishment filled him with a ridiculous degree of elation. It was as if the small red fencer unit, with its brightly winking eye, had assumed a malicious persona. Or perhaps it was just easier to perceive it that way rather than as an insentient mechanism, delivering its cruel payload with metronomic regularity, untouched by Gideon's pain or frustration.

Watching the flashes, he began to count steadily during the pauses, until the bulb lit on the number six every time, and after the first three or four pulses he started to touch his feet down in between, twisting slightly and pushing himself away from the window and the fencer unit as he did so, to obtain the momentum to swing back.

It wasn't so easy to be accurate once he began to swing properly, because it threw his rhythm, and more than once he received a stinging reminder, but on the forward curve his outstretched feet were within inches of the flex now and, for the first time, deliverance seemed a tangible possibility.

He knew from experience that it was no earthly good trying to break the wire itself. Formed from multiple strands of steel, it was manufactured to withstand the kind of pressure that might be exerted by a thick-skinned steer or horse, and Gideon knew it would stretch before it finally snapped. His only hope lay in the join where the crocodile clip connected to the stock fence, or where the flex exited the fencer unit itself.

With the beam creaking alarmingly above him, Gideon put all his efforts into one final forward-reaching swing, kicking out with his bare feet . . .

And missing.

The effort sent his swing out of control and as he fell back his feet hit the floor, dragging on the tiles and providing the contact for a jolt that added pain to the huge wave of disappointment that swamped him. He received two more jolts before he managed to reorganise himself and lift his toes clear of the ground again.

The effort of that final swing had caused the orange twine to bite ever deeper into his wrists, and his whole being shied away from the idea of beginning the process again, yet what choice did he have?

Turning his head, he began to time the flashes again, and after a few pulses gritted his teeth, pushed off and started to swing.

This time he made it.

On the final desperate swing, he stretched his feet forward, his shoulders burning under the strain, and felt his left heel hook over the flex.

The contact broke his impetus, sending him twisting out of control, and for a split second, as he plunged helplessly into the back swing, he thought that once again he hadn't done enough; that the muscle-wrenching effort had been in vain. Then, as he tried to check his wildly careening progress, there came a crash, and the fencer unit toppled from its position on the winch to land on the tiled floor.

Gideon put a foot down briefly to try and steady himself, and looked at the fallen metal box in desperation. The flex was still intact, as was the connection to the wire above, and, with the unit loose on the floor, it was going to be impossible to put the kind of pressure on the contacts necessary to break them free.

Still twisting erratically, Gideon put his toe down again to try and ease the strain on his arms and shoulders, and discovered two things: the twine around his wrists had apparently stretched a little, allowing him to get his feet almost flat on the floor, and, having done so, the expected jolt had not yet come.

Seconds passed, unbearably tense.

Gideon counted steadily, his eyes fixed on the little orange bulb. He'd reached twelve before he stopped counting, finally allowing himself to believe that the fencer really was dead.

He didn't know what exactly had happened to it, but then he didn't need to know. The flex and connection were still intact, but somehow, somewhere, the electrical circuit had been broken and that was all that mattered. Gideon had other concerns, the most pressing of which being how to free himself from the twine and the hook.

The curve on the S-shaped meat hook was far too deep for there to be any hope of unhooking it from the staple in the beam, so he concentrated his efforts on trying to uncouple the loop of twine between his wrists from the hook.

The extra couple of inches of twine his Tarzan-like swinging efforts had netted him allowed him just enough bend in his legs to spring a little. It wasn't the kind of jump that was going to win him any prizes on sports day, and after a dozen or more failed attempts he was forced to admit defeat. It might have worked if the hook was held rigid, but it wasn't, and when he jumped it had an exasperating tendency to move with him.

Breathing heavily, and more weary than he would have believed possible, Gideon bowed his head and could have wept with pure frustration.

How soon would he be discovered, if he didn't manage to free himself?

The set-up was one strongly suggestive of hordes of young pony-mad girls turning up after school to ride and feed their adored charges, and the idea of being found in this predicament by a handful of teenagers was not one that appealed to Gideon. Parents would have to be called, and then, inevitably, the police and probably an ambulance, and the questions would begin . . .

Gideon screwed his eyes tight shut and groaned. When he opened them again it was to see a blur of red on the edge of his vision.

The fencer. A strong metal box. A potential step.

With renewed energy, Gideon set his body swinging once more until he could hook his foot around the hanging flex. Pulling it closer, he managed to get his toe on the fencer unit itself, and from then on his liberation was a done deal.

With the red box positioned below him, he was able to fit both feet onto it and stand up, taking the weight off his wrists. His legs were ridiculously jelly-like, and as the loop of orange twine finally slid clear of the hook, Gideon overbalanced from his suddenly precarious footing on the fencer, took one stumbling step and pitched forward onto the dirty tiled floor.

It seemed to take for ever for Gideon to get himself on his feet, out of the building and back to the Land Rover, and he spent the first part of that time lying foetus-like on the cold tiles, shaking like an aspen leaf.

Ultimately, it was the sound of Zebedee barking that provided the spur he needed; that and the thought of the round-eyed fascination of those pony-mad kids he was sure would soon be on their way. But, even with the decision made, it wasn't easy. His hands were still bound together and felt clumsy with pins and needles, and his shoulders, freed at last from their unnatural attitude, now screamed their protest at having been obliged to move from it. Added to this he had the odd sensation of having been filleted from top to toe, neither arms nor legs seeming inclined, at first, to take his weight.

At the sitting-up stage, Gideon regarded the small, pulled-tight knots that secured his wrists. Knowing from experience that once this kind of synthetic twine was knotted it generally stayed knotted, he didn't waste any time trying to unpick them, looking around him instead for the means to cut or fray the twine. Nothing suggested itself, but then he remembered there'd been hay bales in one of the other sections of the building, and where there are hay bales, there is almost always a knife.

With this in mind, Gideon pulled himself to his feet with the help of the winch mechanism and held onto it while he looked up at the beam from which he had recently hung. There were ten hooks altogether, rusting a little, but still obviously sound, and contrary to his earlier impression, his was the only one secured by a staple. The others hung over a bar fixed to the underside of the timber and were free to run along its length.

Made of grey galvanised steel, the one staple was shiny underneath where it had, in the not too distant past, been hammered into place. The silvery wire that had delivered the sting so effectively to Gideon's body trailed down beside the hook, its end kinked and curled where it had pulled loose as he fell.

And thank God it *had* pulled loose! Gideon thought as he looked up at it. Wrapped tightly, and with his falling weight powering it, it could have taken off a finger or a hand as easily as a cheese wire slicing through Brie. He shuddered at the thought.

On the pallets in the corner he found his shirt and jacket, but they were useless to him while his wrists were bound, so he scooped them up and headed for the door.

The light in the open air made him blink, even though it was still overcast, and the stiff breeze chilled the moisture on his skin as he made his way shakily along the row of outbuildings to the one with the hay. To his relief he found the expected knife, balanced on the inner window sill among decades of hay dust and the dried-up remains of several generations of spiders. Cutting the twine proved more difficult than he'd foreseen, with fingers rendered stupid by insufficient circulation and very little room to manoeuvre the blade between his wrists. In the end he accomplished the task by wedging the knife handle underneath his foot and rubbing the orange strands up and down until they frayed and parted.

The effort made Gideon's shoulders ache again and he sat on one of the bales for a moment, feeling about ninety and wondering where on earth he was going to find the energy needed for the journey home. He'd no idea what the time was, as his watch had disappeared, no doubt into one of his attackers' pockets. It was a chunky explorer's watch-cum-compass and had been a Christmas present from Pippa. A swift search confirmed that his wallet had disappeared, too. Another score to settle with the bastards, if he ever got the chance. Thankfully, he'd left his mobile in the Land Rover.

Wishing he didn't feel as though he'd drunk half a bottle of vodka on an empty stomach, Gideon put his shirt and jacket on and headed for his car.

Zebedee almost turned himself inside out with excitement when Gideon finally pulled himself into the driving seat of the Land Rover, and he had to endure having his ears and the side of his face thoroughly washed as the dog greeted him.

'All right lad, that's enough,' he said eventually, leaning his head against the bodywork and fighting the powerful impulse to close his eyes for a few blissful moments. His head was pounding, whether as a result of the shocks or whatever he'd been forced to inhale he wasn't sure, and his chest felt a little tight, as if he were perpetually on the verge of coughing. But in spite of these discomforts, and a host of overstretched muscles and overstimu-lated nerve endings, his main problem was staying awake.

Best keep moving.

The keys were in the ignition where he'd left them, and he started the engine, put the Land Rover into gear and let in the handbrake. At the end of the long and bumpy drive, Gideon hesi-tated at the junction with the road.

Left, up to the A354 and the sixteen or more miles to Tarrant Grayling, or right, and take the six or seven miles of back roads to Wareham, and Eve?

There was never any contest. Even without the added attrac-tion of a spot of TLC, he seriously doubted his ability to steer between the hedges and the cars for sixteen miles along a busy main road in his present state.

It wasn't until he was about halfway to Wareham that it occurred to him that he should probably have brought the fencer with him as evidence, but there was no way he was going to go back for it.

Eve's home was the top floor of a large Georgian town house, reached by an outside stair with an ornamental black wrought-iron banister.

Gideon stood with his foot on the first step, gazing up, and wished heartily that she'd bought the whole house.

Taking a deep breath he started the climb.

'Gideon? What on earth are you doing?'

Gideon opened his eyes and blinked, trying to focus on Eve's face. She was frowning in bewilderment, which wasn't altogether surprising, as he was sitting on her doorstep, leaning against the glossy red paint of her front door, and he very much suspected he'd been asleep.

'You look terrible,' she added, before he could answer her opening query. 'Where are your boots?'

'I'm not sure,' he mumbled, becoming vaguely aware of another figure standing behind her. He screwed his eyes shut, then looked again. A man – perhaps fiftyish – jeans, a well-cut jacket, and thick, wavy, greying hair. Urbanity personified.

'Are you drunk? No, of course not,' Eve answered herself. 'Come on. Let's go inside.'

Gideon got his feet under him and discovered that her companion was holding a hand down towards him. It wasn't the moment for pride; he took the help it offered.

Inside, he paused by the inner door and Eve gestured to the sofa, a huge squashy affair of black leather, scattered with a multitude of tasselled and beaded cushions in rich Indian silks.

Gideon looked down significantly at his filthy jeans and boot-less feet.

'Oh, for goodness sake! Don't worry about that. Sit down before you fall down. What on earth happened to you? No – before you answer that – would you like something to drink? Coffee, or something stronger?'

'Better be coffee, I think,' Gideon decided. He wasn't sure his body could cope with alcohol, at this juncture. He already felt as though he had the mother and father of all hangovers.

The grey-haired man cleared his throat.

'Ah, I think perhaps I'd better be going . . .' he began, hesitating between the sofa and the front door.

Eve stopped, halfway to the kitchen, and turned back.

'Trevor, I'm sorry. I haven't even introduced you to Gideon. Gideon, this is Trevor Erskine. You remember, I told you about him.'

'Oh, the artist? Pleased to meet you.' Gideon held out a hand, which, after a moment's hesitation, Erskine shook.

'Um . . . Unusual wristwear,' he remarked diffidently, gesturing with his other hand.

Eve came up to Gideon's shoulder, and they all peered in silence at the bloodstained orange twine bracelets just visible under the cuffs of his jacket.

ELEVEN

'SO, WHAT NOW? ARE you going to tell the police?' Eve asked, when Gideon had completed his tale. She was sitting sideways on the sofa next to him and had listened with an expression of growing horror as he spoke. She was no fool, and his attempts to gloss over the details had received short shrift, the full facts leaving her compassionate and furious by turns.

Trevor Erskine had long gone, diplomatically taking his leave soon after the discovery of the baling twine. Eve had seen him to the door, promising to call the next day, and they exchanged kisses, cheek to cheek, before he stepped outside.

When she'd returned to Gideon, he'd looked up at her, holding his wrists forward, and said, simply, 'I'm sorry.'

She'd returned his gaze, her expression unreadable, then moved into business mode.

'Right, first I cut that stuff off, then you have a bath, and then you can tell me all about it. And I mean *all*.'

She'd used her kitchen scissors to cut the orange twine, hissing through her teeth at the mess it had made of his wrists. Initially agonising, the hot bathwater had eased the stiffness in his muscles and cleansed the bloody sores on his arms, and by the time he'd settled down on the sofa, wrapped in a whiter-than-white towelling bathrobe, his natural resilience had kicked in and recovery had begun.

Now, as Eve asked the inevitable question about calling the police, he looked down at his bandaged wrists and the still-warm, empty mug he was cradling.

'I can't.'

'Of course you can. I'll do it for you, if you want. You can't just let something like this happen and not do anything. It's . . . it's barbaric!'

'But just think of all the questions,' Gideon protested. 'And I'd have to see a doctor—'

'And that's a bad idea?' Eve broke in. 'You were almost dead on your feet an hour ago!'

'That was then,' Gideon pointed out. 'I'm a lot better now.'

Eve groaned in sheer frustration.

'Well, apart from the question of a doctor – don't you *want* to see these people caught?'

'Of course I do. But what I want even more is to find out who sent them.'

'I agree. But let someone else do it! I'm serious, Gideon! Look at what could have happened today. As bad as it was, you were lucky. What if you hadn't managed to get free?'

That was something Gideon didn't care to contemplate, but he tried to make light of Eve's anxiety. 'It was a warning. Don't worry; now I know the stakes are high I'll be more careful.'

Eve made another exasperated noise. 'You can't just let it go . . . What about your policeman friend you were telling me about the other night?'

'Logan?' Gideon considered the idea. 'Well, I'd rather not, he's a bit of a pit bull when he latches onto something, but I guess it'd be a stage better than Rockley or Coogan.'

'For God's sake, Gideon! How far do you intend going to protect Lloyd and Pippa? It's not as if you've any evidence that

Lloyd's done anything wrong. I can't see why you don't just come right out and ask him about it. Or is there something you're not telling me?'

'No, nothing. And I think I will ask Lloyd. But I'd rather do that before I turn the list over to the police.'

'Well, if *you* don't ring this Logan, *I'm* going to ring the local lot, so the choice is yours,' Eve told him. 'But meantime, I'm going to call the deli and get them to bring something round. I take it you don't fancy going out to eat?'

'My clothes are in the washing machine.'

'Ah. So they are. By the way, where are you parked? They're getting quite strict about that in this road.'

'Round the back, half on the pavement. Which reminds me ... Zeb's still in the Land Rover. I don't suppose he could come in, could he? He could stay in the kitchen ...'

Logan's mobile phone routed Gideon straight through to the answering service when he first tried to ring, so he left a message for the policeman to call back, which he did, twenty minutes later.

'OK, what is it this time? A car number plate you want traced? Somebody's criminal record checked?'

'No, not exactly.' Gideon wished it was, then at least he might be getting somewhere, instead of feeling stiff and sore and having little idea who he'd upset and why. 'I er ... ran into a bit of trouble.'

'Why doesn't that surprise me? Are you OK?'

'Yeah, just about. Can I talk, off the record?'

'I guess so. But I've just finished a double shift, so it better be good! Do you want me to come over?'

'Well, I'm not at home,' Gideon warned. He explained where he was and gave Logan a very brief outline of the afternoon's events. 'Um ... I don't suppose you could take a look at the place on your way over?'

'You don't want much, do you?' Logan grumbled, but Gideon guessed that wild horses wouldn't keep him away now he'd heard Gideon's tale.

'Will he come?' Eve wanted to know, coming through from the kitchen with the deli meal on two red-and-gold-edged plates. 'By the way, your clothes are in the dryer.'

'Yeah, he'll come,' Gideon said, rubbing Zebedee's upturned belly with his foot. 'Though he's just finished a double shift. God knows when he sleeps; I think he must do it standing up!'

PC Mark Logan arrived around eight, carrying Gideon's boots; five feet ten of unflappable calm, with razor-cut fair hair and blue eyes. He'd been Gideon's salvation on one previous occasion, and Gideon trusted him implicitly, but he had to keep reminding himself that Logan's first duty was to the law and while he was sometimes prepared to stretch the rules in certain circumstances, it was no good asking him to ignore them completely.

'Interesting,' Logan said, when he'd been introduced to Eve, and accepted the offer of a coffee. 'I've taken some photographs and I've got the electric fencer in my van. We might be able to lift some prints off that but I doubt if we'll be able to trace it; it looks pretty old and there are dozens of them lying about on farms. Could have been bought twenty or thirty years ago. We might have more chance with the battery. The building at the end – where you said you saw the Land Rover – was empty, and there were tracks, so it looks as though you were right about that. Not much else to see. There were a couple of people up there feeding their horses, and I had a chat with them. The place was an old abattoir, did you know that?'

'Guessed it might be, what with the meat hooks, and there was a kind of gutter down the middle of the floor.'

'Yeah. Well, I got the name and address of the guy that owns the place and I'll follow that up, but I wouldn't hold my breath, if I were you. It's hardly likely that either of the men will have any known connection with the property. That would be very careless.'

'Well, thanks, anyway,' Gideon said.

'If you'd called it in, we could have sent in CSI and done the job properly,' Logan observed.

'Yeah . . . It's a bit complicated . . .'

'Isn't it always, with you? So are you going to let me in on the secret? Presumably this wasn't entirely unprovoked, so what have you been up to?'

'It was apparently in the nature of a warning.'

'I guessed that, but from whom and about what?'

'I can't give you names,' Gideon warned. 'At least, not all of them.'

'Can't or won't?'

'All right, won't.'

'So it involves someone you know,' Logan stated.

Gideon hesitated.

'Not Barrington-Whatsisname, your landlord?'

'No. Not Giles. Or Pippa. Look, I'm not sure this is going to work.'

'Sorry, but you can't stop me thinking. It's my job, after all. Thanks.' This last was to Eve, who had handed him a mug of coffee.

'I made it strong, as you asked, but are you sure it's all right? It looks revolting!'

'It's fine, I'm a caffeine junkie,' Logan told her, with a flash of his appealing boyish grin. 'If you filtered all the caffeine out of my bloodstream, I'd probably keel over and sleep for about a year!'

Eve laughed, handed Gideon his third mug of coffee and sat down.

'You're not joking. I think that's all that's keeping Gideon awake, too. He was asleep on my doorstep when I found him.'

'Some solvents have that effect,' Logan said, nodding. 'It's not unlike getting drunk, I'm told, complete with the hangover, although far more dangerous, of course. You can quite easily wake up dead.' He took a mouthful of coffee. 'So has this got something to do with Garth Stephenson?'

'What?' Gideon was startled. 'Oh, of course, the other night.'

'Garth Stephenson; aged thirty-four; teaches PE and history at Montague Park School, Charlton Montague. Born in Aylesbury, Buckinghamshire. Unmarried; no kids; former competitive swimmer who represented England several times in the Nineties; how am I doing?'

'Better than me. I didn't know about Aylesbury or the swimming,' Gideon said. 'I might have known you'd follow it up.'

Logan shrugged. 'It's what I do. Do you think he might have had something to do with what happened to you? What did you want him for, the other night?'

Having promised Logan information, Gideon now found himself in a quandary, unable to think of anything he could say that wouldn't lead the policeman to make a connection with Damien Daniels and there, by progression, to the murder inquiry. He knew that if that happened Logan would have no choice but to immediately turn the whole thing over to DI Rockley.

'I found a list of initials and phone numbers – at least, that's what it turned out to be, it had been disguised – and I've been trying to find out what the connection is between them. Garth Stephenson was one of them.' Even as he said it, Gideon knew Logan wasn't going to settle for such a vague explanation, and wished he hadn't let Eve talk him into phoning the man.

'You found it? Where?'

Gideon knew if he mentioned the horse, Logan would soon unearth details of its owner.

'Well it was given to me, amongst some other bits and pieces of paperwork.'

'By whom?'

'I'd rather not say, just at the moment.'

'So why didn't you ask this mystery person about it?'

'I did. They didn't seem interested, and it turned out it wasn't theirs.'

'Most people would have left it at that . . .'

'I thought I recognised one of the phone numbers, and I was curious.'

'So you started asking questions? You must have had some idea what connected the names on the list.'

'I thought I had, but I turned out to be wrong,' Gideon said.

'So what was it?' From the tone of his voice, Logan's patience was wearing understandably thin.

Gideon hesitated. 'I can't tell you, right now. I need to speak to someone first.'

'Oh, come on, Gideon! You haven't told me a bloody thing! You say you've got no idea what it's all about, but you must know enough to worry someone. You don't get done over like you were for nothing, and I didn't come all this way to listen to a load of meaningless bullshit! Tell me something. What did you speak to Stephenson about?'

'I asked him about some of the other names on the list.'

'And?'

'And I think he knew what it was all about, but he wasn't telling. I got the impression that whatever it was happened a long time ago. He didn't want to tell me because it wasn't just him involved, but he didn't show any aggression towards me. I'd be very surprised if today was anything to do with him.'

'OK, so who else have you talked to?'

'Someone called Sam Bentley. He owns a health club called Bentley's of Bath. He wasn't nearly as laid-back. He actually tried to buy me off until he realised I didn't have the first idea what was going on.'

'It's not such ancient history, then,' Logan observed, writing the name in his pocketbook. 'What was it you said that got him so worried — or is that something else you can't tell me?'

'I asked him about the other names on the list, too.'

'But he didn't tell you anything?'

'I think he knew them.'

'Did you tell him who wrote the list?'

'Yes, I did.'

'And?'

'He said he didn't know the person.' Gideon was uncomfortably

207

certain that if ever the time *was* right to divulge the identity of the list's author, Logan was going to be a long way short of happy with him.

'So who else was on this list?'

'Robin Tate. I'm told he's very well off, works in London and is married to Vanessa. Apparently they live at Wimborne St Giles. I haven't spoken to him yet.'

'But one of the others might have,' Logan pointed out, writing the names down. 'And . . . ?'

'Julian Norris. But he died last year in a car crash and his name was crossed out.'

'So the list is at least a year or more old.'

'Looks like it.'

'How many names in total?'

'Six,' Gideon said slowly.

'And you've given me four.'

'Mm.'

Logan tapped his pen on his teeth.

'OK, was there anything else on the paper?'

If he told Logan the truth, would he make the connection with racing and from there to Damien Daniels? Gideon had a feeling he might.

'Just some doodles,' he said. 'The sort of thing you do when you're on the phone.'

Out of the corner of his eye he could see Eve glance sharply at him, but ignored her. Although he wasn't happy deceiving Logan, he told himself it was only temporarily. It was becoming fairly obvious that, sooner or later, he'd have to hand the whole business over to the police.

Logan watched him thoughtfully.

'You know I can't help you unless you tell me the whole story . . .'

'Yeah, I know, and I'm sorry. I will, but I have to speak to someone first.'

'Well, you'd better hurry up and do it, mate. These guys weren't playing around today. Who's to say that next time they won't take it a step further?'

'Yeah, believe me, I know.'

'Well, I hope whoever you're protecting appreciates the risk you're taking on his or her behalf,' Logan said heavily. 'As for your list, I'd say it has all the hallmarks of blackmail. Whoever wrote it has got something on these people and is making them pay. Have you spoken to that person? Do they know you have the list? Because I imagine *they* might be quite keen to have it back, and possibly shut you up in the process.'

'The break-ins!' Eve exclaimed.

'Break-ins?'

'Yeah, I thought someone had been in the house one evening when I was out,' Gideon told him, wishing Eve had kept quiet. 'And we had a prowler the other night, but nothing was taken, either time.'

'And you called it in, of course,' Logan's cynicism was obvious.

'Nothing was taken. I didn't think your lot would be all that interested, and I didn't want the hassle. It didn't occur to me that it might have anything to do with the list, at that time. It didn't seem that important.'

'If I had a tenner for every time someone has said that to me, I'd have retired to the South of France by now,' Logan said. 'Well, all I can suggest is that you try and find something that links two or three of the names. If you do, it's a fair bet that if you look hard enough you'll find the others fit into the pattern, too. But do me a favour and be discreet, huh? You're a stubborn bastard, but I don't particularly want to be investigating your murder; I've got enough to do!'

'You're all heart,' Gideon said. 'But I will be careful.'

'Well, I think it would be far better for him just to leave the whole thing alone,' Eve stated vehemently. 'And I'm surprised you don't tell him the same!'

'I would, if I thought it would do any good,' Logan told her. 'But with this guy it's more about damage limitation.'

'I don't actually go *looking* for trouble,' Gideon protested. 'But on the other hand, I can hardly just leave it at that, can I?'

'I don't see why not!' Eve declared. 'It hasn't really got anything to do with you, after all.'

'I think this is probably where I bow out,' Logan said wisely.

'And if you turn up anything on the fencer . . . ?' Gideon asked.

'I'll maybe let you know,' Logan said. 'It works both ways, mister. You should remember that.'

Before he left, Logan got Eve to remove the dressings from Gideon's wrists so he could take some photographs. He then thanked her courteously for the coffee, and went on his way.

When the door shut behind him, Eve returned to Gideon on the sofa.

'I think he was remarkably patient, considering he'd come all the way out here and you patently weren't being straight with him.'

'I *was* being straight. I warned him I couldn't tell him all the names.'

'All right. Not co-operating with him, then. I thought he'd be a lot tougher on you, from what you told me about him.'

'Yeah, so did I,' Gideon said. 'And that's a bit worrying. It makes me wonder what he thinks he knows . . .'

Gideon spent the night at Eve's, a phone call to Pippa ensuring that Elsa would be fed, and Zebedee dining on minced beef and pasta from Eve's fridge. To Gideon's surprise, she even took the dog out for his late night 'comfort' walk, and came back reporting that he'd tried to chase a neighbour's cat, and almost pulled her into a row of dustbins.

'Funny how they live quite happily with their own cat but see everyone else's as fair game,' Gideon remarked.

'What I think is funny is how you can call yourself an animal behaviourist and yet own such a crazy and ill-disciplined dog!' she retorted.

By the morning, Gideon's throbbing headache had settled down to a dull muzziness but, by contrast, his ill-treated arm and shoulder muscles had become doubly stiff and sore, and the skin felt tender, as though someone had given him a stiff brushing over with a wire brush.

Taking one look at his face, Eve made him lie face down and proceeded to work at his back and shoulders with her fingers and palms, rubbing in some strong-smelling ointment at the same time.

'What *is* that?' Gideon asked, turning his head to one side.

'Arnica. It'll help. Now, lie still, will you?'

It did indeed help. When she'd finished, Gideon sat up gingerly, pulled her towards him and kissed her.

'Mmm,' she murmured. 'Why don't we have a lovely lazy day, doing nothing? I can call Sarah – she'll look after the gallery for me and we can just eat, drink, make love and maybe take old Zeb for a walk along the beach later.'

Gideon stroked her hair. 'Oh, I'm sorry. I'd love to, but . . .'

'But . . . ?'

'I promised I'd take a look at one of Tilly's horses this morning.'

'Can't you just call her and tell her you can't make it?'

'And then there's Angie Bowen. I'm supposed to be helping her with a new horse that has a blacksmith phobia . . .'

'You're hardly in a fit state to wrestle with a phobic horse!' Eve pointed out. 'Why can't you do it tomorrow? Give yourself a chance to recover.'

'Because the blacksmith is booked for today,' he said gently. 'I'm really sorry, but I have to go.'

'OK. Suit yourself. I'll go and rustle up something for breakfast,' she said, pulling away and disappearing towards the kitchen. She spoke lightly but Gideon wasn't deceived.

Sighing, he slid off the bed and followed, finding her putting slices of bread in a big chrome toaster.

'Eve . . . ?'

'Scrambled egg on toast?' she suggested without turning round.

'Lovely.' He went across and stood behind her, drawing her curtain of dark hair aside and kissing her neck, just below her ear. 'I will be careful, you know. I promise.'

'I still don't understand why you can't just turn it all over to the police and have done with it.' She turned to face him and the words burst out as though suddenly she could no longer hold them back. 'Or tell Lloyd and Pippa, and let it be their problem. It's got nothing to do with you – but you're the one getting hurt here!'

Gideon shook his head, sliding his hands down to rest on her hips.

'It's not that simple. You heard what Mark said. It sounds like whoever made the list was blackmailing the people on it, and I think he's right; it's the only thing that fits. I came to that conclusion myself, after I'd spoken to Bentley the other day.'

'You didn't say anything to me.'

'I think I've been trying to find another explanation; I didn't like that one, it makes everything very messy. Which is exactly why I can't tell the police just yet. Imagine what this would do to Tilly and her family. Bad enough that they've lost Damien, without finding out that he had another side to him that they knew nothing about! *I* feel a bit let down, myself, and *I* only knew the guy for a few weeks.'

'But . . .' Eve clearly saw the force of this reasoning. 'But . . . where does that leave you? If you don't want the family to get hurt, can't you just tear up the list and forget about it? Damien's dead and they've caught the guy that did it – even found the gun, for goodness sake – so presumably the blackmailing is over. Who's to know, or care? Isn't it better to leave it at that?'

Gideon shook his head, helplessly. 'I don't know. Something just doesn't feel right here.'

'Well, you're the only one who thinks so,' Eve exclaimed with a touch of impatience. 'You say you're worried about Tilly and her family finding out about Damien – but who's going to tell them? Only you.' She punctuated the last word by prodding him in the chest with her forefinger, then eased out of his grasp and went across to her huge American-style fridge for butter and eggs.

Frowning, Gideon leaned on the marble worktop and thought about it.

'You're right, of course,' he said eventually. 'I've lost track of what's important. In fact, I'm not really sure how all this got started, any more.'

Eve broke eggs into a bowl.

'OK, I think I was to blame for that,' she admitted. 'I think I may have been the one who suggested you ring the numbers, but it was only an off-the-cuff remark. I didn't really expect you to do it, and I certainly never expected any of this to happen. Can you put some plates to warm?'

'I think I had some vague idea that it might have something to do with the murder,' Gideon said, switching the oven on. 'And, come to that, it still might. What if Tetley found out who was blackmailing him and decided to put a stop to it, once and for all?'

'I suppose it's possible. But does the motive really matter? If the police are happy with the one they've got, why not leave it at that?'

'Well, because of yesterday,' Gideon said. '*That* can't have been Tetley because he's locked up, so it must have been one of the others.'

The atmosphere at Puddlestone Farm was so much lighter when Gideon visited, later that morning, that the wisdom of Eve's logic was brought home to him. The arrest of Adam Tetley had clearly brought with it some form of closure and the grieving process had moved on a stage. Even Damien's mother seemed to have begun to adjust to her loss.

'We're having the kitchen done,' Tilly told Gideon when he cocked an inquisitive eye at the three vans that were drawn up in front of the farmhouse. 'It was all put in motion months ago, and they were due to start the week that – well, you know. So then, of course, it was put on hold indefinitely. Mummy didn't really seem interested until a few days ago, and then suddenly, she must have it, right now! I must say the fitters have been really good; I just hope someone somewhere hasn't been abandoned mid-job.'

'It's good that she's taking an interest,' Gideon said. 'Even if it's only to take her mind off things. It'll all help. So, where's this young horse of yours?'

'Luigi,' Tilly said, leading the way into the yard. 'He only arrived a couple of days ago. One of my owners bought him at a sale in Ireland, but he's got a real problem with having his hind feet touched. He panics and lashes out as soon as you get down below his hock. He caught Melanie the first evening and broke a bone in her hand.'

'Oh dear. And how old is he?'

'Just five.'

'I wonder if he's got caught in wire at some point. Or it could be as simple as having fidgeted as a baby and someone having walloped him for it. Let's have a look at him.'

Luigi turned out to be a light-framed brown gelding with an intense, slightly anxious air about him. He eyed Gideon and Tilly when they entered his stable but accepted a Polo mint, and made no fuss about being caught. He was watchful but calm as Gideon patted his glossy neck and ran a hand down his shoulder and front legs. However, as soon as Gideon moved to his hind-quarters and his hand approached the horse's lower hind leg, Luigi stopped chewing his mint and became as taut as a bowstring.

Gideon straightened up with an effort.

'There's no sense in pushing it. I can see how worried he is.'

'What do you suggest we do?' Tilly asked. 'We haven't even been able to pick his feet out properly yet. It's a real battle.'

'There is something we could try. I saw it done at a demo once, and it's worked several times since . . . I shall need a broom handle, without the head, a glove, some sawdust and some string.'

'I think I can manage that. What kind of glove?'

'Oh, anything'll do. But one you're not using every day, because this may take a while.'

Ten minutes later, with a riding glove stuffed full of sawdust and tied tightly to the end of the pole, Tilly and Gideon led Luigi into Puddlestone Farm's covered schooling area. Holding a long lead rein in one hand, Gideon used the other to guide the pole like an extended arm and gently stroke the gelding all over.

At first the horse sidled away, distrustful of the broom handle alongside him, but gradually he relaxed and stood still, appearing to enjoy the sensation of the glove rubbing his satiny coat. This peaceful status quo lasted right up to the point when Gideon ventured to slide the false hand over the animal's hock joint and on down the leg.

Luigi exploded.

He lashed out with the leg that had been touched, and then leapt in the air and kicked out with both hind feet together before plunging forward and circling Gideon, who loosely held the end of the rein and waited for him to calm down.

When he slowed to a halt and faced Gideon warily, Gideon moved closer, spoke calmly to him and began the process again. The result was more or less the same, as it was the third, fourth and fifth times, but on the sixth attempt, although Luigi snatched his foot up, he didn't kick out.

Gideon rested the pole down and patted the horse's sweaty neck, murmuring words of praise. After a moment, he tried again. Once more the foot was lifted but not kicked, and he decided to end the session there.

'That's a really clever idea!' Tilly said, coming forward from her viewing position by the wall.

'Yeah, well, as I said, I can't claim the credit for it, but it's worked every time so far. I think, because there's no danger, you relax and the horse picks up on that. After a while he realises that nothing terrible is actually happening and the only one getting worked up is himself, and then *he* starts to relax as well.'

'It's not rocket science, is it? So why didn't I think of it, instead of getting stressed and making the animal ten times worse?'

'Like most things, it's easy when you know how,' Gideon said, rubbing Luigi behind the ears. The brown horse was totally relaxed now, his head low and eyes half closed.

Tilly watched him, smiling.

'There you go again, making my highly strung racehorses look like beach donkeys,' she said. 'I haven't seen him look so chilled-out since he got here.'

'I expect you need them to be a bit fired up to run their best, so maybe it's a good thing you don't have this effect on them.'

'Come on. Let's put the lad away and go and have a coffee. I've got quite cold standing watching. Are you OK?' she added, as Gideon went to pick up the glove pole and found that his muscles had stiffened again.

'Yeah. Just took some unaccustomed exercise yesterday, and I'm paying for it this morning,' he said, glad that he'd taken the time to call in at the Gatehouse and change into a cream-coloured long-sleeved tee shirt. This, whilst not an immensely practical colour for working with horses, effectively disguised the bandages on his wrists.

'Come into the cottage,' Tilly said as she and Gideon headed out of the yard. 'Mum's kitchen is in complete chaos with the builders. But mind your head, people were smaller when this place was built!'

Gideon did indeed have to duck to get under the stone lintel in the cottage doorway. There was no hall, the front door leading straight into the lounge, where the beamed ceiling was also too low to allow him to straighten up.

'Oh, dear. You'd better come into the kitchen and sit down,' Tilly said, laughing. 'Dad has that problem, too.'

Damien's widow, Beth, was emptying the dishwasher when they went in, and she looked up with a smile.

'The kettle's on; I saw you coming,' she said.

Gideon thought she looked pale.

'Where's Freddy today?' he asked, to make conversation.

'Out somewhere with his granddad. He loves the farm. He's going to hate it when he has to go to school.'

'Freddy's going to have a little brother,' Tilly announced, taking a jar of instant coffee from the cupboard.

'You're pregnant, Beth? Congratulations!' Gideon said. 'I bet he's excited about that.'

'He keeps asking when we're going to get the baby,' Beth replied. 'As if we just have to pop out to the shops and buy one. I wish!'

'The other day he asked if you could get two, didn't he?' Tilly said, and Beth nodded, smiling.

'Buy one get one free at Mothercare,' Gideon suggested. 'Or a free baby coupon for every ten pounds spent at the super-market.'

They all laughed, and no mention was made of the tragedy of a child who would never know his father, and a father who'd died unaware.

As they chatted over coffee, Gideon's eye was caught by three photographs on the middle shelf of the pine dresser opposite him. One was of a boy jumping a breedy pony over a white gate; the second, of a group of fifteen or twenty young men posing for the camera in front of a stately home – some kind of team photo, Gideon supposed; and the third was of a much younger Damien, standing with his arm round a fair-haired boy of perhaps fifteen or sixteen, with a wayward fringe and a shy smile.

'Damien and Marcus,' Tilly said, seeing his interest.

'I wondered if it was. Doesn't Marcus look like Freddy?'

'Freddy's the image of him,' she agreed. 'That was taken the day before he went off to the Olympics training camp. He was terribly nervous but determined to go through with it. Damien kept telling him he'd be OK, and I think he'd have done anything to earn his big brother's respect. I don't think Damien ever really forgave himself when . . . well, you know.'

'He looks very young.'

'Actually, he was almost eighteen, though I admit he doesn't look it. He never had half the confidence that Damien had; he was much more sensitive. If only we'd known just *how* sensitive . . .'

'And the group picture?' Gideon asked.

'Taken at the camp. They held it at Ponsonby Castle; lovely place. And the one on the end is Marcus, competing at the Junior Championships.'

'How did he get into pentathlon? It's not a sport you hear of every day, is it? In fact, usually not from one Olympics to the next.'

'No. His school was very much into it,' Tilly said. 'You know how some schools are into rowing or rugby? Well, his was into pentathlon. In fact, they said three out of the four Olympic team members were old boys of his school, that year. Marcus could already ride and he was a very good runner and swimmer; no doubt the masters were rubbing their hands in glee when he came along. He really was very good; tipped for the team. But to be honest, I always wondered if he had enough competitive spirit to make the very top. I guess we'll never know.'

Gideon would have liked to hear more about Marcus, as it had been him that both Bentley and Stephenson had mentioned, but he had no wish to delve into what had to be very painful memories for Tilly.

Beth changed the subject, asking about their progress with Luigi, and the moment passed.

By the time Gideon drove away from Puddlestone Farm, he was in two minds about whether to ring Angie Bowen and excuse himself from helping out with her farrier-phobic horse. His head was aching fiercely once again and he felt dog-tired, but he hated to let her down.

Maybe the horse would behave itself and the whole business would be over in half an hour or so, he thought with little optimism, as he painfully hauled the Land Rover's steering wheel round to send the vehicle in the direction of the Radcliffe Trust stables. Power-assisted steering had never seemed like such a good idea as it did now.

At first it appeared that he might be in luck. The chestnut mare offered no objections to the farrier paring her hooves and tidying them up with the rasp in readiness to fit the shoes. She even stood quietly while the man tapped her feet with the hammer.

Angie looked pleased.

'Seems pretty quiet,' the farrier grunted, fishing a glowing shoe from the white-hot heart of the mobile forge in the back of his van, and doing a little preparatory shaping on the anvil.

From that point onward, things went sharply downhill. From the moment the farrier approached with the hot shoe the mare began to look anxious, but the problem came when he pressed the metal to her hoof. With a sizzle, a cloud of acrid smoke began to billow through and around his arms and the chestnut stood straight up on her hind legs, pulling her foreleg free of the farrier's grasp and almost ripping the lead rein out of Gideon's hands.

The farrier swore and dodged out from under the flailing hooves, and the horse touched down and rose again, her eyes white-rimmed and fearful. She repeated the action three or four times more in quick succession, rising a little less high each time, until Gideon was able to step forward and put his hand on her neck, soothing her with his voice.

The chestnut threw up her head but after a tense, twitchy moment, she stood still, nostrils flaring.

'Sorry, mate,' Gideon said quietly to the farrier, who retrieved the shoe with a pair of tongs and threw it back into the forge. 'Caught me napping.'

'Couldn't have stopped her, anyway,' the man said. 'They wanna stand up – they stand up.'

'Should think she must have got burned at some time, accidentally,' Angie said. 'Never had one react quite that badly before.'

'What d'you wanna do?' the farrier asked.

'Gideon?'

Gideon wanted nothing so much as to take a good, strong painkiller and lie down in a darkened room. The violence of the chestnut's protest had done his shoulders and headache no favours at all.

'OK. Let's see if we can get her front shoes on cold, and then do some work on the smoke problem another day. Perhaps we can borrow a bee-smoker, or something.'

It took three-quarters of an hour and an enormous amount of patience to get the mare to consent to having front shoes fitted and Gideon was regretting the suggestion long before they'd finished, but finally it was done.

They turned the mare out to roll in the sand of the school, and went into the staffroom.

'All I seem to have done today is drink coffee,' Gideon remarked, collapsing thankfully into one of the comfortable chairs. The farrier had gone on his way, already late for his next appointment, and they were the only occupants of the room.

'Well, if you'll pardon me saying so, you look as though you could do with it,' Angie said frankly. 'I was going to ask a favour, but I'm not sure I should, after all that. You look a bit under the weather.'

'Well, you can try but I'm not making any promises.'

'Actually, it wasn't for me, it was for a friend. Vanessa Tate – you met her last time you were here.'

'I remember.'

'She wondered if you'd call in and have a look at her dog . . .'

'Today?'

'Well, she said she'd be there all afternoon.'

At least it wasn't another wild and unpredictable horse, Gideon supposed. A dog, he might just be able to cope with.

But should he?

In view of yesterday's events and the accompanying warning, should he really go anywhere near Robin Tate or his wife, however innocent the context?

'Don't feel you have to, if you'd rather not; I just said I'd ask,' Angie said, seeing his hesitation and misunderstanding the reason for it. 'You don't mind?'

'No, of course not,' Gideon heard himself say.

'I'd have to show you where she lives, on the map.'

'OK.' Somehow, it seemed, his acquiescence had been assumed, and suppressing the memory of Eve's pleas, he nodded. After all, he was going to see a dog; Vanessa's husband probably wouldn't even be there.

TWELVE

THE TATES' HOME WAS, as Lloyd had once said, massive. Gideon drove the Land Rover between magnificent wrought-iron gates and stopped, his eyes taking in the three-storey stone-built manor house with its immaculate sweep of gravel and swathes of daffodils, and his mind toying with the idea that the people on the list were all in regular contact with one another, and this was a ruse to lure him in and shut him up for good.

But that was rubbish, of course. Why go to all the bother of delivering such an extravagant warning one day, if they'd been planning to bump him off the next? He'd been at their mercy – if they had wanted to take it further, they could have. He was getting fanciful. Besides, they'd hardly have involved Angie Bowen in their scheme, or invited him to Tate's own home.

Perhaps it was a test, to see whether he did, in fact, heed the warning, or whether he took the opportunity to question Robin Tate.

Gideon put his foot on the accelerator and moved forward slowly, as three springer spaniels and a golden retriever came bounding down the drive to meet him.

Perhaps it was just that they had a problem with one of their dogs . . .

Vanessa Tate came down the front steps of the house to meet him, slim, dark and attractive, as he remembered.

'Gideon, thank you so much for coming,' she called, as he got out of the car.

He was immediately mobbed by the four dogs, the spaniels jumping up and wagging ecstatically round his legs and the goldie standing back and barking his deep bark at one-second intervals.

'Oh, I'm sorry! Purdey, Minnie, get down! Lewis, do be quiet! Gideon, come on in. They'll settle in a minute.'

Gideon followed her through the imposing front doorway into an equally impressive hall, and from there to a kitchen straight out of a fitter's brochure: all gleaming chrome, cream-painted timber and polished marble.

'Have a seat, Gideon. Isn't it daft? No matter what size the house is, we always end up in the kitchen. Can I get you a coffee? Or tea?'

'Thanks, but no. I've just had one at Angie's. So what's your problem? Angie said it's a dog; not one of these surely?'

The four dogs had trooped in with them and two of the spaniels had already settled down on a purpose-built bed under one of the worktops. The goldie pushed forward for a fuss and was then supplanted by the third springer.

'You wait,' Vanessa said.

Sure enough, as Gideon began to stroke the spaniel's ears, the goldie backed off a step or two and the barking started again.

'Lewis, stop it!' his owner said after a moment. 'Minnie, go and lie down.'

The spaniel cast Gideon a wistful look and did as it was told, but the goldie carried on barking.

'Lewis! Go and lie down!' Vanessa raised her voice to be heard over the noise of the dog.

Lewis didn't take any notice whatever, each bark reverberating in Gideon's throbbing head like a physical blow. Next time he saw Logan he'd update him on the lingering effects of solvent abuse, he thought.

'It's classic attention-seeking behaviour, of course,' he said after a moment.

'Yes, I know. But what can I do about it?'

'Have you tried ignoring him?'

'Well, I've tried, but someone usually gives in before he does. Robin hasn't got a lot of patience, especially when we've got visitors. He usually gives Lewis a bone to shut him up.'

'Which is rewarding the behaviour,' Gideon pointed out.

'Well, shouting doesn't stop him.'

'For an attention-seeker, any attention is better than none. The best way to punish this kind of behaviour is to withdraw the very thing the dog wants: attention. So you just say firmly, "Lewis. No!" Then, if he carries on, take hold of his collar without looking at him, lead him out of the room and shut the door.'

'He'll just bark outside the door,' Vanessa stated.

'Well, let him.' Gideon got up and led Lewis from the room, shutting the door when he would have come back in. The dog immediately started barking again.

'Don't shout or talk to him,' he said returning to his seat. 'He'll have to stop sometime, and when he does, give it a moment and then quietly let him back in, tell him he's a good lad – without any fuss – and get him to lie down. Once he's settled down, you can give him a little attention. That way you're rewarding the good behaviour, not the bad.'

'I see what you mean. But he's very stubborn.'

'He won't learn overnight, the habit is too ingrained for that, and has been too successful. But you'll be surprised how soon he works out what's best for him. Dogs aren't stupid, in spite of what some people would have us believe. But you must stop your husband giving him bones to shut him up. What more could a dog ask for?'

Outside the door Lewis barked on, monotonously.

'Perhaps I will have that cuppa, if it's still on offer,' Gideon said.

'Tea, this time, and I don't suppose you've got a couple of paracetamol . . . ?'

'Oh, dear! Have you got a headache?' Vanessa asked sympathetically. 'I'm sorry. What rotten timing for a job like this!'

Five minutes later Lewis was still barking, although to Gideon's ears there was slightly less conviction in the tone.

'Of course, you can get collars that puff air or citronella at the dog whenever he barks, and I believe they do work, but I don't feel that Lewis would have learned anything if you did it that way, because you're treating the symptom, not the cause. I'd be surprised if a bright dog like Lewis didn't just find some other way to get your attention.'

'Oh, he would. It's funny, most people don't think he's very bright – just a big lovable teddy bear – but he is, you know. Oh, listen . . . He's stopped.'

He had indeed. After a couple of dejected whines they heard a deep sigh, and then the door rattled as Lewis flopped against it.

'OK, leave him a moment, then go and let him in,' Gideon told Vanessa. 'Don't make a big fuss. Just talk normally to him and tell him to go to his bed.'

Vanessa did as he suggested, and Lewis came in happily waving his plume of a tail. He walked up to Gideon who carefully didn't look at him, and on the second time of asking, the dog lay on his bed with a gusty sigh and put his nose on his paws.

'That's brilliant. I don't think it'll take him long to get the idea, but you must be consistent, and so must everyone else in the house. Dogs are just like kids, they're past masters at playing one person off against the other.'

'Robin does like to make a fuss of him,' Vanessa admitted. 'Lewis's his dog, really.'

'That's OK. I'm not saying don't make a fuss of him, far from it, but for the moment, it must be on your terms. Call him to you for a fuss, or go to him, but don't let him initiate it and make sure that he knows when it's over. It's best to find a word to end it: "OK lad, that's it," or something like that. It might seem hard, but it's kinder in the long run. Dogs need boundaries, just the same as everyone else.'

At that moment, an outer door banged and footsteps were heard approaching the kitchen.

'Where is everyone? Nessie? Lewis?'

The four dogs leapt up and when the door opened they were all there, fawning round the feet of a tall slim man of about Gideon's age, with thinning brown hair and glasses. He was wearing a pair of oil-stained jeans and a faded sweatshirt, and looked nothing like the successful City businessman Lloyd had described.

'Hello, my beauties!' he exclaimed, and the dogs went wild with delight.

'Robin, this is Gideon Blake. Remember, I told you about him?'

Her husband looked up.

'Oh, yes; the animal shrink,' Tate said, but his smile seemed friendly. 'Have you cured him?'

As if to answer him, Lewis backed off and began to bark once more.

'Apparently not,' Tate observed. 'There's nothing else for it; we'll have to wire his jaws together!'

Gideon smiled, tolerantly.

'When you want him to stop, tell him so, and send him to his bed.'

Tate tried it but, predictably, Lewis took no notice whatsoever, and Gideon suspected that the dog regarded him as a playmate rather than the pack leader.

Gideon looked at Vanessa.

'So, what are you going to do about it?'

To his gratification, she proceeded to follow his instructions to the letter, and within moments the spaniels were in their beds and Lewis was barking on the other side of the door once more.

'Poor old lad!' Robin said. 'He was just pleased to see me.'

'Shhh!' his wife said.

Gideon could see that training the husband might be more time-consuming than training the dog.

It took slightly longer for Lewis to calm down this time, but calm down he did, and went to his bed when he was told, with no more than a sideways look at Robin.

'Yup, he's bright, all right,' Gideon said with satisfaction. 'And you did that exactly right. You wouldn't believe how long it takes to get through to some people. The dogs themselves are a doddle!'

He refused a second cup of tea, saying he had to be on his way, but somehow motorbikes crept into the conversation, and before he knew it he was having a conducted tour of Robin Tate's collection of new and antique machines, which he kept in a purpose-built stone barn.

'You like?' Tate asked, as Gideon gazed in admiration at a 1948 Ariel Square Four.

'Oh, yes.'

Tate grinned.

'I thought you did. You've turned a particularly interesting shade of green.'

Gideon laughed. By the time he tore himself away, some three-quarters of an hour later, he and Tate were well on the way to becoming friends, and had made tentative plans to meet up for a ride one day and take Vanessa and Eve out for a meal.

'Funny, your name came up in conversation the other day,' Gideon said as they strolled out to the Land Rover. 'Lloyd mentioned you – do you remember Henry Lloyd-Ellis? Can't remember how we got round to it, but we were talking about pentathlon, and he said you were on the bronze medal team in Dubai.' He could hardly tell Tate he'd done an Internet search.

'Lloyd? Haven't seen him for years. Yes, he tried out for the team that year and was absolutely gutted when he wasn't selected. Should have been really, on merit, but Harry Saddler – the coach – picked a young team, and Lloyd was five or six years older than most of us.'

Hoping his instincts weren't wide of the mark, Gideon took a chance.

'Adam Tetley was on the team, too, wasn't he? Did you know they've arrested him for Damien Daniels' murder?'

'Yes, I heard. Frankly, I find that hard to believe. Adam was always a bit of a chancer, but there was no real harm in him, I would have sworn to it.'

'They found the gun.'

'Yes, I know. Do you know him, then?'

Gideon shook his head.

'No. I know – knew – Damien, and I know his sister, too. That family has had more than their fair share of tragedy.'

'You mean Marcus, I suppose? Yeah, that was awful. I didn't know him well, because he was quite a bit younger than me, but it affected everyone at the camp. It was bound to. Morale wasn't good anyway that year.'

'Why not?'

'One of the coaches had a sadistic streak – at least, that was how it seemed – and a lot of the younger lads were terrified of him.'

'Marcus, too?'

'Difficult to say. As I said, I didn't know him very well, but in view of what happened it looks as though he must have been.'

'Was there a chap called Sam Bentley at the camp, too?' Gideon couldn't resist asking, in spite of what Eve had said. He thought Tate looked at him a little more closely.

'There might have been,' he said slowly. 'There were around twenty of us; I can't remember all the names. He certainly wasn't picked for the team. Why the interest?'

Gideon shrugged, his hand on the door of the Land Rover. 'Just something someone said.'

'I see.' Tate looked at his watch. 'Look, sorry, I'd better go. We're going out to dinner with friends tonight.'

'Of course. Sorry.'

'No worries. We'll go for that ride one day though, OK?'

Gideon slept long and deeply that night, and woke to the sound of his telephone ringing. He opened a blurry eye and picked up the receiver, his bedside clock telling him that it was ten past ten.

'Gideon?' It was Logan.

'Hi, Mark.' Gideon propped himself up on one elbow.

'You sound half asleep.'

'That's because I am. What's doing?'

'Not a lot. I called in a favour and got one of the CSI boys to dust the fencer and battery but they didn't turn up much – a few partial prints but nothing very recent. It looks as though your guys kept their gloves on the whole time. I ran a check on the serial number and apparently that particular model went out of production in '78.'

'Damn.'

'How're you feeling? Been to see a doctor?'

'No. It's getting better all the time,' Gideon said truthfully.

'Nothing else you feel you want to tell me?'

'Not at the moment.'

'Done any more detective work?'

'Not really . . .'

'Listen Gideon, you want to be very careful. Someone on your list of suspects has obviously got a great deal to lose. I'm within an inch of giving what I've got to Rockley and letting him drum it out of you, and if I didn't know how stubborn you can be, that's probably what I'd do.'

Gideon felt Logan overrated his resilience. Having experienced the hours of questioning on the day of Damien's murder, he wasn't at all sure he wouldn't just hand everything over to Rockley, if it came to that, and let Lloyd take his chances.

'I don't intend taking any unnecessary risks,' he assured him. 'And I promise that as soon as I *can* tell, you'll be the first to know.'

'Well, I hope you know what you're doing, mister.'

I *wish* I knew what I was doing! Gideon thought.

Gideon finally made it to the Priory around midday and got a mild shock when he found Giles in the yard, in company with a man dressed in a navy blue uniform. Even though he had so recently spoken to Logan, he thought for a moment the policeman had reneged on his word and told Rockley after all. Then he noticed the dark blue van parked by the house wall with *Norris Security Systems* in white script on the side.

'Gideon. Glad you're here,' Giles said, seeing him. 'Could do with your input. Pippa's out exercising with Lloyd. This is John Norris, from Norris Security – you know – come to see about the new alarm system.'

'Hi,' Gideon said, walking forward and offering a hand. 'John Norris? Family, then.'

'Yes, Julian was my brother.'

'I'm sorry.'

John Norris pursed his lips and inclined his head. 'It happens.'

'Well, I'm not sure what good I can be,' Gideon said. 'But I'll give it my best shot. Pippa's the one with the plan.'

'My fault,' the man confessed. 'I'm early. Finished this morning's job sooner than I thought.'

He proceeded to run through the basics of yard security, giving his opinion of what was necessary, and sensibly joining with Gideon in toning down Giles' more far-fetched suggestions, until Pippa and Lloyd returned twenty minutes later.

Gideon had gone to the Priory with the idea of spending an enjoyable hour or two riding and working with Nero, who was due to go home within the week, and joining Pippa and Giles for lunch somewhere along the way, as was his habit. It soon became clear that, with the exception of the lunch part of it, this plan was doomed to failure. After John Norris had surveyed the yard and the house, and accepted their invitation to bring his sandwich lunch into the warmth of the Priory kitchen, Giles suggested that Gideon show him the Gatehouse.

'I'd do it myself, but I've got someone coming about a possible Sparkler order.'

'So have we actually decided which level of security to go for?' Norris enquired, patting his bewildering sheaf of price lists, order forms and brochures.

'Well, more or less, but if you leave the details with me I'd just like to go over them again, to get it all quite straight in my mind,' Giles said.

'Ah,' the security man said. 'Normally I would, but for some reason I've come out without any copies and I've got another customer to see after I finish here. I'll have to mail them to you.'

'Oh. OK.' Giles hated to have to wait once he'd set his mind on something.

Probably because he'd never really had to, Gideon mused, watching him. Just now, though, it had worked in Gideon's favour. Ever since he'd found Norris with Giles he'd been grappling with the problem of how to wangle a visit to Julian Norris' widow, and now he saw his chance.

'Actually, I could drop in and pick them up, if you like. I've got to go out that way this afternoon,' he said, with a shameful disregard for the truth. He'd already gleaned the information that John's sister-in-law ran the company from an office at her home in Sturminster Newton.

'Oh, OK then. I'll give Marion a ring and let her know you're coming,' Norris said, plainly a little bemused by the unexpected urgency of events.

When Norris had finished at the Gatehouse, Gideon set out for Sturminster Newton with a scribbled note of directions to the office of Norris Security Systems and absolutely no idea of what he was going to say to Julian Norris' widow.

The office was in a single-storey, flat-roofed extension to Marion Norris' modern detached home, and reached by a green-painted wrought-iron gate in a wall on the right-hand side.

As Gideon let himself through the gate he was greeted by a pair of snuffling Pekinese dogs, who thoroughly investigated the hems of his jeans and then accompanied him down the path to the office, yapping alternately to announce his presence.

They stopped yapping when he pressed the buzzer beside the office door, standing with their heads on one side, as if waiting to see who came. Gideon had to press it again before it was answered, and then a stocky, thirty-something woman with a shock of frizzy red hair appeared, a phone wedged between her ear and her shoulder.

'Listen! I have a customer waiting for us to complete their installation before they go away on holiday; what am I supposed to tell them?' She stood back and waved Gideon in. 'No, don't give me that! We promised we'd be finished in time on the strength of your promise to deliver the unit, and now my company is in danger of failing to honour its contract because of some cock-up at your end! . . . I don't care; that's your problem, not mine . . . Well, try somewhere else then. Send a courier to pick it up. If you want to keep our account, you'd better do whatever it takes, because I don't intend letting my customers down . . . Yes. Well, see that you do . . . All right, Jim. Speak to you later. Bye.'

She took the receiver away from her ear, glared at it as if it were the inefficient Jim, and said, 'Bloody cowboys! I won't use them again.'

Gideon wasn't sure what to say, so he merely waited, looking around the square room at the desk, chairs, cupboards and filing cabinets that were common to all businesses, small or large. On one wall was a display of various alarm components and warning notices, one other was lined with shelves bearing row upon row of box files, and most of the floor was covered by a pile of cardboard boxes and paper packages, apparently just delivered.

After a moment the red-haired woman put the handset down, shook her head and held out her hand, smiling briefly.

'Marion Norris. Sorry. I'm just having one of those days. You've come for the brochures, haven't you? Well, I'm afraid I haven't got round to sorting them out yet.' She indicated the chaos on the floor. 'They'll be in one of those. Are you in a dreadful hurry?'

Gideon assured her that he wasn't.

'Well, then, would you mind very much if I made a cup of tea first? I haven't had one since before lunch, and I'm parched. You'll have one too?'

'Well . . . thanks.' Gideon didn't really need one, but the chance to linger was too good to miss. He'd been afraid that Marion Norris would open the door, hand him the leaflets and expect him to be on his way.

'Come in, come in,' she said, going through an inner door into her kitchen, and Gideon followed her, thinking she was remarkably trusting – if not foolhardy – to invite a complete stranger into her house, even if she had been expecting him to call.

At a table in the adjoining breakfast room two young boys sat doing their homework, surrounded by textbooks, pens and crayons. Gideon was impressed, and said so.

'They know they have to do their homework before they do anything else,' Marion said. 'If they know where they stand, they knuckle down quite happily. I use the same system for kids, horses and dogs, really, and it seems to work.'

'Do you ride?' Gideon asked, seizing the opportunity to steer the subject into fruitful territory.

'I do, but not as much as I'd like to. I have a horse at livery, half a mile down the road, but there never seem enough hours in the day. And now there's this . . .' She was wearing a long denim skirt and a loose tunic, which she smoothed down before patting her abdomen.

'A baby? I'm sorry, I thought . . .' Gideon stumbled to a halt, wondering if he'd been mistaken, and this wasn't Julian Norris' widow after all.

'John and I are planning to get married next year,' she stated, with just the merest hint of defensiveness in her eyes. 'We thought we'd keep it in the family, you know. Don't have to change the letterheads that way.'

The jokey declaration made Gideon think that Marion had become used to dealing with a measure of censure over the matter.

'Congratulations! He seems like a nice guy,' he said, wondering if the new development had any bearing on the list. He couldn't see how it could have, for the fact remained that Julian's was the one name that had been crossed off. The initials could have been those of John Norris, but the fact that they *had* been crossed off appeared to indicate that Damien's beef had been solely with Julian.

'He's a smashing guy,' she said, but without the shining-eyed enthusiasm of the newly infatuated.

Gideon supposed that she must have known her brother-in-law too long for that, especially if they had worked together.

'I don't think I could have got through last year without him,' she said frankly, pouring hot water into mugs. 'Well, the last few years really. Julian wasn't the easiest man to live with – not that it was his fault,' she added loyally. 'Depression is an illness, just like any other, but . . .'

'But it's not, is it?' Gideon said. 'Not like any other, I mean. It affects everything, your relationship, your social life, and it changes everything. Chronic depression is more like alcoholism or Alzheimer's.'

Marion Norris paused in the act of fishing a tea bag out on a spoon and turned to look at him.

'That's it. That's exactly it. Friends are very supportive at first, but after a while they stop dropping in and the invitations stop coming. You can't blame them, can you? The last thing you want when you arrange a dinner party is someone who's uncomfortable to be around. And he'd started to drink, too. The family became more and more segregated. It was no wonder I looked to John for support, was it?'

'It would have been more surprising if you hadn't,' Gideon agreed.

'Exactly,' she said, and then seemed to remember that she was talking to someone who was, to all intents and purposes, a complete stranger. She blushed slightly and turned back to the mugs on the worktop. 'Oh, God! I don't know why I'm telling you all this, you must think me very odd.'

Gideon didn't know why she was telling him either, but it wasn't the first time it had happened to him by any means. It was as if there was some kind of label pinned to him that he couldn't see, which proclaimed, '*Over here! Shoulder to cry on!*'

'No, I don't think you're odd,' he said. And then, because this was a chance such as he couldn't afford to pass up, 'Had he been drinking the night he died?'

'No.' She handed him a mug. 'Oh, sorry! Sugar?'

'No, thanks, that's fine.'

Marion led the way back into the office, and Gideon thought she wasn't going to elaborate any further, but after clearing a seat for him to sit on, she did.

'No. He hadn't. It's the first thing they check, isn't it. That and drugs. But he hadn't been drinking; he never did when he was working. It was the only time he really held it together.'

'He'd been to visit Damien, hadn't he? Tilly told me.'

'Oh, you know Tilly? God! That was a terrible thing, wasn't it?' Marion sat in another seat, wedging herself between two packages.

'I was with Damien when it happened,' Gideon told her, more to ensure that the thread of conversation continued than for any sensation value. 'I was helping him with one of his horses.'

'Were you? What a horrible shock. They *have* been unlucky, haven't they? What with Marcus and now this. I mean, it's so easy to feel sorry for yourself, but there's always someone worse off, isn't there? I knew them quite well at one time. Julian used to be very friendly with the family and Marcus' death hit him very hard. Especially as there was a kind of understanding that he'd keep an eye on the boy while he was away from home. Not that Damien ever blamed him, but he blamed himself. He was like that. Dwelt on things far too much.'

'Wait a minute – your husband was at the training camp with Marcus?'

'Yes, he was. It was his last year in competition. After what happened, he lost heart and gave up pentathlon.'

She sat silently for a moment, apparently lost in her memories.

'It was suicide, wasn't it?' Gideon prompted.

'What was?' Marion asked sharply.

'Marcus.'

'Oh, yes. Sorry. The thing is, after Julian's crash, somebody started a rumour that *that* was suicide, but there was absolutely no evidence. I mean, I know he was depressed, but that doesn't automatically mean that he took his own life. I didn't want the kids growing up with that hanging over their heads, but in the end they got to hear of it anyway from other children at their school. Of course, they were devastated – you know how cruel kids can be – and that made me really angry.'

Gideon had an idea that Marion Norris in a rage would be a force to be reckoned with.

'Anyway, the police were quite satisfied it was an accident,' she added with a touch of defiance. 'The thing was, he was supposed to be on his way home, but the accident happened in Winterbourne Whitechurch, and nobody knows why he was there. But he must have had a reason; maybe he was visiting a customer or something, who knows?'

'People are always looking for something to gossip about,' Gideon said, soothingly.

'Yeah, and now it's me and John,' she said, confirming Gideon's earlier supposition. 'Oh, well. You certainly get to know who your real friends are. But you were asking about Marcus; yes, he jumped off the top of some building after they'd all been out drinking one night. Some kind of ruin in the grounds of the castle they were staying at. No-one quite knows why, even to this day. He was the youngest at the camp and a couple of the other guys said he'd been a little homesick, but I can't see that that's a reason to kill yourself, can you? I mean, if the worst comes to the worst, you can always ask to go home, can't you?'

Gideon shrugged. 'Kids tend to get things way out of proportion, don't they? Maybe he was scared of letting everyone down, or maybe it was the drink that got to him; it can affect some people that way, especially if they're not used to it. Did Julian ever talk about it?'

Marion shook her red frizz. 'Not much. All I know is that they'd been out drinking and on the way home the boy went off on his own. Nobody knew what had happened until he didn't turn up back at their rooms and one of the coaches went looking. It was a horrible shock, but nobody's fault, as far as I can see. I never did succeed in getting Julian to see that, though.'

'Do the names Sam Bentley or Garth Stephenson mean anything to you?' Gideon asked. They were so far into confidences that he didn't feel that subtlety was called for.

Marion frowned. 'They do seem familiar. I think I've heard Julian mention them in the past. Sam Bentley, definitely. In fact, I think he might have been on that same course. Why?'

'Well, Tilly found a list of names in Damien's things and she has no idea what it's to do with, or even whether it's important or not. I said I'd try and find out, that's all.'

'Are you saying Julian was on it?'

'Yes, but crossed out.'

'Because of the crash.'

'I imagine so.'

'And what *have* you found out?'

'Not much.' His recent experiences had made Gideon cautious. 'I think I shall have to admit defeat.'

Marion put her cup down, apparently losing interest.

'Well, I suppose I'd better try and find those brochures for you – no, you sit there and finish your tea.'

She rummaged among the parcels, keeping up a running commentary, and, after a minute or two, pulled out a medium-sized cardboard box from the middle of the pile.

'This could be it. God! They really went to town on the sticky tape, didn't they? Anyone would think they were being dropped in by helicopter, the way this is wrapped! It's always one extreme or the other. Would you be a love and pass that knife from the shelf behind you?'

Gideon turned to locate it, and his eye fell on a row of box files, each labelled neatly in black ink. He picked up the Stanley knife that lay in front of them, and then paused to give the files a second look. The writing touched a chord in his memory but – like meeting someone where you don't expect to – he couldn't remember where he'd seen it before.

'Whose handwriting is that on the files?' he asked, leaning forward to hand the knife to Marion.

She looked.

'Julian's. Why?'

'It's beautiful. I wondered if it was yours.'

'I wish! No, mine's very ordinary. Julian did quite a bit of calligraphy – even the illuminated stuff. I'll show you some in a moment, if you like.'

'Thanks, but actually, I'd better be on my way. I've taken up too much of your time as it is.'

'Not at all. It's been nice to talk.'

As Gideon left the NSS offices five minutes later with a handful of brochures, Marion Norris was already back to business, sorting through paperwork with her mobile phone tucked under her ear. She didn't even look up when he raised a hand before shutting the door.

Gideon walked back to the Land Rover, busily assimilating the new information he'd gleaned. Logan had said to find a common denominator for two or three of the names and then try to see where the others fitted in. It was looking pretty certain that the common denominator was the Modern Pentathlon and, more specifically, the training course before the Dubai Olympic Games, in which it seemed Lloyd, Robin Tate, Adam Tetley, Sam Bentley and Julian Norris had all taken part. That just left the schoolteacher, but Gideon was willing to bet that if he dug a little deeper, he would find that Stephenson had been there too.

The only connection with Damien that they all shared appeared to be Marcus, who'd tragically committed suicide on that same course. Marcus, the sensitive young man who Gideon suspected had kept a diary detailing the bullying he'd suffered while he was away from home.

Gideon got into the Land Rover and shut the door, putting the sheaf of brochures on the passenger seat.

There was something staring him in the face but he just wasn't seeing it. He decided it was time he took another look at the photocopied page and, if necessary, ask Tilly if she had any idea where Marcus' diary might be.

He sat gazing through the windscreen at a patch of tulips in the Norrises' front garden, but they only registered as a red blur as his thoughts raced this way and that. The people named on the list knew he had a copy of it; what if they thought he had the diary, too? Was that why he'd been attacked? But if that was the case, why hadn't they tried to make him give it up?

Gideon ran his fingers through his hair and dragged his gaze back into focus. Maybe he was getting carried away. Tetley had shot Damien. The police had incontrovertible evidence against him; they had the gun.

But what if he hadn't been in it alone? There were five names on that list, if you discounted Norris. What if more than one were involved? What if they *all* were?

Oh, God! Lloyd!

It was high time he confronted Lloyd.

With this in mind, he backed the Land Rover out of the drive and set off back to the Priory.

The sky had clouded over while he'd been in talking to Marion Norris and, by the time Gideon turned into the long winding lane that led to Tarrant Grayling, a steady drizzle had set in and patchy fog had begun to form in the river valleys.

About a mile from the Gatehouse, where the road was not much more than a single track, he saw a large green and yellow tractor nosing out of a field gateway.

'No,' he muttered. 'Stay there. Oh, you imbecile!'

When he was not more than twenty yards distant, the tractor lumbered out in front of Gideon's Land Rover, coming to a halt diagonally across the tarmac so that he was forced to slow up and stop.

'Oh, bugger!' he muttered. He repressed an urge to lean on the horn, knowing that with some farmers that was all that was needed to make them go even slower. Hopefully, the driver was just pausing to shut the gate.

Sure enough, the cab door opened and a figure in a grubby green boiler suit jumped down, raised a hand in Gideon's direction, and hurried back through the gateway, his cap pulled well down against the rain.

'Yeah, well, get on with it.' Gideon sighed and tapped his fingers on the steering wheel, listening to the irritating squeak and scrape of the wipers. On each side of the narrow lane, soft grassy verges and shaggy unkempt hedges put paid to any thoughts of squeezing past, four-wheeled drive or no, and as there was no sensible alternative route to the Gatehouse, he had no choice but to wait.

In his wing mirror he caught sight of the approaching headlights of another vehicle, which in due course pulled up behind the Land Rover and waited in its turn.

Peering through his streaky windscreen, Gideon watched in vain for the return of the tractor driver and suddenly the vehicle started to rock as Zebedee broke out in a furious spate of barking.

'Quiet, Zeb!' he said, his patience beginning to wear thin. Where was the bloody man?

A movement in his wing mirror caught his eye and he saw that the occupant of the car behind had got out and was walking forward to see what the hold-up was. Gideon wound down his window a little but as he drew level, instead of leaning down to speak to him, the man yanked the Land Rover door open, put a meaty fist in to grasp Gideon's jacket and hauled him out onto the verge.

Caught entirely unawares, Gideon went sprawling in the long wet grass and, in the back of the Land Rover, Zebedee went absolutely crazy.

THIRTEEN

G IDEON'S FIRST INSTINCT WAS to get to his feet as
soon as possible but the owner of the meaty fist plainly
had other ideas, and he found himself flattened, face down,
amongst last year's bramble runners at the foot of the hedge, with
what felt like a knee in the small of his back.

His first thought was to curse himself for a stupid, unwary fool.
It wasn't as if he hadn't been warned, for God's sake!

There was no sense in struggling. It was impossible to mount
any form of resistance from the position he found himself in.
Shouting was still an option, but there was only the tractor driver
within earshot, and Gideon wasn't naïve enough to continue
supposing that the blockage was anything other than part of the
whole set-up.

'You jest lie still, matey,' a rough voice advised unneccessarily,
then shouted, 'Hurry up, for Christ's sake!'

Suffering from a severely restricted lung capacity, all Gideon
could hear for a moment was his own breathing and the patter
of the worsening rain. Then, above it, came the sound of footsteps running on the road.

'Right,' his captor said briskly. 'Let's get 'im up before some-body comes. But watch 'im though!'

Gideon's upper arms were grasped and the weight lifted cautiously from his back, but if they expected him to scramble instantly to his feet, they were forced to think again. As they pulled on his arms he remained limp, the whole of his six foot four, fourteen-stone frame dragging downwards.

One of the men muttered a curse.

'Come on, get up, you bastard!'

They hauled him to his knees, but hadn't got the height to raise him any further. Gideon let his head slump forward, as if unconscious, hoping that if they thought him incapacitated, they'd be lulled into a false sense of security and lower their guard.

'What's the matter with 'im?'

'Buggered if I know. C'mon, stand up! Stop fuckin' around!'

The rain was fairly pelting down now, soaking coldly through Gideon's guernsey and running through his hair. It drummed on the hollow metal of the vehicles and blattered on the road, and it was a moment before he recognised the swishing hiss for what it was . . .

An approaching car.

'Shit! Someone's coming! Leave him and go. Quickly!'

Abruptly, Gideon's arms were released and he had to put his hands down to save himself from falling on his face in the grass once more.

He scrambled to his feet and raced after the two men, who were both heading for the dirty blue hatchback, but they weren't hanging around. When Gideon was still some yards away they were in the car and had the engine started, and as he came level with the driver's door, the hatchback went into rapid reverse and the approaching Range Rover had to swerve to avoid being hit.

The blue car reversed into a gateway, then drove out and away with a spray of mud and a squeal of tyres.

'Bugger!' Gideon said forcefully, staring up into the rain. He hadn't even been able to read the number plate of the blue car, due to a combination of mud and the rapidly failing visibility. He thought back over the last couple of minutes. '*Matey*' the man had called him. Where had he heard that before?

'Gideon? Are you OK? What the hell was all that about?'

The Range Rover had stopped a little way behind his own vehicle, with two wheels sunk into the soft grass of the verge, and as luck would have it, its driver was Lloyd. He came striding towards Gideon with a look of bewilderment on his face.

'Yeah, I'm OK,' Gideon told him. 'Just cold, wet and distinctly pissed off!'

'So what was all that about? What did they want?'

Gideon came to an abrupt decision. 'Look, it's a long story. You're getting wet and I'm getting wetter. Why don't you come back to the Gatehouse and I'll try and explain.' He looked at the tractor, still blocking the lane. 'I don't suppose you know how to drive one of those things . . . ?'

Lloyd did, and while he set about moving it off the road so they could get past, Gideon rang the police and reported it abandoned.

The Gatehouse was blessedly warm and dry after the foggy dampness outside. Gideon showed Lloyd through to the kitchen, where Elsa took one look at him, jumped off the Aga and disappeared into the sitting room.

Gideon laughed. 'Don't take it personally. She's a bit set in her ways, and not too fond of strangers. It took her almost a month to accept Eve.'

'That's all right. I'm not really a cat person, anyway. Dogs are more my line. Aren't they, boy?' Lloyd added, scratching Zebedee behind the ears. The dog sat down beside him and assumed an expression of euphoria.

'Something to drink? Coffee, tea? Something stronger?'

'The last would be nice. I've only got to drive up to the house.'

'Think I might join you. I'm not sure tea would quite hit the mark.'

Gideon fetched a half-bottle of malt from the sitting room, soothing the cat's ruffled nerves as he passed. He put the bottle and two glasses down on the table beside Lloyd.

'Help yourself. There's water in the tap, and ice in the top of the fridge. No soda, I'm afraid, but you might find lemonade somewhere. Look, I'm just going to go and put something dry on. Won't be a minute.'

When he came back downstairs in a clean pair of jeans and a dry rugby shirt, Gideon found Lloyd leaning back in his chair, with a large measure of what looked like neat whisky in his tumbler. He reached for the remaining glass and poured himself one.

'So, tell me what I walked — or drove — in on,' Lloyd said. 'Those two men looked as though they meant business. Who were they?'

'I wish I knew.' Gideon paused, looking thoughtfully at Pippa's boyfriend, and then decided to go for it. 'If I gave you the names Sam Bentley, Garth Stephenson, Robin Tate, Adam Tetley and Julian Norris, what would you make of it?'

'Sam Bentley? You were asking about him the other day, weren't you? I'm not sure about him, but the others all did pentathlon at around about the time I did.'

'Even Garth?'

'Yes.' Lloyd nodded.

'Were they all on that training course you went on?'

'Yes, they were. Why?'

'But not Sam Bentley?'

'I'm not sure. There were about twenty of us and I don't remember all the names. Look, what's this all about?'

Gideon took a deep breath.

'Remember that list of numbers and letters that we found in Nero's things? Those were all initials and telephone numbers. Yours were on there, too.'

'*Mine* were? How come I didn't notice that?'

'It was the way it was written out.' Gideon explained. 'Actually it was your old number — your wife's.'

Lloyd looked mystified.

'Why on earth would Damien have had all our names on a list? It doesn't make sense.'

'I hoped *you* might be able to tell *me* . . .'

'Well – no, I'm sorry, I can't.'

'I – er, wondered if it could have anything to do with Marcus . . .'

'Marcus Daniels?' Lloyd sounded incredulous. 'But he committed suicide.'

'On that training course . . .'

'Well – yes, but the list must be ages old, if it's got anything to do with that business. I mean, that was all – what? – twelve or fifteen years ago. And as I said, there were twenty or more of us. Christ! I haven't seen those guys for donkey's years. Some of them could be dead by now – well, yes, Julian Norris *is*, isn't he?'

'Ah, but his name was crossed off, so that argues that the list wasn't so very old, or at least that it had been updated. And however out of date it might be, someone would still much rather I didn't ask questions about it.'

'Someone on the list?'

'Well . . . yes, I suppose so. I just assumed it was.' Gideon hadn't considered the alternative. The idea made the whole thing even more worrying. If not one of the names on the list, then where the hell would he begin looking?

'So what do *you* think it's all about?'

'Blackmail?' Gideon tossed the word into the conversation like a stone into a pool, and watched to see what ripples it produced.

Lloyd appeared momentarily stunned.

'*Blackmail?* But don't you think I'd know something about that – as my name's on the list, I mean?'

'And you don't.'

Lloyd shook his head emphatically.

'*No.* And while we're on the subject, what am I – we – supposed to have done that we're so ashamed of?'

Gideon hesitated. This was where it could get awkward.

'I don't know. I haven't got that far. I'm probably barking up the wrong tree altogether, but there's definitely something to hide, because I've been warned off – and pretty forcefully, too.'

'You mean those men today?' Lloyd asked, watching him closely.

'No, it was a couple of days ago. I got a call to go and see a pony and found two men waiting for me, instead. It was obviously a set-up. I'm not sure whether it was the same guys, it might have been, but there was no doubt about the message – stop poking your nose in where it's not wanted, or else!'

Lloyd took a long considering sip of his whisky.

'You told the police, of course.'

'Yeah, I did.' Gideon didn't elaborate.

'Good. And?'

'They're looking into it but there isn't a lot to go on.'

'And what did *they* make of the list?'

'I didn't show it to them.'

'Why ever not?'

'Because I didn't want to make more trouble for Tilly and her family,' Gideon hedged. He fancied Lloyd relaxed a degree or two at the words, but then, guilty or not, he wouldn't welcome the publicity that a police investigation would bring.

'So why didn't you tell anyone about the attack?'

'I told Eve. There didn't seem any point in worrying Pippa and Giles.' Gideon drained the last of his drink and stood up, collecting Lloyd's empty tumbler along with his own on his way to the sink, and rather hoping he'd take the hint and be on his way.

No such luck.

'So how long have you known about the list – the names and numbers, I mean?' Lloyd asked.

'Oh, not long.'

'Why didn't you tell me? Don't you think I had a right to know, as my name's on there?' Lloyd sounded a bit peeved, and Gideon couldn't really blame him.

'I wanted to try and find out what it was all about, first.'

'Well, I might have been able to tell you.'

'Or not,' Gideon couldn't resist saying.

'As it turns out, but you didn't know that. Don't you trust me?'

About as far as I could spit you, Gideon thought, but he merely said, 'I'm telling you now.'

'So have you spoken to the others? What did *they* make of it?'

'I spoke to a couple of them,' Gideon said, deliberately vague. He shrugged. 'They either didn't know, or they weren't telling; it's difficult to say which. But one of them must know something, else why go to the trouble of warning me off?'

Lloyd was silent for a moment, and Gideon leaned back against the range, enjoying the warmth and thinking over what had been said. If Lloyd knew anything, he was hiding it well. He'd volunteered the information about the connection between the names, and seemed more upset about being kept in the dark than at the prospect of Gideon's investigations.

'Well, all I can say is if there is something going on, nobody's let me in on the secret,' Lloyd said suddenly. 'It's strange that Tetley's name is on the list. I suppose you didn't get a chance to speak to him?'

'No, I didn't.'

'So what are you going to do now? It seems to me that whatever reason Damien might have had for making that list, it's probably died with him. Is it really worth getting yourself beaten up for?'

Gideon shook his head and sighed.

'Probably not. I really don't know any more.'

'Will you give the list to the police?'

'I haven't decided. I guess I should ask Tilly what she wants to do.'

'Well, speaking for myself, I'd just as soon you didn't,' Lloyd said, getting to his feet. 'Give it to the police, I mean. The less of that kind of attention I get, the better it is for my political career. But, of course, that's purely selfish. If you think it's important . . .' He smiled. 'Well, I guess I'd better be going. Pippa's expecting me.'

Lloyd walked through to the hall, took his coat off its hook and then paused with his hand on the front-door handle.

'Look,' he said, with a touch of awkwardness, 'I know Pippa's pretty special to you, but she is to me, too, and I will take good care of her, I can promise you that. The thing is, we're not saying anything just yet, but we intend getting married when my divorce comes through, and I'm going to do everything I can to make her happy.'

'Married? Congratulations!' Gideon managed a smile, even though he had the strangest sensation that someone had clamped an iron band round his heart and lungs. 'What does Giles say to that?'

'Actually, we haven't told him yet. I shouldn't really have said anything to you, so don't breathe a word, eh? Not even to Pippa. I just wanted you to know that I'm serious.'

Gideon shrugged. 'It's none of *my* business – surely you should be talking to Giles, not me. But, anyway, I hope you'll be very happy.'

He opened the door and stood to one side.

'Oh, I'm sure we will. Well, see you later. Let me know if you figure anything else out, yeah? And if you want any help . . .'

Gideon watched as Lloyd climbed into the Range Rover and disappeared up the drive to the Priory. Then, stepping backwards into the hall, he slammed the heavy oak front door with as much force as he could muster, causing Zebedee to retreat into the kitchen with his tail between his legs.

At the Priory, the next morning, Pippa seemed a little out of sorts. Her reply to Gideon's usual greeting was decidedly short on warmth and her conversation was stilted, to say the least.

'Have I done something to upset you?' he enquired eventually, tired of trying to draw her out. He was helping her prepare the midday feeds.

'What, you mean apart from lying to me and sneaking around behind Lloyd's back?'

'Oh, he ran straight to you with that little lot, did he?'

'And why shouldn't he? Perhaps he felt I had a right to know!' she suggested icily, pausing with a scoopful of molassed chaff in her hand.

'And exactly when have I lied to you?'

'All along, it seems. Asking me if Lloyd had worked out what that list was about, when you knew all the time.'

'I didn't know *all the time*,' Gideon protested. 'And how is that lying? I just wanted to know if he'd made any sense of it, that's all.'

'You thought he was hiding something.'

'Is that what he told you?'

'He didn't have to. It's obvious, isn't it? Else why didn't you just ask him, instead of going to everyone else first? Maybe you wouldn't have got yourself beaten up, if you'd done that.'

'I didn't get beaten up. Anyway, I did ask Lloyd what he knew about Sam Bentley and Robin Tate, after hunting the other day. You were there, you heard me.'

'But you didn't say *why* you wanted to know.'

'Well, does it matter so much? Lloyd didn't seem too bothered when I told him last night. Why does it matter to you?'

'Because you've never liked him, and you'd love to find something against him, just so you could say "I told you so" to me!'

'Well, it's nice to know you've got such a flattering opinion of my character.' He picked up Nero's bucket and began to stir the feed with a wooden spoon.

'Well, you can't deny you've never liked him,' Pippa declared, turning slightly pink, but pressing on nevertheless.

'He's not my choice of a lifelong buddy, if that's what you mean, but that's got nothing to do with it. If you must know, I didn't bring the subject up because I thought you might take it the wrong way. Can't think why,' he added, turning away to pick up another feed bucket.

'Well, how am I supposed to take it when I find out that someone who's meant to be my friend is digging up dirt on my boyfriend? And what's this about blackmail? Who's blackmailing who? Damien?' she asked incredulously. 'Is that what you're trying to say? That he was going to blackmail the people on the list? That's ridiculous! For God's sake don't try that one on Tilly, it'd just about finish her!'

'Which is exactly the reason why I was trying to find out what it was all about before I said anything.' Gideon straightened up with a bucket in his hand. 'I didn't want anyone to get hurt. But if you want to believe I'd do it just to spite you and Lloyd, then you go ahead! And don't go thinking it makes any difference to me if you want to spend the rest of your life with him – I've got my own life to live.'

'With Eve.'

'Yes – *with Eve*,' he retorted, shaken by the depth of her indignation. 'Do you have a problem with that?'

'No. Why should I?'

'Well, you seem to have a problem with everything else I do.'

Gideon was aware the argument was degenerating into a childish slanging match, but he'd gone too far to draw back. Blast Lloyd and his tale-telling! He'd never fallen out with Pippa in such a wholesale fashion before. They'd had disagreements, certainly, but nothing like this.

'Perhaps it's a good thing Nero's going back tomorrow,' Pippa said, and the implication was plain: without Tilly's horse to work on, Gideon wouldn't necessarily have to visit the yard every day.

With an effort, Gideon finally regained control of himself, biting back the heated response he'd been on the point of uttering and gathering up four of the feed buckets. He'd been in danger of doing the very thing he'd been trying to avoid all this time.

'These are ready,' he said coolly.

Pippa stared angrily at him, conscious perhaps that in withdrawing quietly from the fray, Gideon had left her last stinging remark underlined. But she was clearly too steamed up to take it back. She picked up the remaining buckets and stalked past him out of the feed store.

Gideon's row with Pippa left him feeling uncharacteristically wound up for the rest of the day, and when Eve arrived in the evening she picked up on his mood straight away.

The truth was, he was annoyed with Pippa for suspecting him of base motives and equally annoyed with himself for allowing her to draw him into such an unproductive argument. They had both, he was sure, reacted in exactly the way that Lloyd had hoped they would, and that annoyed him most of all. In spite of his friendly overtures the evening before, Gideon had no doubt that Lloyd would like nothing better than to see them fall out. His frequent, overt demonstrations of affection towards Pippa showed his insecurity all too clearly.

'She'll come round.' Eve moved her fingers up the back of his neck and into his hair. She'd arrived at seven thirty with tortellini and garlic bread from her local deli, and they'd eaten well, before refilling their wine glasses and moving into the sitting room.

He rolled his head on the sofa-back to look at her.

'Sorry. Am I being rotten company?'

'Just a bit preoccupied, that's all. Tell me again about yesterday.'

Gideon repeated what he'd told her earlier, making light of the affair and merely saying that Lloyd had turned up in time to save his bacon, albeit in a passive manner.

Eve wasn't deceived.

'I don't know what you're not telling me,' she said shrewdly, 'but I have absolutely no sympathy anyway. I warned you not to go on poking your nose in where it so obviously wasn't wanted, but I might just as well have saved my breath.'

'I didn't intend to investigate any further, but the opportunity was there and it seemed a shame not to take it,' Gideon said apologetically.

'Make a good epitaph, that,' Eve mused, nestling closer and resting her head on his shoulder. '*It was a shame*. So, what did you find out?

Do you think this Norris woman was having an affair before her husband committed suicide? We do agree he committed suicide, right?'

'Yeah, it looks like it. But if she *was* getting it on with the brother-in-law, I'm not sure we can really blame her. From what she told me, life with Julian was pretty dire. It sounds as though he was chronically depressed and only functioned properly on a business level. Her social life was non-existent, and it's hardly surprising she turned to his brother for support. I just hope it works out for her now.'

'You don't think she could have tipped those men off?'

Gideon shook his head.

'I suppose it's possible but, to be honest, she just didn't seem that interested. She's a very busy lady.' Remembering the office, he suddenly recalled the rows of files and the handwriting that had intrigued him. With an apology to Eve, he slid out of her embrace and went to retrieve Nero's file from under the cushions of the armchair across the room.

Eve raised her eyebrows.

'Novel filing system.'

'I shoved it under there last night, when Lloyd was here.'

'You still don't trust him, then . . . ?'

'Oh, I don't know. I did it without thinking, really.'

Gideon sat down and opened the file, leafing through until he found the underexposed photocopy. As soon as he looked at it, he knew he'd found a match. Even if the beautiful, flowing handwriting hadn't been unusual enough in itself, Julian had had a singular way of forming his aitches – taking the tail down below the line and back, in an old English or Gothic style.

'Well. That puts a new slant on it,' he told Eve. 'It wasn't Marcus that kept the diary; it was Julian Norris. I recognise his handwriting from the files in his office. Where does that leave us?'

'Read it out to me again.'

Gideon did so.

'That first bit,' Eve said, when he finished. 'About Major Clemence and the running – that just sounds like someone whingeing because the training's getting tough. Then it says something about promising Damien . . . Read it again.'

'"*I'd leave, but I promised Damien and I don't want to let . . .*" Then it fades,' Gideon said. 'Actually, it makes a kind of sense, because Julian was supposed to be keeping an eye on Marcus – so maybe that's what he meant by promising Damien. And he didn't want to let – *him down*, perhaps?'

'Could be. And the next bit, where he gets all agitated and says it's a nightmare, and he's scared, and all that stuff. Could that be after Marcus' suicide?'

'I suppose it could, but why should he be scared? What of? Not Damien, surely? He couldn't *really* blame Julian, could he?'

'Unless . . .' Eve said slowly.

'Yeah. Go on.'

'Well. What if Julian felt he *was* to blame – not just him but all of them? What's that bit? Something about telling the truth . . .'

'Er . . .' Gideon scanned the blurry script. 'It says "*I still want to tell the truth. Gary wants . . .*" Gary; I wonder if that could possibly have been Garth – you know, the teacher I told you about. But why should they be to blame? The poor kid committed suicide. Are you saying they drove him to it?'

'Oh, God, I don't know!' Eve sounded as frustrated as Gideon felt. 'We really need that diary. It's the key to everything. If you're right about it being blackmail, then Damien must have found something in that diary – maybe even on that page – that incriminated the six people on the list.'

Gideon put the photocopy back in its sleeve and leaned back in the chair.

'If we're right, then the diary is the key to everything from Damien's murder onwards. It could even explain the original break-in. What if they were trying to find the diary before the police or anybody else did? Someone is obviously desperate to get their hands on it and equally desperate that I don't. I can't see that it's going to stop until either he or I find it.'

'A diary?'

Tilly Daniels had driven the horsebox over to pick up Nero and, by dint of waiting in the lane outside the Gatehouse, Gideon had hitched a lift up to the Priory with her. His question had clearly taken her by surprise.

'You were asking about diaries the other day, weren't you?' she remembered. 'Did that have something to do with this?'

'Yes, it did. You see, I found a photocopied page from a diary in Nero's file, but I didn't know whose it was . . .'

'In Nero's file? Why didn't *I* notice it?'

'It was a duff copy − underexposed − and Damien had used the other side for scrap, to scribble a note. You wouldn't have even seen it unless you'd taken it out of the sleeve.'

'So whose diary is it?'

'Well, at first, I thought it might have been Marcus',' Gideon said. 'That's why I asked if he'd kept one.'

'Only when he was a kid.'

They were approaching the Priory stableyard, and Gideon wished the drive had been three times the length.

'Well, now I'm pretty sure it belonged to Julian Norris.'

'It was *Julian's*? But why on earth did Damien have it?'

She swung the lorry round in a sweeping curve and pulled up, looking curiously at Gideon as she applied the handbrake.

'I think Julian gave it to him. Look, I'd rather not talk about this in front of the others. Can I pop over and see you sometime?'

'Sure. Why not come in the morning and ride out again? We're still short-staffed and Ivan's got a dentist's appointment.'

'OK − but not with the first lot. That's way too early; I need my beauty sleep.'

'But I don't understand why you're even interested in this diary,' Tilly said, carefully reversing towards the archway into the yard.

'It's a bit complicated. I'll tell you tomorrow.'

'OK.' She shrugged slightly. 'But if there was anything like that amongst Damien's things, the police would have it now. They came and bagged up everything they could find, the day he was shot. All his personal papers, bank statements, correspondence, the lot. Just carried it off with them.'

The following morning brought no repeat of the crisp misty conditions of Gideon's first ride out. He awakened to the sound of rain spattering against his bedroom window and it was still raining when he stepped out of the Land Rover in the yard at Puddlestone Farm.

'Hello. Wasn't sure you'd come,' Tilly called from a stable doorway. 'Isn't it foul? I hope you've got waterproofs!'

'I've brought a change of clothes. Who am I riding? Comet again?'

'Well, you could, but I was rather hoping you might take Nero for me, as it's his first time back on the gallops. None of the girls are too keen, and Gavin . . . Well – you saw him last time!'

'OK.' Gideon spoke lightly, hiding his misgivings. Nero, on the gallops, on a cold, wet, windy day, and with an audience, wasn't a very appealing idea. 'Did you have this in mind when you suggested I ride out this morning?'

'No!' Tilly exclaimed indignantly. Then added, with a twinkle, 'Well, yes – actually, it did occur to me. Do you mind?'

'No, that's OK. Bring him on.'

It wasn't until they were on their way back from the gallops that Gideon had a chance to speak privately with Damien's sister. Nero had behaved like a perfect gentleman, and they had been discussing his future and the possibility of running him at Towcester at the end of the week, when Tilly suddenly switched subjects and asked about the diary.

'I don't understand why Julian should have given it to Damien,' she said. 'What possible interest could it have been to him?'

'I think it had to do with what went on at the training camp at Ponsonby Castle.'

It was still pouring and Gideon's jacket had long since stopped repelling the rain. Water had permeated his soft suede chaps and soaked the jeans underneath, and as he spoke he felt the first icy trickle run into his left boot.

'You mean Marcus.'

'Yes, I think so, but until I see the rest of it I can't be sure.'

'I see. Well, I wish I could help, but I certainly don't remember ever having seen anything like that among Damien's things. I could ask Beth, if you like. Why didn't you tell me before?'

'To be honest, I didn't realise what it was until a day or two ago.'

'So why do you want to see it? What does it say?'

'That's just the problem; it's only one page and so much of it is illegible that I'm not sure. But if Damien went to the trouble of photocopying it, it must be something important, don't you think?'

'If he photocopied it, perhaps he gave it back. Have you thought of that?'

Gideon nodded.

'Yeah. I thought I might call in on Marion on my way home. Look, I'm sorry to bother you with this after everything that's happened, it's just that I've been asking around about that list we found, and it seems that someone would much rather I didn't. And now I'm pretty sure the list and the diary are connected in some way. All six names were on that Olympic selection course with Marcus, and I'm pretty sure that's what the extract from the diary is all about. It seems too much of a coincidence to be one – if you know what I mean.'

Tilly rode in silence for a moment or two, frowning.

'You're saying that Damien made the list after reading Julian's diary?'

'That's what it looks like.'

'Then it's got to be something about Marcus, hasn't it?'

'I'm afraid so.'

'But I don't understand. I mean, I know Julian took it badly

– we all did – but it was no-one's fault. Damien understood that.'

'I think we need to find the diary,' Gideon stated. 'I'll call on Marion and, in the meantime, if you think of anywhere it could possibly be . . .'

'But I *can't*. We went through practically everything after we had the break-in, because the police wanted to know what was missing.' She hesitated, and Gideon saw the dawning of an idea. 'Oh my God! You don't think that's what the burglar was looking for?'

'It's just possible.'

Tilly's horse stumbled and she shortened her reins and pushed it on, looking at Gideon in mounting horror.

'What on earth's in it then, to make someone take a chance like that to get hold of it? Oh, God, Gideon! You don't think . . . ? This doesn't have anything to do with the shooting, does it? You don't think Damien found something out . . . ?'

'I thought that, at first, but it doesn't really add up, because whoever it was that tried to warn me off, did it *after* Adam Tetley was arrested. I can only think that whatever it was that Julian Norris wanted Damien to see concerned all of them: all six names on the list.'

Tilly had turned quite pale.

'Oh, my God! This is a nightmare! You don't think they were all involved? That they plotted to kill Damien? I can't believe that – *you* don't believe that, do you? I mean, there's Lloyd, for one; we've known him for ever.'

Gideon thought of Garth Stephenson and Robin Tate. He'd liked them both, but how far could he trust his own judgement of character?

'No. I don't think it was a plot, but I can't help wondering if the diary didn't have something to do with it.'

'But what? And why didn't Damien tell us – tell me, at least?'

'Perhaps he wanted to get to the bottom of it before he said anything. I expect he didn't want to upset you,' Gideon suggested gently. Quite naturally, the thought that Damien might have been using the information for less honourable purposes hadn't occurred to her; after all, *he* still found the idea difficult to accept, himself.

'But he must have had it a year by then. When *was* he going to tell us?'

They were approaching the yard now, and Gideon shrugged, helplessly. 'I'm sorry, Tilly. I don't have the answers. We really need to find the diary.' He hesitated. 'Look, this might sound a strange thing to ask, and you don't have to answer if you'd rather not, but did you find any unexplained transactions on Damien's bank statements for the last year or so?'

'No, it was all in order. As I said, the police took everything and went through it with a fine-toothed comb, but we didn't have any secrets within the family, anyway. I had full access to the business account, and his private one was a joint account with Beth. There was nothing irregular. Why?'

Gideon had expected the question.

'Well, I was talking to Angie Bowen at the Radcliffe Trust, and she told me they have a mystery benefactor who's been sending cash donations in an unmarked envelope, and she'd got it into her head that it was Damien.'

'Damien?' Tilly was astounded. 'But I told you, we'd barely scrape through if it wasn't for the sponsorship! Much as he'd have liked to help, he certainly didn't have any spare cash to hand out.'

'That's what I told her,' Gideon agreed. 'They were fairly hefty amounts too, I gather.'

'No. No way. But I'm glad someone is helping her, anyway.' To Gideon's relief, she seemed to dismiss the subject almost immediately. 'Look, come in for a coffee after we get this lot settled, and we'll ask Beth about the diary. But let's not give her the whole story just now. She's having a bit of a rough time with the pregnancy and everything.'

Ahead there was a sudden flurry of hooves and swishing tails as the horses bunched at the gate into the yard, and Tilly swore.

'Gavin! Get Tremelo away from Benny's backside, you idiot! If he gets kicked, the vet's bill will come out of your wage packet!

Honestly, that boy's a complete waste of space,' she said quietly to Gideon. 'If I had someone to replace him, I'd have got rid of him weeks ago.'

Gideon stayed to lunch at Puddlestone Farm, but, like Tilly, Beth couldn't shed any light on the possible whereabouts of the diary. To Gideon's relief, she accepted their vague explanation as to why they wanted it without question, their cause aided by the distraction of Freddy having toothache.

'What did it look like?' she asked, trying unsuccessfully to make the youngster swallow an aspirin solution.

Gideon had to admit that they didn't know, and after repeating Tilly's assurance that everything had been sorted through after the burglary, she seemed to lose interest.

Leaving the farm, Gideon drove through worsening rain to Sturminster Newton to try his luck with Marion Norris once again.

'I'm afraid I haven't got it.'

Marion Norris faced Gideon across the width of her office, her shock of red hair dragged back into a ponytail that resembled an explosion on the back of her head, and her swelling abdomen hidden under a pair of baggy dungarees.

'But you know what I'm talking about.'

'Yes, but I haven't got any of his diaries. Julian burned them all. The day he died, he went out into the field behind the house and had a bonfire. They all went up in smoke. Twenty-three years' worth; what a waste of time!'

'Are you sure he burnt them all? Because I think he gave one to Damien.'

There was a pause. Marion regarded him warily. 'What makes you think that?'

'Damien photocopied one of the pages. I've seen a copy.'

She frowned. 'So that's why you were asking about his handwriting the other day. But why would he do that?'

'I think it had something to do with Marcus' death, and I was hoping you might be able to tell me what.'

Marion shook her head, an errant curl bobbing on her forehead.

'I'm sorry, I can't. He never told me. But you're right, he did take one diary to Damien. I saw him wrapping it in a bag and asked him what he was doing. He said it was just something for Damien but he wouldn't tell me what.'

'Could you describe it to me? What did it look like?'

'Oh, it was a proper journal: a navy hardback with a red spine, and a ribbon to mark your place – you know the kind of thing. It was about so big.' With her hands she indicated something approximately eight inches by six, and then moved across to her desk and sat down at it abruptly, as if the strength had suddenly left her limbs. 'All right, I'm sorry. What I told you the other day wasn't strictly true. I knew he wasn't coming back, that day. I should have tried to stop him, but I was just so tired. I was tired of all the sighing and self-hate and I just let him go. It was what he wanted, after all. He wouldn't have thanked me. D'you think I was wicked?' She looked up at Gideon, appearing curiously unconcerned, as if she'd just asked his opinion on some mundane matter, but a tear gathered in her eye, spilled over and ran down her cheek, leaving a glistening trail.

He shook his head.

'If he'd made up his mind, I should think there was little you could have done to stop him.'

'Nothing at all. He'd have found a way, sooner or later. But you mustn't tell anyone. You won't, will you? Promise me.' Her eyes beseeched him.

'No, I won't tell.' Gideon felt sorry for her. She must have thought the whole business over and done with, and now he was here dragging it all out into the light of day once more. 'But it *was* about Marcus, wasn't it?'

'Yes, I think so.' The curl bobbed again and she wiped the tear from her chin. 'Julian was convinced he'd let him down. I wanted him to talk to Damien – to get it out of his system. I begged him to, but he said he couldn't face him. I'm afraid he wasn't very strong.'

'And Damien never mentioned the diary to you?'

'No. He came to the funeral but he never said a word about it, and neither did I. I just wanted it all to be over.' She was silent for a moment, staring at the desktop. 'Do you know what I felt when the policeman came to tell me Julian was dead?'

Gideon didn't answer, and she looked up, meeting his eyes.

'Relief,' she stated. 'It sounds terrible but that's what I felt: relief. Oh, I cried – of course I did – but the man I lost that day wasn't the man I fell in love with. *He'd* died gradually over the last ten years or so, until there was nothing left that I either knew or wanted. It sounds brutal, but it's the truth and I'm not going to apologise.'

Gideon shook his head.

'I'm not about to judge you, Marion. I just wanted to know if there was anything more you could tell me about what happened at that training camp, because I'm very much afraid that it isn't over, and won't be until the facts become known. It all hinges on something Julian wrote in that diary but I don't know what, and I don't know where it is.'

There was a click as the door behind him opened, and he turned to find John Norris stepping into the office from outside. He looked surprised to see Gideon there.

'Oh! Hello. Sorry to barge in but I left my mobile behind.' He paused. 'Is everything all right, love?'

'Yes, fine.' Marion sniffed and wiped her eyes with a corner of her handkerchief. 'We were just talking about Julian.'

Norris' face hardened.

'I didn't realise you knew my brother,' he said to Gideon.

'I didn't.'

'Then what . . . ?'

'It's all right, John,' Marion put in quickly. '*I* brought the subject up.'

'I see.' Norris didn't look overpleased. 'Well, it's up to you I suppose, but I would have thought my brother's affairs were family business and best left that way.'

'I'm sorry.' Marion's freckled skin reddened. 'I think perhaps you'd better go, Gideon. I really can't help you.'

'OK.' Gideon glanced at each of them in turn, finding Marion apologetic and her fiancé plainly not. 'Thanks, anyway.'

He left the office and was escorted to the gate by the triumphantly yapping Pekinese.

FOURTEEN

T HE FRIDAY FOLLOWING GIDEON'S visit to Marion
Norris was the day of the race meeting at Towcester, to
which Tilly's owner had invited them all to share her private box.
Throwing caution to the wind, Tilly decided to take a chance
and run Nero. He wasn't at the peak of fitness, even though
Gideon and Pippa had been working on it over the last couple
of weeks that he was at the Priory, but Tilly thought that might
actually be an advantage after so long away from the track.

Gideon had been intending to travel to the meeting with Pippa
and the others, but a slightly anxious telephone call from Tilly
on the Thursday evening resulted in him promising to help her
with Nero during the preparation for the race. As this included
loading him into the lorry at the start of the journey and being
there to unload at the course, it made sense for Gideon to travel
with Tilly and the horses, which he didn't mind in the least. It
was almost a week since his row with Pippa, and although he'd
seen her several times over that period, the atmosphere was still
decidedly frosty.

Eve had been included in Tilly's original invitation, so ten thirty on the Friday morning found both of them arriving at Puddlestone Farm, where the day's three runners were being prettied up in readiness for their public appearance.

'It's a pity you haven't got a jockey's licence,' Tilly said wistfully, as they looked over Nero's stable door. 'It'd be useful if you could ride him in the race, too.'

'Apart from the little matter of my being six foot four and about four stone over the weight allowance,' Gideon said laughing.

'A few hours in the sauna . . .'

'A few *months* in the sauna, maybe! And I'd be so weak I probably wouldn't be able to pull myself on board, let alone ride in a race!'

'Gosh, I've been to the races a couple of times, but you forget how much work goes on behind the scenes,' Eve commented. 'I mean, I don't think the average person thinks about it at all. The horses are just there, saddled and ready to run. You don't imagine them standing in their stables having their feet washed and oiled, and the straw brushed out of their hair. They always look so perfect.'

'Sorry to disillusion you,' Tilly said, slanting a quizzical look at Gideon.

'No, it's fascinating,' she replied. 'Like seeing actors in their dressing rooms before they get made up.'

No doubt picking up on the buzz of anticipation, Nero put up a show of resistance to entering the horsebox, but it was only a token affair and he very soon allowed Gideon to persuade him in.

Two of the stable lads climbed in the back with the horses, Gideon and Eve joined Tilly in the cab and they were on their way.

At Towcester there was no mistaking Nero's excitement, but under Gideon's supervision he behaved himself well, and two hours after arriving at the course he was saddled and walking briskly round the parade ring at Gideon's side, Gideon having changed into corduroy trousers and a jacket for the occasion.

Considering the last-minute nature of the decision, Tilly had been exceedingly lucky to secure the services of a top jockey in the person of Rollo Gallagher, but unfortunately a heavy fall in the previous race rendered him unable to honour his commitments for the rest of the afternoon.

After a minor panic, a replacement was found, and as the jockeys filed into the paddock Gideon led Nero across to where Tilly was briefing a good-looking youngster with golden-blond hair and dazzling blue eyes. He noticed that the lad was listening closely and nodding, but without ever meeting her eyes.

Tilly introduced him to Gideon as Mikey Copperfield, and when Gideon said 'Hi', the jockey mumbled a reply and turned his attention to the horse.

Boosted expertly into the saddle by Tilly, Mikey immediately looked more at home, and Gideon was impressed by the quiet way he managed the animal.

As he led the horse down the pathway to the track itself, Gideon turned and smiled at the jockey.

'OK?'

The boy nodded. 'Fine.'

Once on the turf, Nero's feet began to dance and he tossed his head in impatience, grinding his teeth noisily.

Gideon glanced up at Mikey, but under the orange-silk-covered helmet the youngster's face appeared unconcerned, and when Gideon asked him if he was ready to go, he returned a confident affirmative.

Within seconds the brown horse was away and moving easily down the broad grassy racetrack towards the start. Mikey shifted from sitting to standing in the stirrups, his hands resting quietly on the horse's withers, and after diving his nose forward a couple of times, Nero settled into his stride and proceeded in an exemplary fashion. Gideon turned away, satisfied that the horse was in good hands, and made his way back to join Tilly and the others in the stands.

Agatha Twineham, the owner who had so generously invited them all to share her box, was a wonderfully sprightly octogenarian with a roguish twinkle in her eye. Barely five feet tall, she defiantly wore a real fur coat over her tweed suit, and a jaunty hat on her faintly blue curls.

'I didn't kill the blasted things,' she proclaimed, when Pippa's gaze dwelt slightly longer than it might have on her mink. 'And since they're long dead it seems more of a waste not to wear it, wouldn't you say?'

Whatever Pippa thought, she could hardly start the day by entering into a heated debate with their host and, by the time the coat had been discarded and the first of the refreshments appeared, Agatha had won them all over with her deliciously wicked sense of humour.

Her own party consisted of a rather prim female whom she introduced as a cousin, and a plump teenage boy who was apparently her great-grandson, but who disappeared five minutes after they arrived and wasn't seen for the rest of the day.

Tilly's guests were Pippa, Giles and Lloyd, Gideon and Eve, Barbara and Hamish Daniels, and Beth and Freddy.

'I feel slightly awkward,' she confided in Gideon, as they hurried rather breathlessly up the stairs. 'She's paying for all this, and I've got four times as many guests as she has.'

'But that's what she wanted, and she's loving it. You can see she's in her element,' he pointed out.

When they finally reached the warmth of the box, the television screen was showing the runners circling at the start, and they were pleased to see that Nero was still behaving himself well.

'That kid's got a way with him,' Gideon told Eve as he slipped into a seat between her and Giles, ready to watch the race. 'Considering it was the first time he'd sat on Nero, it was amazing. He's got a real talent.'

'Oh, God! Not another witchdoctor, surely!' Giles exclaimed in horror.

'He's dreadfully shy,' Tilly put in, taking the seat on the other side of Giles. 'But I'd heard he was very good with the horses, and he certainly is.'

In due course the starter called them in and they jumped off in a ragged line, heading down the back-straight at a steady pace. Nero ran his race with controlled enthusiasm, gaining half a length on his opponents at every fence to stay in the leading group for a circuit and a half, before his lack of race-fitness caught up with him in coming round the final bend and he fell back to cross the line a very creditable fifth. His young jockey followed Tilly's instructions to the letter, not pushing him when it became obvious he was tiring.

Tilly was ecstatic. 'That was bloody brilliant! Just what I wanted. I'll be using that boy again, I can tell you. And thanks again to you guys, you've done a fantastic job with him.'

Gideon looked across at Pippa and smiled, forgetting their quarrel in the joy of the moment, but it seemed she wasn't able to forget. She turned away, cutting him dead, and linked her arm through Lloyd's, giving him a kiss for good measure.

Saddened, Gideon found Eve watching him and smiled at her instead, before hurrying down to the course with Tilly to meet Mikey and Nero as they left the track.

Tilly repeated her comments to the jockey.

'He jumped beautifully!' Mikey told her happily, patting the horse's steaming neck. 'I think he'll be really good.'

'Well, the ride is yours for as long as you want it,' she replied. 'You did really well!'

In the unsaddling area water was poured over Nero's sweaty head and body, and then Gideon held him while his groom squeegeed off the excess with a sweat scraper and covered him with a sheet.

Agatha's own horse, Arctic Tremelo, ran in the next race but one, which was the feature race of the afternoon. A big, light grey gelding, he was the rising star of the Puddlestone yard, and although no-one actually said as much, Gideon knew that a great deal of Tilly's credibility as a trainer rested on the horse giving a good account of himself.

While everyone else had thrown themselves into the party

atmosphere of Agatha's box, he noticed that Tilly herself ate little and was unusually quiet. Even Giles' company, which she normally enjoyed, failed to draw her out, and when she disappeared to oversee the horse's preparation, Gideon reassured his friend that her preoccupation was no reflection on him.

Tilly needn't have worried.

Tremelo won his race with ease, drawing six lengths clear of the rest of the field in the finishing straight to win pulling up. She led him in, slapping his grey neck delightedly and beaming from ear to ear, and didn't stop smiling for the remainder of the afternoon.

Agatha was overjoyed at the success of her beloved horse, and when she made her way down to proudly accept a cut-glass decanter for his win, all her new-found friends accompanied her. On the way back to the box after the presentation, Tilly – with no runners for an hour or so – was walking beside Giles, and Gideon smiled secretly, noticing that he'd slipped his arm round her waist.

'Gideon?' a voice said, just behind him.

He turned to find Beth, neat in a navy skirt-suit, her dark eyes barely level with his shoulder. Freddy was astride her left hip.

She held up her racecard.

'There's a horse here called Reuben Jones,' she said quietly. 'And it reminded me of the Reuben at home. You've heard about him, right?'

'Sorry.' He shook his head. 'You've lost me.'

'Reuben – you know – the recluse who lives in the charcoal burner's hut on the farm and looks after the gallops. Hasn't Tilly mentioned him?'

Light dawned.

'Oh, yes, of course. I remember now.'

'You were asking where Dàmien might have hidden this diary you're looking for. Well, he liked Reuben and used to visit him from time to time. What if he left the diary there, with him? I know he once told me he'd trust him with anything . . .'

'That's an idea,' Gideon said. 'You could have something there.'

At this point Freddy, who'd been uncharacteristically quiet so far, picked up on the name and began to chant loudly, 'Reuben Bones, Reuben Bones, Reuben Bones!'

'*Jones*,' his mother amended, smiling. 'Sshh!' But Freddy liked his own version, and carried on chanting.

Hearing him, Tilly looked over her shoulder at Gideon.

'Are you thinking what I'm thinking?' she asked quietly.

Gideon nodded. 'It's worth a try, don't you think? When could we go and see?'

'It'll be too dark tonight. Perhaps if you came over in the morning you could ride out again and we could go on from there.'

'I shall be out with Eve tomorrow,' he said regretfully. 'We've got to be in London for twelve.'

'There's a gallery owner I want Gideon to meet,' Eve put in.

Tilly raised her eyebrows and smiled sweetly.

'First lot's at half past six.'

Gideon groaned.

Bed had never seemed so alluring as it did at five o'clock the next morning, and if it hadn't been for Eve pulling the duvet off him, Gideon would probably have turned the alarm off and gone back to sleep.

However, at six forty-five, with the sun sparkling on the dew-laden, cobwebby turf, and banishing wispy high clouds from a clear blue sky, he was glad he'd made the effort, and filled with a kind of self-righteous superiority over all those still under the covers. He rode Nero again, and the brown horse strode out next to Tilly's mount, apparently none the worse for his exertions the day before.

Tilly was relating some of the positive feedback she'd received after Tremelo's impressive performance at Towcester when she was interrupted by Ivan calling back from his position at the head of the string.

'Sheep's out, guv!'

'That's strange . . .' She frowned and pushed her horse forward to come alongside the ex-jockey. 'I wonder if Reuben's ill. He's never forgotten before.'

'What d'you wanna do? Can't work 'em with sheep all over the place,' Ivan stated.

'They'll probably move if they see you coming,' Tilly told him. 'As we were only giving this lot easy work today, Ivan, can I leave you to organise that, while Gideon and I go and check on Reuben?'

Ivan nodded. 'No worries.'

Trotting Nero next to Tilly's horse along the valley bottom, Gideon had a feeling of deep foreboding.

'Well, I don't have to think up an excuse to visit him now,' Tilly said. 'But I hope he's OK. He's never been ill before – at least, not so ill that he hasn't looked after the gallops.'

She clearly didn't suspect anything more sinister, and Gideon could only hope that his own burgeoning suspicions were proven unfounded.

They weren't.

The old charcoal burner's hut was located in a clearing deep in the hazel copse that bordered the field next to the gallops. They approached it in single file down a grassy path, leaning over the horses' necks to avoid the low, whippy branches. Tilly was in front and as soon as she reached the open area she reined in sharply, causing her horse to throw its head up in surprise.

'Oh, my God!'

Although Gideon had never seen the place before, it was impossible to miss the signs of the wholesale ransacking that had taken place. The clearing, extending to perhaps a quarter of an acre, was dominated by three round corrugated-iron structures, some twelve feet in diameter, two of which were smoking sluggishly. On the far side was a thatched wooden hut, so old that it blended almost seamlessly into the fabric of the woodland. It was fronted by a raised deck with a lean-to roof, which was currently sagging crookedly, one of its supports having been smashed away. A further covered area at the side of the hut was strewn with all manner of tools, pots, pans and utensils, with a rack of shelves thrown down on top, and a little way off a hen house had been overturned and broken, a few of its occupants remaining to peck hopefully amongst the scattered ruins.

The hut stood forlornly in the midst of the disorder, its one visible window shattered, and its chimney showing no sign of life.

'Oh, my God!' Tilly said again. 'What on earth . . . ?'

'We'd better see if he's all right,' Gideon said, urging Nero forward. 'He may have got away and be hiding in the woods.'

'Who could have done this?' Tilly was following, her horse baulking and shying at the smoking charcoal burners. 'Nobody knows it's here, even.'

Somebody clearly did, Gideon reflected.

They left the horses tied to two separate posts and, between them, managed to raise the sagging roof of the lean-to enough for Gideon to prop it temporarily on a broom handle. With this done, they could see that the hut's door was standing open six inches or so and, when Tilly pushed it wider, they were greeted by a low rumbling growl from within.

'That's his dog,' she said softly, glancing at Gideon. 'He's not terribly friendly.'

'Do you know his name?'

'Um . . . Buddy, I think. Yes, Buddy.'

'OK. Let me go first.'

She stood back and he went past her into the gloomy interior of the hut, pausing to let his eyes become accustomed to the poor light. His movement was greeted by a second, more menacing growl.

The inside of the hut was in much the same state as the outside had been. It appeared that everything that could have been tipped over or thrown on the floor, had been. Even the small black potbellied stove had been toppled from its stone slab in the corner of the room, wrenched away from the flue pipe, which now hung bent and redundant. Against the far wall the pallet bed was also broken, its mattress lying on top of the splintered remains, and on top of that Gideon could see what at first he took to be just a tumbled pile of blankets. Then, with a shock, he realised that beneath the covers lay the motionless body of a man. In front of the bed stood a black and white sheepdog, head and tail low and lips drawn back from a set of undoubtedly sharp, white teeth.

First things first. Gideon crouched down sideways on, and averted his face.

'Hello, Buddy,' he said, quietly. He was rewarded by a repetition of the growl but sensed no real aggression, only a wash of fear and anxiety as tangible as a physical embrace.

Holding one hand out, palm downward, he closed his eyes to block out any distraction, and pictured the dog coming towards him, head down, ears flat and tail wagging.

There was another growl, but with a measure of uncertainty this time, and tailing off into a whine.

'Good boy. Good Buddy. It's all right now. No-one's gonna hurt you, little fella.'

Another wave of fear and doubt reached him, and he had to suppress the instinctive response of pity. Pity wasn't what Buddy needed right now. What he craved was someone to offer him security and strength, to take away the awful confusion in his mind.

'It's all right, little dog. We'll take care of you. Don't worry, little fella.'

The dog was coming. Gideon sensed the decision moments before he felt the whiskery muzzle touch the back of his outstretched hand.

'Good boy.'

He waited a few moments longer before opening his eyes, unwilling to scare the animal by making his move too soon. He found Buddy sitting beside him but looking back at the bed and its unmoving occupant.

'Good boy,' he said again, slowly straightening up. 'Let's go and see what we can do for your master, shall we?'

As soon as he stepped forward, the dog trotted back to Reuben's side and stood with his chin on the blankets, but he made no attempt to warn Gideon off again.

Even in the dimly lit hut, Gideon could see that Reuben was in a bad way. He was lying on his side with a blanket pulled roughly over him, and the side of his face that was visible was darkened by two massive bruises, one of which was crusted with dried blood.

Gideon leaned over the man on the pallet bed and spoke his name, softly at first and then progressively louder, but there was no response.

'Tilly. We need an ambulance,' Gideon said over his shoulder. 'And the police, too. Have you got your mobile? Good. Tell them he's been assaulted.'

Tilly nodded and went back out into the sunshine to make the call and, with the dog looking on, Gideon gently shook the man's shoulder.

He was rewarded by a low groan, but repeating Reuben's name brought the same negative result as before. In case the wounded man was able to hear him, Gideon crouched by the bed and began to reassure him that everything was going to be all right.

'Buddy's here. He's fine, and we'll look after him until you're better,' he promised, hoping that Tilly would agree to put the dog up. He had an idea Elsa wouldn't be too chuffed about having a strange house guest foisted on her.

'They're on their way,' Tilly said, coming back into the hut. 'They're sending a helicopter and want me to go out into the field and guide them down. Will you be all right?'

'Sure.'

'How is he?'

'Pretty rough, I think. He's only semi-conscious. Look, if you ride back, be careful with the horse when the chopper comes down, we don't want another accident!'

★

273

It was just over twenty minutes before the helicopter paramedic reached the hut in the clearing, and during that time Reuben gave no sign of a return to consciousness.

Gideon sat with him and the dog, talking to both, and taking in the details of his surroundings as his eyes adjusted fully to the poor light. In spite of the chaos left by whoever had trashed the place, there was no sign of dirt or neglect. As a home, the hut was spartan, to say the least, but there was no smell beyond the inevitable tang of woodsmoke and a rather pleasant overtone of pine resin.

These things he noticed almost in passing, his brain being occupied with the worrying question of just who had carried out this vicious attack. According to Tilly, Reuben had been on the gallops the morning before, standing watching the horses as he often did, so the attack had taken place in the last twenty-four hours. It was difficult to believe it was a coincidence that his name had come up at Towcester.

On the other hand, if it wasn't a coincidence, then someone at the racecourse had overheard their conversation and moved exceedingly fast.

Who?

As far as Gideon was concerned, the finger of suspicion fairly stabbed in the direction of Lloyd. However one looked at it, there really wasn't any other option. Aside from Pippa, Giles and Eve, the others had all been members of Damien's family. Gideon didn't think Lloyd had been close enough to overhear the conversation between Beth, Tilly and himself, but he would have had to be deaf not to have heard Freddy's enthusiastic chanting of Reuben Bones. As a long-time friend of Damien's, it might well have reminded him of the charcoal burner at the farm, and led him to have drawn the same conclusions as had Beth and Tilly.

Lloyd.

The ramifications didn't bear thinking about.

He looked down at the battered face of the man on the bed. It was difficult to tell how old he might be, but although he remembered Tilly saying he could be anything from fifty to seventy, Gideon thought he looked nearer the lower end of that estimate. From what he could see, he got the impression of a strong face, lined but not wasted. Could the Lloyd he knew *really* do something like this? In spite of his dislike for the man, he found it hard to believe.

Gradually the heavy throb of the approaching helicopter intruded onto his deliberations, and he abandoned the unpalatable train of thought in anticipation of the paramedic's arrival.

'Help is on its way. They'll soon be here,' he told the unconscious man, reflecting, even as he did so, that to a man such as Reuben the information was likely to be more painful than soothing. Having successfully shut himself away from the world for thirty years or more, it would surely be a mental torment to have the world, in its most busy, authoritarian guise, invading his tranquil haven.

From that point of view, Gideon thought it was probably a good thing Reuben *was* unconscious.

'But I don't understand. Why would someone do that to a man like Reuben?' Tilly asked, frowning.

She and Gideon were riding back to the farm on horses that had grown cold and fidgety with waiting while Reuben had been examined, transferred to the air ambulance and borne away. The police observer who had accompanied the paramedic had taken their details and remained at the hut to await the arrival of a forensic team.

'I mean, he doesn't trouble anyone,' she went on. 'Hardly anyone even knows he's there. And he's got nothing to steal, you can see that.'

'Except perhaps the diary,' Gideon pointed out.

Tilly's head snapped round.

'Do you think that's what they were after?'

'It's possible, don't you think? Probable, even.'

'But why now, suddenly? Just when . . .' She broke off as her thought processes caught up. 'You don't think someone overheard us?'

'It's possible. After all, Freddy was shouting Reuben Bones at the top of his voice.'

'But hardly anyone knows about Reuben. In fact, outside the family and staff, probably only you.'

And Lloyd, Gideon thought, but he didn't say it. In spite of his suspicions, he had no proof. Much better to let Tilly work it out for herself. He looked back at the hermit's sheepdog, which was trotting quietly behind Tilly's horse at the end of a long piece of rope. 'Good lad, Buddy.'

'What are we going to do with him?' Tilly asked, her attention momentarily diverted. 'I expect he'd be all right with us, just as long as someone didn't let him out by mistake. There are so many comings and goings at our place.'

'Well, I'd offer to take him, but I'm not sure Elsa would be too happy, and I'm not going to be there today – oh, shit! I'm supposed to be back by half past nine – what time is it?'

'Ten to. You'll be all right – just.'

'When I say back by half past nine I mean home, showered and changed, ready to set out for London.'

'Oh, I see. Might be tight, then,' Tilly agreed. 'Well, don't worry about Buddy. We'll look after him. He'd probably be happiest tied up in the barn. At least it's warm and quiet.'

In the event, Gideon and Eve were a quarter of an hour late setting out for London, a circumstance that Eve bore with good grace after Gideon had filled her in on the events of the morning.

'If you seriously think Lloyd has something to do with all this, why would he have helped you out the other day?'

Gideon shrugged. 'It made him look good.'

'You mean he set the whole thing up? Don't you think you might be allowing your personal feelings to get in the way here?'

'I don't know. I hope not . . . Maybe.'

Eve turned the Aston Martin onto the main road and accelerated hard.

'I don't think it's fair to assume it's Lloyd, just because you
can't think who else it might be. I mean, what if someone was
watching our party yesterday? The way that kid was shouting,
almost anyone within fifty feet could have heard him.'

'But the name wouldn't have meant anything, if they didn't
know about the guy in the hut,' Gideon pointed out. 'That's what
it comes down to.'

Eve sighed. 'Well, the police are involved now, so maybe you
should tell them what you know and leave it to them, huh?'

'Yeah, maybe.'

She looked sideways, but Gideon's face was giving nothing
away.

'What? Come on, I know that look.'

'Oh, I don't know − it's this diary thing. If Damien was using
it to blackmail the people on the list, it's going to be a hell of a
shock for his family. They don't need that.'

'*Gideon!*' Eve's tone was loaded with frustration. 'This isn't just
a bit of amateur sleuthing any more; we could be talking murder
here! I know you wanted to keep Damien's name clean, if you
could, but enough's enough, surely. While you're so busy trying
to keep everybody else's name clean, you're going to end up with
your own name on a gravestone if you're not careful!'

'I will be careful. I just want to find this diary first. Tilly and
I are going to visit Reuben tonight, if he's well enough for visi-
tors. If he says the diary has gone, I'll go straight to the police,
OK?'

'And if it hasn't?'

'Then maybe he'll tell us where it is . . .'

Eve just shook her head in defeat.

When Gideon picked Tilly up that evening, he collected Buddy,
too.

'I thought Reuben would be worrying about him,' Gideon

told her, pulling into a muddy gateway to allow a large four-by-four to pass. The blonde at the wheel turned her head and waved.

'Oh, it's Harriet!' Tilly exclaimed, and waved back cheerily. 'Harriet Lloyd-Ellis, Lloyd's ex.' She lives just a couple of miles away. We'll be passing their place. I'll point it out.'

They had left the lanes and were travelling along the main road when Tilly pointed to a tree-flanked gateway.

'It's down there. The drive's about half a mile long, and they have stables and quite a bit of land, or rather she does. It's still hard to imagine that they've split up. They were always sniping at one another, but most of us would have taken odds that they'd stay together; they'd been married for twelve years. Their squabbles were part of life – I mean, we used to laugh at them; nobody took them seriously.'

The hospital was starkly bright after the soft twilight country-side they had been travelling through, and Tilly's shoes squeaked on the shiny grey-and-white-squared lino. She and Gideon got several sideways looks as they traversed its myriad corridors, but it wasn't until they were at the doorway of Reuben's room that anyone questioned the presence of the dog.

'I'm sorry. No animals,' the nurse said. She was middle-aged and wore an air of authority.

'He's a PAT dog,' Gideon said, without so much as a flicker.

'Oh,' she said, looking doubtfully down at Buddy, who was straining towards the door, possibly sensing that his master was inside. 'So where's his official jacket?'

'On the kitchen table,' Gideon said with a smile that was somewhere between apologetic and charming.

The nurse gave him a long look, clearly not fooled, but allowed herself to be won over. 'All right. Just this once. But if anyone catches you, I'll deny all knowledge and have you thrown out, I warn you!'

They thanked her and went on in.

'You're shameless!' Tilly exclaimed, as the door shut behind them.

The collie, on seeing who occupied the bed, threw all his weight into his collar in an effort to reach it.

Reuben was lying propped up against a bank of pillows, his bruised, weather-beaten face looking swarthy against the crisp white bandage that was wound about his head. Seeing his dog, he held out his hands delightedly.

'Here, boy! Come to me,' he said huskily, and the dog whimpered its eagerness.

Gideon let go of the lead and, seconds later, Buddy was on the bed, snuggling close to Reuben and licking his face enthusiastically.

'Oh, crikey! I hope the nurse doesn't come back and see that,' Tilly said fervently, glancing towards the door. 'I think that's taking Pets As Therapy a bit too far!'

While Reuben was occupied with his dog, Gideon had a chance to look at him properly for the first time and saw a man who appeared to be in his fifties, with a strong face and a couple of millimetres of dark hair.

Even in a hospital bed, it was clear that this man in no way conformed to Gideon's image of a hermit. If not particularly tall, he was well built and looked as though he possessed considerable strength. Far from shrinking, his gaze was direct and unafraid, and the look he levelled at Gideon over the collie's black and white head was full of gratitude.

'Thanks,' he said gruffly.

'No problem. How are you?'

'I'll live. You're the ones who found me.' It was more of a statement than a question, and Gideon guessed that the police had told him.

'Yeah. This morning, early. The sheep were out on the gallops.' Reuben nodded.

'So when did this happen?' Gideon indicated his injuries.

'Last night. I was feedin' Buddy.'

'Do you know who did it?'

'No.' He shook his head. 'But I know why.'

'The diary?' Tilly asked.

Reuben shifted to reposition Buddy's weight, wincing as he did so. The bandage on his head was matched by one on his right hand, and there was clearly unseen damage, too.

'Ribs?' Gideon asked, with sympathy.

The injured man grunted.

'Must be gettin' old. Could've took 'im once. Would've then if he 'adn't fuckin' jumped me.' He flashed a look at Tilly. 'Sorry.'

She shook her head dismissively. 'Doesn't matter. Reuben, did Damien give you the diary?'

Reuben's brows dipped and he looked down.

'Didn't want no-one to see it, so I kep' it for him.'

'Do you still have it?' Gideon asked. 'Or did they take it from you?'

Reuben looked pointedly at Gideon. 'Need to talk to you. Alone.'

'To me?' Gideon was surprised. He glanced at Tilly, eyebrows raised and shrugging slightly.

'Oh, all right,' she said reluctantly. 'I'll go and get a coffee.'

When she'd gone, Gideon looked thoughtfully at the man in the bed.

'Do you know who I am?'

'You brought Buddy to me,' he stated simply. 'And I've seen what you do with the horses. Damien spoke of you.'

'I was with him when he died,' Gideon said softly.

'I know.'

'Do you know what's in the diary?'

'Damien told me. He didn't want *them* to know.' Reuben nodded towards the door. 'His family – reckon he didn't want them hurt.'

'Did they take the diary? Whoever did this to you – did they find it?'

He shook his head with certainty.

'I had it hid. Nobody won't have found it.'

'Will you tell me where it is?'

Reuben rubbed the dog's fur contemplatively.

'What'll you do with it?'

'I don't know, yet,' Gideon admitted. 'I need to see it first.'

'Knew it would be trouble. Got him killed, it did.'

Even though he had suspected this, hearing it confirmed gave Gideon a jolt.

'Damien? Are you sure?'

Reuben grunted.

'Of course – Damien. He wanted to make 'em pay.'

He regarded Gideon intensely for several long seconds, then sighed. 'I don't want it any more. The lad's gone and I should've burnt the bloody thing! But he trusted me.' Reuben shook his head in an apparent agony of indecision, and then said abruptly, 'I'll tell you where it is.'

His directions were precise, and easy to remember, which was as well, because he warned Gideon against committing them to paper.

'He'll know you've been here. Watch your back.'

'You keep saying he, was there only one?'

'Dunno. One guy hit me from behind and held me down, but there might have been more. He wanted to know where the book was, but I wasn't about to tell him. Then the bastard did this . . .' With the hand that wasn't stroking the dog, he gestured at his injuries.

'Were you an army man?' Something about his neatness, his composure, suggested it.

'I was . . . once.' Reuben looked down at the dog, which was lying with its muzzle on its master's chest, and his body language plainly said that the subject was closed.

Gideon wandered to the end of the bed. At the top of the form on the clipboard somebody had written *Reuben (?)* It seemed that, so far, their patient had managed to protect his anonymity.

'I guess, for you – after the copse – this must be hell,' he said sympathetically, leaning on the rail.

'I'll leave, tomorrow.'

Gideon had an idea the staff might have something to say about that, but he didn't give much for their chances of stopping him.

'What did you tell the police?'

'Nothin'. Said I couldn't remember.'

'Where will you go?'

'Home. Back to the woods.'

'It's a crime scene . . . They'll have it taped off.'

'I'll wait. Will you bring Buddy, in a day or two?'

'Yes, of course, but what if whoever did this comes back? If you didn't give him the diary, aren't you afraid he'll try again?'

'If he does, I'll be ready.'

Gideon nodded. He had a feeling it was no more than the truth.

FIFTEEN

W HEN GIDEON LEFT REUBEN, leading a very reluctant Buddy, he found Tilly seated in a waiting area a little
way down the corridor, drinking coffee from a polystyrene cup.

'What did you find out? Does he still have the diary?'

'He's hidden it. He told me where it is, and he wants me to
take it off his hands.'

'So why couldn't he tell you that with me there? I mean - no
offence – but it hasn't really got anything to do with you. After
all, Damien was *my* brother.'

'I think it was because Damien told Reuben he didn't want
you involved. Perhaps he guessed it might be dangerous.'

'So you *do* think it has something to do with his death.'

It seemed only fair to tell her.

'It looks that way, yes. Reuben thought so.'

Looking suddenly bleak, Tilly squashed her empty cup and
dropped it in a nearby bin. Together they began to retrace their
steps towards the exit, the dog padding resignedly behind. After
a moment, Tilly pulled a handkerchief from her pocket and blew
her nose.

'Sorry, it still catches me unawares sometimes,' she said, straightening her back determinedly.

Gideon gave her arm a brief rub but said nothing.

'What I don't understand,' she went on, 'is why Damien didn't just go to the police if he found something important in the diary.'

Gideon pursed his lips and shrugged.

'Perhaps he was intending to but just asked one question too many before he had a chance. Who knows?' he said, still evading the blackmail issue.

They walked in silence for a spell, Gideon wishing he knew what Tilly intended doing. If there were any way to avoid it, he would still prefer not to hand the matter over to the authorities just yet, at least until he had had time to judge the importance of the diary for himself.

'What do you want to do?' he asked finally.

'Well, the first step is obviously to find this bloody diary and see just what it does say. Then we can decide what's best to do with it.'

'And the police?'

'If it's got anything to do with Damien's murder, then we have to give it to them, don't we? But I want to see it first. If you're right, and it *is* about Marcus and what happened at Ponsonby, it's family business and we have a right to know.' She paused, shaking her head. 'I still find it hard to believe that Damien would keep something like that to himself. We were always so close.'

Turning a corner, they came face to face with a grey-haired man wearing a raincoat over a rather tired-looking suit. The man stopped, a look of recognition spreading over his features.

Detective Inspector Rockley.

Gideon cursed inwardly. He'd guessed Rockley would seek them out sooner or later, but he'd hoped it would be later. It was fortunate that, as yet, he knew nothing of the existence of Julian Norris' diary, but Gideon was painfully conscious of what they had been saying just moments before.

If Rockley had overheard, he gave no sign of it.

'Ah! Miss Daniels; Mr Blake. I was going to come and find you tomorrow. I understand you found our mystery man in the woods. Would you by any chance have a minute to spare?'

'Er, well, we were just trying to sneak the dog out,' Gideon confided. 'He really shouldn't be here.'

'Well, in that case, we could either talk outside in the cold, or maybe I could find someone to let us have the use of an office or something for five minutes. I'm sure there are several empty, this time of night, and I should think the dog would be excused for a short time. Ah – nurse, have you got a moment?'

Because he was waiting to see whether Tilly stood by their half-formed agreement to keep the existence of the diary a secret, the interview with Rockley, though not long, was uncomfortable, for Gideon at least. Honest by nature and upbringing, he didn't relish the idea of being less than truthful with the detective, for whom he had a great deal of respect.

Rockley didn't seem overly surprised that Tilly could give him no further information on the charcoal burner, not even to the extent of being able to say for sure whether Reuben was his first or last name.

The nurse had brought tea and a plate of bourbon biscuits for them, and, seated at the desk of some absent consultant, the policeman took full advantage of both. He listened while Gideon and Tilly gave him their account of the morning's events and, probably because it was the partial truth, he accepted without demur their story of the sheep's presence on the gallops having led them to search the woodsman out.

'Has he told you anything about the attack?' Rockley asked. 'He was particularly unforthcoming when I visited him earlier. I think he would have liked me to believe he was a few peas short of a pod, but I don't think there's a lot wrong with his intellect. Did you get on any better?'

'He said they took him by surprise,' Gideon reported.

'Apparently he was feeding his dog – this dog – when they hit him from behind. He doesn't know who it was. Or if he does, he wasn't telling.'

'And he doesn't know why?'

Gideon shrugged. 'He's not a talkative kind of bloke.'

'You know . . .' Rockley said, dunking a biscuit in his tea for what Gideon felt was a dangerously long time. 'I can't help thinking there must be more to this than meets the eye. First your brother's murder,' this with a nod towards Tilly, 'then the house is broken into, and now this . . .'

'You think it's connected?' Gideon injected incredulity into his tone. 'But I thought you were satisfied that Tetley shot Damien.'

'Well, it seems that way.' Rockley took another bourbon cream. 'But what I'm seeing is a whole bunch of loose ends, and I don't like loose ends. I don't like 'em at all.'

The diary was hidden in a large plastic sandwich box, ten feet up in the hollow trunk of a gnarled ash on the edge of Reuben's copse.

Gideon had made his way to the wood the morning after visiting the hospital and, mindful of Reuben's warning, he'd gone alone. Just supposing someone really *was* watching, it would be virtually impossible to reach the copse undetected, starting out from the farm. Gideon thought it unlikely that Reuben's attacker would be in a hurry to return to the scene of his crime, but on the other hand, if he suspected that Gideon knew where to find the diary, he might quite well lie in wait to relieve him of it on his return.

Leaving the Gatehouse by the way of the Priory drive and Home Farm Lane, and setting off in the opposite direction to that of his destination, Gideon arrived on the outskirts of Puddlestone Farm's land feeling fairly confident that he hadn't been followed. He parked in a field gateway, some two miles from Reuben's copse, and with Zebedee bounding happily at his heels and an Ordnance Survey Explorer map in his hand, found his way across country to the south corner of the wood. Here, following Reuben's efficient directions, he almost immediately happened upon the stile beside which grew the hollow ash he'd come to find.

Having called upon almost forgotten childhood tree-climbing skills in order to retrieve the plastic box, Gideon lost no time in opening it. It had, in the months it had lain hidden, accumulated on its surface a partial coating of algae, several rotting leaves and a deposit left by a sheltering bird, and, in spite of being water-tight, the inside was clammy with condensation. Luckily, Damien had had the foresight to seal the diary itself in a plastic bag, through which Gideon could make out Julian Norris' initials and a date written on the spine.

Suddenly, he found himself feeling rather vulnerable. Someone had wanted this handwritten journal so badly that he'd been prepared to beat a man half to death to discover its whereabouts. Where was that someone now?

Gideon couldn't resist glancing around him, but there was nothing to be seen except the budding hazel coppice with its carpet of bluebell leaves promising glory to come. Zebedee, who'd been wandering to and fro, happily snuffling amongst the wet leaf mould, was now sitting about a yard away, nose up scenting the air. Gideon took comfort from the thought that the dog's sharp eyes and ears would discern any approaching person at some distance.

Wondering if Reuben had indeed discharged himself from the hospital, he tucked the grubby box in the poacher's pocket of his oiled-cotton coat and had turned to retrace his steps before a disturbing thought struck him.

Damien had been shot, and although Gideon could derive some reassurance from the knowledge that his murderer was accounted for, was this false security? There were four more men on the list he'd made who were still alive and at large, and, by the very nature of their sport, all four would be expert marksmen.

But surely, he reasoned as he trudged back across the wet grass, however great the provocation, the chances of finding more than one man who was prepared to commit murder, in a group of five unrelated men, had to be infinitesimal.

Trying to ignore the slightly uncomfortable sensation between his shoulder blades, Gideon let himself through a gate in the hedge and started across the open space beyond.

Friday April 23rd – Day Six

Six days down, eight to go. It was my turn to ride the grey this morning. I wasn't looking forward to it after he played up with Robin yesterday, but actually, it was OK. I got a clear round and Harry said he went well for me. Got a bollocking this afternoon, though. That Major Clemence is a bastard. I was running as fast as I could but there's no way I could keep up with Marcus and Timothy Landless. Even Lloyd was struggling. Clemence keeps calling him 'Old Man' which is really making him mad!

I don't know what I'm doing here. I'm worst at everything except the shooting and fencing. If it wasn't for Marcus, I think I'd leave, but I promised Damien and I don't want to let him down. Marcus has been quiet all day ~ it was his eighteenth birthday and I think maybe he was homesick, poor kid. Chef made him a cake at tea, which we all helped him eat. Bed early tonight, the others were teasing me but I need all the sleep I can get!

Monday April 26th

Oh God, this is a nightmare! I still can't believe it. We got drunk and played a stupid game and now Marcus is dead!

How can this have happened? I keep thinking I'll wake up ~ God, I wish I could! What the hell am I going to say to Damien? They were here yesterday ~ the whole family ~ but I didn't have a chance to speak to them. I don't think I could have faced them, anyway.

What have we done?

I haven't slept since Friday because every time I close my eyes I hear that terrible scream. The police were here again today and I was terri-fied they would want to see us but as Sam said, why should they? They don't know what we know. Nobody knows except us.

Sam and Adam seem really calm. How can they be? I'm so scared. I still want to tell the truth. Gary wants to as well but the others agree with Lloyd.

Oh God! Why did we start that bloody stupid game? It is my fault, whatever they say. I was supposed to be looking after Marcus. I knew he'd had too much to drink and I should have brought him straight back here.

Oh God, why did this have to happen? Why??? I'd do anything if I could go back and undo what we've done.

God I swear I'll never drink again! But that won't bring Marcus back. I don't know how I'm going to live with myself.

Gideon lowered the book to his knee. After the drama of the entry on that Monday there were nothing but blank pages. If Julian Norris had continued to keep a journal, he hadn't done it in this book. Maybe he feared discovery and had hidden it away somewhere. One thing was for sure: if the others had known then that he'd committed the story of the tragedy to paper, complete with names, they'd have been considerably less than happy. Gideon imagined their dismay when Damien's photocopies had arrived on their doormats, years later, with their accompanying ransom demand.

There was now little doubt in his mind that this was what had happened, and although Gideon couldn't entirely condone Damien's actions, he found it hard to blame him, too. It was almost impossible to imagine how Damien must have felt reading the diary for the first time, and Gideon couldn't decide whether Julian's decision to finally come clean had been the right one. However wrong it had been to withhold the truth originally, after twelve years, wouldn't it have been kinder to the family to let the matter rest? Or was it more important that the record be put straight, whatever the consequences?

Gideon wasn't sure, and it was academic now. Besides this, he was pretty certain, from what Marion had told him, that Julian's motive in revealing the truth was by that time more selfish than anything. He had made the decision to take his own life and wished to depart the world with the slate wiped clean, regardless of the turmoil he might leave behind.

Gideon had read the journal from start to finish, not knowing at what point he would come across the familiar page, and, in doing so, had gained considerable insight into its author's troubled soul. 'Nervous Norris' had indeed been an apt, if not especially kind, nickname for someone who privately agonised over the kinds of issues and daily events for which the average young man barely spared a thought.

Outside the windows the light had faded into twilight while he was reading, and on the table beside his chair a mug of coffee stood, cold and uninviting. Looking at his watch, Gideon rose a little stiffly to his feet and stretched the kinks out of his joints. On the rug in front of the wood-burning stove, Zebedee looked up, hopefully. It was gone seven o'clock and past his teatime.

'Any dog worth its salt would have pulled the curtains, made up the fire and brought me another cup of coffee,' Gideon told him, and was rewarded by Zeb's feathery tail thumping on the mat. 'OK, come on, I'll feed you.'

In the kitchen Gideon forked meat into bowls for Zeb and also Elsa, who had appeared – as if by magic – at the sound of the fridge door shutting.

Having found and read the diary, he was faced with another problem. What to do with it? And what to do with the knowledge he had gained?

Tilly would, understandably, want to see the book. Should he let her? Or would the best course of action be to destroy it and deny finding it? *I should've burnt the bloody thing!* Reuben had said, and Gideon half-wished he had. He thought he could probably convince Tilly that the search had proved fruitless, but was it the right thing to do?

The phone rang, interrupting his thoughts, and he went into the hall. Caller display announced Puddlestone Farm, and he paused with his hand extended towards the receiver. If it was Tilly, what was he going to say?

He withdrew his hand and stood staring into space. She would ring again. He needed to gather his thoughts. The diary had revealed a lot about Julian's state of mind following Marcus' death but very little detail concerning the actual event. Gideon found he wanted to know more, and he felt sure that, if she saw the diary, Tilly would, too.

The telephone bell cut off mid-ring and Gideon reached a decision. Fetching Damien's list, he returned to the phone and keyed in a number.

When Gideon met Garth Stephenson in the Goose and Ferret some forty minutes later, the teacher looked tense and ill at ease. He had been inclined to hang up on Gideon when he rang, until Gideon said, 'I know about the game you played at Ponsonby Castle.'

There had been a pause, then Stephenson had replied, 'All right. I'll meet you. Half an hour, at the pub in the village?'

Now he took a long draught of his beer and looked at Gideon warily across the dark wood table, with its token carnation and fern frond in a slim glass vase. There were far fewer people in the bar than there had been on Gideon's last visit, and they were virtually alone in their corner by the fire.

'How do you know about Ponsonby?'

'I've seen one of the photocopies.' Gideon watched him for a reaction but saw only a deepening resignation.

'Where did you get it?'

'Damien had it.' Of the five, Gideon suspected the teacher least of all, but he was not about to take the chance of telling him he'd found the diary.

'So now you know, what are you going to do about it?'

'I'm not sure yet. I expect it'll be up to Tilly.'

For a moment, Stephenson looked puzzled.

'Damien's sister,' Gideon supplied.

'Oh . . . yes.' Stephenson bowed his head and regarded his beer glass gloomily. 'I'm not sure I understand why you got involved in all this. What is it to you? I mean, it all happened so long ago.'

'Damien's murder didn't.'

The teacher's blue eyes rose to meet Gideon's.

'Is that what this is about?'

'You tell me.'

'What? I didn't have anything to do with that! I wasn't even sure it was him who . . .' His voice faded.

'You weren't sure it was Damien who was blackmailing you?' Gideon said. 'Is that what you were going to say? But I've a strong suspicion someone did know.'

'I had nothing to do with it!' Stephenson whispered fiercely. 'I'm not a criminal! It was all an accident – you saw the page from the diary – it was a stupid game that went wrong. The only thing I'm guilty of was covering it up. I never wanted to do it and I've regretted it ever since.'

'That was Lloyd's idea, wasn't it?'

Stephenson looked swiftly about him, as if expecting to see one of his co-conspirators lurking at an adjoining table. Apparently reassured, he continued, low-voiced.

'Originally, but the others agreed – except Julian, of course. We put it to the vote. It was awful, with poor Marcus just lying there. But Lloyd said us owning up wasn't going to do *him* any good. He said there'd be hell to pay, and we'd probably get chucked off the team. He said Marcus wouldn't have wanted that and, after all, he'd asked to join in the game.'

'Tell me about the game,' Gideon prompted. 'How did it start?'

Stephenson frowned slightly, remembering. 'It was Saturday and we'd been given the evening off, so we all went down to the pub in the village – the Iron Kettle, I think it was called. We'd been training really hard all week and we were on a bit of a high, like kids let out of school. Of course we all drank too much. I guess there was a little one-upmanship going on; a bunch of guys, in our late teens and early twenties, all trying to prove how grown-up we were.' He broke off and laughed bitterly.

'A recipe for disaster,' Gideon agreed.

'Well, there were one or two older; I mean, Lloyd was nearly thirty but he was very fit because he'd been doing triathlon, and he was the best rider among us, and one of the best swimmers. We all thought he was a cert to make the team, though our fitness coach, Major Clemence, was pretty down on him, I must say. Kept calling him "the old man" but I think that was just to make him try even harder. You know, the way you're sometimes harder on a promising pupil, just because you know he can do better − no, perhaps you don't . . .'

'So you all got drunk. What then?'

'Well, I don't suppose we were *all* drunk,' Stephenson said, thinking back. 'There were fifteen or twenty of us there that night. I expect one or two stayed fairly sober, but not in our group. It was the day after Marcus' eighteenth birthday, and the first time he'd been legally allowed to drink, so we made sure it was a night he'd remember. God, you're so bloody stupid at that age, aren't you?'

'How old were you?'

'Me? I was twenty-one. Robin was twenty; Adam, Sam and Julian were about twenty-four or twenty-five.'

'So what happened then?'

It appeared Stephenson had long since stopped worrying about the wisdom of confessing all. In fact, now he'd started, he seemed almost eager to unburden himself.

'Most of the boys went back by the road. One or two of them were feeling rather the worse for wear and just wanted to get back as quickly as possible, I think, but a few of us decided to go across country − across the castle grounds − and that's when we started playing that stupid game.'

'What was the game?'

'I don't know really. I think we made the rules up as we went along, but then it doesn't have to make sense when it's nearly midnight and you're plastered.'

'Can you remember who started it?'

His brow creased. 'I think it was Robin. We were walking along beside the lake and he dared Sam to dive in off the bridge, so he did, and when he got out he dared Robin to swim across the lake, naked. Then I did it. Bloody stupid, really. That lake was incredibly cold. Any one of us could have got into trouble and drowned or even died of the shock. But it had to be Marcus.'

'So did Marcus go in the lake? I thought the diary said he fell.'

'No, he didn't go in the lake. We'd moved on, by then, and we were passing this kind of folly. It was like a ruined castle, only it wasn't really old – not medieval, I mean. Anyway, Lloyd looked at it and said, "What about that, then?" So then Adam – I think it was Adam – dared him to walk up and round the perimeter wall. It wasn't very big; there was a tower and a couple of arches and this wall, with stones around the base as if they'd fallen. It didn't have a roof or anything; I don't imagine it ever had one. It was built to look romantic – probably by the Victorians.'

'And Lloyd walked along the wall?'

'Yes, easily. And then he dared Marcus to do it. It was only about twelve feet tall, maybe a little more over the arch, and there was good footing. It was bright moonlight. Anyone could have done it.'

'Unless they were drunk,' Gideon said.

'Yes, or scared of heights.'

'And Marcus was?'

'Well, he *looked* petrified. I didn't realise at first, we were all chanting his name – it was part of the game, which just goes to prove how smashed we all were. But when he got up there and had to let go of the tower, he kind of froze. Gradually we all stopped chanting and someone – I'm not sure if it was Lloyd or Sam – called out, "Go on, Marcus! You can do it." And then Julian said, "He doesn't have to, if he doesn't want to." But he did really, didn't he . . . ?'

'What do you mean?'

'Well, because he was the youngest, and desperate to fit in.'

'He wanted your respect?'

'Yes, and especially Lloyd's. He idolised Lloyd – I think because he was older and more experienced, and one of his brother's friends. I think Marcus would have done almost anything Lloyd asked him to, that night.'

'Poor little bastard!'

The teacher nodded sadly.

'Anyway, he edged away from the tower and looked down, and then he stepped forward and just seemed to miss the wall altogether. It was horrible.' Stephenson grimaced, as if seeing it again, and his fingers whitened around his beer glass. 'He fell so slowly but he didn't try to save himself, and suddenly he was there, lying on the stones at the bottom of the wall, dead.'

'What did you do then?'

'Well, Julian went to feel for a pulse but we all knew he was dead. It was the way he was lying, and there was blood coming from his nose and his ears.' Stephenson shook his head. 'I've seen him so many times in my dreams. He looked so young and – well, so peaceful. Apart from the blood, he could have been sleeping.'

'So you had a vote and decided . . . what? To say he went off on his own?'

'Yeah. We just walked on back to the castle as if nothing had happened, and when we went in we were all laughing and mucking about – that was Lloyd's idea – to look as though we'd been doing it all the way home. One of the trainers was there, he ticked our names off and asked if we'd seen Marcus. I nearly cracked then, but Sam said, cool as you like, "No, we thought he was with the others." It was that easy.'

He paused and drained his beer.

'Clemence woke us at six the next morning to give us the news. He said they didn't know how it happened. God, that was an awful moment, waking up and remembering! It was like it had happened all over again. Everybody was devastated, and a couple of people said he'd seemed quiet lately. Some of the younger guys were crying – I think I was – and the coaches were so nice, so supportive, it made me feel even guiltier. I wanted to scream out the truth, but I couldn't because of the others, and every minute that passed made it more impossible to own up. That was the longest day of my life.'

Gideon regarded him with a certain amount of compassion. There was no doubt at all in his mind that Stephenson was telling the truth. It would have been natural, aged twenty-one and scared witless, to follow the lead of an older, more experienced man, and so difficult to break out of the group and assert himself. He could only wish that Damien had enquired further before he made the fateful decision to make the group suffer. But then, maybe not. The story as told by Sam or Lloyd might have been entirely different.

'Another drink, gentlemen?'

The barman had stopped in passing, and Stephenson looked momentarily blank, as if he'd forgotten where he was.

The offer was repeated. Stephenson accepted, Gideon declined, and their empty glasses were whisked away towards the bar.

'You didn't guess it was Damien who was blackmailing you, then?' Gideon asked.

'I thought it might be but I wasn't sure. I thought it could have been Julian's widow or brother, as it started after Julian died, but whoever it was, there wasn't much I could do except pay. It wasn't as if he was asking for a huge amount, and I don't think the head would have been too pleased with that kind of publicity. In a way, I felt I deserved to be punished – does that sound ridiculous?'

'No. But I think you're being too hard on yourself. Marcus' death was an accident and all you did was succumb to peer pressure. If anyone was to blame, it was Lloyd. He was old enough to know better.'

Stephenson sat staring broodingly at the beer mat he was twiddling between forefinger and thumb.

'I know you're right. It's what I'd tell any of my boys, but somehow it's different when it happens to you, isn't it?'

In due course his beer arrived, and he took a grateful swallow, running his tongue along his top lip to remove the froth.

There was little more to say, really. Gideon sighed and got to his feet.

'Well, you can stop paying now, I guess, and get on with your life.'

'Yeah.' Stephenson didn't look overjoyed at the news. 'What will you do? Will you tell the police?'

Gideon shook his head and shrugged.

'As I said, it's up to Tilly. Personally, I won't do anything, but I can't answer for her. And if it has any bearing on Damien's murder, I guess the police will have to be told. Sorry.'

'No, it's all right,' Stephenson said dully, shaking his head, and Gideon lifted his jacket off the back of the chair and put it on.

'You sent the cash to a PO box, in an unmarked envelope . . .'

'Yeah. Once a month.'

'Well, if it's any consolation, it all went straight to Damien's favourite charity, so some good came out of it.'

Gideon drove home with the story of Marcus' tragic death playing and replaying in his mind like a film.

Had that been Damien's intention in blackmailing the culprits? Was it so he could be sure they'd never forget? '*It wasn't as if he was asking for a huge amount,*' Stephenson had said. Had he perhaps asked what he felt each individual could afford? After all, what would seem a crippling amount to a nightwatchman like Tetley would be just so much pocket money to 'something in the City' Robin Tate, with his manor house and motorbike museum. And the consequence of revelation would surely be less for Tetley than the owner of a health spa or a would-be politician; it probably wouldn't even make the news. This made it all the more ironic that it should have been Tetley who'd reacted with such catastrophic violence.

On the seat beside him Gideon's mobile phone chirruped several times, announcing messages left while he was out of range, and then began to ring. The display told him it was Tilly and, having ignored her call earlier, he felt it was only fair to pick up.

'Gideon! I've been trying to get you for ages. Where have you been?'

'Sorry.'

'I was getting a bit worried. Did you get the diary?'

'Yes, I did. Look, we need to talk but I'm in the car at the moment . . .'

'Well, where are you? Could you come over?'

'I could do but I'm not terribly close. I might be rather late.' Gideon knew it had been close on half past nine when he'd left the Goose and Ferret.

'I don't mind, if you don't.'

'OK.' He did a quick calculation. 'I'll probably be about thirty – thirty-five minutes.'

'I'll put the kettle on.'

By the time Gideon reached Puddlestone Farm it was getting on for half past ten, and he apologised to Tilly.

'The Land Rover is more of a staying chaser than a five-furlong beast,' he said lightly. 'Hope I haven't woken your parents.'

'They're in the front room watching a film. Or at least Mum is. It's a fair bet Dad nodded off about ten minutes after it started. Come in and sit down.'

Gideon followed her through to the newly refurbished kitchen and sat while she made them each a mug of coffee. She put a biscuit tin on the table beside his mug and it was only then that he realised he hadn't eaten since a sandwich lunch at midday.

Tilly sat opposite him, and quickly spotted the bag-wrapped package he'd laid on the table.

'Is that it?'

'Yeah.' Gideon took the book out and pushed it towards her.

'What you want is on the last written page, where the ribbon is. It seems he abandoned the diary after that.'

She reached for it with shaking hands, and he helped himself to a biscuit and watched the frown grow on her face as she read.

She reached the bottom of the page, glanced briefly at Gideon, and then started again at the top, as if needing a second chance to take it in. When she finished, this time, she put the book down and fished in her pocket for a handkerchief.

'I don't know what I expected,' she said a little unsteadily. 'It wasn't suicide, was it? Marcus didn't kill himself?'

'No, he didn't.' Gideon couldn't quite gauge her mood.

Her eyes were swimming with unshed tears but suddenly she smiled and they spilled over and down her cheeks.

'He didn't kill himself!' she repeated, and what Gideon heard in her voice was immense relief. It completely vindicated his decision to tell her what Damien had discovered.

'We always worried, you know?' she went on. 'We thought perhaps it was because he was away from home; that he was homesick. He didn't want to go, you see. At the last moment he got cold feet but Damien persuaded him – no, that's not fair – we all did. We all wanted him to do it, because we thought he'd always regret it if he didn't. And then, when . . .' She plied the handkerchief again. 'We all felt so *guilty*! It was awful!' she concluded with a rush of remembered grief.

Gideon didn't know what to say, but he felt he'd lived through so many emotions with this family that he knew them well enough for silence, and so just waited, occupied with his own, far from pleasant, thoughts. The journey from Charlton Montague had given him plenty of time to reflect on the sequence of events since Damien's death and, finally, he felt he was beginning to see just a glimmer of light at the end of the long and very dark tunnel.

After a few moments, Tilly picked up the diary and looked at the page again.

'It's amazing to finally know, after all this time, but there's a lot he doesn't say. I mean, this game they were playing . . .'

'I think I can help you there. That's where I was this evening. I went to see one of the guys who was there that night. The one Julian calls Gary. He filled me in.' And starting from the beginning, much as Stephenson had, he told Tilly exactly how her younger brother had died.

She listened, for the most part in silence, until he reached the part about Marcus looking scared, then she broke in, 'Yes, he would have been. He never liked heights.'

When Gideon came to the end, she frowned. 'Tell me again. That part about the ruined castle. *Who* did he say dared Marcus to climb the wall?'

Gideon searched his memory.

'Lloyd, I think. Yes, I'm sure he said it was Lloyd. Why?'

All at once, Tilly looked bitterly angry.

'Why would he do that? He knew very well that Marcus was terrified of heights! Why did Lloyd pick the one thing he knew he would really hate?'

SIXTEEN

'YOU THINK LLOYD KNEW he'd be scared?'

'I don't just think it, I know it,' Tilly asserted. 'When Marcus was fifteen, he and a friend climbed up a haystack Dad had made down in the lower pasture, and when Marcus got to the top he just froze and wouldn't come down. In the end we had to dismantle half the stack so that it was like giant steps and he managed to kind of shuffle down those on his bottom. But he was in a hell of a state; he almost fainted and he was as white as a sheet.'

'And Lloyd knew about that?'

'He was here. He helped us with the bales. So he knew damn well Marcus couldn't have walked along that wall!'

She faced Gideon over the old pine table, her expression a mixture of anger and bewilderment.

'They'd all been drinking,' Gideon pointed out, in Lloyd's defence. 'I don't think any of them were capable of being very rational.'

'But that was deliberately cruel! He was our friend.'

'I know. But reading that diary this afternoon, I think I got a

301

pretty good idea of what it was like on that course; Julian wrote in some detail and he wasn't enjoying it much. Most of the trainers were ex-army, and they were pretty tough, especially on the fitness side of things. From what he said, Lloyd came in for quite a bit of teasing from them because he was the oldest, while Marcus seems to have done extremely well. Julian wasn't even sure that Lloyd would make the team . . .'

Tilly was watching him intensely.

'You're saying he was jealous of Marcus?'

'Well, it wouldn't have been surprising, would it? Lloyd probably saw it as his last chance for glory – at thirty-odd, he wasn't going to be in contention for another Olympic team – and it's quite possible that he saw Marcus as the young gun who was going to cost him his place . . .'

'Gideon! You don't think he did it on purpose? That he *meant* him to fall?'

'No, I wouldn't go that far. I don't think he *planned* it, as such. I think it's more likely that it was a spur of the moment thing, brought on by the drink and a fair bit of resentment. Basically, it was a chance to get back at the boy. If Marcus bunked out and didn't try, he'd be humiliated in front of his peers. If he tried and fell, there was always the chance that he might be put out of action, which would have been all to the good from Lloyd's point of view, but to be fair, I'd guess he was thinking more along the lines of a sprained ankle or a broken arm. I should imagine Lloyd was probably as shocked as the rest of them by what actually happened. No wonder he was so keen to cover it up. If Damien had found out that it was him who suggested the dare – knowing what he did – he'd really have been in hot water!'

'But he was our *friend* . . .' Tilly said, brokenly, the sense of betrayal bringing tears to her eyes again. 'And what about yesterday? Do you still think he attacked Reuben?'

'I don't like the idea, but I can't really think who else, can you?'

Tilly shook her head.

'No, I suppose not. But I still find it hard to believe Lloyd would do something like that. I mean, it's one thing to goad someone into a dangerous situation – if that's how it was – but quite another to go to them with the cold-blooded intention of beating them up! I'm sorry, I just can't get my head round it.'

'He may not have done the physical part himself,' Gideon suggested. 'I've a fair idea Lloyd knows where he can get his hands on a bit of extra muscle when he needs it and, unless I'm very much mistaken, this isn't the first time he's tried to get hold of the diary.'

Then, realising that if Lloyd was to be brought to book, Tilly would almost certainly find out anyway, he took a deep breath and told her everything he knew, from the break-ins, the attacks on himself, and what he'd discovered about Damien's blackmailing activities.

Strangely, she accepted this last information more readily than he'd expected, especially when he explained his theory as to where the money had gone.

'He just wanted them to suffer like we did,' Tilly said when he came to the end. 'Oh, God! This is a nightmare!' She buried her face in her hands momentarily, then rubbed her eyes and looked up at Gideon. 'What are we going to do?'

'Well, I've got the beginnings of an idea,' he said slowly. 'I was thinking about it on the way over. The thing is, although we've got a lot of pointers, we haven't actually got much evidence, so we're going to have to trick Lloyd into showing his hand. It may not work, but I think our ace in the hole is the fact that, as yet, he doesn't know that *we know* about the diary . . .'

The grand opening of the Dorset Cottage restaurant was at lunchtime on Friday, five days after Gideon retrieved Julian Norris' diary from its hiding place in the hollow tree. Owned by friends of Eve's who had entered, at her instigation, into a mutually bene-ficial business relationship with Giles and his sparkling apple wine, all the Priory crowd had been invited to its launch, and it was at this function that Gideon intended to set his plan in motion.

In the intervening time he worked on a portrait commission, saw a woman about a dog with a travel phobia, rode work with Tilly twice, and took Blackbird over the cross-country course on Home Farm, practising for the upcoming team chase.

His relationship with Pippa was still strained and for the most part she seemed to be avoiding him, but the upside to this unhappy state of affairs was that it made it easier to keep his newfound knowledge about Lloyd to himself.

On Thursday evening, which was unseasonably mild, he and Eve took the motorbike out, collected fish and chips, and ate them from the paper on the seafront at Lyme Regis.

Despite his busy schedule, barely an hour passed when Gideon didn't find himself going over the plan that he and Tilly had hatched in the early hours of the Monday morning, searching for possible flaws or loopholes. Gazing out over a calm sea, with Eve leaning against him, the leather of her motorcycle jacket creaking as she unashamedly picked the crispest chips from their joint portion, Gideon's mind wandered once again. It seemed to him there must be a myriad of opportunities for their scheme to fail, but he could see no way they could make it any more watertight.

Beside him, Eve sighed deeply.

'You OK?' he asked, giving her shoulder a squeeze.

'Yeah, just thinking.'

''Bout what?'

'Things.'

'What kind of things?' Gideon felt a little uneasy. It was the kind of non-conversation that he felt sure was shared by lovers everywhere and which, in his experience, often presaged a discussion of some importance. 'Is something wrong?'

She turned her head to look at him, her heavy loose plait flopping over her shoulder.

'No, not really. It's perfect. Almost *too* perfect. That's what makes me feel a little sad. It's like . . . nothing this good can last. It reminds me of those films where the hero and his girlfriend are just blissfully happy at the beginning, and you think – uh-oh, that can't last. Trouble ahead!' She smiled. 'Listen to me – what am I waffling on about? Take no notice.'

Gideon squeezed her shoulder again, harder this time. Considering his plans for the next day, it wasn't really what he needed to hear.

'C'mon, it's turning cold,' he said cheerfully, slapping her leather-clad rump. 'Let's get back and have something deeply warming and disgracefully alcoholic!'

The Dorset Cottage stood in a prime position, just off the main road, in a village outside Chilminster. Eve was all for creating a splash by turning up on the Triumph, but Gideon managed to talk her out of it; for his purposes, it would have been far from ideal. He argued that her sleek, cream Aston Martin was just as much of a head-turner, and would probably do the reputation of her friends' new restaurant far more good, but, when they came to set off, it stubbornly refused to start. In the end they went, to her evident disgust, in Gideon's Land Rover.

'It wouldn't be so bad if it was one of those shiny new ones,' she complained as she gathered her long skirts in before slamming the door. 'But this one looks as though it's seen service in both world wars!'

'Think of it as shabby chic,' Gideon advised.

Giles, Pippa and Lloyd were already there when Gideon and Eve arrived, although when they met up, glasses of Graylings Sparkler in hand, Giles was nowhere to be seen.

'Networking,' Pippa explained. 'It's probably a good thing Tilly *couldn't* make it. I think he's going to be talking business all day.'

Gideon also felt it was as well she wasn't there. Even had the scheme he'd evolved with Tilly not relied on her being at home, he wasn't at all sure she could have carried off meeting Lloyd without betraying her changed feelings towards him. He wasn't finding it easy himself, and he wasn't nearly so emotionally involved, to say nothing of never having liked the man in the first place.

The party was encouragingly well attended, with a significant media presence. Gideon thought he detected Eve's hand in the organisation, and mentioned it.

'Well, what use are contacts, if you don't use 'em?' she replied.

Her artist friend, the effortlessly urbane Trevor Erskine, was present, and came up to speak to them, glancing quizzically at Gideon as they shook hands.

'No unusual fashion accessories this time, then?'

Gideon grinned.

'No. It didn't catch on, for some reason.'

He caught Pippa looking at him curiously, but she apparently couldn't bring herself to ask.

'Private joke,' he said lightly, and wasn't fooled by her bright, brisk change of subject.

A little later, returning from the loo, Eve leaned close to Gideon and, pointing discreetly, asked, 'Who's that, over there by the window? The blonde woman in the grey trouser suit?'

Gideon glanced across and saw a tall, slim, attractive woman with long, ash-blonde hair and aquiline features. She looked smart, sophisticated and vaguely familiar. He searched his memory.

'I'm not sure, but I think it might be Harriet Lloyd-Ellis. Why?'

'Oh, Lloyd's ex?'

'Yes, it is,' Pippa said, overhearing. Lloyd had deserted her some five or ten minutes earlier, ostensibly to go and talk to Giles, but Giles was now in plain view, and Lloyd had not as yet reappeared. 'Why do you ask?'

Eve returned some vague answer, but when Pippa herself drifted away to talk with an acquaintance, she explained.

'I didn't want to say anything with Pippa here, but when I went to find the loo I took a wrong turning and ended up out the back, and who should I see out there but Lloyd and the blonde.'

'Yeah, I think they still see quite a lot of each other because of the kids.'

'Hmm, well, I shouldn't think there was much of each other that they don't see, judging by the way they were carrying on when I spotted them,' Eve remarked dryly. 'Luckily they didn't see me. I just stepped backwards and pulled the door to.'

'You're kidding! Poor Pips!'

'Yeah. He's a twenty-four-carat bastard, isn't he?' Eve agreed. 'I hate to admit it, but you might have been right about him all along.'

Gideon's mind was racing. That was a development he hadn't expected. Why separate if they still felt that way about each other? Or had absence made the heart grow fonder, as the saying went? The thought that Lloyd might have been cheating on Pippa, all along, made his blood boil, and made him all the more eager to reveal Lloyd for the criminal he believed he was.

But, silently, Gideon was beginning to fret.

His plan relied on Lloyd being within earshot when Tilly phoned, and so far he hadn't stayed close long enough for Gideon to set it up. Any moment now they'd be asked to take their places for the meal, and by the time that was over the general exodus would no doubt start.

Looking around, he saw that Lloyd had joined Pippa, in a small group that included Giles. Touching Eve on the arm to alert her to his departure, Gideon worked his way through the throng of happy, chattering faces until he was just a couple of feet away. Eve caught up and looked over his shoulder as he took his mobile phone from his pocket and scrolled through the menu.

'What's up?'

'Oh, nothing. Just a message. Nothing important.'

Finding Tilly's number, Gideon pressed a couple more buttons and sent a blank text message winging its way to her, then – praying that this wouldn't be one of the times when the phone company inexplicably kept the message for half an hour or more before delivering it – he sidled, with apologies, into Giles' group, making room for Eve at his side.

The conversation seemed to be about drag hunting, and Lloyd was holding forth with some amusing tale of his past exploits when Gideon's phone began to ring.

'Oh, sorry!' he exclaimed, digging it out of his pocket. 'Should've switched it off. Oh, it's Tilly! Excuse me . . .' Half turning away, he put the phone to his ear.

'Hi Tilly. Is everything all right?'

'How's it going?' she asked. 'I thought you were never going to text me. Is he listening?'

'Yes.'

'OK. Well, I've dropped it off.'

'*Reuben* did?' Gideon said loudly, launching into his half of their prearranged conversation. Behind him, he sensed a pause in the chatter as the group heard his exclamation. 'For me? What kind of package?'

'Just a package, done up in paper. He was adamant that you should have it.'

'Well, did he say what was in it?'

'No, not a word. Is Lloyd listening?' she added, in a lower voice.

'Yeah. OK. Yeah, we're all at the restaurant . . . No, it'll be OK there. Yeah, sure . . . OK. Well, thanks, Tilly . . . You too. Bye.'

He switched the phone off and rejoined the group. Just before he'd cut the connection he'd heard her say, with a catch in her voice, 'Get the bastard for me, Gideon!'

'Tilly all right?' Giles asked, concerned.

Silently Gideon blessed him for providing the opening he needed.

'Yeah. Odd though . . .'

'What is?' Eve asked. Gideon hadn't let her in on the scheme, for the simple reason that he knew she'd do everything in her power to stop him going through with it, and, given her resource-fulness, he thought it more than likely that she'd succeed.

'Well, you remember I told you about Reuben, the old char-coal burner that lives on Tilly's farm?' he said now.

'The one that was attacked the day we went to London?'

'Yes, that's right. Well, he discharged himself from hospital the other day, and now Tilly says he's gone; moved on. They don't know where.'

'You can't blame him,' Pippa said. 'I don't suppose he'd ever feel safe again, poor man.'

Gideon had told her about the attack on Reuben, feeling that Lloyd would think it strange if he didn't.

'Well, what's odd is that he apparently left a package behind with Tilly, with instructions to give it to me.'

'A token of his gratitude, perhaps,' Eve said.

'What's in it?' Lloyd asked, watching Gideon intently.

'I've no idea. Tilly hasn't opened it. She rang to say that she had to come over this way, so she's dropped it in at the Priory. She would have left it at the Gatehouse but, of course, I haven't got a letter box and she didn't like to leave it in the porch, not knowing how valuable it might be. She said Reuben was pretty insistent that I get it. Apparently it's something in a padded envelope.'

'Shouldn't think it'd be very valuable if that old tramp had it,' Lloyd remarked dismissively.

'You don't know. He might be a nobleman who's denounced modern ways and gone back to nature,' Giles suggested, tongue in cheek. 'He's probably had the family diamonds squirreled away in a hollow tree somewhere for decades.'

Gideon smiled and saw Lloyd glance thoughtfully at Giles. None of them knew how close his jokey remark had landed.

'Tilly said there didn't seem to be anyone about. I suppose Mrs Morecambe has gone to visit her sister.' It had been her custom on a Friday for as long as he could remember. She left about noon and cycled down to her sister in the village for the afternoon, getting back around five.

Conversation moved on. Gideon had begun to wonder if all his planning had been for nothing, when Lloyd suddenly exclaimed, put his hand in his pocket and drew out his own mobile phone.

'It's on silent,' he explained, thumbing a key and putting it to his ear.

The small circle of friends fell quiet once more, each striving not to appear to be listening.

Lloyd's conversation was short and to the point.

'Oh. Hi, Simon . . . What . . . ? When . . . ? Have you called the vet? Well, it's a bit awkward but yes, of course I'll come. Yes, I'll be there right away. Make sure you keep him on his feet. Yes, yes . . . OK. In about twenty minutes. Yes. Bye.' He snapped the lid of his phone shut and looked round the circle apologetically. 'I'm going to have to scoot. That was Simon, the kennelman. Badger's got colic. The vet's on his way, but I'd rather be there. Sorry, folks.'

'I'll come with you,' Pippa said instantly.

Lloyd shook his head.

'No need. You stop here and enjoy the lunch. There's nothing you can do — especially dressed like that. I expect the vet'll get there before I do.'

'Oh, OK.' Pippa looked a little disappointed. 'I hope old Badger's all right.'

'Me too.' Lloyd gave her a kiss on the cheek, waved to the rest of them and left, edging his way through the crowd towards the door.

'Looks like I'll be cadging a lift with you guys,' Pippa said, forcing a smile.

Somewhere at the top of the room, somebody announced that the meal would be served shortly, if guests would like to take their places, and — thanking providence for the timing — Gideon declared his intention of nipping to the toilet before he sat down to eat.

Going out to the foyer, he waylaid a member of staff and asked him if he could wait five minutes, and then tell the diners at table eight that he'd had to nip out for twenty minutes but would be back. Then he went through to the back of the building, where he found the door that Eve had inadvertently opened earlier, and slipped down the corridor beyond towards the open air.

Once outside, Gideon ran across the yard, knowing from a previous fact-finding mission that on this side there were no overlooking windows from the restaurant, and vaulted over a stone wall onto the road. The Land Rover was parked on the verge, a little way back up the road, and, as he climbed in and slotted the key into the ignition, he sent a silent apology to Giles and the girls, who would now probably have to call themselves a taxi.

Lloyd was nowhere to be seen, his sage green Range Rover absent from the space he'd collared close to the door of the restaurant. If Gideon hadn't known where he was going the cause would have been lost at the outset, but Gideon knew exactly where Lloyd was going.

He drove as fast as he dared, knowing that Lloyd's vehicle was significantly faster than his own. Either the bike or Eve's Aston Martin would have been much more suited to this pursuit, but if he'd accidentally got too close behind Lloyd in either of those distinctive vehicles, the game would have been up. This reminded him that he must replace the Aston's distributor cap when he got back.

Turning off the main road towards Tarrant Grayling, Gideon hoped against hope that Tilly had remembered to alert Logan as they'd arranged.

Out of necessity, he'd spoken to the policeman on the Monday, telling him enough to get his interest, and seeking his advice. Logan was no fool, and had initially refused to co-operate until he'd had the full story. When Gideon had called his bluff and threatened to go it alone, he'd finally agreed.

Almost of its own volition, Gideon's hand came off the steering wheel and checked the presence of the matchbox-sized transmitter that was hidden in the breast pocket of his shirt. Logan had bought it from an Internet website, explaining that red tape rendered obtaining one from police stores virtually impossible. Rostered off duty from six on the Friday morning, he'd promised to be in the vicinity of Tarrant Grayling from noon onwards with the receiver, waiting for Tilly to confirm that the plan was in motion.

As the Land Rover swayed round a tight bend, barely holding the road, Gideon's phone began to ring.

Tilly again.

'Hello, yeah?' This was no time for pleasantries.

'I can't get hold of Logan!' Tilly sounded agitated. 'I've been trying ever since I spoke to you, but all I get is his answering service.'

'Shit! Well, keep trying! But if you can't reach him in the next minute or two, you'd better ring Rockley – though God knows how far away *he'll* be! And God only knows how you'll explain it all to him, come to that!'

'But you can't do it without Logan, he's got the receiver!' Tilly protested.

'I know,' Gideon said grimly. 'So keep trying!'

The thought of going after Lloyd without Logan on hand as back-up didn't appeal to Gideon at all, even though on this occasion Lloyd wouldn't have had the time or seen the necessity to mobilise the heavy mob, but the idea of drawing back and trying again another day wasn't one Gideon was prepared to entertain. They'd never again be able to set up such a brilliant opportunity to catch the man red-handed. Also, crucially, they'd made the decision to use the real diary as bait because Gideon was pretty sure that if Lloyd tore open the package, then and there, and discovered he'd been duped, there would be no hope of getting him to talk.

As it was, he wasn't quite sure what Lloyd's course of action would be. To remove the package entirely would doubtless give rise to much speculation, but maybe, as he believed them ignorant of the diary's existence, he would take a chance on that. After all, he had no reason to think they suspected him, and Gideon had told him that Reuben was long gone.

Gideon swung the Land Rover into the drive of Graylings Priory, gritting his teeth as it skidded on the damp tarmac under the trees. His first priority was to get to the house while Lloyd was still inside.

At the top of the drive he slowed down, pulling into the cover of the rhododendrons just out of sight of the house. There he stopped the Land Rover, switched off the ignition and got out, leaving the door open so as not to make a noise.

Lloyd would have entered the house through the boot room into the kitchen, making use of the back-door key, which Mrs Morecambe habitually left in one of the old wellies. The Priory's keys were large in size and few in number, and it was a general rule that the less often they left the property, the better. In fact, John Norris had tutted in horror at their scarcity and recommended that Giles arrange to get some copies made as soon as he could.

Ducking low under the level of the window sills, Gideon made his way through the stableyard, noting the presence of Lloyd's Range Rover with a strange mixture of satisfaction and apprehension.

Unsure how close on Lloyd's heels he might be, he peered cautiously into the boot room before entering. It was empty, and he moved forward to the door into the kitchen, his heart beginning to thud uncomfortably hard.

What if Lloyd had somehow seen his approach and was waiting on the other side of the door, with heaven knew what in his hands? A carving knife, perhaps, or the poker from beside the fire?

He steeled himself to open it, and saw at once that there was nothing to fear. Pippa's dogs, Fanny and Bella, and Giles' two terriers were all standing by the far door that led into the hall, those who had tails waving them gently. No clearer indication was needed of where Lloyd had gone.

When Gideon shut the boot room door, all four dogs turned and bounded across, bodies wriggling and squirming their delight. He was heartily glad that he'd left his own dog at the Gatehouse, because he was almost certain that Zebedee would have given voice to his joy with a series of loud barks.

To be sure of leaving the kitchen without inadvertently letting one or more of the dogs escape, he gave them each a Bonio from the cupboard, and then opened the door a crack and looked through into the entrance hall beyond.

It was empty.

Light poured in by way of the tall, ornate leaded window to the side of the huge front door, illuminating gently whirling dust motes, and he could see that the mat in front of it was unadorned by a parcel of any kind.

Lloyd was clearly in the building, but where?

Gideon stepped quietly into the hall and closed the door behind him, his mind running through the possibilities. He had half-expected to meet Lloyd coming back out with the diary under his arm, or failing that, to find him ripping the padded envelope open in the hallway. The worst scenario he'd contemplated was being altogether too far behind and for Lloyd to have put the whole thing in the Aga without stopping to look at it, but he felt this was the least likely outcome. The lure of reading the journal after all these years would surely be too strong for anyone with an interest in it, and besides, as far as Lloyd knew, he had all afternoon.

So where was he now?

Perhaps, Gideon reasoned, Lloyd hadn't been one hundred per cent sure the package *did* contain Julian Norris' diary. Perhaps he had decided to open it carefully and make sure, before taking any further action. If that *was* the case, Gideon had a good idea where he might have gone: the one place he could be sure of finding scissors, Sellotape and the like. Giles' study.

Moving to the foot of the grand staircase, he peered up, wishing he could see beyond the turn. He knew from experience that the stairs creaked badly – after close on five hundred years, they could be excused that – but, just now, a nice straight modern flight would have been a godsend.

Gideon hesitated. If he was right, and Lloyd *had* taken the diary to Giles' study, then he should be some distance from the head of the main staircase. On the other hand, if he waited in the hall, then surely, sooner or later, Lloyd would have to pass him on his way out. Where was the hurry?

Even as he thought it, he heard a door bang and the sound of someone walking across the old floorboards overhead. Another door opened and shut, and the footsteps moved over the landing towards the top of the stairs, accompanied by the jauntily whistled strains of 'Greensleeves'. Hurriedly, Gideon moved back out of sight as the whistler began to descend.

Lloyd came down the lower flight of stairs casually carrying the padded envelope in one hand, and headed for the front door, presumably to replace it on the mat.

'Curiosity get the better of you, Lloyd?' Gideon said, stepping out of hiding behind him.

Lloyd paused, then turned smoothly, faint surprise showing on his misleadingly pleasant face.

'Gideon! Well, well. What happened? Didn't you like the menu?'

'Ha ha,' Gideon said humourlessly. 'I might ask the same of you. Weren't you supposed to be rushing to the side of a sick horse? Badger, wasn't it? How is the poor old boy?'

'In a bad way,' Lloyd said feigning concern. 'But I couldn't do much in my Sunday best, so I called in to pick up a change of clothes.'

'Which you appear to have forgotten,' Gideon observed. Lloyd still wore the cream trousers and brown wool blazer he'd been wearing when he left the restaurant. 'Christ, Lloyd! Give it up, I'm not buying it. You left the lunch early because you were desperate to see what was in the package Reuben sent me. Why was that, I wonder?'

'Looks like I wasn't the only one.'

'Ah, but that's where you're wrong. I don't need to look at the package, because I know what's in it.'

Lloyd's eyes narrowed and he stood perfectly still, haloed by the sunlight from the window. Gideon imagined his brain racing, wondering how much Gideon knew and whether there was still a way out with honour, or if all was lost.

'He told you? Well, I don't know why the old tramp sent it to you. It's just the ramblings of a manic depressive who's no longer around. Here, you might as well have it.' He tossed the envelope to Gideon, frisbee fashion.

Gideon caught it, pulled the tape away from the flap and took out the diary. Leafing through to the end of the written pages he discovered that the entries now stopped at the twenty-first of April. He looked up and found Lloyd watching with apparent nonchalance.

'So, what did you do with the pages you cut out?' he asked, and had the satisfaction of seeing Lloyd's composure slip for a moment.

'What are you talking about?'

'The pages where Julian explains what happened the night Marcus Daniels died. The pages Damien photocopied and sent to you and the others.'

'You don't know what you're talking about,' Lloyd scoffed, but Gideon could see he was shaken. 'Look, I don't have time for this. I've got a horse to see to.' He started moving towards the kitchen door.

'Oh, come on! We both know that's rubbish! I've read those pages you so carefully removed.'

Lloyd paused and turned. 'You're bluffing . . . How could you have?'

'Easy. Just before I wrapped it up.'

'*You* sent it?' Lloyd's mask of indifference was showing cracks. 'Oh, I suppose you think you're a real smart-arse, don't you? But it doesn't prove a bloody thing. And now you haven't even got the evidence.'

'Damien's not the only one who's got a photocopier,' Gideon pointed out.

There was a pause while Lloyd visibly regrouped.

'And who do you think's going to be interested in something that happened twelve years ago?'

'Well, *you* appear to be pretty worked up about it. *Now why would that be?* I ask myself. Perhaps there's more to this than meets the eye . . .'

'You're talking complete crap! It was an accident. The boy was drunk, tried to balance on the wall, slipped and banged his head. So – we covered it up . . . yeah, maybe that was wrong, but it was nobody's *fault*.'

'On the face of it, maybe, but what if one of his mates – and I use the term loosely – what if one of them, the one, in fact, who suggested the dare, knew damn well that the boy had no head for heights? What if it was known that the mate in question had seen the lad absolutely paralysed with fear on top of a haystack? Don't you think that might make a difference when the inquest is reopened?'

'You've got no proof.'

'I've got a witness, who'll testify if needs be,' Gideon stated, reflecting that Stephenson might've been less than happy to hear him say that, but it was academic, at the moment.

'I'd say your political career was looking a little shaky now, wouldn't you?' he went on. 'And that's what this has all been about, hasn't it? Protecting your ambition, your status, your *standing* within the community. Oh yes, Damien knew just how to make you suffer, didn't he?'

'You know fuck all!'

Lloyd moved towards the door to the kitchen, grabbing the handle and then flattening himself against the heavy wooden panels when it didn't open.

'You looking for the key, by any chance?' Gideon enquired. He was almost enjoying himself.

'Give it to me,' Lloyd said low-voiced.

'Or else?' Gideon wasn't a habitual fighter, but he knew a few moves remembered from a couple of years in his university karate club and, besides that, he reckoned his extra height and reach must count for something.

Lloyd advanced on him, no longer troubling to disguise his loathing.

'You think you're so fucking clever, don't you? Well, you're not. I was in the study when you drove up – oh, so carefully – and parked under the rhododendrons. I guessed you were up to something, and I was waiting for you. That's why I picked up this!'

On the final word he produced from his left pocket a slim shiny blade, some six or seven inches in length, which Gideon recognised as Giles' antique paperknife from the desk in his study.

He stepped back hurriedly as Lloyd jabbed the point towards his face. As knives went, the cutting edge wouldn't win any accolades, but Gideon was uncomfortably certain that it had the potential to be an exceedingly efficient stabbing weapon and, from the expression on Lloyd's face, he was within a hair's breadth of finding out.

'So, what now?' he asked, watching the knife and striving, for pride's sake, to keep his voice steady.

'Now you give me the key,' Lloyd hissed.

'And you go . . . where exactly?'

'Just shut up and give me the key!'

Gideon took a deep breath.

'I haven't got it,' he lied, his eyes glued to the blade that now hovered at neck level.

'Then where the fuck is it?'

'On the ledge.' Gideon glanced past Lloyd at the top of the door frame, and had the satisfaction of seeing him draw back slightly and follow his gaze, but the knife remained alarmingly close.

'Why would you put it up there?' he demanded suspiciously.

'To slow you down if you tried to make a run for it. And it worked.'

'OK. Well, you can just get it down again. Go on,' Lloyd said, gesturing with the blade.

'Sure.' Gideon moved cautiously past him. 'You know, that thing you did with the clock was really clever, I have to admit.'

'What clock?'

'The one in the Daniels' house, when you broke in on the day of the memorial service.'

'You're crazy! I was at the service, remember?'

'I remember you turned up late,' Gideon said, reaching up to feel along the ledge above the door. 'But you gave yourself an alibi, didn't you? You made it look as though the clock had accidentally got broken, knowing that the police would assume that the burglar had still been in the house at that time. But *I* think you moved the hands on, so it would look like you were at the minster mourning your lifelong friend while the thieves were still in the farmhouse.'

Lloyd sneered and shook his head.

'You're crazy,' he repeated. 'Come on, hurry up! Where's the bloody key?'

Gideon turned, shrugged, and threw Julian Norris' diary in Lloyd's face.

He was so close and had done it so quickly that Lloyd had no time to duck, and didn't. The hardback book caught him somewhere around the bridge of his nose and, as his hands rose instinctively towards his face, Gideon caught the one that held the knife with both of his own. Bearing Lloyd backwards, off balance, he rammed his wrist against the spindle-turned posts of the banisters a couple of times and saw the paperknife drop from his fingers.

With Gideon concentrating his efforts on the hand that held the knife, however, Lloyd's other hand was left free, and he made good use of it by burying it with some force between Gideon's left hip and ribs. It wasn't a particularly debilitating blow, being delivered, as it was, from close quarters by the right hand of a left-handed person, but it was enough to momentarily wind him.

Still holding onto Lloyd's left wrist, Gideon leaned back and swivelled on his heels, pulling Lloyd off balance and releasing him to go staggering across the hall and crash into the dark oak coffer that stood against the wall.

Lloyd recovered quickly, rubbing his wrist and regarding Gideon with intense loathing.

'Whatever you might think I've done, you've got no proof. No fingerprints or witnesses. It's only your word against mine, and when they find out that you had it in for me because I got to

319

shag the girl you've always wanted, I don't think they'll take you too seriously, do you?'

'Are you out of your mind? Is that what you really think?'

'Oh, don't play the innocent with me! I could see it from the start and it made fucking her oh so sweet!'

Quite suddenly, Gideon was seething, and it must have shown in his face, because Lloyd took a step back and put his hands forward as if to fend him off.

'Oh, no! You don't want to fight me. Sure, you're a big guy and you'd probably beat me, but what would Pippa think of that? You touch me and you'll never get her; let me go, and forget all this nonsense about diaries, and maybe . . . just maybe . . .' Lloyd had been edging sideways as he spoke, and was now level with the door to the hall. He paused, producing a false expression of sympathy. ' . . . if you're very lucky, she'll come back to you when I've finished with her.'

As Gideon started forward, Lloyd lifted the latch, pushed the heavy hall door open and slipped through.

It only took Gideon a moment to realise what he was up to. From the far end of the hall a door accessed the garden room with its French windows onto the patio, from where the guests had watched the fireworks on the night of the launch party. He knew, as Lloyd obviously did, that the key to the windows was kept in a pot on the mantelpiece. He also knew that the hall door could be bolted from the inside, and he put his shoulder to it before Lloyd could do so.

There was a yelp of pain, and he pushed it wide to find Lloyd backing away, rubbing one hand in the other.

'For God's sake, Gideon! I don't want to fight. Leave me alone!'

'Nobody's asking you to fight. Just stand still and give me some answers. It was you, the night of the Sparkler launch, wasn't it? It has to have been. You didn't find the diary when you searched the farmhouse, and you knew we'd found the list amongst Nero's things, so you thought you'd look and see what else there was to find. Not the diary itself, perhaps, but a reference to where it was, am I right? But what I don't understand is why you didn't just search during the day. I mean you're in the yard quite a lot. Surely you could have found a moment when no-one was around. Why the hurry?'

'It was that bloody policeman, Rockley,' Lloyd said suddenly, bitterly, as if the words burst from him of their own volition. 'He was snooping round all the time, asking questions, poking his nose into everyone's business.'

'Well, he's a detective,' Gideon observed, amused in spite of the situation, and secretly triumphant; Lloyd had started to talk.

'So you thought you'd sneak out while everyone was watching the fireworks and have a good look round, uninterrupted. Only you weren't uninterrupted, were you? Because I went out to check on Nero.'

'I wish I'd hit you harder!'

Lloyd was still backing slowly away but Gideon was following at the same pace, keeping the gap between them a constant six or seven feet.

'Yeah, I bet you do. But it explains how the door was opened: Pippa didn't forget to lock it, you just borrowed the key, as you did, I imagine, when you searched the Gatehouse the night I was at the gallery with Eve. But Nero's file was in the Land Rover and it wasn't there that evening, was it? So you came back in the middle of the night to have another look, but by that time I'd taken it in, so you drew another blank. I should've listened to Eve and set the dog on you!'

'He wouldn't hurt me, he likes me.'

'Yeah, and I caught him rolling on a dead bird the other day, so I guess we can't rely on *his* good taste,' Gideon responded.

'I was in the Gatehouse again, the morning you were up here doing your mumbo-jumbo stuff with Nero,' Lloyd declared, ignoring his taunt. 'You didn't know that did you, Hercule fucking Poirot? And you'd left your little notepad out for me to see.'

Gideon remembered. That had been the day after he'd visited Bentley and Stephenson. He'd been trying to make sense of things when Tilly had rung about Nero, and he'd left the notepad on the kitchen table.

'You realised I was on your trail, so that's when you set up that business with your two pals and the fencer, was it?'

Lloyd grinned. He'd backed right across the hall now, skirting the table and benches in the centre, and was near the door to the garden room.

'Begging for mercy, the lads said you were. Jesus! What wouldn't I have given to see it?'

Gideon didn't waste his breath denying it.

'And Reuben? Was that you or one of your bullyboys? You thought he'd be a pushover, didn't you? But he wouldn't tell you where the diary was, so you beat him up. If there's any justice, that alone should see you put away for a good few years.'

'But you can't *prove* it — any of it!' Lloyd spoke to him as if trying to explain something to a small and not very bright child. 'All this supposition — it's pointless. If you've got some idea that I'll hold my hands up and confess everything, you'd better think again. I'll do whatever it takes to keep my name clear, believe me; anything at all. That's the mistake Damien made.'

Somewhere deep inside Gideon, something froze.

'So ... Why do you think Adam Tetley shot Damien?' he asked, striving to keep his voice calm. 'On the face of it, he didn't appear to have much to lose, even if the truth *had* come out.'

'He and Damien had history,' Lloyd answered, without hesitation. 'Damien used to train a horse for him and they fell out, big-time. Damien dumped him in it with the company he worked for and he lost his job.'

'Oh, so you knew about that, did you?'

'Of course. I've known the family for years.'

'So if you were looking for a scapegoat, Adam Tetley would be the obvious choice ...'

Lloyd became very still.

'What are you talking about? I was miles away when Damien was killed. Out hunting, with dozens of witnesses; it's a cast-iron alibi.'

'Except that you weren't all that far away, as the crow flies, were you? And at the end of the first line, your horse was lame and you had to walk it back to the lorry and get a fresh one.'

'So what are you saying? That I tied Lady to a tree and sprinted three or four miles to shoot Damien, then sprinted back? I'm flattered you think I'm that fit, but get *real*!'

He laughed, but Gideon thought he detected a thread of unease mingled with the scorn.

'No, I don't think you did that,' he said. 'But I found out something interesting the other day. I found out that your ex-wife lives just down the road from where Damien was shot.'

Now he was sure he was onto something. Everything about Lloyd's body language became guarded, and the muscles in his face tightened.

'What's that got to do with anything? She's my *ex*-wife. We're hardly on speaking terms. I wouldn't see her at all if it wasn't for my kids.'

Lloyd moved a few steps away from the garden-room door, towards the end of the hall.

'So it wasn't Harriet that Eve saw you kissing, this morning? She was surprised; said you looked pretty wrapped up in one another . . .'

'She's a lying bitch!'

Gideon's eyes narrowed.

'Well, one of you's lying, that's for sure, and I know where I'd put *my* money. I'm saying maybe you rode your "*lame*" horse to your old home and then borrowed a car. How does that sound? I think you'd have had plenty of time to ride back afterwards and then walk the last bit on foot. The police were looking for a red hatchback at one point – does Harriet have a red hatchback tucked away in her garage somewhere, I wonder?'

Lloyd began to sweat.

'You're crazy! The police have found the gun, remember? It was in Tetley's locker and he had the key. Tetley shot Damien, not me.'

He was moving with purpose now, across to the far wall, and Gideon began to follow, unsure what he was planning.

He found out all too soon.

A huge oak carver chair stood against the golden stone, tapestry-hung wall, and Lloyd jumped onto this, reaching high above his head to where a pair of swords was displayed. Standing on tiptoe, he managed to lift one off the brackets that held it.

Still on the chair, he hefted the sword in his left hand, raising it and squinting down the thirty-inch blade. He looked disturbingly at home with the weapon, and Gideon slowed and stopped where he was, halfway across the hall.

'British naval cutlass, late eighteenth century. Beautifully balanced,' Lloyd said appreciatively.

The blade was slim, subtly curved near the point, and the hilt handsome, with a finely chased knucklebow, but just at that moment Gideon couldn't share his enthusiasm. He watched, heart thumping, while Lloyd reached the second one down.

'That's not bad, either. Try it,' he invited, and the next moment the sword came flying in a deadly silver arc, straight towards Gideon.

SEVENTEEN

GIDEON DODGED.
Duellists in films might catch swords deftly by the hilt but he certainly wasn't about to try, and, even had he done so, he would only have been able to hack and chop with a complete absence of skill.

The weapon landed on the worn carpet behind him, vibration making the blade ring.

Lloyd laughed out loud, his eyes glittering.

'It won't bite you! Pick it up. Let's see what you're made of.'

Flesh and bone, Gideon thought mordantly, neither of which stood much chance of resisting the finely crafted steel blade of the cutlass.

Why hadn't he kept his mouth shut? So much better to have let Lloyd go, not suspecting that Gideon had guessed the truth, and then laid his theory in front of Logan or Rockley. If he'd had more time to think that was undoubtedly what he would have done, but the revelation had come in a flash and he couldn't resist trying for a reaction. Now he was faced with a man who not

only loathed him with a passion, but who also felt he had little
to lose by killing him.

'I'm not going to make it self-defence,' Gideon said, backing
away from the fallen sword.

'Oh, *go on*,' Lloyd urged, dropping down from the carver. He
smiled in a manner that did nothing to reassure. 'It's ages since I
used one of these. I might have forgotten how – you never know.'

Passing the sword from one hand to the other, he shed his
jacket and tossed it aside.

Modern Pentathlon, Gideon remembered with uncomfortable
clarity, consisted of shooting, running, swimming, riding and
fencing. Any hope that Lloyd's knowledge of swordplay was superficial vanished like a drop of water on a hotplate.

Lloyd advanced, bringing the point of his cutlass altogether too
close for Gideon's comfort. He took another step or two backward.

'You didn't really think I came on my own, unprepared?' he
asked, trying to keep his voice and breathing steady. He pointed
towards his chest, where the transmitter nestled comfortingly in
his pocket. 'I'm wired. The police have heard every word we've
said. I should think they'll be here any moment now, wouldn't
you?' Remembering Tilly's last, panic-stricken call, he fervently
hoped it was true.

'Nice try,' Lloyd said. 'Almost believable.' He stepped forward
and brandished the cutlass, its point describing a neat figure of
eight in the air just inches in front of Gideon, who moved back
smartly, almost falling as one of the benches for the refectory
table caught him behind the knees. It tipped over with a bang,
and Gideon stumbled sideways. Now it was *his* turn to sweat.

Lloyd seemed to find it highly amusing.

'Not quite so keen to fight now, are we?'

'Give it up, Lloyd. I'm telling the truth. You'll never get away
with this. Too many people knew I was coming here.' Gideon
looked around for inspiration and found it over the fireplace on
the opposite side of the hall, where were displayed two crossed

pikes and a shield. The pikes combined a spearhead and an ugly-looking elongated axe, mounted on a wooden staff of some six feet in length. They were polished to gleaming perfection, and had probably not been wielded in anger for the best part of five hundred years, but to Gideon, at that moment, they represented possible salvation.

'What if I don't care?' Lloyd said, the sword still in dazzling motion. 'I'll say you were determined to fight. I had to defend myself. I'll put the sword in your hand. What'll I get for self-defence? Five or six years, halved for good behaviour – what if I thought it was worth it, to get you out of my life?'

The sword sliced through the ether, so close that Gideon felt the wind of its passing. A look at Lloyd's face revealed that he was deadly serious; his hatred of Gideon was greater than his fear of the consequences.

Gideon turned and sprinted for the fireplace, hoping against hope that the weapons were merely resting in their brackets as the cutlasses had been.

They were. Within moments he had his hands on one of them, lifted it and pulled, bringing the other clattering down with it as it came free. Gripping the wooden shaft, he whirled to meet his opponent.

He was only just in time. Lloyd had followed him and, even as he turned, he saw the cutlass lancing towards him. The pikestaff swept across, knocking the blade aside, and Gideon leapt side-ways and ran towards the table in the centre of the room.

His counter-attack had unbalanced Lloyd and with his burst of speed, Gideon managed to get into a position where the table was between them, in which situation he felt marginally happier. He tried reason again.

'Look Lloyd . . .' he said, his heart thumping heavily. 'If you injure me, you'll just make things ten times worse for yourself . . . Why don't you give it up?'

'And what? Turn myself in? Let you play the hero? Wired? What do you fucking take me for?'

A murderer, Gideon thought, but he didn't say it; he didn't think it would help.

Lloyd seemed to feel compelled to fill the silence.

'All right. If you're telling the truth – where are they? I don't see them. Wouldn't you think they'd be here by now?'

He had a point. *Where indeed?* Was anyone even listening?

'You know what I think?' Lloyd went on without waiting for an answer. 'I think you're a fucking liar! You're shit-scared and you're lying to buy time. Well, the way I see it, we've got at least another hour before the others finish their meal, maybe two before they make it back here. Do you think you can last that long?' He swung the cutlass horizontally so that it whipped through the space between them, cleaving the air with a hissing sound, and Gideon swayed back out of reach, bringing the staff up way too late.

Before he could recover fully, Lloyd had stepped up onto the bench and table and launched himself from the top in a flying leap. In desperation, Gideon threw up both hands with the pikestaff spanning the gap, overbalancing and falling back with most of Lloyd's descending weight on top of him.

The stone floor hit Gideon gruntingly hard between the shoulder blades and his head followed through to connect with a crack that left him momentarily disoriented. Pain stabbed through his right hand and through the blotchy daze of semi-consciousness, he became aware of a hard ridge of pressure across his chest. As his head cleared he realised that he'd fallen with the pikestaff across him and Lloyd was now leaning on it, crushing Gideon's hand between the end of the wooden staff and the stone floor. He grinned unpleasantly, no doubt enjoying the grimace that Gideon couldn't prevent.

After a final push on the staff, Lloyd got to his feet, mercifully lifting his weight off Gideon, but his attempt to sit up was foiled by the discovery that the point of the naval cutlass was floating menacingly around his upper chest region, and he lay back, breathing hard.

Where the hell was Logan? If no-one was listening, then his carefully crafted trap had come to nothing, and his predicament was dire.

'So what now?' Lloyd mocked, looking down the blade of the sword. 'What's the next part of your oh-so-clever plan?'

With no way of knowing if help was indeed on the way, Gideon rapidly came to the conclusion that his best and only resource was the age-old favourite of the out-gunned: flight. Somehow, he had to try and stave off Lloyd's attack long enough to reach one of the doors or windows.

'Well?'

Suddenly the sword point flicked towards Gideon's face and away, but although he flinched, instinctively, it was several moments before a burning pain told him that the steel had actually scored his skin.

'What d'you want me to say?' he said, feeling blood trickle over his cheek to his right ear. Deep inside he could feel tremors of tension, and prayed that it didn't show.

Lloyd rolled his eyes towards the ceiling, as if in preface to some declaration or action, and in that moment Gideon moved, bringing the blunt end of the pikestaff upward to thud into Lloyd's groin with all the force he could muster.

With a cry of agony Lloyd crumpled, face screwed up like a baby with colic, one hand clasping the source of his distress. He still held the sword, but for the moment it posed no threat, and Gideon lost no time in rolling away and regaining his feet.

'That's from Pippa!' Gideon told him. 'And this . . .' he swung the pike again, ' . . . is from me!'

Lloyd grunted and dropped to his knees as the wooden shaft landed across his shoulders and neck with some considerable force. Unfortunately he retained his hold on the cutlass and Gideon was reluctant to waste time in what might be a fruitless tussle to wrest it from him, so, resisting the almost overwhelming temptation to land another, more final blow, he sprinted for the door they'd come in by.

He should have made sure of his man.

Gideon only just had time to reach the entrance hall and pull the heavy door shut behind him before Lloyd, having arrived at the other side, was throwing all his weight into pulling it open again. With his crushed fingers still stiff and painful, Gideon felt his grip on the knurled metal ring slipping fast and glanced up and down the hall in desperation.

For the first time he regretted having removed the key from the kitchen door. Even if his hand had been in perfect working order, the chances of his being able to fend off the cutlass while he fished in his trouser pocket for the key and then used it, were somewhere between extremely unlikely and non-existent. As it was . . .

Abruptly relinquishing his hold on the door, Gideon hefted the pike and ran for the staircase. Halfway up the first flight he turned, fighting for balance, and faced the hall, the pike, with its lethal steel tip, held awkwardly in his left hand and pointing defensively down the stairs. Sure enough, Lloyd was close behind him, but was forced to halt two or three steps up, the naval sword held before him and fury in his eyes.

Hatred seemed to have overridden reason in Lloyd's mind, because he didn't let the disadvantage of lower ground and shorter reach put him off. The cutlass snaked round the wavering point and hit the staff with a juddering blow, almost jarring it from Gideon's grasp. A chip of wood flew off and the point swung sideways to hit the wall.

Barely had Gideon got it back on track, when again the blade clove into the staff, and he realised that his only hope was to attack. Bringing his semi-useless right hand into play, he grasped the staff and stabbed downward at Lloyd, trying to force him off balance and back down the stairs.

As a plan it was spectacularly unsuccessful.

With the grace and dexterity that had almost won him a place on the Olympic team all those years before, Lloyd swayed to one side, grasped the pikestaff close behind its deadly chopping blade, and pulled Gideon off balance instead.

Gideon let go of the weapon and grabbed at the banister to try and save himself, but to no avail. He felt himself falling and, in an effort to salvage something from the pathetic ruins of his intentions, launched a flying leap at Lloyd.

With a bone-jarring crash, they hit the stone floor at the foot of the stairs in a mess of arms, legs, wood and steel, Gideon's landing made marginally softer by his being partly on top of Lloyd.

At close quarters the weapons were rendered useless and fell by the wayside as the two of them rolled and scrambled across the floor, locked together in a vicious, heavy-breathing struggle.

Gideon had temporarily gained the ascendancy, pinning one of Lloyd's wrists to the floor with his left hand and battling to secure the other, when the dogs started barking.

Someone was coming.

He instinctively glanced across at the kitchen door and, as he looked back, was stunned by a brutal headbutt that knocked him back and away, leaving Lloyd to scramble to his feet unchallenged and deliver a few hefty kicks for good measure.

Consciousness drifted and returned, and Gideon found himself lying on his back on a cold stone floor that seemed to be rolling under him in a nauseous manner.

The dogs were still kicking up a fuss, and someone somewhere was shouting his name with a fair degree of urgency.

'In here!' he croaked, rolling over and getting to all fours.

'Gideon! Is that you? Open the door!' a male voice shouted. Not Logan, Gideon thought, as the floor began to settle down and come into focus. There were a couple of dark spots on it and as he watched, head hung low, another appeared. Blood, he realised with a woolly detachment.

'Gideon?' Tilly's voice. 'Are you all right? Where's Lloyd?'

A good question. Where indeed?

'Gideon!' The male voice once more, and followed by a crashing bang against the heavy wooden panels of the door. 'Open the door!'

'Coming,' he muttered. Raising his head muzzily to scan the entrance hall, Gideon found it empty, and the door to the great hall standing open.

'Gideon!'

'*Coming!*' In spite of his relief, Gideon's tone was tetchy. He was doing his best. He decided it would be safest to make his way across to the door on his hands and knees and, once there, used the wall to steady himself as he got to his feet and felt in his pocket for the key.

Where *was* Lloyd? Had he got right away? Gideon wasn't sure if he'd lost consciousness for several minutes or just a few seconds. His fingers located the key and he withdrew it, swearing under his breath as the fabric tightened on his swollen fist. Transferring the key to his left hand, he fitted it into the lock and turned it, grasping the doorpost to save falling through the opening as the door was yanked away from him.

A huge man filled the opening. Definitely not Logan.

'Where is the bastard?' he demanded, and Gideon recognised Hamish Daniels, Tilly's father. He waved a hand in the general direction of the main hall and Hamish brushed past him and disappeared.

'Gideon, are you all right? Oh, God! What happened?' Tilly, this time, putting a hand on his arm and peering anxiously into his face.

'Where's Logan?' Gideon asked, ignoring her questions. 'Did he hear everything?'

'He went to find another way in. Round the front. Are you OK?'

'Did he hear? Was the bug working? I wasn't sure . . .'

'Yes, he heard. We all heard. Dad too.'

'How come *he's* here?'

'I'm sorry. He heard me trying to get hold of Logan,' she cried. 'Gideon, we have to stop him! He says he's going to kill him!'

'Oh, shit!' Gideon groaned and, cautiously leaving the support of the doorpost, he went after Tilly's father.

When he entered the hall, with Tilly close on his heels, it was to see Hamish, with the second of the pikes held threateningly in front of him, advancing towards Lloyd who waited at the far end with his back to the wall, for all the world like some defenceless animal hunted to exhaustion.

'Dad, no!' Tilly screamed, and Gideon broke into a stumbling run with no thought of how, in his feeble state, he was going to prevent the burly farmer from exacting rough justice on the man who'd killed both his sons.

'Think what you're doing, man!' Gideon urged, reaching Hamish and grabbing his arm. 'Think of your family!'

'I'm not letting the bastard get away with it. Let go!' He jabbed backward with the end of the pikestaff, catching Gideon in the chest and sending him reeling back, gasping.

'Dad, please! Don't!'

Tilly had come closer, and Hamish hesitated, not ten feet from Lloyd.

'Stay out of it, girl!' he commanded, his gaze fixed on the man in front of him.

With no clear plan, Gideon began to move out to one side, desperately hoping that if it came to it, he could find some way to prevent Hamish from carrying out his intention.

Tilly's father stepped forward once more, coldly determined, his knuckles white on the pikestaff, and Lloyd waited, breathing deeply.

Gideon moved further out and his eyes narrowed as his new angle of sight revealed a gleam of metal between Lloyd's trouser leg and the wall.

'Hamish, look out!'

Even as realisation dawned, Gideon was moving. Two paces took him close to the outside wall, where he grasped the lower edge of one of the Priory's antique tapestries and yanked it downward as hard as he could. The age-rotted stitching gave way noiselessly and Gideon gathered the yards of musty fabric in his arms, racing to reach Lloyd before Hamish did.

Lloyd kept the sword hidden until Tilly's father was almost upon him, then swept it out from behind his leg and brought it round in a slashing attack aimed at Hamish's upper body.

Catching the blade in the copious folds of the priceless tapestry, Gideon flung all his weight onto Lloyd's sword arm and bore it down, hoping that Hamish wouldn't take advantage of the situation to deliver his own coup de grâce.

As Gideon pulled him down Lloyd twisted violently, spitting furious curses at him, and he felt his hold rapidly loosening, but suddenly, mercifully, Logan was there. He hauled Lloyd off Gideon and, in one efficient move, fielded his free arm, twisting it expertly up behind his back and forcing him face down onto the floor.

With a sigh, Gideon relaxed in the sudden stillness, rolling off the crumpled fabric to lie on his back for a moment, staring up at the magnificence of the hall's beamed ceiling and trying to get his breath back.

'Thanks. I could have done with you twenty minutes ago,' he told the policeman wearily. He sat up. 'I must get you to teach me that move. Might come in handy.'

'Should'a let me have him,' Hamish said bitterly, shaking his head. He still held the pike but his other arm was around Tilly's shoulders, squeezing tight, and his heightened colour and glittering eyes showed the depth of his emotion.

'Oh, no. We don't want you banged up, too,' Logan said prosaically. 'Prisons are too full as it is.'

'Prison's too bloody good for that worm; he should be hanged!'

With handcuffs fitted, Lloyd was hauled to his feet, protesting his innocence.

'Look, you've got it all wrong! There's absolutely no proof. Blake attacked me with no warning. What was I supposed to do? I had to protect myself.'

'Yeah, yeah. Tell it to the judge,' Logan advised. 'And as for proof – there's the little matter of a tape recording I think the jury might be interested to hear.'

That took the wind out of his sails. Logan used the ensuing

silence to read Lloyd his rights and then handed him over to a pair of uniformed officers who had appeared, right on cue, and stood looking in understandable bewilderment at the weaponry on show.

As Lloyd was led away, he twisted round and looked back at Gideon.

'I should have shot you right at the start – when I had the chance!' he hissed. 'I had you in my sights.'

'That's enough, sir. Come on,' one of the officers said.

Gideon bowed his head. It was a sobering thought, even so long after the event, to know that he'd been that close to joining Damien. He looked up at Logan.

'If you needed any more proof . . .'

'It all helps,' Logan said, offering him a hand to get to his feet. 'Sorry. I had to call it in this time, and I've got a feeling DI Rockley might want a word or two with you.'

The words Rockley chose to open his dialogue with Gideon were not, he suspected, to be found in any official police hand-book or code of practice. The DI had had, perforce, to wait until the paramedics had dealt with Gideon's sundry cuts and bruises, and the waiting hadn't improved his mood.

It had been previously agreed that, to prevent Logan's super-iors coming down on him like a ton of bricks, Gideon and Tilly should say the policeman had been recruited at the last minute to man the receiver, knowing little of what he was to hear, but Gideon suspected the inspector wasn't deceived.

On the subject of his own part in the proceedings, Gideon was on the receiving end of a lengthy diatribe, peppered with such words as *foolhardy, ill considered* and *bloody stupid,* and such phrases as *interfering with an official investigation* and *withholding vital information.*

Gideon listened with half an ear, aware that Rockley was well within his rights to tear a strip off him and, moreover, that he had earned it, but wondering, at the same time, how Pippa was going to take this complete upheaval of her personal life.

When Rockley had said his piece, taken Gideon's statement and departed, presumably to follow Lloyd and his escort back to the station, Gideon sat on one of the benches in the deserted great hall, feeling depressed, sore, and unutterably weary.

Police officers had bagged and labelled the swords and pikes, carrying them away as evidence, and now only the tumbled bench and the untidy heap of faded fabric by the far wall remained to tell of the drama that had been played out. Even to Gideon, the events of the afternoon had assumed a strangely distant and dream-like quality.

After a couple of minutes, he heard the scrape of a shoe on the stone floor and looked up to see Eve approaching, still wearing the long brown velvet skirt and old-gold linen jacket she'd worn to the restaurant.

'Hey, you,' she said softly.

'Hiyah. Sorry I ran out on you at the restaurant.'

'We wondered where the hell you'd gone.'

'Yeah, sorry about that. I've seen Giles but I haven't seen Pippa. How's she taking all this? Does she know the full story?'

'Tilly told her.' Eve came round in front of him and put out a gentle hand to tilt his chin up, with a soft hiss of indrawn breath. 'She took it pretty well, all things considered, but then I never believed theirs was a grand passion in the first place.'

'She'll hate me . . .'

Eve shook her head.

'For a while, maybe, she'll find it hard to forgive you for being right about him, but she'll come round. But what about you? Are you OK?'

'OK in the way that someone who's been run over by a bus is OK,' he said with resurfacing humour. 'How do I look?'

She put her head on one side.

'I wish I could say romantically scarred, but one eye is almost shut and you've got what looks like a train track running up your cheek. What happened to your hand?'

'Oh, it's nothing much. They don't think there's anything broken.' Gideon flexed the fingers of his swollen hand experimentally. Because he'd refused to go to hospital the paramedic had carried out *in situ* repairs to the sword cut on his face, but he would have to go to casualty to get his hand checked out properly.

'Was Rockley very rough with you?' She put a hand on his shoulder and bent to kiss him.

'No more than I deserved, probably.'

'I wish you'd told me what you were going to do.'

'You would have tried to stop me,' he pointed out.

'And that would have been a bad thing?'

Gideon shrugged. 'I'm sorry. I couldn't see any other way to get to the truth; Lloyd had covered his tracks too well. I couldn't just stand by and let him get away with it.'

Eve stroked his hair.

'You know, for a quiet bloke, you're surprisingly bloody-minded! I thought life with you was going to be peaceful and undemanding. How wrong can a person be?'

'That from a newly hatched biker chick,' he teased. 'Oh, come on – you know peaceful and undemanding would bore you stiff! But anyway, it's all over now. We'll probably dwindle into old age in perfect tranquillity.'

'Maybe,' she said, and Gideon was struck by an uncharacteristic note of reserve in her voice. 'Anyway, I came to tell you that Mrs Morecambe's back and making cups of tea in the kitchen.'

'Perfect.' Gideon climbed stiffly to his feet. 'Life is back to normal.'

In the kitchen they found Pippa, Giles, Tilly and Hamish sitting round the table drinking tea, and Mrs Morecambe making sandwiches with doorstep slices of bread and cheese.

It was the first time either Pippa or Mrs Morecambe had seen Gideon's battered face, and their reactions couldn't have been more different.

The housekeeper hurried forward, full of concern, fussing over him until he was safely seated with a mug of tea in his hand. Pippa glanced up when he first came in, then her gaze dropped to the mug in front of her, her expression strained and unhappy.

Clearly envious, Giles was inclined to view the revelations as a drama from which he'd been unfairly excluded, and was eager to hear the mechanics of the confrontation.

'You do realise you've got me into trouble,' he said. 'It's quite possible I could be charged for the improper storage and display of weapons.'

'Yeah. Sorry about that, but I must admit, it wasn't a consideration at the time.'

'So whose idea was it to grab the swords and halberds?'

'Lloyd's – look, do we have to talk about this now?' Gideon protested, seeing Pippa beginning to look intensely uncomfortable.

'What? Oh, I see.' Belatedly, Giles caught on. 'But we can't just pretend it didn't happen.'

Suddenly, Pippa pushed her chair back and stood up.

'No. Don't mind me,' she said with brittle brightness and suspiciously sparkling eyes. 'I've got things to do, anyway. It'll be easier for you to rake it all over if I'm not here.'

She left the room without so much as looking at Gideon, brushing past Logan in the doorway with a muttered apology, and leaving behind an uncomfortable silence.

Life, it seemed, would take a little while to return to normal.

'Should I go after her, do you think?' Giles asked, doubtfully, and seemed relieved when the general consensus was that she probably needed a little space.

Logan had come to take his leave, but accepted, with no noticeable reluctance, an invitation to stay for tea and sandwiches.

'How's it going?' he asked Gideon.

'OK, all things considered.'

'Sorry I didn't get here sooner, but I was stuck at work,' Logan explained, tucking into one of the wedge-shaped offerings. 'Just before I came off shift we were called out to a post office raid, and then there was the report to write up. I can't just down tools and leave if I'm in the middle of something. But then I thought we had an agreement that you wouldn't do anything until you knew I was in place?'

'Yeah, I know, but if I'd waited it would have all been for nothing, so I just took a chance. I guessed you'd get here as soon as you could. So where *did* you come in — as a matter of interest?'

'Something about a dog and a dead bird, if I remember rightly. You know, it's not always the best idea to antagonise someone you suspect of murder — especially when you're on your own without back-up!'

'No, I guess not, but you can't deny I got results.'

'You bloody nearly got yourself killed — that's what you got!' Logan said. 'Again!'

'He was brilliant!' Tilly said, jumping to his defence. 'We got here just after PC Logan did,' she told Gideon. 'So we listened in. It was pretty scary not being able to see what was happening, but we were only just down the drive . . .'

'I wanted to be sure Lloyd-Ellis would incriminate himself,' Logan put in. 'I knew you'd blow your top if I breezed in before we had enough to nail him, and it didn't sound as though there was any violent activity at that point. But when he offered you a sword, I decided the time had come to step in. Would've been easier if you hadn't locked the door, though.'

'I didn't want him getting away,' Gideon admitted sheepishly. 'If I'd had any idea he would go so completely off the rails, I don't think I'd have gone in, in the first place. But then I thought it was just going to be about Marcus and the diary, and it wasn't until he all but admitted to killing Damien that I realised just how dangerous he really was.'

'But I don't understand. I thought the case against Adam Tetley was cut and dried,' Tilly put in. 'DI Rockley said you'd found the gun in a locker and Tetley had the key . . .'

'Yeah, but Rockley was never completely happy about that,'

Logan said. 'It was just too easy. Plus, Tetley was on nights and he said he slept most of the morning. Neighbours told us that his car was on the drive all day, and he was there when a man from the electricity company called just after noon to read the meter. He could have done it, but it would have been extremely tight. The facts didn't quite fit.'

'So how did he come to have the key?' Hamish wanted to know.

Logan swallowed a mouthful of tea.

'He told us it came in the post, in a plain brown envelope, addressed to him, and I guess he was probably telling the truth. I mean, what would *you* do if something like that turned up? Most people would do what he did — look at it, wonder where the hell it came from, and then put it on the window sill and forget all about it. It was a clever move on Lloyd–Ellis' part. It seems he's been pretty clever all along. We underestimated him. Not that he was ever really a suspect, because we didn't have a motive and, in any case, he seemed to have a watertight alibi for the shooting. Mind you — if we'd known about the list of names from the start, it might have been a different matter.' He slanted a look at Gideon under his brows. 'Our friend here has something of a history of withholding information.'

'I just wanted to find out whether it was actually relevant before dumping everyone in it,' Gideon explained. 'I thought Damien's family had had enough to deal with. How was I to know I was lighting the blue touchpaper?'

The day of the Tarrant and Stour Team Chase dawned fine, clear and windy. In the absence of Lloyd, Tilly had offered to step into the breach, riding Comet.

Waiting at the start with Pippa, Tilly and Steve Pettet, the hunt dragsman, Gideon shivered with nervous anticipation and wondered, for the umpteenth time that morning, just what the hell he was doing there.

Blackbird sidled restlessly beneath him, ducking his head down and grinding his teeth. Gideon had visions of him exploding into a frenzy of bucking as soon as they got under way, and could only be glad that there would be nobody amongst the spectators who knew him. Giles had had business commitments – a new and satisfying concept for him. Even Eve had had to cry off, having promised to see her friend Trevor Erskine off in his yacht for a six-month painting odyssey to the Mediterranean.

'Two minutes,' the starter called, and Tilly gave Gideon a reassuring smile. They were all wearing matching purple rugby shirts with the team name, Stour Grapes, emblazoned across the shoulders. The name had been Giles' idea.

Pippa was walking Skylark in circles next to Steve, who rode a lean grey horse with a casual ease that Gideon envied. The arrest of the Master of the Tarrant and Stour Hunt was, inevitably, the talk of the day, unfortunately for Pippa. Knowing of her relationship with Lloyd, a number of people had approached her, agog for news. Gideon was full of admiration for the way she had politely denied any knowledge of his misdemeanours and suggested they ask his wife.

In the fortnight since the showdown at the Priory, Gideon's working relationship with Pippa had gradually settled back into something approaching its former status. Away from the horses, however, she avoided him whenever she could, and seemed depressed and unhappy. They hadn't talked about what had happened and Gideon decided that Eve had been wrong for once, and that Pippa had been more deeply attached to Lloyd than any of them had suspected. Whatever the case, the discovery of Lloyd's duplicity seemed to have hit her hard, and, as the one who'd been instrumental in bringing it out into the open, Gideon was reluctant to offer his support for fear of being rebuffed.

For himself, his scars were healing, even the worst bruises not much more now than yellowing remnants, and the sword slash a thin red line. His hand was still tender, and strapped on this occasion, but it was fully functional, and his attempts to use it as an excuse for not riding in the team had received short shrift.

'Thirty seconds,' the starter called, and they began to manoeuvre the horses so that they were at least all facing the same way.

'OK?' Tilly asked brightly.

'Sure.' Gideon smiled. 'But if I disappear into the wide blue yonder, just carry on without me! It's only the first three riders that count.'

'You'll be all right!'

All four horses stood stock-still while the starter counted them down, then with a whoop from Steve they were away, Blackbird accelerating so swiftly that Gideon was almost thrown out the back door. Now that would have been *really* embarrassing, he thought, as they powered up a slight incline to the first of the twenty-two fences on the course; Pippa in the lead, side by side with Steve, Gideon third and Tilly bringing up the rear.

They flew the first hedge in that order, all the horses jumping high and wide, and swung left-handed across the next field towards a stile in the far corner.

So began the most exhilarating ride of Gideon's career. Fences loomed, one after another, with bewildering rapidity: post and rails, hedges, walls, ditches and tree trunks. Low branches were dodged, muddy gateways floundered through and even a stream forded. Mud flew, coating all of them in turn as the running order changed and changed again; horses stumbled in the rough ground, slipped on the turns and occasionally bumped one another over the narrower fences, but somehow they all stayed on their feet and their riders remained, more or less, in control.

Blackbird was in his element and, as they approached the last two obstacles on the run in, speeding up all the time, his competitive spirit rose to the fore and he put on a spurt to take the lead. Gideon let him run, putting his trust in the horse's sure-footedness, and Blackbird didn't let him down. They crossed the finish line with all four horses more or less in line and pulled up laughing, swearing, mud-splattered and out of breath, to hear the loudspeaker announce that the Stour Grapes had, at the moment, gone into second place.

Moments later the four team members had dismounted and were exchanging hugs, kisses and slaps on the back, the horses trailing at the ends of their reins, flanks heaving and bodies wet with sweat.

Caught up on a high, Gideon and Pippa embraced and kissed.

'You were brilliant!' she cried, her eyes shining. 'And wasn't Blackbird wonderful?'

'You weren't so shabby yourself,' Gideon told her, laughing, and suddenly it seemed the most natural thing in the world to take her in his arms and kiss her soundly.

Moments later, still standing close, they looked each other in the eye and Gideon bowed his head.

'Oh Lord,' he said. 'Sorry.'

'Are you?'

Gideon looked at her again.

'No,' he said, slowly. 'No, I'm not. But we can't, you know. Not just now.'

'Eve?'

'Yes; Eve. I won't hurt her, you know.'

'No, you mustn't.'

Blackbird interrupted, rubbing his sweaty face on Gideon's arm and shoving him violently sideways in the process so that contact with Pippa was broken.

'We should see to these horses,' she said, practicality surfacing once more. She turned towards the others, who were reliving the round, fence by fence.

Back at the lorry, with the horses washed down, rugged up and pulling at haynets, Gideon remembered his good-luck gift from Eve that morning. He climbed up into the cab and retrieved a boxed bottle of Moët et Chandon from behind the seats. Pippa dug out plastic mugs from the picnic hamper and set them out in a row on the step.

Opening the box, Gideon found a twist of pale gold paper attached to the neck of the bottle with a ribbon. Mystified, he removed it, passing the bottle to Steve to uncork.

It was a sheet of paper, such as might be torn from a writing pad, and the words on it were written in Eve's stylish hand. Gideon read it, his heart beating suddenly faster.

Gideon, my love, I'm going with Trevor. I'm a free spirit who needs to stretch her wings again. I have loved you but I'm not leaving you, for you were never mine. Pippa needs you now, and she can give you what I cannot. I was right, you know – it was too perfect, but this way nothing will ever spoil it. Goodbye, my gentle giant!

Eve xx

He read it through again, struggling to take in the words.

Eve had gone.

Eve, tall and willowy, effortlessly elegant in shades of gold and bronze silk; she'd gone, leaving him free, and in that moment he probably loved her more than he ever had before.

'What's wrong?'

Pippa was beside him, holding out a green plastic mug, a smudge of drying mud on her nose.

Wordlessly he handed her the note and watched her read it, seeing her hands begin to shake. Finally she looked up at him, her hazel eyes glistening with tears.

'She knew,' she said. 'How did she know? And what was it she couldn't give you?'

Gideon remembered Eve's reaction to the news of his sister's pregnancy and hesitated, meeting Pippa's gaze with his own.

One step at a time, perhaps.

'I'll tell you, one day,' he said, and raised his plastic mug of champagne. 'To Eve!'